Lorca's Experimental Theater

NEW HISPANISMS

Cultural and Literary Studies

ANNE J. CRUZ, SERIES EDITOR

LORCA'S
EXPERIMENTAL THEATER
Breaking the Guardrails
of Convention

ANDREW A. ANDERSON

Louisiana State University Press
Baton Rouge

Published by Louisiana State University Press
lsupress.org

DESIGNER: Barbara Neely Bourgoyne
TYPEFACE: Ingeborg

Jacket illustration: Scene from *El público,* photograph by Chicho, courtesy
of the Centro de Documentación de las Artes Escénicas y de la Música

LIBRARY OF CONGRESS CATALOGING-IN-PUBLICATION DATA
Names: Anderson, Andrew A., 1953– author.
Title: Lorca's experimental theater : breaking the guardrails of convention /
   Andrew A. Anderson.
Description: Baton Rouge : Louisiana State University Press, [2024] |
   Series: New Hispanisms : cultural and literary studies | Includes
   bibliographical references and index.
Identifiers: LCCN 2024009570 (print) | LCCN 2024009571 (ebook) | ISBN
   978-0-8071-8250-5 (cloth) | ISBN 978-0-8071-8325-0 (pdf) | ISBN 978-
   0-8071-8324-3 (epub)
Subjects: LCSH: García Lorca, Federico, 1898–1936—Criticism and
   interpretation. | Experimental drama, Spanish—History and criticism.
Classification: LCC PQ6613.A763 Z53819 2024 (print) | LCC PQ6613.A763
   (ebook) | DDC 862/.62—dc23/eng/20240726
LC record available at https://lccn.loc.gov/2024009570
LC ebook record available at https://lccn.loc.gov/2024009571

DIRECTOR: ¿Qué hago con el público si quito las barandas al puente? (*El público,* "Cuadro Primero")

DIRECTOR: What do I do with the audience if I remove the railings from the bridge?

CONTENTS

ACKNOWLEDGMENTS

My sincere thanks to Anne J. Cruz, series editor of New Hispanisms; James W. Long, senior editor at LSU Press; Catherine L. Kadair, managing editor at LSU Press; and Elizabeth Gratch, copyeditor, for their wholehearted enthusiasm and support for this project from its inception to completion.

Previous versions of six chapters in this book appeared originally as articles or book chapters. Their full publication details are as follows:

Chapter 2: "Undecidability in Lorca's *Amor de don Perlimplín con Belisa en su jardín.*" *Hispanic Studies Review* 3 (2018): 1–13. Reproduced by kind permission of *Hispanic Studies Review.*

Chapter 3: "On Broadway, Off Broadway: García Lorca and the New York Theatre, 1929–1930." *Gestos* 8, no. 16 (1993): 135–48.

Chapter 4: "*El público, Así que pasen cinco años, El sueño de la vida:* tres dramas expresionistas de García Lorca." In *El teatro en España entre la tradición y la vanguardia (1918–1939)*, edited by Dru Dougherty and María Francisca Vilches de Frutos, 215–26. Madrid: CSIC / Fundación Federico García Lorca / Tabacalera, SA, 1992.

Chapter 5: "'Un dificilísimo juego poético': Theme and Symbol in Lorca's *El público.*" *Romance Quarterly* 39, no. 3 (1992): 331–46. Reproduced by kind permission of *Romance Quarterly* and Taylor & Francis Group, https://www.tandfonline.com/.

Chapter 6: "'Una desorientación absoluta': Juliet and the Shifting Sands of García Lorca's *El público*." *Revista Hispánica Moderna* 50, no. 1 (1997): 67–85. Reproduced by kind permission of *Revista Hispánica Moderna*.

Chapter 9: "Lorca's *El sueño de la vida:* Social Concern, Metatheatrical Subversion, and the Audience's Experience." *Hispanófila* 197 (Spring 2023): 129–44. Reproduced by kind permission of *Hispanófila*.

NOTE ON TRANSLATIONS

Titles of plays, books, newspapers, magazines, and articles published in Spanish are given only in their original form. Quotations originally in Spanish are normally followed by an English translation. Rather than relying on the published English versions of the four plays, many of which can be in one way or another problematic, I have provided all my own translations. They have no literary pretensions: in general, I have aimed for fairly literal accuracy while balancing this goal with avoiding the production of overly stilted versions.

Lorca's Experimental Theater

Introduction

None of Lorca's plays can be considered as entirely conventional when judged by the standards of his day, but they bucked convention to varying degrees and in a range of different ways.[1] As a result, some were—and still remain—more approachable for mainstream audiences than others. In this volume, I shall be concerned with the mature examples of Lorca's work for the theater that pushed the boundaries most forcefully and did indeed break the guardrails of acceptability. But first I want to sketch briefly the overall history of Lorca's dramatic output to better situate the four plays that are the focus of this study.

When Lorca was eighteen, he shifted his major endeavors from music to literature, and the following year—1917—he started writing plays. In rapid succession, he produced more than a dozen.[2] Many are short, exploratory first drafts, petering out after just a few pages, and only a couple achieve the length of what might be considered a fully developed play. Likewise, the earliest texts found in this corpus—essentially dialogues or earnest discussions presented in theatrical format—are lacking in dramatic qualities and rather resemble quite closely the prose pieces that Lorca was writing over the same period. As their titles suggest, a good number of them are centrally preoccupied with fundamental issues of a personal, philosophical, or religious nature. However, others—*La viudita que se quería casar, Comedia de la carbonerita,* and *Elenita*—connect with elements of Romantic drama, the ballad tradition, folklore, popular and children's song, and puppetry. Lorca was just beginning to learn his craft, and he made no attempt to have any of these works performed.

Lorca's first play to receive a theatrical premiere—*El maleficio de la mariposa*—has been written about extensively and only requires brief mention here. Commissioned by Gregorio Martínez Sierra and based on a narrative poem by Lorca (now lost), he worked on it over the latter half of 1919 and beginning of 1920, and after several postponements, it opened at the Teatro Eslava on March 22, 1920, and flopped badly. After a total of four performances, it was hurriedly removed from the repertoire. Martínez Sierra was one of the very few impresarios—probably the only one—who at that time would have been enthusiastic about bringing to the Madrid stage a play written in verse and whose characters were mainly cockroaches, joined by a butterfly, a scorpion, and glowworms. It is worth mentioning that Lorca had originally called the play "La ínfima comedia," a title ill suited to commercial promotion. This was changed to "La estrella del prado" and then to *El maleficio de la mariposa*. Lorca had conceived of "La ínfima comedia" as being performed by puppets, and the change to actors was imposed by Martínez Sierra at a fairly late point in the preparations for its staging. It is tempting to think that a production using puppets might have met with somewhat less resistance. Of course, the work's evident unconventionality goes a long way toward explaining its lack of success with critics and public alike—its intrinsic dramatic qualities are more debatable, and in hindsight we can see how it falls squarely within the tradition of Symbolist theater that at the time had only made relatively minor inroads in Spain.[3]

If we follow through the decade of the 1920s the sequence of the composition of plays by Lorca that are well known today, he now turned back to popular traditions and puppetry, first with an unfinished piece that he titled *Cristobícal* or *Cristobítal* (1921) and then with *Los títeres de Cachiporra* (also known as *Tragicomedia de don Cristóbal y la señá Rosita*, 1922). Again, these were hardly standard fare, and despite a whole series of attempts by Lorca to see *Los títeres* produced by several different theatrical companies, it remained unperformed at the time of his death. It was followed by the historical verse drama *Mariana Pineda* (written 1923–24, performed 1927) and the two-act "Farsa violenta" *La zapatera prodigiosa* (written 1924–25, performed 1930), both of which proved somewhat more palatable to impresarios, actors, critics, and audiences alike, and while neither were flops, nor could they be counted as huge successes.

Next would come *Amor de don Perlimplín con Belisa en su jardín* (written 1925–26, performed 1933), which is the first of the plays to be treated in this book. Besides *Amor de don Perlimplín,* there are manuscript traces of several other theatrical works that Lorca drafted over the period 1925–29, whose incomplete, fragmentary nature recalls that of the dramatic *juvenilia.* Based on the textual evidence that is often no more than a page or two in length, most of these plays were again distinctly unconventional in their conception: *Diego Corrientes. Tópico andaluz en tres actos* (ca. 1925–26), *Ampliación fotográfica. Drama* (1926), *Drama fotográfico* (1926), *Rosa mudable. Drama fotografiado* (ca. 1927–29), *Posada* (second half of 1920s), and *Dragón* (ca. 1928–29).[4] The surviving fragment of *Dragón* consists of a substantial prologue that has important connections with both *La zapatera prodigiosa* and *El sueño de la vida.*

When we reach the decade of the 1930s, the divide between experimentalism and approachability seems to become clearer. To the one side stand *El público, Así que pasen cinco años,* and *El sueño de la vida,* and to the other the plays with which Lorca achieved real recognition, thanks to their box office success: *Bodas de sangre, Yerma,* and *Doña Rosita la soltera. La casa de Bernarda Alba,* completed in the summer of 1936, but not performed until 1945, clearly falls into this second category, as is demonstrated by its celebrity nowadays, while somewhere in the margins we can situate the second of the puppet plays that Lorca completed, *El retablillo de don Cristóbal* (1931), which, unlike the earlier work, did see performances during his lifetime (twice in 1934 and once in 1935).

However, this appearance of a distinct dichotomy between the two groups can be misleading. In his study of Lorca's drama and its reception in Spain over the 1920s and 1930s, Luis Fernández-Cifuentes argued that

las obras dramáticas que García Lorca estrenó en vida (1920–1936) no constituyeron una transgresión tan estruendosa o absoluta que obligara a los críticos a formular expresamente su desconcierto. Se diría, más bien, que con tales obras modificó considerablemente los paradigmas existentes sin llegar a desplazarlos con un paradigma decididamente nuevo y revolucionario.[5]

the dramatic works that García Lorca premiered during his lifetime (1920–1936) did not constitute such an outrageous or absolute transgression that it obliged the critics to specifically formulate their discomposure. One would say, rather, that with these works he modified considerably the existing paradigms without ever arriving at the point of supplanting them with a decidedly new and revolutionary paradigm.

In particular, in the chapters of his book on *Bodas de sangre, Yerma,* and *Doña Rosita la soltera,* Cifuentes demonstrated how these works also diverged significantly from the contemporaneous standard fare yet at the same time met with broad acceptance and in many cases acclaim. They achieved this by various means, not straying too far from the established norms, introducing the innovations that they contained with a certain degree of moderation or subtlety, and compensating for any disconcerting features with a range of strong dramatic qualities.

Coincidentally, in the same year of publication as Cifuentes's book, I argued in an article that Lorca was perfectly aware of what he was doing and that the differences observable between, for instance, *El público* and *Bodas de sangre* were attributable to a conscious strategy on his part.[6] Not only did Lorca value his experimental works over his other plays, as we shall see in greater detail in chapter 1, but he had also realized that if he ever wanted to see them performed onstage, he would first have to build a solid reputation as a successful playwright and accumulate enough "cultural capital" in order to insist that they be produced and to convince a dramatic company to take the risk. And if he needed to acquire real status in the cutthroat world of the Spanish theater, he would have to write plays that were sufficiently approachable to be commercial successes. As he told a journalist in the spring of 1936: "Yo en el teatro he seguido una trayectoria definida. Mis primeras comedias son irrepresentables. [. . .] En estas comedias imposibles está mi verdadero propósito. Pero para demostrar una personalidad y tener derecho al respeto he dado otras cosas" (In the theater, I have followed a clear trajectory. My foremost plays are unperformable. [. . .] My true purpose is in these impossible plays. But in order to establish a personality and have the right to be respected I have given other things).[7] In this key statement, *personalidad* and *respeto* imply authority and "bankability," concepts that are also reflected in a comment that Lorca reportedly made to Rafael Martínez Nadal apropos of *El público:* "Es el tipo de teatro que quiero imponer cuando termine la trilogía bíblica que estoy preparando" (It is the type of theater that I want to impose once I have finished the biblical trilogy that I am preparing).[8] While Nadal's memory may not be exact, the verb *imponer* certainly rings true.

After *El público,* the next play, *Así que pasen cinco años,* does give the impression of Lorca pulling back and attempting to moderate his extreme experimentalism just a little; it is not quite as daring as *El público,* but it certainly stands well outside the boundaries of mainstream theater and brings its own substantial challenges to performance and interpretation. While the one extant act of *Un sueño de la vida* is also somewhat more approachable, at least on first encounter, it creates its own complexities with a redoubling of the metatheatrical dimension and the addition of sociopolitical themes. Furthermore, the outlines of the action of acts 2 and 3 that have come down to us suggest that, had it been completed, it might well have been just as radical, disquieting, and revolutionary as *El público.*

Structure of This Volume

My engagement with Lorca's dramatic production dates back to 1985. Over the years, I have written short monographs on *La zapatera prodigiosa* (1991) and *Yerma* (2003) as well as articles and essays concerned with *Bodas de sangre, Doña Rosita la soltera,* and *La casa de Bernarda Alba* and a variety of other aspects of Lorca's writings for the stage and the troupes with which he worked.

In the present volume, I have chosen to focus on *Amor de don Perlimplín con Belisa en su jardín* plus the three experimental works from the 1930s. Chapter 1, entitled "Staging the Unstageable," gives details concerning the chronology of composition of the four plays, the texts that have survived, what Lorca had to say about these works in newspaper interviews, and most importantly, his numerous attempts to get what he called his "unperformable plays" actually performed. After a chapter on *Amor de don Perlimplín,* two further contextual chapters cover what I would consider the two most significant factors that encouraged Lorca to venture further down the path already embarked upon with *Amor de don Perlimplín,* namely his exposure to theater in New York over 1929–30 and his increasing familiarity with Expressionist drama that he both read and heard about from other theater professionals. Thereafter, two chapters each are devoted to *El público* and *Así que pasen cinco años,* and the book ends with a chapter on *El sueño de la vida*. Six previously published studies are reprinted here in revised form (full bibliographical details are given in the acknowledgments) in combination with three newly composed chapters plus this introduction.

The only mildly controversial feature here, I imagine, would be my decision to include *Amor de don Perlimplín* as part of the chosen corpus. As I see it, the play straddles the two decades in a number of ways: it was composed in the 1920s and was revised in the 1930s; it was nearly performed in 1929 but in the event was not staged until 1933; more importantly, from the technical and thematic perspectives, it glances back but at the same time clearly anticipates what would come in the 1930s. Thus, *Amor de don Perlimplín* retains a few ties with *La zapatera prodigiosa*. There the dramatic situation is of an older man married to a younger woman, and the denouement is decidedly open-ended: have the main characters grown psychologically over the course of the action, or will they go back to their old ways? has each of them achieved a greater acceptance of the other, and if so, to what extent? how happy or conflictive will their marriage be from this point forward? However, in *Amor de don Perlimplín,* as I argue in chapter 2, thematic ambiguity gives way to a kind of pervasive and unsettling undecidability, in which the spectator or reader is left with various competing options as to what to take away from the play, an aspect that situates it closer to the experimental pieces of the 1930s. Likewise, stylization increasingly topples over into unreality in the characters, sets, and costumes that Lorca prescribes, culminating in the two Duendes who come onstage to draw a veil over the wedding night, the "grandes cuernos de ciervo" (large antlers) with which Perlimplín awakes adorning his head, and the dining room where "las perspectivas están equivocadas deliciosamente. La mesa con todos los objetos pintados como en una 'Cena' primitiva" (the perspectives are delightfully wrong. The table with all the objects painted as if in a primitive "Last Supper").[9] With all this, it is clear that we are moving ever closer to the world of *El público* and *Así que pasen cinco años.*

1

Staging the Unstageable

Efforts to Perform the Experimental Plays, 1929–1936

Amor de don Perlimplín con Belisa en su jardín was completed by early 1926 but had to wait over seven years to be performed, just twice, in the spring of 1933, brought to the stage by an amateur drama group (Anfistora), with which Lorca was a close collaborator. *El público*, whose first version was completed in the summer of 1930, never made it past the selection process of a theatrical company. *Así que pasen cinco años*, finished in summer 1931, entered initial rehearsals in the fall of 1933 and a final phase in the spring of 1936; its premiere, again by Anfistora, was eventually postponed to the fall of 1936 and hence never took place. Lorca worked on *El sueño de la vida* over the second half of 1935 and into 1936, but the play was never completed because of his assassination in the opening weeks of the Civil War. The following sections present a detailed overview of what we know about these plays' chronologies of composition, their texts, Lorca's plans for them, his descriptions of them, and his various attempts to have them publicly performed.

Amor de don Perlimplín con Belisa en su jardín

Lorca may have written a first draft of a plot outline for *Amor de don Perlimplín* as early as 1922 or 1923 and the first surviving fragment of dialogue might be dated to somewhere between 1923 and 1925.[1] But he did not start working on the play in earnest until 1925, immediately after completing, or coming close to completing, *La zapatera prodigiosa*.[2] In a letter from the summer of 1924, he refers to his work on *La zapatera* and then

7

asks his correspondent, Melchor Fernández Almagro, to do something for him: "Léele el reparto a Cipriano [Rivas Cherif] el *simpático y culto* comediógrafo y dile si quiere colaborar conmigo en otra cosa que preparo, que ya le diré" (Read the cast list to Cipriano, the likable and cultured playwright, and ask him if he wants to collaborate with me on another thing that I am preparing, which I will tell him about in due course). That "other thing" could well be *Perlimplín*. Likewise, announcing to his family in April 1925 his upcoming visit to Salvador Dalí's home for Easter, he told them that "me voy antes con objeto de en el silencio del pueblo [Cadaqués] trabajar en una nueva obra teatral que he comenzado y hacer la última escena de la Zapatera" (I am going early so that in the silence of the village, I can work on a new theatrical work that I have started and write the last scene of *La zapatera prodigiosa*). That "new work" was very likely *Perlimplín*. Its first mention by name comes in a letter to Fernández Almagro from September 1925, where the line break points up the fact that the title forms a pair of rhyming octosyllabic lines:

> Y hago ahora una obra de teatro grotesca:
> "Amor de Don Perlimplín
> con Belisa en su jardín."
> Son las aleluyas que te expliqué en [el café] Savoia, ¿recuerdas? Disfruto como un idiota. No tienes idea.[3]

> And now I am writing a grotesque play:
> "The Love of Don Perlimplín
> with Belisa in His Garden."
> These are the rhyming couplets of a strip cartoon that I explained to you in the [café] Savoia, do you remember? I am having a crazy amount of fun. You have no idea.

A few months later—January 1926—Lorca followed up by transcribing a substantial passage that in the final version of the text would form the central section of "Cuadro Cuarto." He referred to it as a "sample" ("botón [de muestra]") and also here specified its subtitle as an "aleluya erótica."[4]

By the early spring of 1926, then, the writing of *Amor de don Perlimplín* was doubtless completed. Around this time, Lorca finally gave up on

Gregorio Martínez Sierra and his Teatro Eslava as an option—till that time his main possibility—for getting his plays performed. After the production and flop of *El maleficio de la mariposa* (March 1920), Martínez Sierra had nevertheless continued to show interest in staging Lorca's subsequent plays, *Mariana Pineda, Los títeres de Cachiporra,* and *La zapatera prodigiosa,* and of these, primarily *Mariana Pineda.* However, six years had passed, nothing after *El maleficio* had seen the light of day, and Lorca's hopefulness and patience had finally snapped: "Ahora quisiera resolver la *Mariana Pineda* ya que el cabrón de Martínez Sierra se ha portado como tal. Pero Martínez Sierra *ignora mi fantasía.* No sabe él, la *que se ha echado* encima conmigo. Cabrón" (Now I would like to resolve the question of *Mariana Pineda* since Martínez Sierra has behaved just like the bastard that he is. But Martínez Sierra *is unaware of my imagination.* He has no idea of *what he has got himself into* with me. Bastard).[5]

Even before this, Lorca had begun to explore other possible channels for performance—for instance, Cipriano Rivas Cherif (as in the letter cited earlier)—and he now contemplated the possibility of turning to Rivas Cherif's amateur group El Mirlo Blanco,[6] both for *Los títeres de Cachiporra* and for another projected but unrealized play, *Ampliación fotográfica,* or *Drama fotográfico.* In May or June 1926, Lorca also read his most recently completed play, *Amor de don Perlimplín,* to Salvador Dalí and Luis Buñuel. Dalí was away from Madrid from the beginning of the summer holidays in 1925 until the beginning of May 1926, when he returned to take his end-of-year exams at the art school in the middle of June. Buñuel moved to Paris in January 1925 and thereafter sporadically visited Madrid, and so these two months are the only period after the completion of *Perlimplín* when all three men were in Madrid simultaneously. However, the event did not go as anticipated: Buñuel reacted very negatively, and Dalí followed his friend's lead.[7]

Over 1927 and 1928, Lorca's struggles to get his plays performed continued. After further irritating delays, he finally managed to see *Mariana Pineda* on the stage in Barcelona (June 1927): this was his first collaboration with Margarita Xirgu, who, in the 1930s, would become his most important actress and leader of a company. *Mariana* transferred to Madrid in October. Despite interest from several actors and companies, no productions of other plays were forthcoming, and a newspaper column from the time of the Madrid opening of *Mariana* listed the "tres obras nuevas, verdaderamente nuevas" (three new plays, truly new) that were ready and waiting but yet to be premiered: *La zapatera, Perlimplín,* and *Los títeres.*[8] In the summer of 1928, Lorca stayed on in Madrid waiting for his *Romancero gitano* to be published—the official date would not be until July 20—and at some moment during the last week in June, he gave a reading of *Perlimplín* to an unspecified "group of friends."[9]

Late that fall, things began to look up. In an interview, Lorca claimed that he was going to publish a volume of theater to include *Los títeres* and *Perlimplín,* but as was often the case, this never came to fruition. More importantly, after El Mirlo Blanco and a brief adventure with El Cántaro Roto, Rivas Cherif was back with yet another minority theater group, El Caracol, which debuted in the Sala Rex in Madrid on November 24.[10] The inaugural performance included a lecture by Azorín ("El teatro moderno"); three plays by him, *Prólogo a lo invisible, La arañita en el espejo,* and *Doctor Death, de tres a cinco;* and also *Un duelo,* by Chekhov. Stagings of other works followed on December 6, 19, and 29, 1928, and January 5, 1929.[11] By the second week of December, Lorca informed his family that "es probable que haya estreno mío y *muy pronto*" (it is probable that I will have a premiere and *very soon*), and subsequently, *Perlimplín* was chosen for the sixth presentation of El Caracol (there was only one performance of each production). By the second half of January, he reported that "han empezado ya los ensayos de mi *Perlimplín,* que pone la compañía 'Caracol.' Creo que resultará bien" (the rehearsals of my *Perlimplín* have already started; it is being put on by the Caracol company. I think it will turn out well).[12] The performance was slated for February 5 (in conjunction with another play, *Las nueve y media o Por qué don Fabián cambia constantemente de cocinera,* by Enrique Suárez de Deza), but then it was postponed to the next day, perhaps because Rivas Cherif and Lorca did not think it quite ready. Unfortunately, overnight between the fifth and the sixth, the Queen Mother, María Cristina, died, and so all theaters' activities for that day were canceled as part of the observation of official mourning. Although the theaters were temporarily closed to the public, a further rehearsal of Lorca's play was held on February 6, and it seems that it was during this event that Colonel Agustín Marzo Balaguer, chief of the Madrid police, entered the auditorium, witnessed part of the rehearsal, and subsequently shut down the production and confiscated the master copy (director's copy) of the text.[13] Various explanations for the reasons behind this action have been proposed and are fully treated by Ucelay.[14] Whatever the case, and despite Rivas Cherif's protestations to the contrary,[15] this also spelled the end for El Caracol. Rivas Cherif joined the company of Irene López Heredia as its artistic advisor, and they set off to Buenos Aires at the beginning of May;[16] Lorca would also cross the Atlantic less than two months later.

Fortunately, Lorca still had in his possession a text of the play, most likely the full autograph manuscript from which a certain number of typed copies would have been made in preparation for the El Caracol rehearsals. This is one of the works in progress that he took with him when he left Spain for New York. Ucelay believes that Lorca reconstructed the play from memory while he was there,[17] but she overlooks the fact that the three typed copies for El Caracol that we know of (plus other actors' copies) must have been made from a (manuscript) base text. Ángel del Río reports that at their summer vacation cabin near Shandaken, in the Catskills, where Lorca spent some time—perhaps up to two weeks—with del Río and his family, he read them "the play *Don Perlimplín,* which he had revised in New York."[18] We do not know the nature of those revisions, whether it was a question of just some minor tinkering with the manuscript that he had brought along or whether it was more extensive and necessitated a complete rewriting. Either way, this process seems to have taken place during the summer and fall of 1929.[19] *Perlimplín* is very likely the play mentioned by Lorca to Carlos Morla Lynch at the end of September or beginning of October: "He escrito mucho. Tengo casi dos libros de poemas y una pieza de teatro" (I have written a lot. I have almost two books of poetry and a play). By later in October, Lorca was again seeing real possibilities of bringing about productions of two of those "three new plays, truly new" that had lingered on since the middle of the decade:

Ahora se empiezan a mover algunos amigos míos ingleses en New York para ver si consiguen que se ponga mi teatro aquí. Esto puede ser muy bueno para mí y ojalá se consiga, porque sería excelente cosa.

De ponerse algo, se pondría el *Perlimplín* y los *Títeres de Cachiporra,* traducidos y con gran decorado.

Now some English friends of mine in New York are beginning to take steps to see if they can manage to get my theater put on here. This could be very good for me and hopefully it can be done, because that would be really excellent.

If something were put on, it would be *Perlimplín* and the *Títeres de Cachiporra,* in translation and with a full-scale staging and set.

He added: "es bonito llegar a New York y que representen aquí lo que en España se prohibió indecentemente o no quieren montar *porque no es de público*" (it is gratifying to arrive in New York and have them perform here what in Spain was indecently prohibited or what they do not want to put on *because it does not have wide audience appeal*).[20] The adverb *indecentemente* refers—with a kind of pun—to the unjustifiable cancellation of the performance in February on the spurious grounds of indecency, but more telling and far-reaching is the other comment: time and time again, when he sent his plays to representatives of theater companies or talked in person with leading actresses and actors, he was told—and would be told—that personally they liked the work but that they judged it to be not commercially viable. This is one reason why Margarita Xirgu was so important for his budding career: she was willing to take a risk on *Mariana Pineda* and again on *La zapatera prodigiosa.*[21]

More readings followed. María Antonieta Rivas Mercado and Emilio Amero were not "English" but rather part of a set of Mexican friends, and in late October, Lorca shared both *Perlimplín* and *Los títeres* with them.[22] A further reading of *Perlimplín* took place at the home of Herschel and Norma Brickell, with Jack Leacock (a linen merchant from Madeira) and Mildred Adams also in attendance.[23] Lorca had already mentioned the idea of translation back in October, and now the reception of the play was so positive that as Adams recalled, "Federico insisted on giving me the script to translate into English."[24]

Back in Spain at the beginning of the new decade, Lorca's success in getting his plays into production was still low. The one bright spot was *La zapatera prodigiosa.* Rivas Cherif had brought El Caracol back into existence in a new and more stable form, in a collaboration with Margarita Xirgu at the Teatro Español, and Lorca's play was staged just before Christmas 1930 in a double bill alongside a piece described as a "fábula china medieval" (medieval Chinese fable), *El príncipe, la princesa y su destino.* In subsequent performances, this was replaced by Calderón's *auto sacramental El gran teatro del mundo,*[25] and the two plays enjoyed a run of almost three weeks. In an interview with the three principals, Lorca, when asked whether he had other plays in waiting, again named *Los títeres* and *Perlimplín,* to which list he was now able to add the newest, *El público.*[26] And once again, true to previous form, there followed another lull of over two years, with no play of his staged until March 1933.

Meanwhile, back in New York, Mildred Adams had been struggling with her translation. Then, on assignment for the *New York Times,* she traveled to Europe in October 1931 and arrived in Madrid in late November or the very beginning of December.[27] We can place her there on December 2, when she attended a homage function at the Círculo de Bellas Artes for the dancer Antonia Mercé, "La Argentina," along with the antiquarian, art dealer, collector, and translator José Weissberger and Adams's friend Margaret Palmer (an American living in Spain and working as a local art agent for the Carnegie Institution).[28] In her biography, she narrates her chance encounter with Lorca in a café, which occurred shortly after she got to Madrid:

> Then "Where is my play?" he demanded. "In my suitcase," was the reply, given with as little explanation as his question. . . . "Good. Then I won't have to rewrite it. They're going to put it on," he said, and with no more talk except to ask where I was staying, he returned to his table.[29]

Along with her unfinished translation, Adams had naturally brought the manuscript that Lorca had left with her in New York, which was the only version of the play that he then had any access to. The next day, Lorca is supposed to have sent his brother Francisco to collect it in person, though we have reason to believe that Adams and Lorca may have made some efforts to work on the translation before the manuscript was finally returned to him.[30]

Seemingly before departing for Europe, Adams had also sent off a copy of her partial translation (likely the carbon copy) to Edith Isaacs, the editor of *Theatre Arts Monthly,* who did not see much prospect for it in the United States and also commented that "I believe that is what you said you thought too."[31] In her later biography, Adams sounds more defeatist in tone: "The process of translation had proved impossible. In Spanish the play was delightful; in English it did not make theater sense. Also there was too much poetry in it for a journalist to cope with, particularly one who has always held to the belief that poetry can be translated properly only by a poet. Baffled, I had brought the play back to Spain."[32] In 1949–50 Adams corresponded with Lorca's sister Concha about her contacts with Lorca and his plays. Adams told her that she had believed that Lorca had left *Los títeres de Cachiporra* with her at the same time as *Perlimplín,* but in a later pencil note to herself (dated May 18, 1959) on a copy of the letter, she writes: "Having returned *Don Perlimplín* as too poetic for translation, he FGL handed this to me and said 'This is prose—you can translate this.'"[33]

In the archive of the Fundación Federico García Lorca, we also find a postcard sent by Adams to Lorca. It gives every indication of having been written in New York (a postscript is signed "M. New York," and she tells Lorca that his friend José Antonio Rubio Sacristán is there; Rubio Sacristán had shared an apartment with Lorca over 1929–30). The missive is addressed to "Ayala, 60, Madrid, Spain," the attic apartment where Lorca lived between the last months of 1930 and the first half of 1933. The stamp cancellation on the postcard is difficult to decipher, but it seems to read "DEC 19 193? 4PM," the last figure of the year being obscured by an excess of ink. Since we know that Adams was already in Madrid by early December 1931 (and had left the States in October), it would appear that this must correspond to another year, either 1930 or 1932. Perhaps significantly, there is a gap in her regular contributions to the *New York Times* between December 18, 1932, and June 18, 1933. In the aforementioned postcard, Adams writes: "Voy a volver a Madrid al fin de esta semana, y si Vd. quiere, podemos acabar esa traducción. Voy a visitar una amiga mía muy simpática, la señorita Palmer, cuya casa tiene una atmósfera mucho más agradable que lo [*sic*] de un hotel" (I am going to return to Madrid at the end of this week, and if you want, we can finish that translation. I am going to visit a very nice friend of mine, Miss Palmer, whose house has a much more pleasant atmosphere than that of a hotel). This is Margaret Palmer, already mentioned alongside Adams in the 1931 *ABC* report, and "that translation" could either be *Perlimplín* or *Los títeres de Cachiporra,* as presumably she was imagining that they could work together on some of the more challenging passages.[34]

However, the vicissitudes of the text of *Amor de don Perlimplín* were only just beginning. At some time between December 1931 (when Lorca got the manuscript back) and the fall of 1932, it went missing again. Given that he told Adams that "they're going to put it on," it seems quite possible that it was lost at some point during this new initiative, which also came to naught. Ucelay plausibly suggests that after the relative success of *La zapatera*, Rivas Cherif might have expressed renewed interest in performing *Perlimplín*, especially as he was now collaborating with Xirgu and working at the Teatro Español.[35] Whatever the case, when Pura Maórtua de Ucelay approached Lorca concerning the possibility of including *La zapatera prodigiosa* in the repertoire of the amateur theater group of the Asociación Femenina de Cultura Cívica (later known as the Club Teatral de Cultura and eventually as the Club Anfistora), he made her a counteroffer. He would authorize the production of *La zapatera* and indeed aid with the directing so long as Maórtua could retrieve from the censorship office a copy of *Perlimplín*, so that the club could offer both in a double bill.[36] Evidently, Lorca no longer had any version of the play in his possession.

Given the change of government from Primo de Rivera's dictatorship to the democratic Second Republic, Maórtua expected the task to be relatively simple, but in the event, she needed to pester the employees on a daily basis for weeks before they acceded to her request. For the Sala Rex production, two typed copies of the play had been submitted beforehand for official scrutiny, as was the case with all performances of all plays in the 1920s, and in addition, the director's working copy had been confiscated during the dress rehearsal. What Maórtua recovered was one of the two "censorship copies," so it must have lacked whatever handwritten changes had been added during the rehearsals of January 1929.[37] This then served as the base text for acting copies to be made, and it was also used as the director's copy in 1933, as it contains a good number of manuscript emendations made by Lorca, Maórtua, and Santiago Ontañón (who designed the sets and played the part of Perlimplín). Many of these emendations match the text of the revised New York version of 1929; although that Spanish original is lost, Adams's translation of it can be used as an indirect witness to the revisions that Lorca made while in New York and possibly, too, in Madrid in late 1931.[38]

Maórtua having fulfilled her half of the bargain, in March 1933 *Perlimplín* went into rehearsal, along with *La zapatera,* and both plays were performed on April 5, 1933, in the Teatro Español in what was described as a Gran Función de Gala.[59] Lorca directed both works and delivered the prologue to *La zapatera.* He also gave a long interview on the importance of amateur theater groups.[40] The production was extensively reviewed in the Madrid press. The double bill was repeated for one more performance on May 3.[41]

Thereafter, Lorca still talked on a number of occasions about publishing *Amor de don Perlimplín* (along with other plays) and about a new staging of it. He envisaged editions of *Mariana Pineda, La zapatera prodigiosa, Amor de don Perlimplín, El público,* and now also *Así que pasen cinco años* and *Bodas de sangre,* with the chronologically most recent play, *Bodas,* to be published first.[42] While in Buenos Aires, he outlined his plan to stage *Don Perlimplín* back in Spain "en la próxima temporada" (during the next theatrical season), in 1934,[43] but then in a letter home from November 1933, he claimed—exaggeratedly, in the case of *Perlimplín*—that "ya empiezan a ensayar la *Zapatera* y el *Perlimplín* para los que hay una gran expectación" (they are already beginning to rehearse the *Zapatera* and *Perlimplín* for both of which there is great anticipation).[44] During his stay in Argentina, Lorca was working on *Yerma,* and when asked about a possible premiere there, he diverted attention away from it: "En cambio es casi seguro que estrene *Amor de don Perlimplín con Belisa en su jardín,* una aleluya, una cosita ligera, en un acto, muy diferente de *Yerma* y de *Bodas de sangre*" (Conversely, it is almost certain that I will premiere *Amor de don Perlimplín con Belisa en su jardín,* an "aleluya," a light little thing, in one act, very different from *Yerma* and *Bodas de sangre*).[45] As the time for his return to Spain approached, Lola Membrives and her company conceived the idea of putting on "una función en mi homenaje y como despedida" (a homage and farewell performance), a special, one-off event to consist of "un acto de cada una de las obras que he estrenado, y después yo haré el *Perlimplín*" (one act of each of the plays that I have premiered, and afterward I will do *Perlimplín*),[46] the latter phrase meaning that Lorca himself would give a dramatic reading of the text. As the date approached, the program was firmed up: first as one act of *Bodas de sangre,* one act of *La zapatera prodigiosa,* and the reading of *Amor de don Perlimplín,* and then as act 3 of *Mariana Pineda,* act 2 of *La zapatera,* the last scene of *Bodas de sangre,* and Lorca's reading of act 1 of *Yerma.*[47] Once again, *Amor de don Perlimplín* was sidelined. In light of this, Lorca's last mention of the play, in a broadcast radio interview from 1935, was particularly poignant:

> Ahora, si me pregunta usted qué obra mía me gusta más, le diré que es una obra pequeña que por su lirismo verdadero ninguna compañía profesional se atreve a poner y que se llama *Amor de don Perlimplín con Belisa en su jardín.*[48]

> Now, if you ask me which play of mine I like the most, I will tell you that it is a small work that because of its true lyricism no professional company dares to put on and which is called *Amor de don Perlimplín con Belisa en su jardín.*

Of the four plays under consideration in this book, *Amor de don Perlimplín con Belisa en su jardín* was the only one to be performed by a theatrical company in front of an audience during Lorca's lifetime, and then only twice, on two evenings in April and May 1933.

El público

What we know about the compositional history of *El público* is frustratingly incomplete. It is possible, perhaps even likely, that Lorca may have made some preliminary sketches for parts of the play while he was in New York. Ángel del Río reports that "at the farm [. . .] he also read to us [. . .] fragments of [. . .] *The Public.*"[49] This was around the first week of September 1929. Writing to his family in the second half of October, he told them about what he had been working on and also explained why he was doing so: "he empezado a escribir una cosa de teatro que puede ser interesante. Hay que pensar en el teatro del porvenir. Todo lo que existe ahora en España está muerto. O se cambia el teatro de raíz o se acaba para siempre. No hay otra solución" (I have begun to write a thing for the theater that could be interesting. We must think about the theater of the future. Everything that exists nowadays in Spain is dead. Either the theater is changed at its root or it's finished for good. There is no other solution).[50] It is plausible to think that this "thing for the theater" that might bring about a radical change could have been the beginnings of *El público,* but we cannot be certain.

The first solid fact is provided by the sole surviving manuscript of the play. Martínez Nadal has repeated many times his account of how the manuscript came to be in his possession—left with him in July 1936 just before Lorca's fateful return to Granada—but a number of critics have questioned its accuracy and pointed out historical flaws in his version of events. The letterhead paper on which the opening scene and the start of the next scene are written is from the Hotel "La Unión" in Havana.[51] Lorca was in Cuba from March 7 through June 12, 1930. The text is titled *El público. Drama en veinte cuadros y un asesinato,* but there is no indication of scene or act, only the opening stage direction, "Cuarto del Director," and then the subsequent one, "Ruina romana," that indicate the two locations of the action. "Ruina romana" would later be adopted—mistakenly, I believe—as the name or title for this scene; the sequence of the manuscript indicates that this must be the second one in the play, just as "Cuarto del Director" was the first. Despite this confusion, given the problematical nature of the numbering of the scenes, these opening stage directions remain useful as shorthand for referring to a given scene. The pages that contain the first scene have a good number of crossings-out and emendations on them, suggesting that this could indeed be a first draft, while the few pages of the opening of "Ruina romana" are very clean, indicating perhaps that this was already a fair copy of a previous draft.

It seems probable that Lorca composed a good deal of *El público* while in Cuba, and the continuation of "Ruina romana" as well as the long untitled scene that opens with the stage direction "Muro de arena" are written on much larger sheets of paper with faint printed horizontal lines. While in Havana, Lorca spent a lot of time at the house of a family of two brothers and two sisters, Enrique, Carlos Manuel, Flor, and Dulce María Loynaz. According to Flor, "aquí escribió poemas y también leía y corregía páginas de su obra teatral *El público*" (here he wrote poems and also read and corrected pages of his play *El público*), and he gave a reading of what he had written to her and Carlos Manuel.[52] Before leaving, he presented a manuscript of the play (almost certainly unfinished at that time) to Carlos Manuel, who in later life destroyed it.[53] It is impossible to know whether those pages represented a draft earlier than the manuscript that has been preserved or whether they were a copy of it—up to the point that he had reached—that he made in order to offer it as a gift. Likewise, Luis Cardoza y Aragón, another frequent and close companion during the weeks in Havana, reports that "mi memoria me dicta que escribió escenas de *El público* [. . .]. Me leyó pasajes en estado de fusión, caóticos, que no acierto a clasificar su pertenencia. Buscaba cómo ordenarlos, cómo continuarlos" (my memory tells me that he wrote scenes of *El público* [. . .]. He read to me passages that were in a state of flux, chaotic, and I am not able to say where they belonged. He was trying to work out how to order them, to continue them), and also that "me refirió que iba a escribir el teatro que nadie se había atrevido a escribir por cobardía" (he told me that he was going to write the kind of theater that no one had dared to write out of cowardice).[54] A reference made by Cardoza to Oscar Wilde suggests that he was referring, implicitly, to themes connected with homosexuality.

Lorca arrived back in Granada at the beginning of July 1930. Sometime during that month, he wrote to Rafael Martínez Nadal, reestablishing contact with his friend after his absence and summarizing his recent work: "Tengo muchos versos de *escándalo* y teatro de escándalo también"; "He escrito un drama que daría algo por leértelo en compañía de Miguel [Benítez Inglott]. De tema *francamente* homosexual. Creo que es mi mejor poema" (I have many *scandalous* lines of poetry and scandalous theater as well; I have written a drama that I would love to read to you with Miguel. With an *openly* homosexual theme. I think that it is my best poem).[55] But perhaps "I have written" was a slight exaggeration because the last segment of the manuscript of *El público,* comprised of "Cuadro 5," the brief section opening with the stage direction "Cortina azul," and then "Cuadro 6," all now written on plain paper larger than the letterhead but smaller than the lined sheets, is dated at the very end of August, "Sábado 22 de agosto 1930" (the twenty-second was actually a Friday).

As we shall see, Lorca revised the play on more than one occasion, and there were at least two, perhaps more, subsequent versions of the text, one or more handwritten and at least one typed. But none of these has ever come to light, and they are now presumed lost. Consequently, for modern-day productions and for critical readings, we are obliged to utilize the one script at our disposal, this early, composite manuscript version from 1930. The play as it stands appears to be more or less complete, though it has its internal inconsistencies. For instance, only two of the scenes are numbered by Lorca, 5 and 6, while the four others open simply with a stage direction. This adds up to six, but the section headed "Cortina azul," baptized by Martínez Nadal as the "Solo del pastor bobo" (it could also be considered a kind of "Loa"), occupies less than two manuscript pages, so it is hard to consider it as a fully fledged scene. Several critics have proposed different theories to account for or resolve this numerical conundrum, none of which is entirely convincing. Later versions of the subtitle would reduce the total number of scenes to five.

With the composition of *El público,* Lorca met head-on the difficulties of bringing about real change in the theater culture of the period and of getting what he considered authentic theater staged, challenges that stemmed from what he saw as a rampant and near-ubiquitous culture of commercialism wherein the criterion of success at the box office reigned supreme. And this was based on firsthand experience. After the seemingly endless delays and disappointments of the 1920s and emboldened perhaps by the theatrical scene that he encountered in New York, he now adopted a distinctly confrontational attitude, writing a play that not only took these very issues and problems as one of its own points of departure, given its many metatheatrical features, but which at its core was concerned with various taboo themes and utilized many avant-garde theatrical techniques that would immediately set off a host of red flags for almost any theater company of the time. Jacinto Grau also aimed to challenge the status quo with his play *El señor de Pigmalión* (1921), which was performed in Paris (1923), Prague (1925), and Rome (1926), before being finally premiered in Madrid (1928). The lengthy, complex, and lyrical stage directions in Ramón del Valle-Inclán's *esperpentos* can be understood as another kind of protest.

For the following six years, Lorca's attitude toward the play might appear somewhat ambivalent: on the one hand, he continued working on and revising the text, he gave a number of private readings of the play (which was part of his standard compositional practice), and he approached some actors and companies with a view to its possible staging. On the other hand, simultaneously, to the press he made several comments regarding its unperformability, in the sense that no theater company would want to touch it. The contradiction is only, I believe, superficial: these latter disclaimers were intended to be disarming and strategic, partially explaining why, after *La zapatera,* there were no more premieres immediately forthcoming and at the same time ramping up curiosity and preparing the ground for the moment when some daring theatrical troupe might actually take on the challenge.

In the first interview given shortly after his return to Madrid from Granada, in October 1930, the "twenty acts" of the manuscript were now reduced to six: "se compone de seis actos y un asesinato. [. . .] No sé si será muy representable en el orden material. Los principales personajes del drama son caballos" (it is composed of six acts and an assassination. [. . .] I do not know if it will be very performable from a practical point of view. The main characters of the drama are horses).[56] Just before the first night of *La zapatera,* Lorca distanced himself from the play that was about to open: "No, no es *mi obra.* Mi obra vendrá . . . ; ya tengo algo . . . , algo. Lo que venga será *mi obra.* ¿Sabes cómo titulo *mi obra? El público.* Ésa sí, ésa sí. . . . Dramatismo profundo, profundísimo." (No, it is not *my work.* My work will come . . . ; I already have something . . . , something. What may come will be *my work.* Do you know how I have titled *my work? El público.* That's it, that's it. . . . Deep, very deep dramatism).[57] Right around this time, Lorca gave his first reported reading of *El público* to a group of friends gathered at the residence of Carlos Morla Lynch. Marcelle Auclair misdates this reading to June 22, 1930, when Lorca was still on the liner that would arrive in Cádiz at the end of the month.[58] Martínez Nadal's recollection of the event given to Auclair paints a very negative reaction on the part of Morla Lynch and his wife, Bebé. Perhaps significantly, Morla Lynch himself does not include an account of the evening in his diary. If Martínez Nadal's memory is correct, namely that the script that Lorca read from was "escrita a tinta en pequeñas hojas en octavo" (written in ink on small octavo sheets of paper),[59] then this means that already within something like four months there was a new version of the play or at the very least a fair copy of it.

The subtitle and Lorca's thumbnail description of the contents of the play varied over time. In January 1931, it was characterized as "un drama en seis actos, *El público,* donde se plantea el conflicto de las máscaras y el espíritu" (a drama in six acts, *El público,* where the conflict of masks and the mind is explored),[60] with the "assassination" now suppressed. By spring, a double initiative was launched by an unidentified group of people to whom Lorca must have read the text: "Un grupo de amigos y poetas jóvenes quieren representar mi drama *El público* si la Irene López Heredia, a quien se lo han llevado, no aceptara" (A group of friends and young poets want to perform my drama *El público* if Irene López Heredia, to whom they have taken it, will not agree to do so).[61] López Heredia was a rather more conventional actress than Xirgu, but she had worked with both Ricardo Baeza (1928) and Rivas Cherif (1929).[62] Evidently, she rejected *El público,* and the plan to go it alone did not pan out either. In the summer, it is a little curious to find an upcoming reading announced publicly in the press: listed as attending are the actor Antonio Vico; the artist and designer Santiago Ontañón; the guitarist Regino Sainz de la Maza; writer, journalist, and playwright Samuel Ros; the writer and journalist Miguel Pérez Ferrero; and the architect Carlos Arniches, son of the playwright of the same name.[63] In a much later article, the poet and writer José María Alfaro recalled a reading of the play, given by Lorca on a hot summer's afternoon in his apartment on the top floor of calle Ayala, 60, attended by him, the artists Jesús Olasagasti and Juan Manuel Díaz-Caneja, and Sainz de la Maza.[64] Everything points to this being the same event.

The year 1932 brought a new plan from Rivas Cherif. The summer was traditionally low season for Spanish theaters; he proposed that a group be formed of out-of-work actors and that a committee of writers and dramatists select by voting a series of plays to be performed by them during the summer months at the Teatro Español. One of those already chosen by the committee (of which Lorca was himself a member) was *El público.*[65] The whole project seems to have been sunk—unintentionally—a few days later, when Rivas Cherif was named to an additional position as artistic director of the Teatro Lírico Nacional.[66]

A year later, Lorca brought out two of the scenes in the last number, no. 3, of the literary magazine *Los Cuatro Vientos* (June 1933). A note after the main title gave the important information that this was now "un drama en cinco actos" (a drama in five acts), matching the number of surviving scenes. In the case of the scene that opens with "Ruina romana," the stage direction was converted into a title and then misprinted as "REINA ROMANA" (61–67); "Cuadro 5" was printed unproblematically as "CUADRO

QUINTO" (68–78). The handwritten manuscripts that Lorca sent to Jorge Guillén (one of the editors of the magazine) for this publication are preserved among Guillén's papers lodged in the Biblioteca Nacional, and they constitute one more (incomplete) stage in the history of revisions and versions. On the occasion of this publication, Martínez Nadal asked Lorca why he did not publish the whole piece, to which he reportedly replied: "Porque lo estoy retocando y va a quedar formidable, y sin una sola concesión que facilite su estreno" (Because I am retouching it, and it is going to turn out fantastic, without a single concession that might make its being premiered any easier).[67] However, we now know that at precisely this same time, the editors of *Los Cuatro Vientos* were planning to launch a series of editions to be sponsored by the magazine and produced by Editorial Signo; Lorca was to be one of the authors, and his book in the series would have been none other than *El público.*[68] Unfortunately, as was so often the case, the initiative never got off the ground. These developments may be loosely connected with the ambitious plans that Lorca laid out for a journalist in July: a new edition of *Mariana Pineda;* and editions of *La zapatera, Perlimplín,* and *El público;* as well as the more recent *Así que pasen cinco años* and *Bodas de sangre.*[69] Of *El público,* he observed somewhat cryptically: "que no se ha estrenado ni ha de estrenarse nunca, porque . . . 'no se puede' estrenar" (which has not been premiered nor will ever be premiered because . . . "it cannot" be premiered).

Several weeks after Lorca's departure for Argentina, news came of Rivas Cherif's next initiative in Madrid, which he called the Teatro Escuela de Arte (TEA), an independent institution that would be formed by recent theater conservatory graduates and current students and would offer practical training, while at the same time they rehearsed and performed an ambitious list of works.[70] At the very end of that list, Rivas Cherif added *El público, poema trágico para ser silbado.* This time the overall project did go ahead, and starting in the middle of January 1934, for the next two years a good number of productions were successfully mounted. However, Lorca's play was not among them.

Meanwhile, over the six months that Lorca spent in Buenos Aires and Montevideo, the story was largely the same as before. Immediately upon his arrival, an anonymous journalist reported:

Además de sus tres piezas estrenadas, [. . .] tiene escritas otras dos piezas, que no tiene interés ni muchas esperanzas de representar. Y sobre ellas se expresa así:

—[. . .] En cuanto a la otra, que se titula *El público,* no pretendo estrenarla en Buenos Aires ni en ninguna parte, pues creo que no hay compañía que se anime a llevarla a escena ni público que la tolere sin indignarse.[71]

Besides his three plays that have been premiered, [. . .] he has two other plays finished, which he has no interest in seeing performed nor much hope of that happening. And about them he says this:

—[. . .] As for the other one, which is titled *El público,* I do not intend to premiere it in Buenos Aires or anywhere else, because I do not believe that there is any company that would have the courage to bring it to the stage nor any audience that would tolerate it without becoming outraged.

The notion of the audience's resistance to innovation and the unfamiliar had already been treated metatheatrically by Lorca in several texts, notably the prologue to *La zapatera prodigiosa* and the prologue (the only part written) of the unfinished play *Dragón,*[72] but here the confrontation was even more direct. And so when queried as to the reason for his reluctance, Lorca replied at greater length than usual:

—Pues porque es el espejo del público. Es ir haciendo desfilar en escena los dramas propios que cada uno de los espectadores está pensando, mientras está mirando, muchas veces sin fijarse, la representación. Y como el drama de cada uno a veces es muy punzante y generalmente nada honroso, pues los espectadores en seguida se levantarían indignados e impedirían que continuara la representación. Sí; mi pieza no es una obra para representarse: es, como yo la he definido, "un poema para silbarlo."

—Well because it is the mirror of the audience. What it does is to parade across the stage the private dramas that each one of the spectators is thinking, while he or she is watching the performance, often without paying attention. And since the drama of each one of them is very prickly and usually far from honorable, the outraged spectators would immediately rise up and stop the performance from continuing. Yes; my play is not a work to be performed: it is, as I have defined it, "a poem to be booed."

For his part, Pablo Suero confirmed a sentiment that Lorca had expressed back as early as December 1930: "habla con entusiasmo de dos obras que no ha podido representar y que son, según él, el teatro que quiere hacer. Esas obras se titulan *Así que pasen cinco años* y *El público*" (he speaks enthusiastically about two works that he has not been able to perform and which are, according to him, the kind of theater that he wants to create. Those works are titled *Así que pasen cinco años* and *El público*).[73] In Montevideo, a journalist likewise noted that "tiene, hace tiempo escrita, una obra intitulada *El público*—una terrible sátira, que muy difícil—según él encontrará compañía que se atreva a darla y público que la resista. Él lo ha definido de esta suerte: 'Una pieza para no ser representada, y un poema para ser silbado'" (he has a work that he wrote a while back entitled *El público*—a terrible satire, which according to him will have enormous difficulty in finding a company that would dare to stage it and an audience that would withstand it. He has defined it in this way: "A play not to be performed and a poem to be booed").[74] And back again in Buenos Aires, there was a report of another plan for the play's production: "El poeta de *Bodas de sangre* ha decidido brindar a la compañía que dirigirá el escritor Enrique Gustavino una pieza suya titulada *El público* y subtitulada *poema trágico para ser silbado*. Esta obra será estrenada por el poeta español en su país" (The author of *Blood Wedding* has decided to make available to the company that will be directed by Enrique Gustavino a play of his entitled *El público* and subtitled *tragic poem to be booed*. This work will be premiered by the Spanish poet in his own country).[75]

After this, Lorca seems to have essentially shelved *El público* for the next year and a half. As regards his theatrical activity, there was now a great deal else going on, with new plays being prepared (*Yerma,* then *Doña Rosita la soltera*), a number of revivals of other plays performed by both Lola Membrives and Margarita Xirgu, ongoing work with La Barraca (where political tensions were rising), and special productions of works by Lope de Vega for the tercentenary year. When finally the topic returned, in an important interview with Felipe Morales, Lorca's brief comments were entirely consistent with previous statements on the subject: "Yo en el teatro he seguido una trayectoria definida. Mis primeras comedias son irrepresent-ables. [. . .] En estas comedias imposibles está mi verdadero propósito" (In the theater, I have followed a clear trajectory. My foremost plays are unperformable. [. . .] My true purpose lies in these impossible plays).[76]

Only perhaps in the early summer of 1936, after *Así que pasen cinco años* was being regularly rehearsed by the Club Anfistora, did Lorca return once more to *El público* and thoughts of staging it. According to Pura Maór-tua's daughter Margarita Ucelay, he gave Pura the script of the play with a view to its possible performance by Anfistora, but on reading it, she was "consternada" (troubled) and commented that in her opinion "habría que esperar, quizá mucho tiempo" (it will be necessary to wait, perhaps a long time) before it could be staged.[77] Martínez Nadal remembers a final read-ing of the play to a couple of friends in the Restaurante Buenavista. This time the text was typed on "papel tamaño folio" (folio-size paper), with handwritten corrections, and supposedly Lorca was going to get a typed fair copy made of it the following day.[78] Over these same days in early July 1936, Lorca also gave several readings of *La casa de Bernarda Alba,* which he had just finished on June 19, and then left for Granada on July 13.

The manuscript in Martínez Nadal's possession was left behind in Ma-drid when he went into exile and only recovered when it was sent to him in London in 1958. It seems that he initially held off publication in the hope that a more complete and/or advanced version of the play might be found. The surviving manuscript was eventually incorporated piecemeal into his critical study of 1970 and then reproduced in facsimile in 1976.[79] The hybrid nature of the 1970 study was interpreted in some quarters as an attempt to "force the hand" of the Lorca family into granting permis-sion for publication of the surviving text. This notion, though, is highly debatable, and the history of the wide-ranging search for a more advanced version is complex and yet to be brought fully to light. A commercially accessible edition appeared in 1978,[80] after which came many others. Stu-dent productions were given in Murcia and Río Piedras, Puerto Rico (1977, 1978), and a professional staging was mounted in Poland in 1984, but the true "world premiere" of the play in Spanish took place in Milan in 1986, subsequently transferring to Madrid in 1987.[81]

Así que pasen cinco años

What we know of the compositional history of *Así que pasen cinco años* is very incomplete. As with *El público,* Ángel del Río reports that during those late summer holidays of September 1929, "he also read to us, [. . .] fragments of [. . .] *When Five Years Passed.*"[82] Perhaps basing herself on del Río, Auclair states that "il commença à y travailler aux États-Unis ou il lut une première version à des amis" (he started to work on it in the United States, where he read a first version to some friends).[83] For his part, Adolfo Salazar says that while he and Lorca were in Cuba together in the spring of 1930:

> Varias obras de teatro nacieron en La Habana de ese momento de su inspiración, y dos de ellas existen en posesión de grupos de aficionados madrileños que han de conservarlas, seguramente.[84] Una se titulaba *Así que pasen cinco años,* y la otra era ese famoso drama, famoso ya antes de nacer, *El público,* donde ocurren las cosas más inconcebibles en su incongruencia.[85]

> Several plays were born in Havana from that moment of his inspiration, and two of them exist in the possession of groups of Madrid-based enthusiasts who surely will have kept them safe. One was titled *Así que pasen cinco años,* and the other was that famous drama, already famous before being born, *El público,* in which the most incongruously inconceivable things take place.

Whether Lorca really had started drafting *Así que pasen* at the same time as *El público* or whether the two plays were confused in his friends' recollections is hard to say. What is clear, though, is that at a certain point *El público* took priority, and its composition was completed on August 22, 1930, during the summer months that Lorca spent with his family at the Huerta de San Vicente in Granada, while *Así que pasen* was completed almost exactly a year later, on August 19, 1931, under very similar circumstances. In the case of *Así que pasen,* the entire manuscript is written partially in ink and partially in pencil on just one kind of paper—poor-quality, plain octavo sheets, which suggests that it was written in one place over a fairly limited period of time. Crossings-out and revisions are quite frequent and numerous at some points and nonexistent at others, making it difficult to infer whether Lorca was working with earlier, partial drafts in front of him or not.[86]

Lorca's correspondence from the summer of 1931 bears testimony to the flurry of compositional activity that occurred at that time and which may well have accounted for the majority of the play. At the end of July, he announced to Morla Lynch that "yo trabajo mucho. En los últimos días de septiembre haremos en vuestra casa (que es la mía, porque me lo habéis dicho siempre) una lectura de mi nueva pieza con invitados y fotos" (I am working a lot. In the last days of September we will have at your house [which is mine, because you have always said that to me] a reading of my new play with guests and photos), and a few days later, at the beginning of August: "Trabajo. Ya voy por el tercer acto de mi pieza *Así que pasen cinco años,* cuya idea tanto gustó a Bebé. Espero que pronto la leeremos y mi mayor alegría será que os guste" (I am working. I am already on the third act of my play *Así que pasen cinco años,* the idea for which Bebé liked so much. I hope that we will read it soon and my greatest joy would be that you like it). Shortly after August 19, he reported to Regino Sáinz de la Maza: "He terminado mi obra *Así que pasen cinco años,* estoy *en cierto modo* satisfecho" (I have completed my play *Así que pasen cinco años,* and I am *in a certain way* satisfied).[87] Almost immediately after Lorca's return to Madrid from Granada in the fall of 1931, the already proposed reading took place at the home of Carlos and Bebé Morla Lynch, on October 4. The host gave a long and detailed description of the event, his reaction to the play, and a summary of the action.[88]

Thereafter, however, *Así que pasen* disappeared from view for a while. At some point in the 1930s—it is impossible to determine when—Lorca tried to get Margarita Xirgu interested in the play and gave her a private reading. Xirgu remembers that on one of her frequent recreational drives out to the Monte de El Pardo, Lorca accompanied her and read it to her while they sat in the vehicle with the windows rolled down to breathe the country air. Xirgu says that:

No la entendí y se lo dije. Federico procuraba explicármela, pero yo seguía sin entenderla. Independientemente algunas escenas y los versos me parecían bellísimos, pero lo que no entendía era la obra como realización

escénica. No "veía" la comedia. [. . .] Entonces me pareció irrealizable tea-
tralmente, además de incomprensible para el público, y le dije: "Mira, Federico, vamos a dejar esta obra por ahora."[89]

I did not understand it and told him so. Federico tried to explain it to me, but
to no avail. Independently, some scenes and lines of poetry seemed really
beautiful to me, but what I did not understand was the work as a creation
for the stage. I did not "see" the play. [. . .] At that time it seemed to me to be
theatrically impossible to put on, besides being incomprehensible for the
audience, and I told him: "Look, Federico, we are going to set aside this work
for now.

It is possible that this setback may have occurred at some time before
the staging of *Amor de don Perlimplín* because, according to Ucelay, on
April 5, 1933, the very night of its premiere, at the after-party, Lorca announced his intention of continuing to work with the Club Teatral and
handed Pura Maórtua the manuscript of *Así que pasen,* saying "este será
nuestro nuevo estreno" (this will be our new premiere). Maórtua's first job
was to produce a typed copy of the script from which they could work, a
task that took her months.[90] Thereafter, she and Lorca discussed its production, which was scheduled for after he returned from his trip to Argentina and Uruguay (which ended up lasting from October 1933 to March
1934).[91] In July 1933, Lorca mentioned the play as one that he planned to
publish, adding that "*Así que pasen cinco años* será estrenada por el Club
Teatral de Cultura, fundado por mí, cuya alma es una gran artista: Pura
Ucelay" (*Así que pasen cinco años* will be premiered by the Club Teatral de
Cultura, founded by me, whose soul is a great artist: Pura Ucelay).[92] While
his brother was away in Buenos Aires, Francisco García Lorca gave a first
reading of the script to the troupe,[93] Maórtua assigned parts and started
rehearsals,[94] but when Lorca returned to Madrid in April 1934 and became
actively involved again, he was dissatisfied with the actor assigned to the
lead role of the Joven, and this obstacle of finding a suitable replacement
ended up causing a considerable delay in the play's staging.[95]

Lorca's statements to the Argentinian press about *Así que pasen* were
infrequent and always yoked with *El público*. Just as he was arriving, a
journalist reported:

Además de sus tres piezas estrenadas, [. . .] tiene escritas otras dos piezas, que no tiene interés ni muchas esperanzas de representar. Y sobre ellas se expresa así:

—Una que es un misterio, dentro de las características de este género, un misterio sobre el tiempo, escrita en prosa y verso, la traigo en mi valija, aunque no tenga la pretensión de estrenarla en Buenos Aires.[96]

Besides his three plays that have been premiered, [. . .] he has two other plays finished, which he has no interest in seeing performed nor much hope of that happening. And about them he says this:

—One that is a mystery play, within the characteristics of that genre, a mystery play about time, written in prose and verse, I have brought it in my suitcase, although I do not intend to try to have it premiered in Buenos Aires.

And to Pablo Suero he said much the same: "Si le habláis de *Bodas de sangre,* habla con entusiasmo de dos obras que no ha podido representar y que son, según él, el teatro que quiere hacer. Esas obras se titulan *Así que pasen cinco años* y *El público*" (If you talk to him about *Bodas de sangre,* he speaks enthusiastically about two works that he has not been able to perform and which are, according to him, the kind of theater that he wants to do. Those works are titled *Así que pasen cinco años* and *El público*).[97] Later, in 1943, Suero gave, in book form, additional information that dated from later during the Buenos Aires visit but which had not appeared in the newspapers at the time.

> Federico García Lorca me ha leído últimamente su material de teatro inédito. Son dos obras. Una de ellas, *Yerma* . . . [. . .]
> La otra obra es *Así que pasen cinco años* y es un misterio del tiempo. Ignoro si la gran actriz Lola Membrives se atreverá a montar esa obra, que es para mí lo mejor de García Lorca, y abre sobre el teatro actual, ahogado entre las fórmulas y desvanecido en la pátina de lo gastado, una boca de nueva y misteriosa luz, un plano de nuevas posibilidades. [. . .]
> *Así que pasen cinco años* es una obra novísima.[98]

> Just recently Federico García Lorca has read to me his unpublished work for the theater. There are two plays. One of them, *Yerma* . . . [. . .]

The other work is *Así que pasen cinco años,* and it is a mystery play of time. I do not know if the great actress Lola Membrives will dare to stage that work, which is for me the best of García Lorca and which opens over the present-day theater, drowning in formulaic devices and fainting away on the patina of the timeworn, a window of new and mysterious light, a level of new possibilities. [. . .]

Así que pasen cinco años is a very novel work.

At the end of 1934, Pura Maórtua was optimistic about the prospects of public performance; when asked by Agustín de Figueroa about the Club's plans, she replied that "en la primera quincena de enero daremos en Capitol *Peribáñez y el comendador de Ocaña* [. . .]. Luego un estreno de Lorca: *Así que pasen cinco años*" (in the first half of January, we will give in the Capitol Building *Peribáñez y el comendador de Ocaña* [. . .]. Then a premiere of Lorca's *Así que pasen cinco años*).[99] The same day, she was echoed by the child actor Andrés Higueras, who had performed in the first outing of the Club Teatral and now was cast as the Niño in *Así que pasen:* "No era la primera vez que subía al escenario: trabajé en la obra de Federico García Lorca *La zapatera prodigiosa,* y ahora voy a subir en una obra suya, *Así que pasen cinco años*" (It was not the first time that I was on the stage: I acted in Federico García Lorca's work *La zapatera prodigiosa,* and now I am going to appear in another work of his, *Así que pasen cinco años*).[100] However, the whole of 1935 passed with barely another mention: "Tengo dos obras que no doy por demasiado intelectuales" (I have two works that I am not putting forward because they are too intellectual).[101]

In March 1936, there was briefly news of a different initiative. According to reports, Lorca approached the actor Benito Cibrián, who was the leader, together with Pepita Meliá, of a theater company, and offered him "una comedia que he terminado hace unos días" (a play that I have finished a few days ago), a work that was then identified as *Así que pasen cinco años.*[102] The detail regarding its date of composition is patently inaccurate; if we can believe the substance of the information at all, it is unclear whether Lorca might have temporarily thought of withdrawing the work from Anfistora or whether this would have been a second, additional, professional production.[103] The gossip related by the anonymous journalist was closely linked to Cibrián's bid for the lease of the Teatro Español for the spring and summer seasons, and another contemporary column suggests that the addition of the Lorca play to the proposed repertoire would have enhanced his chances of success.[104] In the event, it all turned out to be moot: Ana Adamuz was offered the spring season (April 15 through June 15) and Cibrián only the summer season (June 16 through October 15),[105] while there was already a tacit understanding that the fall season of 1936 would be granted, again, to Margarita Xirgu. Cibrián had been hoping to secure both spring and summer, allowing for a six-month run, and had already stated that three months were insufficient for his plans.[106] On hearing the news, he was disconsolate and, by the middle of April, had rejected the offer of just the three summer months.[107] While Lorca might have had second thoughts, it is also quite possible that the planned production became a victim of the outcome of the leasing competition and Cibrián's subsequent withdrawal.

Meanwhile, the Anfistora company had been undergoing change. The last-minute cancellation of the performance of *Los cuernos de don Friolera*, at Valle-Inclán's widow's request, caused the exodus of several members of the troupe and consequently the recruitment of some new ones. Among them was an actor that Lorca deemed suitable for the role of the Joven, and this in turn spurred the resumption of rehearsals of the play, coinciding with the last rehearsals of Antonio García Gutiérrez's romantic drama *El trovador,* which was the Club's most recent production, performed on April 3.[108] A few days later, therefore, Lorca was able to tell a journalist:

—Yo en el teatro he seguido una trayectoria definida. Mis primeras comedias son irrepresentables. Ahora creo que una de ellas, *Así que pasen cinco años,* va a ser representada por el Club Anfistora. En estas comedias imposibles está mi verdadero propósito.[109]

—In the theater, I have followed a clear trajectory. My foremost plays are unperformable. Now I believe that one of them, *Así que pasen cinco años,* is going to be performed by the Club Anfistora. My true purpose is in these impossible plays.

Likewise, in a report on *El trovador,* a magazine also noted that "Anfistora no cesa en sus actividades, y actualmente ensaya una nueva y bella obra,

esencialmente poética, de Federico García Lorca: *Así que pasen cinco años*"
(Anfistora never stops in its activities, and right now it is rehearsing a new
and beautiful work, essentially poetic in nature, by Federico García Lorca:
Así que pasen cinco años).[110]

One of the actresses cast in *Así que pasen*, playing the Maniquí, was
Ana Mariscal.[111] Decades later, she still remembered what Lorca told her
during those rehearsals:

> Y le oí expresarse [. . .] en contra de un teatro apto sólo para la burguesía.
> Pero él incluía en la burguesía a los pseudo-intelectuales y a los eruditos.
> Le escuché decir también, saliéndole del alma, que su sueño sería que *Así
> que pasen cinco años* se representase un día en [el Teatro] La Latina, y que
> el público que lo viera y comprendiera estuviera integrado por gente del
> pueblo, y mujeres de la plaza de la Cebada.[112]

> And I heard him speak out [. . .] against a theater solely suitable for the
> bourgeoisie. But he included in the bourgeoisie pseudo-intellectuals and
> scholars. I also heard him say, coming from the depths of his soul, that his
> dream would be that *Así que pasen cinco años* might be performed one day
> in [the] La Latina [Theater] and that the audience that saw and under-
> stood it should be made up of people from the working class and women
> from La Cebada square.

The Barrio de la Latina is one of the most historic parts of Madrid and in
Lorca's day was closely associated with the working class. The theater of
the same name was and is located there, precisely in the Plaza de la Cebada,
and over the first decades of the twentieth century, it specialized in popular revue and variety-type shows.

Over those months, Mariscal also played a role in another related event.
Pablo Suero, who had interviewed Lorca in Buenos Aires, was now visiting
Spain, and Lorca wanted to give him a copy of *Así que pasen*. He contacted
Maórtua, and she agreed to send round a spare actor's copy, with the un-
derstanding that none of the emendations from rehearsal were included
on it. Mariscal brought it to the Lorca family apartment on calle Alcalá.[113]
This explains how Suero came to have a copy as of 1937: "también tengo en
mi poder un drama inédito: *Así que pasen 5 años*" (I also have in my pos-

session an unpublished play: *Así que pasen 5 años*),[114] and it also clarifies that it was a spare, uncorrected actor's copy—supplied by Suero—that served as the base text for the 1938 first edition prepared by Guillermo de Torre and published by Losada.[115] In 1943 Suero expanded on his comment of 1937, confirming that "*Así que pasen cinco años* me fue entregada luego por Federico en Madrid en 1936 [. . .] A solicitud del editor Losada, se la entregué y éste la editó" (in Madrid in 1936, Federico then handed me [a copy of] *Así que pasen cinco años* [. . .] At the request of Losada the publisher, I gave it to him and he published it). At the same time he claimed that "me dio la única copia que tenía, para que yo la estrenase aquí [en Buenos Aires]. Ello no me fue posible" (he gave me the only copy that he had, so that I should premiere it here [in Buenos Aires]. That was not possible).[116] *Only copy* is to be understood not in absolute terms but, rather, as the only copy that Lorca had readily to hand.

The performance of *Así que pasen cinco años* was scheduled for June. Normally, productions by Anfistora were prepared meticulously over many months prior to their public presentation, but this was a different case. Rehearsals of the play had been underway since 1933, and even after the problems with the lead role, Maórtua continued rehearsing those parts of the text where the Joven was not onstage. Now, over April and May, it would be necessary to work with the new principal actor and also with those new members of the company assigned to other roles who had recently joined in the spring of that year.[117] By June much of the play was ready, but Lorca was dissatisfied with the scene involving the Maniquí. He seems to have taken with him to Granada the six pages from the working copy that correspond to this scene, as they ended up in the family archive, while pages from a carbon copy are found filling the gap in the full typescript held by the Hispanic Society of America.[118] The complicated act 3, scene 1, needed to be rehearsed on an actual stage, and the music that was to be used for the production had not yet been pinned down.[119]

Eventually, it became clear that the proposed timetable was not going to work, given that the summer was not a good time to put on plays and, in addition, Lorca was going to return to Granada, and so a decision was made to postpone to the end of September or beginning of October.[120] Agustín Penón records the testimony given to him by Maórtua in the mid-

1950s that it was toward the end of June 1936 that she saw Lorca for the last time and that it was only on that occasion when he told her that he preferred a fall debut instead of July.[121] However, these chronological indications may be slightly inaccurate because a newspaper rumor column from the end of May already records the likelihood of postponement:

—Que no es cierto que haya retirado al Club Teatral Anfistora—al que aprecia muchísimo, artísticamente—su poema dramático *Así que pasen cinco años*,[122] escrito hace un lustro y rechazado por Margarita Xirgu y Lola Membrives, que no se atrevieron a montarlo.

—Que lo que ha hecho Federico es pedir que no monten ahora dicha obra, pues él quiere dirigirla personalmente y no estará en Madrid, de asiento, hasta octubre.

—Que entonces, con mucho gusto, ayudará a los del Anfistora a montarla y estrenarla.[123]

—That it is not true that he has withdrawn from the Club Teatral Anfistora—which he thinks very highly of, artistically—his dramatic poem *Así que pasen cinco años*, written five years ago and rejected by Margarita Xirgu and Lola Membrives, who did not dare to stage it.

—That what Federico has done is request that they do not put on this work right now, as he wants to direct it personally, and he will not be settled back in Madrid until October.

—That then, with great pleasure, he will help the members of Anfistora stage it and premiere it.

At all events, as agreed, no performance took place, and Anfistora dissolved shortly after the outbreak of the Civil War.

Martínez Nadal recounts that he had come into possession of the 1931 manuscript in July 1936, very shortly after his return to Spain on the fifth of the month and before Lorca's departure for Granada on the evening of the thirteenth.[124] Thus, according to Nadal, he acquired the manuscripts of both *Así que pasen* and *El público* within the space of just a few days, though under different sets of circumstances. He tells us that he and Lorca had gone round to Maórtua's home, and Lorca had retrieved *Así que pasen*

LORCA'S EXPERIMENTAL THEATER

cinco años from her and handed it over to Nadal for him to make a typed copy, which he should then send to Lorca at the Huerta de San Vicente. This version of events makes little sense, as evidently there were clean but uncorrected typed actors' copies available, and a fair copy of the 1931 manuscript would not incorporate any of the changes made in rehearsals over 1933–36. The manuscript was reproduced in facsimile in 1979, and as far as can be determined, it remains today in the possession of Martínez Nadal's heirs. For her part, Ucelay edited the typed director's copy passed down to her by her mother, which contained all the emendations made during the long rehearsal period.

El sueño de la vida

While Lorca did not start to write *El sueño de la vida* until the latter part of 1935, certain ideas that were incorporated into the play had been incubating for quite some time beforehand. It is evident that Lorca was much affected—and distressed—by the events surrounding the Asturian miners' strike of October 1934: the demonstrations and violent uprising that followed were met by brutal repression by the government, which ordered into the area large numbers of army units as well as the Civil Guard. One of his earliest biographers commented on the constant evolution of his theater, adding that "esta condición tomaba cada vez más evidencia, hasta afrontar un teatro de contenido social, cuyos primeros actos alcanzó a escribir el poeta. En él habría de tener destino epopéyico la vida de los mineros de Asturias" (this condition became increasingly evident, until he tackled a type of theater with social content, whose first acts the poet managed to write. In it the life of the Asturian miners was to have an epic destiny).[125]

This change can also be observed in many of the newspaper interviews that Lorca gave from late 1934 onward. In December he told one journalist:

> Después, quiero hacer otro tipo de cosas, incluso comedia corriente de los tiempos actuales y llevar al teatro temas y problemas que la gente tiene miedo de abordar. Aquí, lo grave es que las gentes que van al teatro no quieren que se les haga pensar sobre ningún tema moral. [. . .] Yo espero para el teatro la llegada de la luz de arriba siempre: del paraíso.[126] En cuanto los de arriba bajen al patio de butacas, todo estará resuelto.[127]

Afterward, I want to do other kinds of things, including a mainstream play about the present day and bring to the theater themes and problems that people are afraid of broaching. Here, the serious thing is that the people who go to the theater do not want to be made to think about any moral theme. [. . .] For the theater, I am always waiting/hoping for the arrival of the light from above: from the "gods." As soon as the people from up above come down to the stalls, everything will be resolved.

In a speech that Lorca gave to theater professionals before a special performance of *Yerma,* he described himself as an "ardiente apasionado del teatro y de su acción social" (ardent devotee of theater and its social action) and decried any kind of theater "que no recoge el latido social, el latido histórico, el drama de sus gentes" (that does not incorporate the social heartbeat, the historical heartbeat, the drama of its peoples).[128] In February 1935, he argued that the dramatic form "nos permite un contacto más directo con las masas" (allows us to have a more direct contact with the masses), expressed his outrage at the "mundo lleno de injusticias y miserias de todo orden" (world full of injustices and misfortunes of all kinds) that he observed around him, and stated that "tengo en proyecto varios dramas de tipo humano y social" (I have in the planning stage several human and social dramas).[129] And Lorca told another journalist that, quite simply, "el teatro ha de recoger el drama total de la vida actual" (the theater is obliged to incorporate the total drama of present-day life).[130]

The leading ideas that emerge here, and which would be repeated in Lorca's subsequent descriptions of the play in progress and in the surviving manuscript of act 1, are that theater must make people think and face up to unpleasant realities; theater must engage with current social issues and the question of social justice; social change is needed, rendered here in terms of the occupants of the cheap seats in the "gods" coming down to occupy the stalls; and the kind of theater that he envisages has an important role to play in bringing about that change.

In 1935 the week of Corpus Christi fell on June 16–23, and on June 27 and 29, Margarita Xirgu and her company gave performances of *Fuenteovejuna* and *El alcalde de Zalamea* in Granada. It is very likely that Lorca would have been there, spending some time with his family at the Huerta de San Vicente. He stayed on for several more days after Xirgu's departure, for a visit from Eduardo Blanco-Amor, which has been dated to June 21 through July 19 (July 18 was Lorca's and his father's saint's day).[131] Meanwhile, Xirgu and her company completed a rapid sweep through Andalucía and were back in Madrid by July 3.[132] The same day, interviewed while he was still in Sevilla, Rivas Cherif announced that "Margarita va a descansar varios días, después de una de las temporadas más duras de su carrera" (Margarita is going to rest for a number of days, after one of the most grueling seasons of her career).[133] A little while later, Xirgu arrived at the Parador de Gredos in the mountains outside Madrid, where she would stay for about a month. Meanwhile, Xirgu's company's manager, Miguel Ortín, gave a journalist various more pieces of information: Xirgu was currently in the Sierra de Gredos, they would open a season in Barcelona in September, they would perform *Yerma,* and they might well debut a new play by Lorca, *Doña Rosita.*[134] By August 10, Xirgu had completed her vacation and was back in Madrid.[135]

Sometime over this summer period, Lorca read *Doña Rosita la soltera* and the first act of another play to Xirgu on successive days while she was staying at the Parador de Gredos.[136] A photograph from the time shows Lorca; Xirgu; her husband, José Arnall; Ortín; and Rivas Cherif sitting around a table. Lorca has a book (rather than a manuscript) in his hands.[137] If Lorca was in Granada until July 19, and thereafter returned to Madrid, and if Xirgu was back in Madrid from the Sierra by August 10, then this leaves a window of some twenty days during which this gathering would have taken place outside the capital. Lorca had been working principally on *Doña Rosita la soltera,* and he read the just completed text to Blanco-Amor during the Galician writer's visit to Granada,[138] but evidently—given the lengthy description of the plot that Xirgu gave to Valentín de Pedro—he had also made a start on a new play, *El sueño de la vida.*

Logically, therefore, from fall 1935 onward, there are periodic reports concerning this new work, as yet untitled. In September, Lorca said that "estoy trabajando en otra tragedia. Una tragedia política" (I am working on another tragedy. A political tragedy),[139] and in a radio broadcast soon after, he elaborated on his intentions and challenges:

Aspiro a recoger el drama social de la época en que vivimos y pretendo que el público no se asuste de situaciones y símbolos. Pretendo que el público haga las paces con fantasmas y con ideas sin las cuales no yo puedo dar un paso como autor.

El poeta dramático tiene obras detrás de cada esquina. Lo que pasa es que nadie se atreve a tirar de los hilos difíciles, porque el hombre teme a verse retratado en el teatro y por eso llena de oro las manos de los autores que lo pintan como no es, en la comedia burguesa.[140]

I aim to show the social drama of the period in which we are living, and my intention is that the audience should not be frightened by situations and symbols. My intention is that the audience should make peace with specters and with ideas without which I cannot take a step as an author.

The dramatic poet has got works around every corner. What happens is that no one dares to pull on the difficult threads, because human beings fear seeing themselves portrayed in the theater and for that reason they fill with gold the hands of authors who paint them not as they [actually] are, in the bourgeois comedy.

And in a wide-ranging and remarkably frank interview from November, he made a number of interesting and sometimes provocative statements:

—Hoy no interesan más que dos clases de problemas: el social y el sexual. La obra que no siga una de esas direcciones está condenada al fracaso, aunque sea muy buena. Yo hago lo sexual, que me atrae más. Pudiera escribir otras cosas porque es ése mi gusto intelectual.

—Nowadays only two types of problems are of interest: the social and the sexual. The work that does not follow one of these directions is condemned to failure, even though it might be very good. I treat the sexual one, which attracts me more. I could write other things because that is my intellectual preference.

In passing, Lorca mentioned *El público* and *Así que pasen cinco años:* "Tengo dos obras que no doy por demasiado intelectuales" (I have two works that I am not putting forward because they are too intellectual). He then turned to what he was working on at that moment:

—En lo formal, acabo de terminar un acto completamente subversivo que supone una verdadera revolución de la técnica, un gran avance.
—¿Con qué asunto?
—Un tema social, mezclado de religioso, en el que irrumpe mi angustia constante del más allá.

—As for the formal aspect, I have just finished a completely subversive act that presupposes a true revolution in technique, a great advance.
—With what subject?
—A social theme, mixed in with a religious one, which my constant anguish about the afterlife bursts into.

He added: "Las gentes a quienes espanta mi realidad son fariseos que viven[,] sin asustarse[,] la misma realidad de mi teatro. [. . .] Quiero provocar revulsivos, a ver si se vomita de una vez todo lo malo del teatro actual" (The people whom my reality scares are hypocrites who are living the very reality of my theater without getting frightened. [. . .] I want to provoke emetics, to see if it is possible to vomit, once and for all, all that is bad in present-day theater).[141] Lorca was with Xirgu and her company in Cataluña for much of fall 1935, and it was likely during that time that he described part of the first act of *El sueño* to Rivas Cherif. While Rivas Cherif thought that the plot details corresponded to *El público*, it is quite clear that this was in fact the later play:

una escena que por lo visto, no llegó a escribir, en que uno del público de lunetas mataba de un tiro a un espectador de la galería, a quien recogían los personajes de Shakespeare que estaban ensayando en el escenario, y al escenario entraban, por el patio de butacas, cargando "el cadáver del obrero asesinado."[142]

a scene that apparently he never came to write, in which a member of the audience in the stalls killed with a shot a spectator in the gallery, who was then picked up by the characters from Shakespeare who were rehearsing on the stage, and entered the stage, through the orchestra level, carrying "the corpse of the assassinated workman."

Around the turn of the year, Lorca started giving further readings. Pablo Suero, whom Lorca had met in 1933, arrived in Spain in mid-December 1935 to cover the upcoming elections.[143] Seemingly, he saw Lorca quite frequently over the subsequent months, well into the spring. With some degree of exaggeration he writes: "Federico me llevaba diariamente a dos tabernas típicas madrileñas. Una en la calle del Pozo y otra en la calle de la Luna. En una de ellas, nos reunimos una noche para leerme, después de comer, sus últimas cosas" (Federico took me on a daily basis to two typical Madrid taverns. One in the calle del Pozo and the other in the calle de la Luna. In one of them we met up one night so that he could read to me, after dinner, his latest things).[144] When Margarita Xirgu arrived in Buenos Aires in May 1937, Suero was waiting for her at the airport. And when he mentioned to her "una pieza formidable, sin título aún" (a fantastic play, still without a title), she responded: "Conozco este acto; me lo leyó a mí en una taberna de la calle de la Luna" (I am familiar with that act; he read it to me in a tavern on the calle de la Luna).[145] The "tavern" in question was Casa Pascual, much favored by Lorca at that time, but the date of Lorca's reading of the act to Xirgu is harder to pin down. After finishing the long fall season in Cataluña, in Badalona, on January 9, 1936, Xirgu immediately undertook a short swing through theaters in Logroño and Vitoria that would take the company to Bilbao by the seventeenth and then Santander by the end of the month, where they embarked on the SS *Orinoco* of the Hamburg-Amerika line for Cuba. If her presence, even very briefly, in Madrid during January is therefore out of the question, this would suggest that the second reading to her, in Madrid, must have taken place after the one at the Parador de Gredos, at some point after August 10 but before the start of the Barcelona theater run that she commenced on September 10, 1935.

By late winter 1936, Lorca was claiming that *El sueño de la vida* was finished: "¿Terminado? Un drama social, aún sin título, con intervención del público de la sala y de la calle, donde estalla una revolución y asaltan el teatro" (Finished? A social drama, still without a title, in which the people in the auditorium and from the street intervene, and where a revolution breaks out and the theater is under assault).[146] By "finished," it is very possible that Lorca meant mentally mapped out but not necessarily written. A "rumor" from February was more realistic:

—Que el gran poeta Federico García Lorca, uno de los grandes prestigios de España, trabaja febrilmente.

—Que está terminando el segundo acto de una obra ultramoderna en la que maneja los más audaces procedimientos y sistemas teatrales.

—Que el espectador no irá a ver lo que pasa, sino a sentir lo que "les pasa."

—Que el escenario y la sala están unidos en el desarrollo de la obra.

—Que la obra es sumamente fuerte; y en previsión de no poderla estrenar en España ha entablado relaciones con una compañía argentina, que la estrenará en Buenos Aires.

—Que la obra no tiene título aún, pero que el que más le cuadraría hubiese sido *La vida es sueño*.

—Que ese título ya lo "utilizó" Calderón . . .

—Que, de todas formas, el título será parecido a ese.

—Que la intensidad emocional de la obra va en aumento y que los espectadores que no puedan mantener el control de sus nervios harán bien en abandonar la sala.

—Que la obra trata de un problema social agudo y latente.

—Que la obra está resuelta de un modo sorprendente.[147]

—That the great Federico García Lorca, one of the most highly regarded writers in Spain, is working feverishly.

—That he is finishing the second act of an ultra-modern work in which he deploys the most audacious theatrical procedures and systems.

—That the spectator will not go to see what happens but, rather, to experience what "happens to them."

—That the stage and the auditorium are combined in the development of the work.

—That the work is enormously powerful; and as a precaution against not being able to premiere it in Spanish, he has established relations with an Argentinian company, which will premiere it in Buenos Aires.

—That the work still has no title but that the one that would fit it best would have been *La vida es sueño*.

—That that title was already "used" by Calderón . . .

—That, in any event, the title will be similar to that one.

—That the emotional intensity of the work increases steadily and that the spectators who cannot control their nerves will be well advised to leave the auditorium.

—That the work treats an acute and latent social problem.

—That the work ends in a surprising way.

Later that month, Lorca added the further detail that he planned to premiere the play later in the fall, in Madrid. Once Margarita Xirgu returned from an extended tour of Cuba and Mexico, they would perform *Doña Rosita la soltera* in the capital and then the new play:

y después el poeta estrenará con la admirable primera actriz una nueva comedia. Un tema nuevo; pero sin salirse de la línea que le ha proporcionado sus resonantes éxitos.

—¿Qué título llevará?

—Hasta ahora no lo tengo. El que le va mejor a la comedia es *La vida es sueño*; pero no quiero tener pleito con ningún otro poeta.[148]

and afterward the poet will premiere with the admirable leading lady a new play. A new theme; but without getting away from the line that has afforded him his resounding successes.

—What will it be called?

—I haven't come up with the title yet. The one that best suits it is *La vida es sueño*; but I don't want a lawsuit with any other poet.

In March, Pedro Salinas sent Jorge Guillén his own piece of gossip: "Mucho me temo que Federico en su carrera de noble emulación con Rafael [Alberti] caiga también en el garlito 'social.' Ya parece que ha escrito un drama comunistísimo para no dejarse pisar" (I greatly fear that Federico in his career of noble emulation of Rafael [Alberti] is also falling into the "social" snare. It already seems that he has written a highly communistic work so as not to be left behind).[149]

Composition continued through the spring, as witnessed by more interviews and newspaper reports:

—Ahora estoy trabajando en una nueva comedia. Ya no será como las anteriores. Ahora es una obra, en la que no puedo escribir nada, ni una línea, porque se han desatado y andan por los aires la verdad y la mentira, el hambre y la poesía. Se me han escapado de las páginas. La verdad de la comedia es un problema religioso y económico-social. El Mundo está detenido ante el hambre que asola a los pueblos. Mientras haya desequilibrio económico, el Mundo no piensa. Yo lo tengo visto. [. . .] El día en que el hambre desaparezca va a producirse en el Mundo la explosión espiritual más grande que jamás conoció la Humanidad. Nunca, jamás, se podrán figurar los hombres la alegría que estallará el día de la Gran Revolución. ¿Verdad que te estoy hablado en socialista puro?

Como final, el poeta nos habla de su obra. De su próxima producción:

—Tengo cuatro libros escritos que van a ser publicados: *Nueva York, Sonetos,* la comedia sin título y otro.[150]

—Now I am working on a new play. It will not be at all like the previous ones. Now it is a work, which I cannot write any part of, not a single line, because truth and falsehood, hunger and poetry, have been unleashed and are traveling through the air. They have made their escape from my pages. The truth of the play is a religious and socioeconomic problem. The world is at a standstill in the face of the hunger that is devastating the peoples. While there is economic imbalance, the world does not think. I have seen it. [. . .] On the day that hunger disappears, the greatest spiritual explosion ever known by humanity will take place in the world. Never, ever, will mankind be able to imagine the joy that will break out on the day of the Great Revolution. I am talking to you like a pure socialist, aren't I?

To end, the poet talks to us about his work. About his forthcoming production:

—I have four books that are written and which are going to be published: *Nueva York, Sonetos,* the play without a title and another one.

Finally, after the mention of Calderón and his famous *comedia* and *auto sacramental* in February, two newspaper columns provided and then confirmed the title of Lorca's new play, in late April and May: "está trabajando. No se lo cuenta a nadie, pero trabaja. Prepara *El sueño de la vida,* comedia de la que ya se ha dado en alguna parte el título. *El sueño de la vida* está escrita mojando la pluma en rebeldías" (he is working. He does not let on to anyone, but he is working. He is preparing *El sueño de la vida,* a play whose title has already been put forward in some place or other. *El sueño de la vida* has been written with a pen dipped in rebellious ideas).[151] And again: "también lleva muy adelantada la labor en su drama social *El sueño de la vida*" (he also is far advanced with work on his social drama *El sueño de la vida*).[152] From the same month, José Luis Cano remembers a reading of a new work, which he, like Rivas Cherif, confuses with *El público* but which, on the basis of the details that he provides, was clearly of that memorable passage from the first act of *El sueño de la vida:*

> Recuerdo que Federico me leyó en aquella ocasión unas escenas de su drama *El público,* y que en una de ellas se producía un choque entre un personaje que se hallaba camuflado en las localidades altas del teatro—el paraíso— y los actores que trabajaban en la escena, contra la cual disparaba aquél, mientras en una atmósfera revolucionaria se escuchaba el rumor de aviones, como si sobrevolasen por encima del techo del teatro.[153]

> I remember that Federico read to me on that occasion some scenes from his drama *El público* and that in one of them there took place a clash between a character who was hiding, camouflaged up in the high seats of the theater—the "gods"—and the actors who were acting on the stage, and he fired down on it, while in a revolutionary atmosphere one could hear the sound of airplanes, as if they were flying over the roof of the theater.

The surviving manuscript of act 1, which is held in the Archivo Federico García Lorca in Granada, is reproduced in facsimile in the edition of his *Teatro inconcluso* (234–83). It consists of twenty-four sheets of paper; twenty-three of them are written on one side only, and the remaining one is folded and written on two of the four sides. Pages 1 through 22 are unproblematic: they are numbered sequentially and written on the same size and type of paper. The only variation is in the use of ink (1–10), then pencil (10–18), and then ink again (18–22), suggesting that the writing was done on three separate occasions not too far apart. The folded sheet is of a different size and type of paper; the first of the written sides is also numbered 22 and the second is numbered 23. The text here is mainly in pencil; three-quarters of the way down 23, it transitions to ink. The very last page, numbered 24, consists of only three lines of text written in ink on yet another size and type of paper. Pages 1–22 have relatively few crossings-out and additions.

There is every indication that almost all the surviving manuscript is a fair copy revision of a previous version, which in turn was quite possibly the first draft.[154] However, for some reason, the very end of the existing manuscript was finished in a composite fashion. Thus, one "double page" (the folded sheet) of the earlier version was incorporated into the closing stages of the text. Given the near-repetition of a particular stage direction from the bottom of the "first" page 22, we can determine that three-quarters of the "second" page 22 contains material that would be unique to the previous (lost) version, and perhaps curiously, it is not crossed out. At that point, the similar stage direction appears, after which the action continues through most of page 23. The last quarter of page 23 was written in ink; this likely was done on a later occasion, and the completion of the act was carried over to the short page 24, which is also in ink and now on a third type of paper.

These determinations are important because various witnesses' recollections of the reported readings of act 1 leave no room for doubt as to the general identification of the play in question, while at the same time they contain many divergent details, details that very likely corresponded to one or more earlier versions of it. In the account that Xirgu gave to Valentín de Pedro, her mention of the reading of *Doña Rosita* allows us to situate this in Gredos.[155] It is too long to reproduce in full here, but some of the most salient details are as follows. Act 1 opened in the middle of a performance of *A Midsummer Night's Dream* taking place in the Teatro Español that was then interrupted by the director, who comes onstage and announces that a revolution has broken out. He urges the audience to remain in their seats and stay safe inside the building. He subsequently produces from his pocket a newspaper cutting about a woman and her child who had frozen to death in the Plaza Mayor on Christmas Eve.[156] Titania comes out, apparently as the actual fairy character in Shakespeare's play, rather than as the actress performing that role. Cooped up and increasingly nervous, the audience starts to argue and rapidly polarizes, one spectator kills another, the revolutionary group outside breaks into the theater, and the director, accompanied by Titania, joins them. According to Xirgu, Lorca had some sketches for parts of act 2, set in a morgue and visited by the director and Titania; none of act 3 was written, but it would take place in heaven, "un cielo con ángeles andaluces, que vestirían con faralaes" (a heaven with Andalusian angels, who would be wearing ruffled dresses).

The account offered by Xirgu to María Teresa León is shorter but generally very similar.[157] It includes a couple of additional or different details: a second child who survived the cold by eating a tin of shoe polish and the fact that the director was himself dying in act 2. Pablo Suero's account, which must date from a few months after the Xirgu readings, is also the one committed to paper soonest after the event.[158] The summary is again brief, but two otherwise undocumented details stand out: "Los revolucionarios aprovechaban una procesión para pasar en la Custodia un contrabando de un poderoso explosivo que iba a asegurar el triunfo a la reacción. Hay un cuadro de las madres en una morgue que alcanza verdadera grandeza" (the revolutionaries took advantage of a procession to smuggle, hidden inside the monstrance, a powerful explosive that was going to ensure their triumph over the forces of reaction. There is a scene of mothers in a morgue that achieves true grandeur). Finally, José Luis Cano's reminiscences from a May 1936 reading (quoted earlier) contain a few details—such as the sound of airplanes flying overhead—that harmonize completely with the action of the surviving manuscript.

If parts of act 2 or even an outline of act 3 ever existed, they do not appear to be extant. The newspaper reports indicate that Lorca was working actively on this project over the months preceding his death, and with the composition of *La casa de Bernarda Alba* completed in June 1936, there is little doubt that under different circumstances *El sueño de la vida* would have been the next principal focus of his attention.

2

Undecidability in *Amor de don Perlimplín con Belisa en su jardín*

BELISA: ¡Nunca creí que fuese tan complicado!

BELISA: I never believed that he was so complicated!

Within Lorca's dramatic output, *Amor de don Perlimplín con Belisa en su jardín* is often situated alongside *La zapatera prodigiosa* and the two puppet plays, *Tragicomedia de don Cristóbal y la señá Rosita* and *Retablillo de don Cristóbal,* partly on the grounds of its elements of farce and partly for its treatment of the topos of *el viejo y la niña* (the old man and the young girl). However, as I hope to demonstrate here, and as I have already proposed in the introduction, such an adscription falls very short of doing the play full justice.

Many essays about *Amor de don Perlimplín con Belisa en su jardín* used to open with the well-worn trope of unjustified neglect, arguing that, because of its short length, difficult generic categorization, and lack of popularity among theater companies, the play had frequently been overlooked or marginalized. However, such an assertion can no longer be sustained today, given the substantial body of critical material that has gradually but steadily accumulated. I have identified and read through sixty-four journal articles and chapters in collective volumes, in addition to at least forty single-authored books that dedicate a chapter or a section to the play; these date from 1941 to 2015. For obvious reasons of space, I have cited and included in the bibliography only those that I consider the most germane to my own considerations.

Over the years, various aspects of the work have received attention: the complex textual and performance histories and the play's initial reception;[1] what *aleluyas* are, their evolution, and the relationship of the play to that tradition;[2] Lorca's modulation of the stock situation of an old man married to a young woman;[3] connections with other literary texts and issues of influence (beyond the long list of works connected with the tradition of *el viejo y la niña,* Edmond Rostand's *Cyrano de Bergerac* and Fernand Crommelynck's *Le Cocu magnifique* are frequently mentioned); and questions of genre (farce, tragedy, tragicomedy, and such). But above all, and as is only to be expected, most efforts have been directed toward understanding the motives of the characters and construing the unusual course of events that unfolds.

Indeed, the majority of commentators hasten to provide their version of a plot summary, after which they then put forward their particular interpretation. What is rarely, if ever, done is to dwell on the dialogue and the onstage action of the play, moment by moment. It will be my contention here that there are many junctures in *Amor de don Perlimplín,* both small and large, at which the spectator or reader encounters unresolved, and perhaps unresolvable, ambiguities, discontinuities, and unknowns and, furthermore, that taken together these constitute an important and pervasive feature of the play that, ultimately, becomes thematized as undecidability.

The uncertainties start to present themselves early on in scene 1. Given Perlimplín's bookish, bachelor lifestyle, we do not know but may conjecture that perhaps, at age fifty, he is still a virgin. Marcolfa is too embarrassed to spell out what the hidden "grandes encantos" (great charms) of marriage are, but her blushing suggests that they may be sexual in nature, a suspicion immediately reinforced by Belisa's erotically charged song issuing from offstage (254, 255). In the Madre's brief lecture to her daughter on the economic advantages of marriage to a rich man, she states, with rather cryptic logic, that "los dineros dan la hermosura. . . . Y la hermosura es codiciada por los demás hombres" (lots of money gives beauty. . . . And beauty is coveted by other men) (257), perhaps pointing out that Belisa can expect a life of leisure that will preserve her good looks or possibly hinting at the likelihood that she will soon be widowed, will inherit, and subsequently will be pursued by other, younger suitors. Here I am thinking of the plan that the mother has for her daughter in Leandro Fernández de Moratín's play *El sí de las niñas,* one of the landmarks in the literary tradition of *el viejo y la niña.*

Having sent her indoors, the Madre stresses her daughter's fair complexion and purity, "es una azucena" (she is a white lily) (257), picking up Marcolfa's adjective, "la blanca Belisa" (the pale Belisa) (255), and then continues on in a more confidential tone: "Pues si la viese por dentro. . . . ¡Como de azúcar!" (If only you could see her on the inside. . . . Just like sugar!) (257). Sugar is also white, but on the face of it, the comment seems addressed more to Belisa's sweet disposition. But why the need for a hushed voice? Could the Madre be referring, indirectly but still indelicately, to her daughter's intimate physical attributes—"on the inside"— rather than her unseen character, an alternative seemingly bolstered by lines from Belisa's song?

> Entre mis muslos cerrados
> nada como un pez el sol.
> Agua tibia entre los juncos,
> amor. (255)

> Between my closed thighs
> the sun swims like a fish.
> Warm water among the reeds,
> love.

Additionally, could this repeated motif of whiteness ("¡Como de azúcar! . . . blanca por dentro" [259]) also gesture, despite her exuberantly sensual nature, to Belisa's virginity? It is hard to say, but given the notional eighteenth-century setting, such an implication is not beyond the bounds of possibility.

As the first stirrings of a new feeling arise in Perlimplín—"siento una sed. . . . ¿Por qué no me traes agua?" (I'm feeling thirsty. . . . Why don't you bring me some water) (258)—Marcolfa whispers something—we have absolutely no idea what—to him: "(MARCOLFA *se le acerca y le da un recado al oído*)" (MARCOLFA *goes up to him and gives him a message in his ear*), but it is sufficiently startling to elicit a reaction of considerable surprise, if not disbelief: "¿Quién lo puede creer?" (Who can believe it?) (258). The recapitulation of Belisa's song again insinuates—but hardly proves—that the message just delivered contains some sexual revelation. And as the song ends, Perlimplín asks semi-rhetorically: "¿Y qué es esto que me pasa? . . . ¿Qué es esto?" (What is this that's happening to me? . . . What is this?) (259). While a good number of critics relate his perplexity to a mixture of anticipation and anxiety hitherto unknown to this newly betrothed fifty-year-old, others have posited that he is actually experiencing an erection—perhaps his first, but of course, whether it is one of these two sensations or something else again, we will never know.

From mild doubts to deeper imponderables, in scene 2 the questions mount. There is no indication of how much time has elapsed between the proposal and the wedding. From within Perlimplín's bedroom, five whistles are heard (262), evidently corresponding to the five men with whom Belisa will, reportedly, have intercourse during the night (274); when the signals are heard again (264), Belisa explains them away as the clock "striking" five. If we posit for the moment a more or less "realistic" sequence of events, this would imply that the multiple illicit rendezvous must have been arranged in advance, a conclusion that perhaps fits with Belisa's statement that "el que me busque con ardor me encontrará" (he who seeks me with ardor will find me) (261) and her apparent lack of surprise that "son cinco" (there are five) (262). When Belisa asks Perlimplín about his past loves, he first responds "¿Qué mujeres?" (What women?) and then "Pero ¿hay otras mujeres?" (But are there other women?) (263). While it is possible to read this as simple, romantic gallantry—there is "no one else but you"—Belisa's astonished reaction ("¡Me estás asombrando!" [You're astounding me!] [263]) may support, though it does not prove, a previous conjecture that at age fifty Perlimplín is still a virgin.

Up to this point, the dialogue, stage design, costumes, musical effects, and other elements have combined to create an effect of heavily stylized realism, but now the lights dim, and two Duendes enter and perch on the hood of the prompter's box. The presence of these supernatural creatures in this liminal space onstage now propels the action into an unreal dimension. Is the audience meant to think that they are somehow "real"?—after all, they claim to have known Perlimplín and Belisa for many years (266), and later Perlimplín mentions "mi madre cuando la visitaron las hadas de los contornos" (my mother when she was visited by fairies from the surrounding area) (281). Or do they fulfill a purely symbolic function, as extraneous and mischievous entities endowed with a superior knowledge of events, as an indirect mouthpiece of the author or a kind of chorus, as well as serving as an expedient way of compressing the hours of the wedding night into a few theatrical moments? Their status is, ultimately, indeterminate and never resolved.

When the curtain is drawn back and dawn starts to break, Perlimplín is found to be wearing a pair of large, gilded antlers (269), a heavy and awkward headdress, of which both he and Belisa make no mention throughout the remainder of the scene, suggesting that it, too, is to be taken symbolically and intended primarily for the benefit of the audience. When Perlimplín first came onstage in scene 2, he was described as "vestido magníficamente" (dressed magnificently) (261), and later he asked his wife for permission to remove his "casaca," presumably the same green dress coat or morning suit of scene 1 (253). However, no stage direction indicates that such an action occurred, and now, on getting out of bed, "va vestido con casaca" (he is wearing a dress coat) (269), seeming to suggest that he has spent the whole night fully clothed. For her part, Belisa is found in an "espléndida toilete [sic]" (splendid toilette) (270), which must reprise the attire in which she appeared the evening before: a "gran traje de dormir lleno de encajes" (an imposing nightgown covered in lace) and "cofia inmensa [con] una cascada de puntillas y entredoses" (huge sleeping cap [with] a cascade of lace edgings and embroidered strips) (261).

The five open balconies, the ladders, and the hats are explained away implausibly by Belisa, and the explicit statement of the supposed events only comes at the beginning of scene 3, when Marcolfa reminds her employer of what she says he already knows, namely that "la noche de boda entraron cinco personas por los balcones" (the wedding night, five persons entered through the balconies). It is, of course, impossible to imagine realistically how Perlimplín and Belisa could have occupied the same bed and yet, at the same time, Belisa could have cuckolded him five times over the course of a single night inside the house and with five different sex partners who were "representantes de las cinco razas de la tierra" (representatives of the five races of the world) (274). Evidently, there is some hyperbolic compression and symbolic representation occurring here;[4] once conveniently married, it is implied, Belisa will soon go on to have adulterous liaisons with a wide range of younger suitors. Another unanswered question has to do with how much, at this precise moment, Perlimplín really knows or suspects or has an inkling of or is in denial about. When Marcolfa later recounts the incident, she adds: "Y usted sin enterarse" (And you without realizing) (274). At all events, after Perlimplín's queries concerning the five balconies, her being kissed, and whether anyone else has kissed her, all of which Belisa cajolingly deflects, he finally seems to decide, mainly on the basis of her first explicit declaration of love for him, that everything else is unimportant (271). However, the adoption of such a positive or optimistic attitude is immediately undercut by the violence and sadness of the imagery of Perlimplín's poem/song that closes the scene (272).

Many critics have asserted that Perlimplín is impotent, but while this is certainly a possibility, it is far from being convincingly substantiated. If he never undresses, as appears to be the case, it seems reasonable to conclude that whatever Belisa may or may not have done, the marriage was not consummated between husband and wife. Nonetheless, in the second of the three brief rounds of questioning that take place, Belisa replies: "¡Tú me has besado!" (You have kissed me!), to which Perlimplín concurs: "¡Sí! Yo te he besado" (Yes! I have kissed you) (270). The reasons why things may not have progressed beyond kissing—if indeed that occurred—are open to speculation. Impotence is certainly one factor to be considered ("Tú eres joven y yo soy viejo. . . . ¡Qué le vamos a hacer!" [You are young, and I am old. . . . There's nothing that we can do about that!] [277]), and fear of his wife is another ("pareces una ola y me das el mismo miedo que de niño tuve al mar" [you look like a wave, and you frighten me in the same way the sea did when I was a child] [261]), but we should not overlook the precise nature of the evolving emotions that he has for Belisa, in which sexual attraction may rapidly be giving way to something else. Such would appear to be the implication of Duende 2's assertion that "el alma de Perlimplín, chica y asustada como un patito recién nacido, se enriquece y sublima en estos instantes" (Perlimplín's soul, small and scared like a newborn duckling, is being enriched and ennobled in these instants) (266). Is Perlimplín an ugly duckling spiritually turning into a beautiful swan? The *Diccionario de la Real Academia Española* (*DRAE*) defines *sub-*

limar as "engrandecer, exaltar, ensalzar, elevar a un grado superior" (ennoble, exalt, extol, elevate to a higher level), implying not only a gain in complexity but also one of moral quality. The Duende's phrase "in these instants," though, is surely premature, in the sense that what is happening at that moment will be the stimulus for a complex psychological process that spans the remainder of the play.

Scene 3 presents a Perlimplín unperturbed by the clear evidence of Belisa's multiple adulteries and positively intrigued by her latest dalliance (274), disconcerting attitudes to which we will return later. After relinquishing to Belisa the letter from her latest admirer (only later do we realize that the stone to which it was attached was thrown by Marcolfa), Perlimplín avers: "Yo sé que tú me eres fiel y lo sigues siendo" (I know that you are faithful to me and continue to be so) (276), a statement that, in the moment, must leave the audience completely baffled and which is still difficult to construe even in light of the denouement. And a similar reaction surely awaits his next declaration that since he now knows "everything," "quiero ayudarte como debe hacer todo buen marido cuando su esposa es un dechado de virtud" (I want to help you as every good husband ought to do when his wife is a model of virtue) (276–77). How can Belisa be conceived of as a perfect example, a veritable paragon, of virtue? What "good husband" aids and abets his wife in her repeated adulteries? There is no irony detectable here. Furthermore, it is almost equally remarkable that she adjusts nearly instantaneously, and with minimal hesitation, not only to the revelation that her husband is fully aware of what is going on but also to his professed inclination to be her close confidant and indeed to his fulsome praise of her latest mystery lover.

Scene 4 brings the denouement that constitutes one of the biggest conundrums posed by the play and is a topic to which we shall likewise return. More locally, Belisa sings her erotically charged song offstage and then emerges in the moonlit garden, expectant for the ten o'clock rendezvous. As she waits, she says: "He sentido tu calor y tu peso, delicioso joven de mi alma" (I have felt your warmth and your weight, oh delightful young man of my soul) (284), but of course, this cannot literally be the case, as they have never even met face to face, save gone further than that, so we are forced to conclude that this has occurred purely in her imagination.

Likewise, a little later, in conversation with Perlimplín, she asserts of her mystery lover that "el olor de su carne le pasa a través de su ropa" (the smell of his body permeates his clothes) (285), yet again they have never been in sufficiently close proximity for Belisa actually to perceive this phenomenon. After Perlimplín shows Belisa his dagger and announces his intention of plunging it into her suitor's heart (285), she tries to restrain him, but he breaks free; she then calls out "desperately" for Marcolfa to bring her the sword from the dining room, as she now intends to "atravesar la garganta de mi marido" (stab through my husband's neck) (286). The phrase also picks up what Perlimplín says to Belisa earlier in describing his first feeling of love toward here, "como un hondo corte de lanceta en mi garganta" (like a deep cut in my neck from a lancet) (263).

Even allowing for the extremity of her emotions at this climactic juncture, such a plan of action—of attacking him with the sword—seems decidedly suspect. But what really casts doubt on all this is her next speech:

> (*A voces.*)
> Don Perlimplín
> marido ruin
> como le mates
> te mato a ti. (286)

> (*Loudly.*)
> Don Perlimplín
> despicable husband
> if you kill him
> I'll kill you.

Her imprecations, shouted out, are couched in five-syllable lines of verse with an insistent assonance in stressed *i*, making them sound more like a children's jingle than a desperate threat of homicidal vengeance. To what extent can the real violence that is unfolding here—the soon-to-be-discovered suicide—be taken seriously? Immediately thereafter, when Belisa encounters the "mystery man" wrapped in the long red cloak, she asks him repeatedly and insistently who has stabbed him, despite her exchange with Perlimplín moments earlier. As the mystery man collapses on the garden bench, it seems that only now does Belisa start to take him seriously, as if in her previous dialogue she had really been under the impression that this was all part of some elaborate sham or pretense, as if from a melodramatic romance: "¿Pero qué es esto? . . . ¡Y estás herido de verdad!" (But what's this? . . . And you're really wounded!) (287). It is far from clear, though, why she should ever have thought that this was make-believe, as there is no indication that Perlimplín's dagger is anything but real.

Although these many individual moments of uncertainty, ambiguity, discontinuity, and disjunction are spread throughout the text, there are several bigger questions arising from a consideration of the play as a whole that are just as hard to pin down and, perhaps, irresolvable. These have to do with a variety of topics: the evolution of Perlimplín's feelings for Belisa and the vocabulary that he uses to designate them; how cuckoldry and happiness can be reconciled and the acquisition of new capabilities that Perlimplín claims the experience has afforded him; his motives and goals for the elaborate plan that he sets in motion during the latter half of the play, his feelings about it, and the inconsistencies within it; the meaning of the denouement and, particularly, how Belisa is affected by what Perlimplín does; to what extent the Christological framework should be understood as having a serious or an ironic import; the unique, jarring mix of genres, from farce through to tragedy; and the representational instability occasioned by various different cases of metatheatrical effects.

As we saw, by the end of scene 1, Perlimplín starts to feel unsettled by Belisa, though he cannot put a name on it (258, 259), and at the beginning of scene 2, he wonders where his "old self" has gone (¡Ay! . . . Perlimplín . . . ¿dónde estás, Perlimplín?" [Oh! . . . Perlimplín . . . where are you, Perlimplín?] [261]). A little later, he makes the momentous announcement: "He tardado en decidirme. . . . Pero . . . [. . .] Belisa . . . ¡yo te amo!" (I have taken a long time to make up my mind . . . But . . . [. . .] Belisa . . . I love you!) (262), and in the dialogue that ensues, he expands on this abrupt declaration:

PERLIMPLÍN: [. . .] Antes de casarme contigo yo no te quería. [. . .]

PERLIMPLÍN: Me casé . . . ¡por lo que fuera!, pero no te quería. Yo no había podido imaginarme tu cuerpo hasta que lo vi por el ojo de la cerradura cuando te vestían de novia. Y entonces fue cuando sentí el amor, ¡entonces!, como un hondo corte de lanceta en mi garganta. (263)

PERLIMPLÍN: [. . .] Before I married you, I did not love you. [. . .]

PERLIMPLÍN: I got married . . . for whatever reason! but I did not love you. I had not been able to imagine your body until I saw it through the keyhole when they were dressing you in your bridal clothes. And it was then that I felt love, then! like a deep cut in my neck from a lancet.

But the inexperienced Perlimplín seems to be confused. Is love really something that one ponders and then makes one's mind up about? And if the first crucial event for him was spying voyeuristically on Belisa and seeing her as she was putting on her bridal attire, then surely the new feeling that he experiences is physical attraction and desire, rather than love. Several lines later, as they get into bed and he puts out the light, he ups the ante still further: "¡Te adoro!" (I adore you) (264) are his last words before the Duendes come onstage.

Many critics assume that Perlimplín has seen Belisa naked, but notice the phrase "cuando te vestían de novia." It is much more likely that he has seen her in her undergarments. In consonance with one of the general propositions made by the play—that concealment generates curiosity and fascination[5]—Perlimplín is at most mildly interested in Belisa on her balcony, where she sits "medio desnuda" (half-naked) (255) and later "casi desnuda" (almost naked) (258).[6] In contrast, for the wedding night, she wears a heavy and elaborately decorated nightgown and a sleeping cap, though her hair is down ("el pelo suelto") and her arms are exposed ("los brazos desnudos") (261). Likewise, in scene 4, she is "espléndidamente vestida" (splendidly dressed) (284), though admittedly, by the end of the scene, she has become considerably disheveled ("medio desnuda" [half-naked] [288]).

Later, in the midst of all his suspicions about the open balconies / ladders / hats, Perlimplín nonetheless also tells Belisa that "yo cada minuto te quiero más" (every minute I love you more) (270), and in a stage direction, he is described as "embobado" (besotted) (270). But all is not well. He earlier characterized the coup de foudre that he experienced as "un hondo corte de lanceta en mi garganta" (263), and the poem/song that closes scene 2 picks up precisely that imagery.

> Amor, amor
> que estoy herido.
> Herido de amor huido,
> herido,
> muerto de amor.
> Decid a todos que ha sido
> el ruiseñor.
> Bisturí de cuatro filos
> garganta rota y olvido. (272)

> Love, love
> I am wounded.
> Wounded by love that has fled,
> wounded,
> dying of love.
> Tell everyone that it was
> the nightingale.
> A scalpel with four cutting edges
> neck broken and oblivion.

Beyond the age-old trope of falling in love as receiving a wound, there is also the suggestion of "love that has fled," a notion that undercuts his apparent satisfaction at Belisa's answers and the sense of expansive well-being that dominated his mood moments earlier.

Marcolfa, too, perceives his words and actions as betokening love: "Mi señor la quiere demasiado" (The master loves her too much), to which he cryptically replies: "No tanto como ella merece" (Not as much as she deserves) (275). Perlimplín convinces Belisa to confide in him, and a key part of his argument is that "ahora te quiero como si fuera tu padre . . . ya estoy lejos de las tonterías" (now I love you as if I were your father . . . I'm well past all that foolishness) (277). These "tonterías" must refer to his previous stirrings of physical desire and also to what he (mis)identified as true marital love. But as Perlimplín bifurcates his personality into the "paternal" husband and the sensual "mystery lover," things become distinctly complicated. Based on the letters that she receives, Belisa concludes that "lo que no cabe duda es que me ama como yo deseo" (what is not in any doubt is that he loves me as I want him to) (278), and she gives us a sample of the kind of thing that he writes to her: "Belisa. ¡No es tu alma lo que yo deseo!, ¡sino tu blanco y mórbido cuerpo estremecido!" (Belisa. It is not your soul that I desire! but rather your white and soft trembling body) (278). Here is Perlimplín in the persona of the unidentified young man channeling his powerful lust, at a distant remove from the fatherly affection professed by the "real" Perlimplín.

This dichotomy reappears in a modified form at the close of the action: "¡Ah, Don Perlimplín! Viejo verde, monigote sin fuerzas, tú no podías gozar el cuerpo de Belisa. . . . El cuerpo de Belisa era para músculos jóvenes y labios de ascuas. . . . Yo en cambio amaba tu cuerpo nada más" (Oh, don Perlimplín! You dirty old man, you powerless weakling, you could not enjoy Belisa's body . . . Belisa's body was for young muscles and fiery lips. . . . I, however, loved your body and nothing more) (287). Perlimplín now characterizes himself as a feeble "dirty old man," only able to "love" but not physically enjoy her body, quite unlike the "father figure" role that he claimed to have adopted. At all events, by killing the mystery lover (and hence, also himself), Perlimplín achieves at one stroke two very different goals: "Él te querrá con el amor infinito de los difuntos y yo quedaré libre de esta oscura pesadilla de tu cuerpo grandioso. (*Abrazándola.*) Tu cuerpo . . . que nunca podría descifrar" (He will love you with the infinite love of the dead, and I will be free of this dark nightmare of your magnificent body. [*Embracing her.*] Your body . . . that I could never decipher) (286). For Belisa he eternalizes the love felt for her by the young man,[7] and for himself he breaks free of the terrible oppression caused by her splendid body and his ultimate inability to make sense of it or possess it. Accordingly, the invention of an alter ego corresponds to an attempt to compartmentalize the uncomfortable mixture of lust and affection that he repeatedly refers to as love. This hardly constitutes the transcendence that we are at moments led to believe he has achieved, as for instance by the Duendes.

Despite Perlimplín's initial apprehension about marriage in general and Belisa in particular, after the wedding night, a remarkable change has come over him. In the midst of his concerns about all the suspicious details, he is still able to announce that "¡Por primera vez en mi vida estoy contento!" (For the first time in my life, I am happy!) (270), and a little later he relishes the sunrise that, apparently, he has never seen before: "Es un espectáculo que . . . parece mentira . . . ¡me conmueve!" (It is a spectacle that . . . it's hard to believe . . . moves me!) (271). On the face of it, it would seem that this transformation has been wrought by the "love" that he has just declared for Belisa. But in scene 3, we are obliged to revise our previous conjecture. Now Perlimplín knows for certain that he has been cuckolded, and yet he tells Marcolfa: "yo soy feliz [. . .]. Feliz como no tienes idea" (I am happy [. . .]. You have no idea how happy). And his explanation of how these two inimical states can coexist within him is that thanks to this new experience, "he aprendido muchas cosas y, sobre todo, puedo imaginarlas" (I have learned many things, and above all, I can imagine them) (275). Love or physical attraction or lust for a highly sexual young woman may have been the catalyst, but it appears that the resulting consequence of being cuckolded is a small price to pay—or perhaps simply becomes irrelevant—compared to the new capabilities that he has acquired. Perlimplín makes repeated reference to them in the rest of the play: "comprendo tu estado de ánimo [. . .]. Yo me doy cuenta de las cosas. Y aunque me hieren profundamente comprendo que vives un drama" (I understand your state of mind [. . .]. I notice things. And although they wound me deeply, I understand that you are living through a drama) (276); "¡Yo lo sé todo! . . . Me di cuenta enseguida. [. . .] lo comprendo perfectamente" (I know everything! . . . I realized immediately. [. . .] I understand perfectly); and he strikes the attitude of the worldly-wise: "¡Qué inocente eres!" (How innocent you are!) (277). *Learning* (and hence knowing, understanding) and *imagining* are intimately linked; imagination is a mode of insight, of knowledge.[8] Perlimplín tells us that "yo no había podido imaginarme tu cuerpo hasta que lo vi por el ojo de la cerradura" (I had not been able to imagine your body until I saw it through the keyhole) (263), and later he contrasts "then" and "now": "Antes no podía pensar en las cosas extraordinarias que tiene el mundo. . . . Me quedaba en las puertas. . . . En cambio ahora. . . . El amor de Belisa me ha dado un tesoro precioso que yo ignoraba. . . . ¿Ves? Ahora cierro los ojos y . . . veo lo que quiero" (Before, I wasn't able to think about the extraordinary things that the world has. . . . I fell short. . . . However now. . . . Love for Belisa has given me a precious treasure that I knew nothing of. . . . Do you see? Now I close my eyes and . . . I see what I want to) (280–81). At the end, he will call the elaborate ruse and its impact on Belisa "el triunfo de mi imaginación" (the triumph of my imagination) (285).

While all this would seem to establish a simple linear trajectory, such a "triumph" might at the very least be considered Pyrrhic, the acquisition of understanding and imagination involving betrayal, suffering, and ultimately self-immolation (as will be explored here), and may possibly be undermined by one of Perlimplín's last utterances: although it is the *sight* of her (partially clothed) body that—he claims—endows him with imagination, he nonetheless admits that his new faculties are not powerful enough to achieve ultimate *understanding* of it: "Tu cuerpo . . . que nunca podría descifrar" (Your body . . . that I could never decipher) (286).

In the wake of Perlimplín's marriage, whatever he experiences—or does not experience—on the wedding night, the upsurge of emotions, both happy and painful, his suspicions and then confirmation of Belisa's adultery, and finally some kind of curiosity concerning his wife's extramarital affairs (the stage directions describe him twice as "intrigado" [intrigued] [274, 278] and once as "inquisitivo" [inquisitive] [278]), he conceives of a plan to induce Belisa to fall in love with a mysterious suitor whom he creates and then brings to life (Perlimplín is the figure only glimpsed in the street, the writer of the letters, and so on). Through the course of scenes 3 and 4, numerous sequences of dialogue appear to throw light on his motives and goals in carrying out this plan.

Perlimplín is cognizant of the large difference in age and its implications (277, 279, 287),[9] and so the fictional young man allows him to play out a role vis-à-vis Belisa that he could never do in "real life." At the same time, it seems that he also intends for the experience of this unusual courtship to have a very particular impact on his wife. Perlimplín calculates correctly that elusiveness and a hint of disdain will pique Belisa's interest and cause her to speculate obsessively about the mysterious figure (275). He stokes her fascination with eloquent descriptions of the young man (277), but it is the letters that he writes anonymously that are the most effective component in his ruse. In stark contrast to the romantic clichés sent by her other admirers, his letters scorn soulful platitudes and concentrate instead on her body, which—as he bluntly states—he desires (278). At the end of scene 3, Perlimplín for the first time refers explicitly to what he is in the process of doing: "Como soy un viejo quiero sacrificarme por ti. Esto que yo hago no lo hizo nadie jamás. Pero ya estoy fuera del mundo y de la moral ridícula de las gentes" (As I am an old man I want to sacrifice myself for you. This thing that I'm doing, no one has ever done. But I am already free of the world and the ridiculous moral code of people) (279). The key concepts here are self-sacrifice, the uniqueness of his scheme, being "fuera del mundo"—whatever that means—and being beyond conventional social morality. He elaborates on his attitude and intentions in conversation with Marcolfa:

MARCOLFA: Su amor debe rayar en la locura.

PERLIMPLÍN: (*Vibrante.*) ¡Eso es! Yo necesito que ella ame a ese joven más que a su propio cuerpo y ¡No hay duda que lo ama!

MARCOLFA: (*Llorando.*) [. . .] ¿cómo es posible? ¡Que usted mismo fomente en su mujer el peor de los pecados!

PERLIMPLÍN: ¡Porque Don Perlimplín no tiene honor y quiere divertirse! [. . .] ¿Qué he de hacer sino cantar?
(*Cantando.*)
> ¡Don Perlimplín no tiene honor!
> ¡No tiene honor! (281–82)

MARCOLFA: Her love must be bordering on madness.

PERLIMPLÍN: (*Vibrant.*) That's it! I need her to love that young man more than her own body, and there is no doubt that she loves him!

MARCOLFA: (*Weeping.*) [. . .] how is it possible? That you yourself encourage in your wife the worst of sins!

PERLIMPLÍN: Because don Perlimplín has no honor and wants to have some fun! [. . .] What am I going to do if not sing?
(*Singing.*)
> Don Perlimplín has no honor!
> He has no honor!

now adding the further ingredients of needing Belisa to be madly in love, his lost honor, and most troublingly, his desire to amuse or entertain himself.

When he surprises Belisa in the garden, Perlimplín is now described as "concupiscente" (lustful), hinting at the salacious, though vicarious, pleasure he takes in this. He is eager for details:

BELISA: [. . .] Le quiero, Perlimplín, ¡le quiero! ¡Me parece que soy otra mujer!

PERLIMPLÍN: Ése es mi triunfo.

BELISA: ¿Qué triunfo?

PERLIMPLÍN: El triunfo de mi imaginación. (285)

BELISA: [. . .] I love him, Perlimplín, I love him! It seems to me that I am another woman!

PERLIMPLÍN: That is my triumph.

BELISA: What triumph?

PERLIMPLÍN: The triumph of my imagination.

Her "transformation" is a marker of success, achieved by the unique plan that he conceived, but this is only step one, as we soon discover: "para que sea tuyo completamente se me ha ocurrido que lo mejor es clavarle este puñal en su corazón galante. ¿Te gusta?" (so that he may be completely yours, it has occurred to me that the best thing is to pierce his gallant heart with this dagger. Do you like that?) (285). Beyond the extremity of his proposed course of action, the final question that he poses to her is, evidently, more than a little disturbing.

In the last part of the scene, Perlimplín appears in character as the young man who has just been stabbed. He lowers his long cloak, and Belisa immediately recognizes her husband, but he continues on firmly in character, claiming that Perlimplín "salió corriendo por el campo y no le verás más nunca. Me mató porque sabía que te amaba como nadie. Mientras me hería . . . gritó: ¡Belisa ya tiene un alma!" (ran off into the countryside, and you will never see him again. He killed me because he knew that I loved you like no one else. While he was stabbing me . . . he cried: Belisa now has a soul!). While Belisa struggles to work out what is going on, he tries to clarify his intent: "¿Entiendes? . . . Yo soy mi alma y tú eres tu cuerpo"

(Do you understand? . . . I am my soul, and you are your body) (287). The mention of her body refocuses his attention in the final moments:

> PERLIMPLÍN: (*Moribundo.*) [. . .] tu cuerpo. Déjame en este último instante, puesto que tanto me has querido, morir abrazado a él.
>
> BELISA: (*Se acerca medio desnuda y lo abraza.*) Sí . . . ¿pero y el joven? . . . ¿Por qué me has engañado?
>
> PERLIMPLÍN: ¿El joven? . . . (*Cierra los ojos.*) (287–88)

> PERLIMPLÍN: (*Dying.*) [. . .] your body. Let me in this last moment, since you have loved me so much, die embracing it.
>
> BELISA: (*She approaches half-naked and embraces him.*) Yes . . . but what about the young man? . . . Why have you deceived me?
>
> PERLIMPLÍN: The young man? . . . (*He closes his eyes.*)

There are several unresolved questions here. Is Perlimplín still talking in character? Does the "me" of "Déjame" refer to Perlimplín or the alter ego? If "Belisa now has a soul," why are the verbs still in the present tense in the subsequent assertion that "I am my soul, and you are your body"? How does this fit with his request for a final, physical embrace, which Belisa grants? Does such a request, at this very point in time, undercut his previous contentions? Furthermore, it is unclear how completely Belisa now understands the situation. When she asks "what about the young man?" is she referring to Perlimplín's scheming, or does she still somehow believe that he exists? And when Perlimplín repeats her penultimate question as his final words—"The young man?" what tone of voice should inflect them as a pointer to how he understands it? Is he incredulous that she is still so confused, frustrated that she continues to obsess about him, disappointed that she has not intuited his purpose, or something else again? Could they even be an indication that just as he expires, he half-grasps that he may actually have failed?

Marcolfa is left to "pick up the pieces." Realization finally seems to be dawning on Belisa as she exclaims: "(*Extrañada y en otro mundo.*) Perlimplín, ¿qué cosa has hecho, Perlimplín?" ([*Puzzled and in another world.*] Perlimplín, what have you done, Perlimplín?) (288). Having fallen in love with the mystery man, Belisa already considered herself "another woman" (285), but now, following this latest experience, Marcolfa asserts that she is changed again: "Belisa, ya eres otra mujer" (Belisa, now you are another woman). More ambiguity arises when, after Marcolfa refers to "mi señor" (my master), Belisa asks: "¿Pero quién era este hombre? ¿Quién era?" (But who was this man? Who was he?) (288). It is possible that she is still unsure regarding the basics of what has just happened (who was the "mystery man"?), but it is more likely that she is asking who the *real* Perlimplín was, the person whom she never got to know. Marcolfa's answer, "El hermoso adolescente al que nunca verás el rostro" (The handsome adolescent whose face you will never see), does nothing to resolve things, and it is unclear why she (re)introduces this idea at this stage—is she suggesting that Perlimplín was both "mi señor" *and* the "hermoso adolescente" (288)? This leads through to Belisa's final statement and question: "Sí, sí, Marcolfa, le quiero, le quiero con toda la fuerza de mi carne y de mi alma. Pero ¿dónde está el joven de la capa roja? . . . Dios mío. ¿Dónde está?" (Yes, yes, Marcolfa, I love him, I love him with all the strength of my body and soul. But where is the young man with the red cape? . . . Oh God. Where is he?). If *le* refers to Perlimplín and she loves him "body *and* soul," he would seem to have been successful, but in the next breath, Belisa is still desperately asking after the "joven." Is this part of Perlimplín's scheme, that she should still remain fixated on the mirage of the young man, or does Belisa continue to genuinely fail to understand the situation? Marcolfa implies the former: "Don Perlimplín, duerme tranquilo. . . . ¡La estás oyendo! . . . Don Perlimplín . . . ¡la estás oyendo? [*sic*]" (Don Perlimplín, sleep easy. . . . You're hearing her! . . . Don Perlimplín . . . Are you hearing her?) (289).

Expressed succinctly, Perlimplín has created a persona designed for Belisa to fall hopelessly in love with, in order that she can become a "whole" person (with an integrated body and soul). This involves her experiencing a powerful love that she has never felt before, which is both a means to an end (that is, integration) and an end in itself, as Perlimplín wants her to feel for him (his alter ego) the same kind of love that he believes he has for her. However, such a love is inevitably and fundamentally problematic: for Perlimplín, its physical fulfillment and reciprocation are unattainable, and he can only experience it, vicariously, through the alter ego; for her part, Belisa unknowingly falls in love with a fiction, and it is highly questionable whether the nature of the love that she feels (physical desire that turns into something obsessive) is really appropriate to the task of bringing out her spiritual dimension. If Perlimplín can be counted as having "succeeded"—and that is far from certain—it is a very mixed success, and of course, it involves his own death; as for the now widowed Belisa, doubts remain as to whether she has truly become that second type of "otra mujer."

John Lyon usefully lists several of Perlimplín's possible—and often contradictory—motives, to which I have added some additional ones of my own.[10] This gives us at least six different ways of interpreting what impels him to act in the way that he does. (1) Perlimplín is grateful to Belisa for having afforded him the new experience of love and, above all, for having unlocked the unsuspected power of his imagination; his actions therefore involve self-sacrifice driven by altruism and selfless love, and their goal is to "repay" Belisa by endowing her with a soul. (2) He is driven by a desire for revenge, conceived in a symmetrical fashion as having Belisa experience exactly the same profound frustration and nonfulfillment caused by unattainable love, in her case, for the nonexistent young suitor who is subsequently done away with, after which she will live on with an unrequited memory of him. Perlimplín's cruel query "¿te gusta?" (285) would seem to support this. Certainly, the proposition that some kind of unconventional retaliation is involved would appear to be suggested by certain statements that Lorca made in 1933: "El héroe, o antihéroe, a quien hacen cornudo, es español y calderoniano; pero [Perlimplín] no quiere reaccionar calderonianamente, y de ahí su lucha, la tragedia grotesca de su caso" (The hero, or antihero, who is cuckolded, is Spanish and Calderonian; but [Perlimplín] does not want to react in a Calderonian fashion, and this is the cause of his struggle, the grotesque tragedy of his case); "Su imaginación dormida se despierta con el tremendo engaño de su mujer; pero él luego hace cornudas a todas las mujeres que existen" (His slumbering imagination is awakened by the tremendous deceit of his wife; but then he cuckolds all the women that exist).[11] (3) His suicide is more self-centered, in that it will liberate him from the frustration of not having the kind of physical relationship with Belisa that he longs for but knows he will never achieve. (4) Less altruistic than interpretation 1, less vengeful than 2, and closer to 3 because of the selfishness involved, one might also argue that his chief aim is to know that he will be loved after death, to live on in Belisa's heart.[12] (5) Another possibility not considered by Lyon is that Perlimplín is mentally unhinged; his comment that "ya estoy fuera del mundo y de la moral ridícula de las gentes" (I am already free of the world and the ridiculous moral code of people) (279) can be read in two ways, and his apparent glee at his loss of honor and how this "frees him up" is striking: "¡Porque don Perlimplín no tiene honor y quiere divertirse! [. . .] ¿Qué he de hacer sino cantar?" (Because don Perlimplín has no honor and wants to have some fun! [. . .] What am I going to do if not sing?) (282). (6) The denouement can be read as kind of modified *liebestod:* in that last embrace with the semi-naked Belisa, Perlimplín achieves a momentary union with her and the conjunction of bodies and souls; this is only attainable through death. It should be clear that it is impossible to opt for just one of these alternative readings over the others, as is demonstrated by the complete lack of critical consensus in interpretations of the play.

Another factor that affects our attempts to determine whether any change really occurred in Belisa—and if so, the precise nature of that change—is the Christological framework present in the text. Marcolfa addresses Perlimplín repeatedly as "señor mío" (253), "mi señor" (255, 255, 275, 280), or "el señor" (275), but the full significance of these appellations only becomes apparent toward the end. The decor for scene 3 includes "La mesa con todos los objetos pintados como en una 'Cena' primitiva" (The table with all the objects painted as if in a primitive "Last Supper") (274), while scene 4 is set in a "Jardín de cipreses y naranjos" (Garden of cypress and orange trees) (280). The two emblematic trees foreshadow the intermingling of death and love that will predominate here, and while neither are olive trees, the garden acquires distinct overtones of Gethsemane as well as the *hortus conclusus.* The key juncture comes when Perlimplín announces to Belisa the arrival of her lover (whom he intends to stab) with the line "Míralo por dónde viene" (Look at where he is coming) (286), the opening line of one of the best-known *saetas* sung during Easter processions to announce the arrival of a float with a sculpture of the Passion of Christ. Minutes later, Marcolfa talks of wrapping Perlimplín in a shroud and then announces to Belisa: "ya eres otra mujer. . . . Estás vestida por la sangre gloriosísima de mi señor" (now you are another woman. . . . You are clothed in the most glorious blood of my master) (288), making explicit the implications of the use here of *señor/Señor* as the formal mode of address used by a servant but also to refer to Christ the Lord.

There are at least two ways of taking this, as an example of serious symbolism or as highly ironic or even parodic. Perlimplín becomes a Christlike figure: out of his love for Belisa, he chooses willingly to lay down his own life in order to "redeem" hers. Perlimplín's spilled blood is shed for Belisa and "clothes" her, a notion from Catholic devotion reinforced by the Last Supper–like dining room table. But this only holds if we accept one line of interpretation of the play and reject all the others. Furthermore, are Perlimplín's lustful urges (as well as his paternalistic affection) for Belisa comparable to Christ's pure love for mankind? Is Belisa really "redeemed"? The *lo* from the line of the *saeta* supposedly refers to the mystery lover and not to Perlimplín. Does this correspond, therefore, just to the particular way that Marcolfa, the loyal servant, has of understanding the unfolding of events,[13] or by introducing these strange, out-of-place, and occasionally jarring elements, does Lorca make a parody of the possible parallels?

In the light of these many considerations, it is no surprise that the generic category of the play also remains indeterminate. Lorca, of course, avoided the issue by calling it an "aleluya erótica" (literally something like "the erotic rhyming couplets of a strip cartoon"). Critics who stress the elements of comedy or farce connect it with popular medieval farce, commedia dell'arte, puppet traditions, Cervantes, Italian comedy (Carlo Goldoni), and so on. Others find more of the grotesque, while it is hard not to agree that as the action progresses, it tips increasingly toward tragedy, though in a rather unconventional fashion.[14] Lorca himself acknowledged that "empieza en burla y acaba en trágico" (it starts out in jest, and it ends in the tragic); of Perlimplín, he referred to "la tragedia grotesca de su caso" (the grotesque tragedy of his case) and stated that "lo que me ha interesado en don Perlimplín es subrayar el contraste entre lo grotesco y lo lírico y aún mezclarlos en todo momento" (what interested me in don Perlimplín is to underline the contrast between the grotesque and the lyrical and even to mix them constantly).[15]

Finally, the various different examples of metatheater should be mentioned, as this phenomenon immediately calls into doubt how the spectator should respond to what is more or less self-consciously being presented onstage, that is, to what extent the theatrical illusion is foregrounded and itself thematized.[16] In scene 1, beyond the stylized pattern of dialogue, from behind a curtain (256), Marcolfa acts exactly as a prompter, feeding Perlimplín his lines, which he then humorously mangles. In scene 2, the episode with the Duendes introduces a very overt metatheatrical element as they draw a curtain, perch on the prompter's box, and refer in their dialogue to the audience.[17] As superior and possibly supernatural beings, they know things about the characters in the play and about the plot, and at moments they assume an almost chorus-like status vaguely reminiscent of the three Leñadores in *Bodas de sangre*. Further, the audience whom they address comes to play the role of society at large.[18] In scenes 3 and 4, Perlimplín invents a character, fosters a belief in his existence, writes (the script of) his letters, and finally performs the role in the garden.

I debated for some time whether to use *ambiguity* or *undecidability* in the title of this essay but eventually opted for the second term. Bennett and Royle write that

> the difference between new critical ambiguity and poststructuralist unde-
> cidability, though apparently minimal, is fundamental. For the new critics,
> ambiguity produces a complex but organic whole, a unity wherein ambi-
> guity brings together disparate elements. For poststructuralist critics, by
> contrast, undecidability opens up a gap, a rift in the text which can never
> be fully sealed. Undecidability opens the text to multiple readings, it de-
> stabilizes the reader's sense of the certainty of any particular reading, and
> ultimately threatens to undermine the very stability of any reading posi-
> tion, the very identity of any reader [. . .]. Suspensions of meaning bypass
> the reductive and constricting determination of what is now recognized to
> be the illusion of a single, final, determined "meaning." To think in terms
> of undecidability, however, is not to advocate the equal legitimacy of any
> and every interpretation: to acknowledge and explore aporias or suspen-
> sions of meaning involves the responsibilities of the most thoughtful and
> scrupulous kinds of reading.[19]

It seems to me that *Amor de don Perlimplín* is poised somewhere between the two extremes adumbrated here. Perlimplín's motives and goals and the effect that his scheme ultimately has on Belisa remain open to speculation; the status of the Duendes remains unresolved; and so on and so forth.

Lorca's intent seems to be to throw into question a variety of commonly held assumptions—whether an individual's psychology and motivations are understandable by others; societal conventions of morality, standards of conduct, and prescribed codes; the relationship of the theatrical illusion to reality; spectator expectations based on theatrical genre—and at the same time, his purpose also appears to be to explore and champion other human capabilities, chief among them the power of the imagination. Wright comes close to my overall view of the play: "the difficulty of locating an ultimate meaning is a function of a text in which univocal referential meaning is constantly undermined by a play of plurivocal signifiers."[20] However, for her, this phenomenon is a consequence of the play's basic theme of "epistemology and its relation to the visual medium" (42), a theme that manifests itself through difficult and shifting layers of meaning involving veils, illusions, dreams, fantasies, and psychological projections.

The entirety of Lorca's dramatic corpus is bound together in sharing an essentially poetic discourse and rich veins of symbolism. However, if we focus on the issue of undecidability, *Amor de don Perlimplín* clearly aligns more closely with Lorca's plays from the 1930s, which are normally thought of as his most innovative, difficult, and challenging pieces: *El público, Así que pasen cinco años*, and *El sueño de la vida. Amor de don Perlimplín*, like those three plays, and also like *El maleficio de la mariposa*, has a male protagonist, whereas what might be thought of as Lorca's more "approachable" plays, from *Mariana Pineda* through *La zapatera prodigiosa* to the three tragedies and *Doña Rosita la soltera*, all feature female protagonists. I would argue that *Amor de don Perlimplín* actually embodies more undecidability than *Así que pasen cinco años* and just as much as *El público*, although its presence in the earlier play is more "stealthy" and less immediately noticeable, a characteristic that marks it as unique in Lorca's dramatic writings.

3

García Lorca and the New York Theater, 1929–1930

"El viaje a Nueva York puede decirse que enriquece y cambia la obra del poeta ya que es la primera vez que este se enfrenta con un mundo nuevo" (The trip to New York could be said to enrich and change the work of the poet since it is the first time that he confronts a new world).[1] Such was Lorca's own expressed opinion, as recorded in a brief autobiographical note that he jotted down sometime during his New York stay for a fellow American student. The "enrichment" and "change" to which he refers can be seen in many aspects of his life and work but perhaps in none more so than in his subsequent writings for the theater.[2] My purpose in this chapter will be to explore in some detail what can be discovered or reconstructed regarding Lorca's exposure to the stimulus of New York theatrical life both On- and Off-Broadway.

The letters home, to his parents and siblings, constitute the single most important source for our knowledge in this area, and yet at the same time, they are frustratingly tantalizing.[3] Federico had been put on a tight budget by his financially cautious father, and it is striking how in these missives the mention of a few extra dollars, either hoped for or garnered, is repeatedly tied to the possibility of theatergoing.[4] "Ya Paquito, que cobre y me gire el dinero de mis libros para tener para ir a teatros, cosa que me interesa enormemente" (Please have Paquito get the payment and wire me the money from my books [the royalties from *Canciones* and *Romancero gitano*] so that I can have enough to go to the theater, which is a thing that interests me enormously); "el dinero de la *Revista de Occidente* no lo he recibido. [. . .] Pero ese dinero lo guardaré para ir al teatro" (I have not received the money from the *Revista de Occidente*. [. . .] But I will reserve that money to go to the theater); "de todos modos, si gano algunos dólares los emplearé en comprarme algunas cosas y en ir a espectáculos, principalmente el teatro" (in any event, if I earn a few dollars, I will use them to buy some things and to go to shows, mainly the theater); "veremos a ver si mi presupuesto me alcanza pare asistir al teatro, en el que tengo tanto interés" (let's see if my budget is sufficient for me to go to the theater, in which I have so much interest).[5]

Furthermore, Lorca's analysis and evaluation of the New York theater scene are enthusiastic and entirely positive: here the theatergoer can see just what can be done, and the putative dramatist can glimpse the artistic directions of the future. "Aquí el teatro es magnífico y yo espero sacar gran partido de él para mis cosas" (Here the theater is magnificent, and I hope to take much advantage of it for my things); "aquí [el teatro] es muy bueno y muy *nuevo* y a mí me interesa en extremo" (here the theater is very good and very *new,* and I'm extremely interested in it); "hay que pensar en el teatro del porvenir. Todo lo que existe ahora en España está muerto. O se cambia el teatro de raíz o se acaba para siempre. No hay otra solución" (we must think about the theater of the future. Everything that exists nowadays in Spain is dead. Either the theater is changed at its root or it's finished for good. There is no other solution); "aquí hay un teatro de vanguardia" (here there is an avant-garde theater); "empiezo a ir al teatro, que es importantísimo en New York, y estoy asombrado de los actores tan buenos que tienen los americanos. En algunos conjuntos os sería difícil saber cuáles son las primeras figuras, ¡tanto y tan bien dirigidos están!" (I'm beginning to go to the theater, which is very important in New York, and I'm astonished at how good the actors are that the Americans have. In some companies, it would be difficult for you to tell who are the leading actors, so carefully and so well are they directed).[6]

So far so good, but what we do not know, and what we shall probably never know, is just what plays Lorca actually saw: unfortunately, the letters home do not name a single, specific title,[7] and none of the memoirs of contemporaries who socialized with Federico during his New York stay contains any reference to performances they might have attended together.[8] Confronted by this impasse, it is nevertheless possible to offer some speculation, as Christopher Maurer and Ian Gibson have already done.[9] In what follows, I shall be venturing further down the same conjectural path: if it is not possible to ascertain which plays and performances Lorca *actually* attended, then nevertheless it certainly *is* still feasible to identify the big hits of the period, the plays people would have been talking about and talking to Lorca about, the authors who were currently the toast of the town, the companies with high artistic reputations, the actors and actresses who received critical acclaim, and so on and so forth.

Lorca arrived in New York in late June 1929 and lodged in Columbia University's Furnald Hall for the summer session. He headed north to Vermont on August 21 and was back in New York, now in John Jay Hall, by September 22. Thereafter, he seems to have remained in Manhattan (except for a very brief visit to Vassar College in Poughkeepsie) until his departure by train on March 4, on the first leg of his journey to Cuba.[10] Lorca therefore spent some eight weeks in New York in the summer of 1929 and some twenty-three weeks there through the fall and winter of 1929–30—just over seven months in total, certainly a long enough period of time to get acclimatized, to find one's way around, and to take in at least a proportion of all that Manhattan had to offer.

Looking at plays and other theatrical entertainments that were already running when Lorca arrived in New York, as well as those that opened or opened and closed during the two periods when he was living there, and adopting the conventional genre categories of the time, we can arrive at the following statistics of productions that he *could* have patronized: 77 dramas, 18 comedy-dramas, 89 comedies, 14 revues, 21 musicals, and 14 light operas.[11] The numbers for revues and musicals are relatively low, as these tended to enjoy longer runs.[12] Overall, this adds up to 233, a figure that can be compared to the approximately 280 productions that opened during the entire 1929–30 theatrical season.[13] Clearly, then, there was no lack of choice.

Even at this time, Broadway productions did not actually mean those playing in theaters located on this famous thoroughfare, dubbed the "Great White Way" (in fact, the great majority of the theaters were not located along Broadway),[14] but rather, that part of the total offering whose nature was, broadly speaking, professional, mainstream, and distinctly commercial in intent.[15] In the summer of 1929, talkies had only just begun to erode the popularity of live performance, and nearly eighty "Broadway" theaters were in operation.[16] Through the fall of 1929, *Billboard* was much exercised over Hollywood financing of "legitimate" Broadway theater, a process whereby successful plays could rapidly be turned into films. The Wall Street crash was certainly felt by the theater world, forcing more plays than usual to offer cut-rate tickets, but this did not stop producers and entrepreneurs from continuing to line up new productions at a dizzying rate.[17] Flops, then, would open and close in a matter of days or weeks, while the most successful productions boasted runs that lasted for years. The longest-running productions that were still going when Lorca arrived in Manhattan were *Skidding,* by Aurania Rouverol, a comedy (opened May 21, 1928, closed June 29, 1929); *The New Moon,* a musical (opened September 19, 1928); and *Hold Everything,* another musical (opened October 10, 1928). In time, all of these would be outstripped by Elmer Rice's *Street Scene* (opened January 1, 1929), and it, in turn, by Marc Connelly's *The Green Pastures* (opened February 26, 1930).[18]

What might be called the "intellectual content" of many of these plays was not particularly high, as can perhaps be gauged from a brief selection of their titles: *Bedfellows, Gambling, Soldiers and Women, Houseparty, The Love Expert, Mountain Fury, Kansas City Kitty,* and so on.[19] Likewise, the thumbnail plot summaries provided by contemporary critic Burns Mantle are often eloquent in this regard. For instance, of *Remote Control,* a drama by Clyde North, Albert Fuller, and Jack Nelson, which opened September 10, 1929, and ran a respectable seventy-nine performances, he wrote: "Walter Brokenchild, announcer for Station WPH, Chicago, agrees to let six Junior League girls broadcast a part of their 'Follies' program. During the broadcasting holdups invade the studio and rob the girls of their jewels. Brokenchild, seeking to do a little amateur detective work, is about to fasten a motive on Dr. Workman, spiritualist, when the doctor is killed at the microphone. Brokenchild is accused of the murder, loyally defended by his secretary-sweetheart, Helen Wright, and eventually cleared. It was the Ghost gang."[20] The principal attraction of this play was, apparently, the innovation of setting the mystery in the broadcasting booth of a radio station.

Frequent also were sexual situations that would certainly have surprised and likely shocked Spanish theatergoers of the time: the gold-digging chorus girl of easy virtue seeking to ensnare the scion of a wealthy family, illegitimate children, and extramarital affairs conducted by both husbands and wives, these were all common plot mechanisms. As the modern-day critic Samuel Leiter has observed: "A significant number of the decade's plays dealt unashamedly with life's most vital concerns: war, politics, religion, sex, alcoholism, Prohibition, drugs, gambling, psychiatry, prostitution, racial bigotry, divorce, adultery, and homosexuality were among the many subjects given comparatively unvarnished treatment. Contemporary issues were often discussed with a frankness previously unheard on the American stage; [. . .] dramatists occasionally overstepped the bounds of what many in the theater-going public considered tasteful, but they persisted nonetheless. Some of their work was clearly written for sensationalistic reasons."[21]

Christopher Maurer has conjectured that in all likelihood Lorca would not have seen many mainstream Broadway plays, a speculation that might be further supported by the fact that the principal interest of most of these productions lay in their English-language dialogue, all but inaccessible to Lorca, and not in their staging, decor, or special effects.[22] On the other hand, it seems reasonable to assume that Lorca, by direct or indirect means, would have acquired some sense of the most typically treated topics and would have heard about—if not actually attended—some of the biggest hits of the season, to which I shall return.

Furthermore, Broadway productions included various other genres beyond the staple fare of straight dramas and comedies. For instance, the Jolson Theatre Musical Comedy Company staged ten operettas during Lorca's stay: *Sweethearts, Mlle. Modiste, Naughty Marietta, The Fortune Teller,* and *Babes in Toyland* (Victor Herbert); *The Merry Widow* and *The Count of Luxembourg* (Franz Lehár); *The Chocolate Soldier* (Oscar Straus); *Robin Hood* (Reginald De Koven); and *The Prince of Pilsen* (Gustav Luders); while an adaptation of Johann Strauss II's *Die Fledermaus* was also given.[23] As Lorca wrote in a letter from the first week of November 1929: "Ahora empieza la sesión de invierno y esto está lleno de teatros, de cinematógrafos, de ópera, y de automóviles" (Now the winter season is starting, and the city is full of theaters, cinemas, opera, and automobiles).[24] Moving into more popular terrain, during his months in Manhattan, Lorca would also have been able to catch, should he have wished, Kern and Hammerstein's *Sweet Adeline*, Eddie Cantor in Florenz Ziegfeld's *Whoopee!*, Noel Coward's *Bitter Sweet*, Rodgers and Hart's *Heads Up!* and *Simple Simon*, Cole Porter's musical *Fifty Million Frenchmen* and his revue *Wake Up and Dream*, Ginger Rogers dancing in *Top Speed*, and George and Ira Gershwin's *Show Girl* and *Strike Up the Band*, alongside a slew of less distinguished musicals and revues.

When we come to consider what might, for want of a better term, be called "quality" drama, we find that a certain portion of it *was* staged in Broadway theaters. The five most successful and most celebrated plays of the period, Elmer Rice's highly innovative *Street Scene*, R. C. Sherriff's First World War drama *Journey's End*, John Drinkwater's comedy-drama of British class distinctions *Bird in Hand*, Preston Sturges's speakeasy comedy-romance *Strictly Dishonorable*, and Marc Connelly's reworking of Old Testament stories *The Green Pastures*, were all Broadway productions; two of them won Pulitzers in successive years, four of them made Burns Mantle's lists of the "ten best plays of the year," and all achieved runs of near or over five hundred performances.[25] In particular, it is hard to imagine that Lorca did not at least hear a good deal about Rice's extraordinary play, if he did not actually witness a performance in New York.[26] A Madrid production of it—*La calle*—opened on November 14, 1930, staged by Cipriano Rivas Cherif and Margarita Xirgu, shortly before Lorca's own *La zapatera prodigiosa*.[27] A film version was made by United Artists in 1931.

Other plays and dramatists of note that reached the public under the auspices of Broadway theaters include Elmer Rice's wisecracking comedy *See Naples and Die*, the Álvarez Quintero brothers' sentimental comedy *A Hundred Years Old (Papá Juan)*, Martin Flavin's grim prison drama *The Criminal Code*, Ring Lardner and George S. Kaufman's satirical Tin Pan Alley comedy *June Moon*, John Drinkwater's biographical drama *Abraham Lincoln*, John L. Balderston's time travel drama *Berkeley Square*, John Kirkpatrick's satirical small-town comedy *Charm*, A. A. Milne's British marital comedy *Michael and Mary*, G. K. Chesterton's British drawing-room comedy *Magic*, Alberto Casella's fantastic Italian comedy-drama *Death Takes a Holiday*, St. John Ervine's British marital comedy *The First Mrs. Fraser*, Edwin Justus Mayer's costume tragicomedy *Children of Darkness*, Donald Ogden Stewart's comedy of manners *Rebound*, Marcel Pagnol's satirical comedy *Topaze*, and John Wexley's violent prison drama *The*

Last Mile. There were also two metatheatrical dramas, Hans Chlumberg's *Out of a Blue Sky* and Monckton Hoffe's *Many Waters.* Leiter summarizes the plots of these two plays thus:

> The curtain rose on the bare stage of a German municipal theatre with stagehands playing poker and fooling with lights. The director [. . .] appears to apologize for an error that has left him with no play or actors to offer and requests that members of the audience come on stage and improvise according to a plot outline. This allows a young couple [. . .] having an affair to act out their adultery while the woman's indulgent husband [. . .] foolishly plays the cuckold in the play-within-a-play.

> [The] episodic plot presented a playwright [. . .] and a producer [. . .] arguing in the latter's office over whether audiences want plays to be realistic mirrors of actuality or escapist fantasy. The producer illustrates his reason for presenting the former by pointing to the dramaless lives of a dull couple, the Barcaldines [. . .], who arrive on the matter of a house rental; a chronicle drama ensues following the Barcaldines through their many faithful years together, during which all of the dramatic elements of which the producer mistakenly believes their lives empty are enacted. Numerous scenes and characters pass by until the dramatist realizes that his preconceptions regarding such supposedly humdrum people are erroneous; he agrees henceforth to write lightweight works for their enjoyment having learned that "many waters cannot quench love, neither can the floods drown it."[28]

This list of plays is necessarily a selective—and subjective—one, but it represents works whose plot or content seems somehow interesting (especially vis-à-vis Lorca) and/or titles or authors who enjoy some "name recognition" today. Of these seventeen pieces that I have singled out, ten were named by Burns Mantle as "best plays" of 1929–30 or, in the case of revivals, of previous years.

However, most interest almost certainly lies in what was later to be termed "Off-Broadway." The actual term *Off-Broadway* was not originated until the 1930s, although the phenomenon had started as far back as 1905 and gathered momentum in the decade of the 1910s.[29] Since early in the century, these small theater groups and independent companies, both professional and semiprofessional, profit making and non-profit making, whose acting ensembles were sometimes linked with drama schools, had begun to proliferate in different parts of New York.[30] It is here that we find, in contrast to Broadway's predilection for contemporary British and American plays, most of the productions of modern foreign classics as well as a much greater disposition to take risks with plays and experimental stagings that, on the face of it at least, were unlikely ever to be commercial money-spinners.[31]

The Neighborhood Playhouse Acting Company and its leading lights, Alice and Irene Lewisohn, have already attracted a good deal of attention.[32] Organized originally in 1912 as an amateur group associated with the Henry Street Settlement House, a professional company was formed for the 1920–21 season but continued to make use of some amateur actors.[33] What is perhaps not generally realized is that the Neighborhood Playhouse stopped producing plays on a regular basis in 1927, had some brief engagements in 1930 and 1931, and then, on a one-off basis, mounted Lorca's *Bodas de sangre* as *Bitter Oleander* in 1935.[34] Over the 1929–30 season, they were active nonetheless but with several dance productions involving Martha Graham: music, dance, and the ritual origins of theater had always been one of the distinguishing features of the Playhouse's offerings.[35] Lorca clearly had contact with the Lewisohn sisters while he was in New York, most likely through Mildred Adams,[36] and he was impressed enough to wax lyrical about them and their endeavors years later in an interview of October 1933: "Es uno de los más interesantes laboratorios de experiencia de arte dramático del mundo" (It is one of the most interesting laboratories experimenting with the dramatic art in the world).[37]

Be this as it may, if we look at the production statistics of these Off-Broadway groups for 1929–30, it is obvious that the most important of them, numerically at least, was the Civic Repertory Theatre. Founded in the fall of 1926 by the famous actress Eva Le Gallienne, financially the group depended largely on subscriptions, and organizationally it was committed to performing plays in repertory using an ensemble company. It was also one of very few groups that survived into the 1930s.[38] While Lorca was living in Manhattan, the group staged Molière's *The Would-Be Gentleman,* Chekhov's *The Sea Gull,* Gregorio Martínez Sierra's *Cradle Song*

(*Canción de cuna*), Ibsen's *The Master Builder,* Chekhov's *The Cherry Orchard,* the Álvarez Quinteros' *The Lady from Alfaqueque* (*La consulesa*) with Chekhov's one-act *On the High Road,* Claude Anet's *Mademoiselle Bourrat,* Susan Glaspell's *Inheritors,* James Barrie's *Peter Pan,* Tolstoy's *The Living Corpse (Redemption),* Goldoni's *La Locandiera,* the Álvarez Quintero brothers' *The Women Have Their Way* (*Puebla de las mujeres*) with Alfred Sutro's one-act *The Open Door,* Jean-Jacques Bernard's *L'Invitation au voyage,* and Ibsen's *Hedda Gabler,* sixteen productions in all. The authors and titles speak for themselves.

In second place came the Theatre Guild Acting Company, which had evolved out of the Washington Square Players.[39] It espoused the principles of repertory, an ensemble company, democratic management, subscription series, taking chances on unknown quantities, and offering good, quality theater at very modest prices.[40] Nine plays were staged by the Theatre Guild during the period in question: Frantisek Langer's *The Camel through the Needle's Eye,* Dorothy and DuBose Heyward's *Porgy,* Leonhard Frank's *Karl and Anna,* Romain Rolland's *The Game of Love and Death,* V. Kirchon and A. Ouspensky's *Red Rust,* S. N. Behrman's *Meteor,* Karel Čapek's *R.U.R.,* and George Bernard Shaw's *The Apple Cart.* Despite this roster of productions, Burns Mantle opined: "neither of those leaders of the better theatre—the Theatre Guild and the Civic Repertory—performed according to promise [during the 1929–30 season]."[41]

Along with the Civic Repertory and the Theatre Guild, we should not forget a variety of lesser—or perhaps just less active—groups that also enriched New York theatrical life over the same period.[42] The New York Theatre Assembly, for instance, offered Fanny Heaslip Lea's *Lolly;* Paul Osborn's *A Ledge;* Shakespeare's *Measure for Measure,* adapted by Olga Katzin as *The Novice and the Duke;* and Don Marquis's *Everything's Jake.* Walter Hampden's company put on Jacinto Benavente's *The Bonds of Interest* (*Los intereses creados*), Arthur Goodrich and Rose A. Palmer's *Caponsacchi,* and Edward Bulwer-Lytton's *Richelieu* (the 1929–30 season was its last).[43] Maurice Schwartz's Yiddish Art Theatre staged Lion Feuchtwanger's *Jew Süss,* Chune Gottesfeld's *Angels on Earth,* and H. Leivick's *Chains* (all performances were, of course, in Yiddish).[44] The Irish Players mounted Sean O'Casey's *The Silver Tassie,* J. M. Synge's *The Playboy of the Western World,* and George E. Birmingham's *General John Regan.* The Provincetown

Players—known since 1923 as the Experimental Theatre, Inc.—produced Michael Gold's *Fiesta* and Thomas H. Dickinson's *Winter Bound* (having recently relocated to the Garrick Theatre, the stock market crash forced them to close the doors on December 14, 1929, and thereafter the group ceased to exist).[45] The American Laboratory Theatre gave Chekhov's *The Three Sisters* (the highly influential ALT was also in its final season);[46] the Ben Greet Players Shakespeare's *Much Ado about Nothing*; the Cooperative Company Chekhov's *The Sea Gull*; Leo Bulgakov Theatre Associates, Inc., Gorky's *At the Bottom (The Lower Depths)*; and the Macdougal Street Playhouse Strindberg's *The Pelican*.

Finally, I want to draw attention to a number of specific titles. In his letters home, in subsequent interviews, in the *conferencia-recital* of *Poeta en Nueva York,* and in poems from that collection, Lorca made repeated mention of Harlem and Black culture, a feature of New York that obviously made a particularly strong impression on him. Besides the cabarets and jazz clubs like Small's Paradise that he frequented, and besides the three Harlem theaters—the Lafayette, Lincoln, and Alhambra—that provided a steady fare of Black revues (the famous Apollo Theater did not become a venue for Black performers until 1934),[47] certain On- and Off-Broadway productions must also have caught Lorca's eye.[48]

For instance, "Fats" Waller provided the music and Louis Armstrong played in the band for a successful Black revue called *Hot Chocolates;* a second one, *Ginger Snaps,* got execrable reviews and folded shortly afterward. D. Frank Marcus's Black musical, *Bamboola,* had only a fairly short run but did better than another Black musical, *Malinda,* which seems to have completely flopped; Marcus's political comedy, *Make Me Know It,* again played by a Black cast, bombed critically and commercially. (Three other productions, the extremely successful and long-running *Blackbirds of 1928* and the much less successful *Messin' Around* and *Pansy,* had all closed shortly before Lorca's arrival.) One of the very few theatrical spectacles that we can be certain that Lorca attended is precisely the Black revue. On October 22 or 23, 1929, Lorca reported that "voy a algunos espectáculos. He visto una revista negra que es una de los espectáculos más bellos y más sensibles que se pueden contemplar" (I am going to some shows. I have seen a Black revue that is one of the most beautiful and most profound spectacles that can be contemplated).[49] It is unfortunately impossible to identify the particular production to which he is referring, though we do know that Lorca did meet members of the Blackbirds dance troupe socially while he was in New York.[50]

On a different note, Wallace Thurman, in conjunction with William Jourdan Rapp, authored one of only two serious full-length dramas by Black writers to reach Broadway in the 1920s, *Harlem,* described by one critic as a "rambunctious melodrama" and by Burns Mantle as "orgiastic" and named by him a "Best Play of 1928–29."[51] Mrs. Jeroline Hemsley's period drama of southern racial tensions, *Wade in de Water,* was staged briefly by the New Negro Art Theatre. An all-Black cast figured in Marc Connelly's Pulitzer-winning comedy, *The Green Pastures,* which presented the Old Testament as told by a rural Black Louisiana Sunday school teacher, while Black actors were also used for the numerous Black roles in Dorothy and DuBose Heyward's *Porgy,* set in the courtyard of Charleston, South Carolina's Black fishing tenement, Catfish Row; this drama was named a "Best Play of 1927–28" and went on, of course, to inspire George Gershwin's famous folk opera. A revival of Garland Anderson's drama *Appearances* had closed shortly before Lorca's arrival.[52]

There is little to add to Maurer's account of the Chinese theater in New York. He notes that a resident company, Sun Sai Gai, performed regularly in the Grand Street Theatre,[53] and it is to this group that Lorca must have been referring when he announced in a letter of August 8, 1929, that "la próxima semana iremos con mis amigas las rusas y su hermano al teatro chino, cosa que espero con gran interes" (next week we will go with my friends the Russian women and their brother to the Chinese theater, something that I am looking forward to with great interest).[54] Several months later, Mei Lan-Fang and the Peking Opera, on a leg of an influential world tour, opened at the Forty-Ninth Street Theatre on February 17, 1930, with six one-act plays that caused something of a sensation. Leiter writes of Mei Lan-Fang: "he was a delicately featured thirty-two-year-old gentleman who specialized in female roles, or what the Chinese call the *tan* classification. His plays employed a performance style dependent upon sparse settings, a highly elaborate code of symbolic movements and gestures, formalized vocal techniques, lavish costumes, and stylized makeups, as well as what seemed extremely uneuphonious music to Western ears. Symbolism (Mei preferred the word 'patternism') prevailed in every facet of the ritual-like performance."[55] This exposure must account for Lorca's assertion, in October 1933, that "uno de los dos grandes bloques que hay en la literatura dramática de todos los pueblos [. . .] es el teatro chino" (one of the two great blocs that exist in the dramatic literature of all peoples [. . .] is the Chinese theater).[56]

Throughout the 1920s, plays produced in New York had also tackled some of the more "difficult" and sensitive sexual issues. Frank Wedekind's *Der Erdgeist*—jazzed up in translation as *The Loves of Lulu*—had opened for a short run on May 11, 1925. Edouard Bourdet's *The Captive (La Prisonnière)* reached 160 performances (opening September 29, 1926) before being shut down by the authorities: it was the first serious treatment of lesbianism seen on Broadway. e. e. cummings's experimental *him* was given by the Provincetown Players, opening on April 18, 1928, and included several homosexual characters in its phantasmagorical goings-on. Very different in intention was Mae West's *Pleasure Man,* a play with a sensationalist plot and a number of overtly effeminate characters: it was closed down on its opening night—October 1, 1928. Many jokes at gays' expense were also evident in the scarcely less salacious *Little Orchid Annie,* a comedy by Hadley Waters and Charles Beahan, which had a short run from April 21, 1930.[57] Finally, while Lorca was in Manhattan, the Provincetown Players staged what would prove to be their swan song: *Winter Bound,* by Thomas H. Dickinson, a drama that addressed, if in distinctly muted tones, both the supposed subordinate position of women to men and the (alternative) possibility of lesbianism. It opened on November 12, 1929, and ran for thirty-nine performances, the last of which also marked the end of the famous "P.-town" group.[58] Lorca would surely have been put in mind of Rivas Cherif's *Un sueño de la razón,* performed in Madrid in early 1929, with a similar basic theme.[59]

What conclusions can we draw from all this? During the seven months that Lorca lived there, New York was teeming with all shapes and forms of theatrical life. Broadway offered a large selection of pretty mindless entertainment, in the form of revues, musicals, farces, comedies, melodramas, murder mysteries, and the like, and these constituted the U.S. equivalent of the established Spanish theater that Lorca—and just about every other Spanish intellectual of the period—complained about vociferously. Broadway, at the same time, *could* offer thoughtful and thought-provoking, quality plays and productions—Elmer Rice's *Street Scene* being perhaps the best example. Off Broadway was also very active, experimenting with different kinds of theatrical organization (repertory versus the long single-run ensemble casts, cooperatives versus hierarchical administration, and so on) and consistently offering quality plays, the large majority of them of foreign origin. Harlem life, Black culture, Black authors, and Black actors were represented, if far from proportionally, on both the On- and Off-Broadway scenes. And finally, many aspects of sexual issues were aired, homosexuality as well as heterosexuality, and many of them would certainly, in 1920s Spain, have fallen foul of Primo de Rivera's censors.

Lorca made a good number of friends during his New York stay and was, it seems, constantly being invited out.[60] Through the likes of Mildred Adams and Hershel Brickell, through Federico de Onís and Ángel del Río, through other Spaniards and Latin Americans resident in New York and others, like him, just passing through, he must have come into contact, directly and indirectly, with some measure of this sprawling New York theater life whose dimensions I have just outlined. Regardless of how many On- or Off-Broadway plays he may actually have gone to see, he would certainly have been able to perceive that the situation in Manhattan was quite different from that in Madrid.

If this is so, then we can hypothesize that New York afforded Lorca a glimpse of the future, an indication of where developments in the modern stage could lead. This in turn likely constituted one of his motivations for collaborating in La Barraca, and, later, in the Club Teatral Anfistora.[61] When Lorca participated in the staging of his own plays with commercial companies, he laid special emphasis on rehearsal and ensemble acting, rare in Spain at the time and clearly superior in the United States.[62] Furthermore, Lorca seems to have started to work in earnest on his own play *El público* immediately after leaving Manhattan and arriving in Havana, in the spring of 1930: both its bold experimentalism and its explicit treatment of homosexual themes may be ascribed, in part at least, to the stimulus of New York.[63] Finally, once back in Spain, Lorca would refer approvingly and enthusiastically to what he had witnessed in the New World and link it to his own writerly preoccupations: "El teatro nuevo, avanzado de formas y teoría, es mi mayor preocupación. Nueva York es un sitio único para tomarle el pulso al nuevo arte teatral" (New theater, progressive in forms and theory, is my greatest concern. New York is a unique place to take the pulse of the new theatrical art); "Los mejores actores que he visto han sido también negros. Mimos insuperables. La revista negra va sustituyendo la revista blanca. El arte blanco se va quedando para las minorías. El público quiere siempre teatro negro, deliran por él" (The best actors that I have seen have been Black. Unsurpassable mimes. The Black revue is in the process of replacing the white revue. White art is being left behind for minorities. The public always wants Black theater; they are crazy for it).[64] Dru Dougherty develops the argument that the mass appeal of Black revues (to white audiences) may have alerted Lorca to the possibility of communicating with large numbers of spectators, something that was certainly one of Lorca's priorities through his theatrical career of the 1930s.[65] Little wonder, then, that right through the 1930s and until his death, Lorca would fight to implement in Spain much of what had so impressed him, On and Off Broadway, for those seven memorable months that he spent in Manhattan.

4

Three Expressionist Dramas
El público, Así que pasen cinco años, and *El sueño de la vida*

The Argentinian journalist and dramatist Pablo Suero, reminiscing about one of the new theatrical compositions that Lorca shared with him during his stay in Buenos Aires over 1933–34, described it years later in these glowing terms:

> *Así que pasen cinco años* es una obra donde todo es imprevisto. [. . .] No busquéis en ella la ilación convencional de asunto y escenas; el desarrollo técnico del teatro de todos los días. Como técnica podría tal vez hallarse antecedentes en algunos instantes de *El espíritu de la tierra* y *Despertar de primavera,* de Wedekind. Pero van más lejos la fantasía y la valentía técnica de autor de García Lorca. *Gas,* de Kaiser; *Hinkemann* y *Los destructores de máquinas,* de Toller, y *La máquina de calcular,* de Elmer Rice, pueden haber servido de punto de partida.[1]

> *Así que pasen cinco años* is a work where everything is unexpected. [. . .] Do not look in it for the conventional linkage between subject matter and scenes; the technical development of everyday theater. As a technique, precedents might perhaps be found in some moments of *Earth-Spirit* and *Spring's Awakening* by Wedekind. But García Lorca's imagination and his technical courage as an author go further. *Gas,* by Kaiser; *Hinkemann* and *The Machine Wreckers,* by Toller, and *The Adding Machine,* by Elmer Rice, may have served as points of departure.

On assignment in Spain to cover the general elections of February 1936, Suero met up again with Lorca and subsequently recalled: "Me leyó primero un acto de una pieza grande. Es un drama social de extraordinaria fuerza. Infinitamente superior a todo lo que Kaiser y Toller han hecho en este género" (He first read to me an act of a great play. It is a social drama of extraordinary power. Infinitely superior to all that Kaiser and Toller have done in this genre).[2] Here, evidently, he was referring to the unfinished *El sueño de la vida*.[3] However, what most interests me in these two quotations are the names of the dramatists that Suero adduces to contextualize Lorca's innovations and orient his readers: Frank Wedekind, Georg Kaiser, Ernst Toller, and Elmer Rice.

It is regrettable that the majority of modern critics, upon approaching Lorca's experimental dramas, have not followed the example given by the Argentinian journalist when they attempt to establish connections between the European avant-garde and the three plays that are the subject of this chapter—*El público, Así que pasen cinco años,* and *El sueño de la vida*. Some scholars mention Expressionism in passing, almost always exclusively in relation to *Así que pasen cinco años,*[4] but there are to my knowledge still only two articles that deal directly with the importance of this movement. Besides these two articles, another important early contribution was made by Alfredo de la Guardia.[5] Although he never uses the terms *Expressionist* or *Expressionism,* he situates *Así que pasen cinco años* by invoking August Strindberg, Georg Kaiser, and Eugene O'Neill, among others. First, back in 1961, Ofelia Kovacci and Nélida Salvador called attention to the many links between *Así que pasen cinco años* and Expressionism in an article that unfortunately has largely gone overlooked or been forgotten,[6] while more recently, Carlos Jerez-Farrán expanded the scope of the issue by identifying the parallel points of contact with *El público*.[7] My purpose here is triple: to carry forward and advance the discussion begun by these critics;[8] to add *El sueño de la vida* to the corpus of texts to be considered under this light; and at the same time to try to combat the excessively frequent and unreflecting location of Lorca's experimental dramas under the aegis of Surrealism. In regard to this third point, this chapter takes as its starting point an earlier study of mine that offered a survey of the reception of Surrealism in Spanish theater of the 1920s and 1930s.[9]

For the purposes of the analysis that is presented here, I shall use the term *Expressionism* in a fairly conventional sense, to refer not only to the nucleus of the movement rooted in Germany but also to include both the most important proto-Expressionists and writers of other nationalities who were strongly influenced by this aesthetic. Almost all critics are agreed in pointing to August Strindberg, above all in his late phase, as the father of Expressionist theater; another significant precursor would be Frank Wedekind.[10] Although Expressionism as it is understood today manifested itself in all the literary genres and, in fact, in almost all art forms, I shall limit myself in the discussion of the main German contingent to the most prominent dramatists and filmmakers, such as Reinhard Sorge, Georg Kaiser, Ernst Toller, Robert Wiene, F. W. Murnau, and Fritz Lang.[11] Sorge, Kaiser, and Toller receive a lot of coverage in all the studies of Expressionism that I am citing here, and the specific influence of Strindberg on them has been documented by several critics. Among figures outside Germany, mention should be made of an Austrian contemporary of theirs, Oskar Kokoschka, and in the category of those not belonging to the movement but most influenced by it, the Americans Eugene O'Neill and Elmer Rice.[12]

Moving now from the exponents of the movement to its history and diffusion, we can say that Expressionism, like other *isms* of the same period, was known reasonably well in the Spain of the 1920s. There were several translations of Strindberg, though most of them were not of the plays that are most important for our present purposes: *The Road to Damascus, A Dream Play,* and *The Ghost Sonata.*[13] Some of his works were staged in Spain, such as *Creditors, The Dance of Death,* and *The Father,* though his fortunes seem to have declined in the 1930s.[14] Others were only translated (*Lucky Peter's Journey, Miss Julie,* and *Cinco dramas en un acto,* for example).[15] A third, although less direct, way to enter into contact with the world of Strindberg would have been through "theater people," both actresses, like Margarita Xirgu, and directors, designers, and impresarios—Gregorio Martínez Sierra, Sigfrido Bürmann, and, more than anyone else, Cipriano Rivas Cherif, whose knowledge of contemporary European theater was very extensive. The situation with Wedekind is less clear: a translation of *Spring's Awakening* was published in 1910 and subsequently reprinted but not performed during this period; his name appears in the Madrid press with a certain frequency through the 1920s, usually in conjunction with reports of productions abroad; Lorca mentions him in his "Charla sobre teatro" ("Talk about Theater"), of February 1935;[16] and the Hispanophile Jean Gebser was working on another translation of *Spring's Awakening* but at a very late date, June 1936.[17]

At the beginning of the 1920s, the Spanish *ultraístas* showed a good deal of interest in German Expressionist literature and painting, publishing translations and critical pieces in the magazines associated with the group.[18] Among translations and essays from the period, we should note several by Jorge Luis Borges and the three by Paul Colin.[19] It was also covered rather more broadly in a number of articles appearing in the journal *España*. In the second half of the decade it was Georg Kaiser who came to dominate the image of Expressionism conveyed to the Spanish reading public.

In 1928 Kaiser visited Barcelona with Max Reinhardt to work on a theater that was installed in the International Exposition there.[20] Meanwhile, three translations appeared in the *Revista de Occidente,* of *From Morn to Midnight, Gas [I],* and *One Day in October,* the first of these preceded by an article by Enrique Díez-Canedo about the German playwright.[21] Not all the dramatic works by Kaiser are equally Expressionist in nature: *From Morn to Midnight* is one of the most typical, while *One Day in October* has relatively little to do with the movement and perhaps owes more to the world of Luigi Pirandello.[22] Perhaps due in part to the publication of these texts, the performance of his plays became quite fashionable in the 1930s. *Un día de octubre* was premiered in May 1931.[23] Performing in the Teatro de Muñoz Seca (where they had transferred toward the end of February), Xirgu worked with Cipriano Rivas Cherif and Sigfrido Bürmann, using the new translation by Luis Fernández-Rica and Ángel Custodio; although they had changed theaters, this was part of the season put on by the El Caracol group that had earlier occupied the Teatro Español. In the days following the play's premiere, it received a lot of press coverage.

For its part, *Gas [I]* was the object of several different productions between 1935 and 1936. Most performances of *Gas [I]* were given by the Teatro Escuela de Arte, founded and directed by Rivas Cherif. Although the play was announced as forming part of the TEA's repertoire on the creation of the company at the beginning of 1934, the first run of performances of *Gas [I]* did not begin until March 2, 1935 (Teatro María Guerrero, translation by Luis Fernández-Rica and Álvaro Arauz). Other performances were given at the Teatro Pavón on May 8, 1935; the Teatro de la Zarzuela on June 22, 1935; and the Teatro Español on May 19, 1936. In February 1935, TEA published in book form the translation the company was using. Juventud de Izquierda Republicana performed the play at the Teatro Pavón on July 10, 1935, and the Federación Cultural Deportiva Obrera del Centro de España also performed it on August 31, 1935.[24] Kaiser, therefore, was well known, and it was no display of specialized knowledge—though perhaps of pride—when Lorca, in an interview of November 1935 and speaking about *El sueño de la vida,* told the journalist that "a Lenormand y a Kaiser creo haber superado yo" (I believe that I have surpassed Lenormand and Kaiser).[25]

A rather different situation exists in regard to Ernst Toller. During the 1920s, he received occasional mentions in the press for both his literary and political activities but, compared to Kaiser, was relatively overlooked or ignored.[26] The various articles included in a number of *La Gaceta Literaria* dedicated to German culture refer to him several times, and a text by him was published in the press in 1929.[27] However, interest in him and his work picked up at the end of the decade and continued into the 1930s. Coincidentally, he arrived in New York at the end of September 1929—just after Lorca returned there from his New England vacation. He had been invited by the Theatre Guild and the International Labor Alliance on a lecture tour.[28] After several days' delay at Ellis Island, he was granted entry, and there is a record of at least one talk—"Social Literature in Germany"— and a reading from his work given for the Freie Volksbühne at Webster Hall on October 9, 1929.[29] In Spain, he seems to have achieved greater visibility with the publication in 1931 of a translation of *Hinkemann* and *The Machine Wreckers.*[30] The previous year, 1930, the same publishing house brought out Piscator's *El teatro político.* César and Irene Falcón and their Compañía de Teatro Proletario performed *Hinkemann* in various cities in the north of Spain over late 1933 and early 1934.[31]

In regard to the North Americans whom we might categorize as Expressionists, Eugene O'Neill seems to have been the most famous. A translation made by Ricardo Baeza of *The Emperor Jones* came out in the *Revista de*

Occidente in 1929, accompanied by a very long and insightful study of his dramatic output, also written by Baeza.[32] It is very unlikely that Lorca saw any of O'Neill's plays while he was in New York; *Strange Interlude* was being performed during this period but at a number of theaters in other cities and towns outside Manhattan. Lola Membrives offered the first Spanish staging of a work by O'Neill, his play *Anna Christie* at the Teatro Fontalba in Madrid on January 20, 1931, in a translation by Isabel de Palencia.[33] His short play *Before Breakfast* was given in February 1934 as a monologue,[34] fully performed the following month by the Teatro Escuela de Arte at the Teatro María Guerrero,[35] and in December 1934, again performed by the Teatro Escuela de Arte.[36] Information on Elmer Rice is rather scarcer: as regards the work mentioned by Pablo Suero, *The Adding Machine,* in Spain there were a few reports of its staging in London and Paris, but *Street Scene,* translated by Juan Chabás as *La calle,* was put on by Cipriano Rivas Cherif and Margarita Xirgu at the Teatro Español, at a date—November 14, 1930—very close to the premiere of Lorca's *La zapatera prodigiosa* as part of that company's same season.[37]

Finally, a few Expressionist films, all originating in Germany, had a certain impact in Spain.[38] *Herr Tartüff* (1926), by F. W. Murnau,[39] and *Greed* (1924), by Erich von Stroheim, were shown at two of the early meetings of the Madrid Cineclub, in 1928–29,[40] but the tastes of Ernesto Giménez Caballero and his companions in the enterprise (notably Luis Buñuel) tended to run more to French avant-garde cinema, and films from this genre tended to dominate the club's offerings. Robert Wiene's *The Cabinet of Dr. Caligari* (1920) was shown in Spain in March 1923, in June 1926, and again by the Cineclub in January 1931, Fritz Lang's *Metropolis* (1927) in January 1928 and in August 1929, but F. W. Murnau's *Nosferatu* had to wait till November–December 1931 for a commercial release in Madrid.[41] A film version of *From Morn to Midnight* was made by Karlheinz Martin and is now held to be one of the most radical examples of Expressionist cinema. Finished in 1920, it received almost no distribution and certainly never reached Spain.[42] In the middle of the decade, Buñuel moved to Paris, and from 1927 for several years he served as the main movie critic for Giménez Caballero's *La Gaceta Literaria.* In one of his articles for that journal (from 1927) he recognized several of the innovative qualities of these German films, calling Lang's *Destiny* (*Der müde Tod,* 1921) an "inefable poema" (ineffable poem) and praising the lyricism and photographic technique of his *Metropolis*.[43]

Clearly, then, Expressionism received sufficiently wide diffusion and attention in Spain in the 1920s for it to have had a direct impact on the experimental drama that Lorca composed during the first half of the 1930s. On the other hand, it would be unwise, and almost certainly wrong, to claim that every feature of Lorca's avant-garde theatrical works that could remind us of characteristics associated with Expressionism did actually derive from that movement, when in certain instances they would much more likely be the result of coincidence, that is, of the German authors and Lorca having arrived at these innovations around the same time but independently of each other. In light of the historical context established in the previous pages, what I would propose regarding the three plays in question is therefore a mixture of influence and coincidence. Let us now turn to identifying exactly where we can find concrete examples of both of these phenomena.[44]

The most obvious similarity is in the portrayal and function of the characters in these plays. As is well known, a fundamental feature of Expressionist characters is that they tend to be generic, lacking a proper name and being distinguished rather by their age, gender, family relationship, or profession.[45] To validate this basic concept, one needs only to review the dramatis personae of some representative works: Strindberg's *The Road to Damascus*; Kokoschka's *Murderer, the Hope of Women*; or Kaiser's *From Morn to Midnight*. The Director, the Criado, the Niño, the Centurión, the Emperador, the Enfermero, the Traspunte, and the Señora (from *El público*); the Joven, the Viejo, Amigo 1°, Amigo 2°, the Mecanógrafa, the Criado, the Novia, the Criada, and the Padre (from *Así que pasen cinco años*); and the Autor, the Actriz, the Criado, the Apuntador, and the Tramoyista (from *El sueño de la vida*) all belong to that same world.

Connected with this tendency toward the generic, we also find the use of blocs of characters who are more or less indistinguishable among themselves.[46] Typical of these blocs are the choruses of Men and Women in *Murderer, the Hope of Women*; the ten Young Ladies and the ten Gentlemen Dressed in Mourning in *Job*, also by Kokoschka; the Newspaper Readers, the Prostitutes, and the Airmen in Johannes Sorge's *The Beggar*; the Five

Jewish Gentlemen and Four Female Masks in *From Morn to Midnight;* and the five Gentlemen in Black in *Gas [I],* whose costumes resemble each other's. The Caballos Blancos, Damas, and Estudiantes (in *El público*); the three Jugadores (in *Así que pasen cinco años*), and the Espectadores and Espectadoras (in *El sueño de la vida*) all function in a similar fashion.

The generic characters and the members of groups often dress in exaggeratedly formal ways, and the same propensity has been identified in Expressionist films, in which the black-and-white photography reinforces the contrast between faces and hands (or gloves) and the typically dark clothing.[47] In Kaiser's *De la mañana a medianoche,* the protagonist—the Cashier—appears in evening dress with a top hat, cloak, silk muffler, white gloves, and gold-headed bamboo cane; the Jewish Gentlemen are in dinner jackets and wear silk hats; and the gentlemen at the cabaret again in evening dress.[48] In *Gas [I]* the Engineer is wearing a frock coat, the Officer has a red uniform, the Gentlemen in Black are in frock coats, and the Government Commissioner has a top hat.[49] These costumes recall the Director's "chaqué" (morning coat) (45), the three Hombres who are "vestidos de frac, exactamente iguales" (dressed in tailcoats, exactly the same) (48), Julieta's "traje blanco de ópera" (white opera dress) (78), Hombre 3's "capa roja" (red cloak) (99), the Damas "vestidas de noche" (in evening attire) (109), and the "frac, capa blanca de raso [. . .] y [. . .] sombrero de copa" (tailcoat, white satin cloak [. . .] and [. . .] top hat) (123) of the Prestidigitador (*El público*);[50] the "chaqué gris" (gray morning coat) of the Viejo (191), the pure white "impecable traje de lana" (impeccable woolen suit) of Amigo 2° (235), the Padre with his "guantes blancos y traje negro" (white gloves and black suit) (260), the three Jugadores who "vienen de frac" (come dressed in tailcoats) and "traen capas largas de raso blanco" (bring long cloaks of white satin) (340), matched by the Joven, now also "vestido de frac" (dressed in a tailcoat) (343) (*Así que pasen cinco años*);[51] and the audience member identified as the Joven, also "de frac" (in a tailcoat) (144), and the easily imaginable evening dress worn by the Autor and the other Espectadores seated in the "butacas" (stalls) (139) in a production of *El sueño de la vida.*[52]

Finally, I should mention certain symbolic figures and the use of masks and disguises.[53] The Gentleman in White in *Gas [I]* is a projection of the Clerk's fear; the grandfather called the Old Reaper in Toller's *The Machine*

Wreckers needs no further explanation; and several Little Formless Fears appear to the protagonist in *The Emperor Jones*. Another famous German Expressionist playwright, Carl Sternheim, created a family with the surname Maske, which then appeared in several of his works, while in another play by O'Neill, *The Great God Brown,* the protagonist is equipped with a mask to hide his face and thus his true personality.[54] Similar in nature are Elena, the Figura de Cascabeles, the Figura de Pámpanos, Julieta, the Desnudo Rojo, and the Prestidigitador (*El público*) and the Niño Muerto, the Gato, the Jugador de Rugby, and the Maniquí (*Así que pasen cinco años*).

In the cabaret scene of Kaiser's *De la mañana a medianoche,* "cabezas con antifaces de seda" (heads with silk masks) (199) peep through the doorway; the first female Mask is "un arlequín de traje a cuadros amarillos y rojos, ceñido al cuerpo, del pecho a los pies, como un muchacho" (a Harlequin's suit of yellow and red lozenges, tightly fitted to her body, from her chest to her feet, like a boy) (200); there are two black Masks; and a Fourth Mask is "una Pierrette, cuya falda le llega a los pies" (a female Pierrot, whose skirt reaches her feet) (204). Furthermore, there is a reference to "disfraces que dejan ver la desnudez" (disguises that reveal nakedness) (193), the question "si se te sondea hasta el fondo, ¿qué tienes?" (if people take deep soundings, what have you got?) (201), and the vision of death as a skeleton, which is there "sentado . . . desnudo hasta los huesos" (seated . . . naked to the bone) (223). In *Gas [I],* at a certain point, the Billionaire's Son tells the Officer what he should do: "Empuja tus miradas hacia ti mismo, y haz que resuene en ti una voz: 'Disfrazado con este traje, estoy ahora vacío para la vida'" (Direct your stare toward yourself and make a voice reverberate within you: "Disguised with this set of cloths, I am now empty for life") (208). In the two plays by Wedekind in which Lulu is the protagonist, she takes different names and rapidly changes clothes to suggest the different roles that she plays as a woman.[55]

Similarly, in *El público,* the Director transforms into "un muchacho vestido de raso blanco" (a boy dressed in white satin) (54), a role played by an actress, and Hombre 2 into "una mujer vestida con pantalones de pijama negro" (a women dressed in black pajama pants) (55); the Figura de Pámpanos "se despoja de los pámpanos y aparece un desnudo blanco de yeso" (sheds the vine shoots, and [underneath] there appears a naked body white like plaster) (68); a costume that has been removed turns into an autonomous character—"el mismo Arlequín blanco con una careta amarillo pálido" (the same white Harlequin with a pale yellow mask) (94); the Pastor Bobo wheels onstage his "gran armario lleno de caretas blancas" (great cupboard full of white masks) (103); while throughout the play, there is a play of images and symbols based on disguise and nakedness, surface and depth, skin and skeleton.[56]

In *Así que pasen cinco años* we encounter the Maniquí clad in the wedding dress (276); the Arlequín with two masks (292–93); the Payaso "lleno de lentejuelas" (covered in sequins), whose "cabeza empolvada da una sensación de calavera" (powdered head gives the impression of a skull) (297); and the Máscara, who "viste un traje 1900 con larga cola amarillo rabioso [. . .] y máscara blanca de yeso: guantes hasta el codo, del mismo color" (is wearing a 1900s-style dress with a long, dazzlingly yellow train [. . .] and a mask white like plaster: gloves up to her elbow, of the same color) (303). In the course of the action of *El sueño de la vida*, various actors come onstage dressed in the costume that corresponds to their role: the Actriz, as Titania and Lady Macbeth, Nick Bottom, the Leñador, the Hada, and the Silfo.

The second important aspect that is shared by Expressionist drama and Lorca's experimental theater is structural innovation, typified in the so-called *Stationendrama*, whose antecedents can be found in Wedekind's *King Nicolo* and Strindberg's *The Road to Damascus*.[57] The majority of Expressionist plays are configured in this way, organized in a succession of episodes, or "stations," that can often appear disconnected one from the other. There are many examples, including Sorge's *The Beggar* and Toller's *Transfiguration* and *Masses and Man*.[58] In Kaiser's *De la mañana a medianoche*, the Cashier even observes: "Así peregriné yo desde la mañana. No quiero aburriros con el cuento de las estaciones donde hice parada. [. . .] Pasé juntas a todas sin detenerme. Estación tras estación, se iban hundiendo detrás de mi espalda de peregrino" (That is how I wandered since morning. I don't want to bore you with the account of all the stations that I visited. [. . .] I passed by next to all of them without stopping. Station after station, they sank behind me as I wandered on) (220). Exactly the same kind of structure can be observed above all in *El público*, which returns, as in *The Road to Damascus*, in its last scene to the point of departure (in Strindberg's play, the Stranger directly refers to the "seventh station," where he and the Lady began their journey).[59] Furthermore, the play on words between the Stations of the Cross and railway stations, incorporated into the dialogue of the Desnudo Rojo and the Enfermero, echoes both literally and symbolically the German term used to describe the technique. Although *Así que pasen cinco años* is configured in the conventional three acts, the various Cuadros, and scenes within Cuadros, that it contains can often appear disconcerting in their sequence or connection, and again the last Cuadro returns to the beginning in the Joven's library.

The principal factor underlying the creation of this new kind of structure was the early interest in the world of dreams evinced by Strindberg and, after him, by the Expressionists, an interest fueled by the writings in German of Freud, all of these developments taking place many years before the "Surrealist revolution." While it is too long to quote here, Strindberg's prologue to *A Dream Play* is crucial in this regard and lays out all the key ideas. The discovery of the power of the oneiric had other consequences too. The Expressionists did not want to reproduce authentic dreams on the stage but, rather, were attracted by the additional expressiveness offered by the adoption of the form and logic of dreams and the resulting elimination of a more rigid plot structure.[60] The repressed desires and the internal struggles and sufferings of a character could in this way be portrayed on the stage with great visual and emotional impact, while at the same time the strong sense of plot that dominated the traditional "well-made play" could be discarded, although not necessarily with the concomitant loss of all internal unity.[61]

Another result of this innovation, related to the *Stationendrama* and to dream, was the arrangement of episodes contrapuntally, with alternating scenes that were relatively "realist" and ones more suggestive of oneiric qualities. This structural model can be seen in *The Beggar, Transfiguration,* and *Masses and Man;*[62] it also comes fairly close to describing the pattern found in *Así que pasen cinco años,* with its intercalated scenes that tend toward the fantastic or unreal: the Niño Muerto with the Gato, the Joven with the Maniquí, and all of "Cuadro 1" in act 3.

From this counterpoint based on the oneiric, it is only a small step to conceiving of the whole action of a play as the representation of a dream taking place in the mind of the protagonist, as a kind of *psychomaquia* played out onstage.[63] The only reality, then, is that of the protagonist, as Strindberg demonstrated at the beginning of the century with *The Road to Damascus* and *A Dream Play*.[64] If what is portrayed is a dream, or obeys dream logic, then the physical laws of time are suspended: the Stranger says that he has experienced some kind of vision, seeing his whole life pass before his eyes,[65] and in the film *Destiny*, a long episode occurs in an instant of "real" time.[66] Critics have already suggested that all of the action of both *El público* and *Así que pasen cinco años* is taking place in the mind of their respective protagonists—the Director and the Joven, very probably only moments before their death.[67] In the initial stage direction for his very early and incomplete dramatic text called *Teatro de almas,* Lorca writes: "(La escena en el teatro maravilloso de nuestro mundo interior)" (The setting in the marvelous theater of our internal world).[68]

If what we see onstage is the enactment of the protagonist's dream, or dream episodes, then all the other "characters" are inventions of his or projections of parts of his psyche. In the multiple doublings and fragmentations of *The Road to Damascus* and *A Dream Play,* Strindberg established the basic model that would then be elaborated upon by the German playwrights.[69] Thus, the dramatis personae of *The Beggar* contains the section "figures [that is, projections] of the Poet"; Friedrich, the central character in *Transfiguration,* assumes in the course of the work various roles, both masculine and feminine, and the protagonist of *The Emperor Jones* suffers a series of visions or hallucinations, which Ricardo Baeza described as "la representación física de realidades puramente psíquicas" (the physical representation of purely psychic realities).[70] Bearing these examples in mind, the relationship between the Joven and the Viejo and Amigos 1° and 2° in *Así que pasen cinco años,* or the "logic" of the different metamorphoses of the Director and Hombre 1° in *El público,* become much clearer.

Beyond these structural principles and their diverse consequences, we also encounter an insistent motif that has to do both with the concept of the *Stationendrama* and with the mode of presentation of the central character and which creates a fundamental symbolism found in Expressionism: the cross, the Crucifixion, and the figure of Christ, all most strongly associated with the protagonist.[71] The Stranger in *The Road to Damascus* sees three crosses in the three empty masts of a ship and gets the idea that he himself needs to take on all the pain and suffering in the world.[72] The denouement of *De la mañana a medianoche* is typical: there is a big black cross on the yellow backdrop against which the Cashier falls on dying by suicide, seeming to utter, gasping and sighing, the two words *Ecce* and *Homo* (209, 224). Toller also repeatedly makes use of this motif, in *Transfiguration, The Machine Wreckers,* and *Hinkemann;* a parallel instance has been identified in Kokoschka's *Murderer, the Hope of Women;* while the use of the same symbol can be observed in some scenes of Lang's *Metropolis*.[73] *El público* is obviously the work that offers the greatest similarities: in "Cuadro 5" there is a "Desnudo Rojo coronado de espinas azules" (Red Nude crowned with blue thorns) lying vertically on "una cama de frente y perpendicular" (a front-facing, vertical bed) (105), and the whole scene plays out as a kind of modernized and stylized version of the Crucifixion, with various references to the gospels.[74]

While the cross would sometimes be mentioned in the course of the dialogue, it also, as we have seen, could form part of the set. Indeed, following the path blazed by the Symbolists, the Expressionists used the whole stage in an anti-realistic way. The set became a projection of an internal self, which implied, in most cases, a radical simplification and distortion of reality. Hence, the decor could represent what the protagonist's mind saw, with the consequent elimination of any suggestion of verisimilitude, as can be observed in the quintessentially Expressionist film *The Cabinet of Dr. Caligari*.[75] Also contributing were the lighting effects, which had already been explored and developed by Max Reinhardt: in Expressionist plays, illumination or darkness might divide the stage, or it might again reflect the mental processes of the protagonist.[76] Chiaroscuro, therefore, was a typical stylistic feature, the strong contrasts between light and dark being reinforced in the films—like *Caligari*—by makeup and costume.[77]

Expressionists also were wont to present onstage, in a visual and literal form, ideas and tropes that normally only had a figurative value.[78] In Kokoschka's *Job. A Drama,* women used to "turn the head" of Job, and so one day it remains stuck—"turned"—in one position, looking off to one side; his wife cheats on him, and he sprouts deer's antlers, on which the lovers dry their underwear.[79] Likewise, the sets can undergo unreal transformations: in *The Beggar* the walls of the living room open and let the cosmos enter, only then to close up again later; in a work by August Stramm, *Awakening,* the wall of a hotel room breaks apart to show the sky; and in Walter Hasenclever's *Humanity,* a room is transformed into a nocturnal landscape.[80]

The parallels with Lorca's works are not difficult to perceive. The quasi-realist action of *Así que pasen cinco años* is twice interrupted, giving way, with highly conspicuous lighting effects, to the scene between the Niño Muerto and the Gato and then to that between the Joven and the Maniquí; a hand—perhaps the hand of God—enters from the wings to take away the Cat and then the Niño; the scene located in the Novia's boudoir requires a whole series of changing lighting effects, different intensities, and various shades of color; in act 3 the set in the wood is quite unreal. In *El sueño de la vida* the artificiality of the stage decor and lighting effects is emphasized, with the successive replacement of the backdrop curtain with another and major changes of lighting, sometimes requested and commented on by the Autor. The purely symbolic use of the set is even more intense in *El público,* with the "gran mano impresa en la pared" (large hand impressed on the wall), "las ventanas [que] son radiografías" (windows [that] are X-rays) (45), the "ojo enorme" (enormous eye) (123), the Roman ruin, and "la luz [que] toma un fuerte tinte plateado de pantalla cinematografica" (light [that] takes on a strong silvery tint like a cinema screen) (117) when the bed turns on its axis to reveal the Hombre 1°. Above all, what most captures our attention is the "muro de arena" (wall of sand) (71, 78), which then opens to reveal Juliet's tomb, and the last scenographic effect, when "todo el ángulo izquierdo de la decoración se parte y aparece un cielo de nubes largas vivamente iluminado" (the whole left corner of the set opens and there appears an intensely illuminated sky with long clouds) (132). In a novel by Max Brod, *The Big Risk* (1919), part of the plot features a "horizontal drama" in which the theater opens and resembles a cemetery.[81]

Lastly, we need to mention the political dimension of the Expressionist movement. The young German writers, who were already at odds with the values of their society under Emperor Wilhelm II, were prompted by the outbreak of the First World War to develop their ideas, now emphasizing pacifism, international socialism, the role of the proletariat, and the need for a regenerated "new man."[82] These preoccupations are clearly reflected in Kaiser's famous trilogy, made up of *The Coral, Gas [I],* and *Gas [II],* and in several works by Toller. An innovative structural element that often accompanies this cluster of themes is the use of crowds onstage, crowds—with their corresponding spokespeople—that were almost always made up of the proletarian masses.[83] The crowd is obviously a development of the "bloc of characters" already mentioned. Act 4 of *Gas [I]* offers a good example of the resulting kind of "orchestrated" scene: an important workers' meeting is also held in *Gas [II]*; in *The Machine Wreckers* the meetings and debates held by the workers constitute a large part of the action; among Expressionist films, one need go no further than *Metropolis* to find many striking scenes involving crowds and large numbers of people.

While *El público* and *Así que pasen cinco años* have no or barely any political content, *El sueño de la vida* demonstrates a clear preoccupation with social justice, class relations, the situation of the proletariat, and a coming revolution and/or counterrevolution. Although we cannot exactly talk about crowds occupying the stage, Lorca's technique here of involving the audience in the action turns the auditorium into part of the acting space, and the summary descriptions that we have of the projected acts 2 and 3 suggest that masses were going to play an increasingly important role there too.[84]

Having arrived at this point, all that now remains is to point to the various conclusions that can be derived from the material described and analyzed in the previous pages. Despite the bald assertion of my title, the demonstration of thematic, structural, and stylistic coincidences and parallels between two groups of literary works is not the equivalent of proving a direct and exclusive connection between them. On the one hand, Lorca's plays do not display all the typical features of Expressionism: for example, they lack the "telegraphic" style of the dialogue and the exaggerated, or "ecstatic," manner of acting that were characteristic of the German dramas. On the other hand, Lorca's works also obviously contain certain elements that have nothing to do with Expressionism and which will have been derived through other diverse channels or are the product of the author's own creativity.

Nevertheless, I do believe that a sufficient number of points in common and similar details have been identified here to justify the use of the adjective *Expressionist* to describe the predominant aesthetic tendency—rather than any complete affiliation—that characterizes Lorca's experimental theater. To be sure, *El público* seems to be the play closest to the movement, but *Así que pasen cinco años* is only slightly behind. The case of *El sueño de la vida,* written a few years later, offers a different aspect: here we can perceive a broader mixture of possible influences, among them some others coming from Pirandello. At the same time, we should not forget that a piece like *The Beggar,* by Sorge, also has a metatheatrical and revolutionary dimension, with its Poet who wants to inaugurate a new theater in which he will premiere a new work that he says he has composed specifically for the people.[85] Furthermore, although some typically Expressionist elements are lacking, they are compensated for by the new political dimension, which could easily have been derived from or been influenced by Kaiser and Toller.

Beyond these important nuances, we should not lose sight of the fundamental point here: if these three dramas are to be categorized as something beyond broadly avant-garde, as works linked to a specific avant-garde movement, it will be a lot less misleading to ascribe them to Expressionism than to any other more or less contemporaneous one. What is more, establishing this connection opens up many promising avenues of analysis and interpretation. Too many critics do not make functional distinctions between the different avant-garde *isms*—and in particular Expressionism and Surrealism—and too many critics use the Surrealist label with excessive frequency and vagueness.[86] This tendency has only increased with the growth of the internet, where unexamined "received truths" are repeated time and again. Claudio Guillén rightly complains about the tendency to make *Surrealist* a synonym of the whole of the avant-garde.[87] And a handful of commentators—still too few—have already rejected the unthinking application of the theory and aesthetic of Surrealism to these works by Lorca.[88] My hope is that this more detailed account of their resemblances to Expressionism will serve to add more force and weight to this argument, an argument that needs to be pursued if we are to arrive at a just appreciation of the multiple, and sometimes surprising, sources of Lorca's theater and its position within the historical avant-garde.

5

Theme and Symbol in *El público*

Man is least himself when he talks in his own person. Give him a
mask and he will tell you the truth.

—Oscar Wilde, "The Critic as Artist"

The last scene of *El público,* the "Cuadro Sexto," provides the Director
with an opportunity to explain at some length his intentions, motives,
and actions: in conversation with the Prestidigitador, he recalls how "yo
me atrevía a realizar un dificilísimo juego poético" (I dared to create a
very difficult, poetic gameplay) (126)[1] in mounting his experimental and
taboo breaking production of Shakespeare's *Romeo and Juliet.* By the same
token, I want to propose that what Lorca achieved in *his* experimental
play, *El público,* is precisely the same—a "dificilísimo juego poético," and
it will be the main goal of this essay to explore what I understand by this
phrase and to demonstrate the ways in which I think it can be applied to
El público. There are a number of parallels to be made between *El público*
and other works by Lorca—the one act of *El sueño de la vida, Viaje a la
luna, Poeta en Nueva York, Así que pasen cinco años,* and so on. However,
to preserve the unity of the present study and to show that *El público* can
absolutely "stand on its own feet," I have not established the many possible
cross-references with these other works.

In approaching most "realistic" nineteenth- and twentieth-century
drama, we tend to look to the characters, their situation and relationships,
what they say and do, the plot and its denouement, for major indicators
as to how we are to construe the play and where to find its chief thematic

burden. However, a broader historical scope (and here I am thinking of playwrights such as Shakespeare or Calderón as well as more modern dramatists in the Symbolist and Expressionist traditions) presents us with many works that really require a more integral approach, wherein the sets and the props, the costume and makeup, and above all the figurative language in which the characters express themselves are factored into the interpretative process. The school of British Shakespeare criticism that grew up in the 1930s around such figures as Caroline Spurgeon and G. Wilson Knight posited the reading of the plays, among other things, as extended poems, with all the richness and complexity of imagery commonly associated with that genre. In *El público,* with its episodic, not to say fragmented, dramatic structure, its generically named figures and allegorical overtones, one indeed finds that traditional concepts of character and plot have surrendered a good deal of their significance, while at the same time one of the principal vehicles of "meaning" has come to be located in the very language of the text, in the multiplicity of images and symbols that Lorca puts both onstage and in the mouths of his characters.[2] For the purposes of this analysis, I have conflated lexical items found in the dialogue and in the stage directions, which together make up the overall "text" of the play; performed faithfully, the effect would of course be both aural and visual in nature.

Reading *El público* with these considerations in mind, it is quite easy to identify several important clusters or paradigms of imagery, the two most highly developed of which are based on the human body and on the theater. In both of these, the constitutive elements of the paradigm do not occur in any kind of jumbled fashion or random order, but rather, they can be clearly articulated in a linear concatenation. Hence, in the first, the sequence of images moves, physically and spatially, from outside the body to deep within it. We start, therefore, with "traje"—outfit, garb, dress, suit (90, 94, 97, 121, 123)—and all the specific kinds and descriptions of clothing that the term subsumes: "chaqué" (morning coat) (45), "frac" (tailcoat) (48, 54, 116, 123, 132), "[muchacho] vestido de raso blanco con una gola al cuello" ([boy] dressed in white satin with a ruff around his neck) (54, = "Arlequín blanco," 89, 94, 128), "pantalones de pijama negro" (black pajama pants) (55, 97), "[Elena] Viste de griega. [. . .] El vestido, abierto totalmente por delante, deja ver sus muslos cubiertos con apretada malla rosa" ([Elena] dresses in the Grecian fashion. [. . .] The dress, completely open at the front, reveals her thighs covered with a tight pink mesh) (56), "una malla roja" (a red mesh) (65), "túnica amarilla" (yellow tunic) (66), "guantes negros" (black gloves) (67), "guantes rojos" (red gloves) (67), "pijama de nubes" (pajama with clouds) (74), "traje blanco de ópera" (white opera dress) (78), "traje de bailarina" (ballerina's tutu) (93–94, 94, = "las gasas" [chiffon], 94), "un maillot todo lleno de pequeños cascabeles" (a leotard completely covered with little bells) (94), "una gran capa roja" (a big red cloak) (97, 99), "mantos negros y becas rojas" (black academic gowns and red hoods) (107), "[Damas] vestidas de noche" ([Ladies] in evening attire) (109), "capa blanca de raso" (white satin cloak) (123, 130), "sombrero de copa" (top hat) (123), "[una Señora] vestida de negro [con la cara cubierta por] un espeso tul" ([a lady] dressed in black [with her face covered by] a thick tulle veil) (128), "guantes" (gloves) (132), and "guantes blancos" (white gloves) (132). The notion of clothes leads to that of changing or removing them, and thence to the image of the "biombo" (folding screen), behind which the garb of various characters in the "Cuadro Primero" is transformed (53–58; and cf. 69).

While different layers of clothing lie on top of the surface of the body, cosmetics are applied directly to it, and in the text there is one allusion to lipstick as "lápiz para los labios" and "carmín" (55; cf. the passing mention of "polvera" [powder compact], 64). On the skin also, principally the face and head, can grow various kinds of hair, referred to here as "el peinado con la raya en medio" (the hairstyle with the parting in the middle) (53), "el cabello blanco" (white hair) (56), "cejas azules" (blue eyebrows) (56), "un bigote rubio" (a blond mustache) (55, 56), "barbas oscuras" (dark beard) (48, 52, 55, 57, 69, 96, 97, 114), and finally, "vello" (fuzz) (47). "False" hair is denoted by a "peluca rubia" (blond wig) (48, 97, 116), "peluca morena" (dark wig) (48), and "un bigote de tinta" (ink mustache) (83).

The bare skin is not named as such, as "piel," but it is suggested by the references to "los tatuajes" (tattoos) (54), "cuero" (hide) (88, 90), and Julieta's naked breasts—"senos," "pechecitos" (78, 87, 88), and above all in the repeated use of the noun and adjective "desnudo" (nude, naked) (61, 68, 72, 91, 93, 105, 108) and the related verb "desnudar" (undress, strip naked) (68, 87, 92, 97, 110, 124). A further, more subtle distinction is made between "un desnudo blanco de yeso" (a naked body white like plaster) into which

Pámpanos transforms himself (68); the Director, described by the Hombre 1 as "un desnudo que yo he hecho blanco a fuerza de lágrimas" (a naked body that I have turned white by dint of my tears) (93); and the Desnudo Rojo (Red Nude) of the "Cuadro Quinto" (esp. 105–16).

Under the skin lies the flesh—"carne," though on both the occasions on which Lorca uses this term (54, 91), he actually seems to make little distinction between *carne* and *piel*. Cutting the skin and piercing the flesh creates a wound, "herida" (46), which in turn may form a scab, "costra" (46). The wound can take the form of a Christlike "herida del costado" (wound in the side) (106); it can be multiplied and cause an actress's death—"un racimo de heridas" (a cluster of wounds) (118)—or simply result from harsh manual work (125). Under the skin also, on the same "layer" as the flesh, and flowing on occasions from these wounds, is blood. *Sangre* and its related forms *ensangrentado, sangriento* (bloodstained; bloody), are mentioned a number of times, often when violence is envisaged or has occurred, but sometimes also as a symbol of the basic life force (51, 61, 71, 74, 85, 90, 106, 124, 128, 129). The Caballo Negro refers to an iterative process of delving further into the body: "Cuando se hayan quitado el último traje de sangre" (When they have removed the last suit of blood) (90). There is a remark, too, concerning a "capa de músculos" (layer/cloak of muscles) (78). Finally, as we move deeper down, we reach the "huesos" (bones) (78, 125) that make up the "esqueleto" (skeleton) (92, 110, 111). An intensification of this last notion is achieved by the unreal coupling of terms—"desnudaré tu esqueleto" (I will strip your skeleton naked) (92), "¿Qué necesidad teníamos de lamer los esqueletos?" (What need had we to lick the skeletons?) (110), and in addition, it is implicitly suggested by "las ventanas [que] son radiografías" (windows [that] are X-rays) that punctuate the walls of the Director's office (45).[3]

The second major paradigm, that of the theater, is rather more complicated than that of the human body, involving as it does the idea of the theater as a structure, a physical space, and also that of performance, as in such a phrase as *live theater*. Indeed, the word *teatro* is used with a wide range of nuanced meanings that acquire their particular shading from the context: as a result, *teatro* can signify a generic or specific building (49, 50, 53, 96, 108, 115, 125, 126, 129), the auditorium (51, 104,105, 107, 110, 129), the stage (47), the overall undertaking or enterprise of mounting and performing plays (50, 75, 79, 112, 113, 125, 126), or playacting, pretense, sham (91, 125).

To take first the category of theater as a physical space, there is a gamut of terms associated with it that give form and substance to the notion of a building in which much of the action of *El público* takes place. Thus, there are "anuncios" (advertisements) outside (49, 89); external doors, "puertas" (49, 96, 109, 115, 121, 128, 131); a foyer, "vestíbulo" (130); with "arcos" (arches) and "escaleras" (stairs) (105, 108, 117, 121). Elsewhere in the structure is the Director's office, "cuarto" (45, 123), and a wardrobe room, "guardarropía" (129), and these are connected by a series of passages and communicating doors (46, 47, 53, 129, 132); the theater also has a number of skylights, "claraboyas" (108, 121, 130), and it is even equipped with "calefacción" (heating) (131). Inside the auditorium the seating is provided by "butacas" (stall seats) (49, 89, 118, 124), also described as "sillas" and "asientos" (seats) (104, 111, 119), "lunetas" (stalls) (104), and "palcos" (boxes) (105, 109, 113). (In Spanish there may not always be a clear distinction between *butacas* and *lunetas,* just as in English exactly what parts of the auditorium are denoted by orchestra, stalls, and circle can vary somewhat from theater to theater.) At the front edge of the acting space hangs the "telón" (curtain) (124, 125, 126), also sometimes referred to as the "cortina" (123, 124, 126); the stage itself is variously "escena" and "escenario" (52, 53, 107, 118), with the set, decor, or scenery—"decoración" (121)—and backdrops, "telones" (115, 124), while above all this hang the spotlights, "focos" (49, 89). In the boards of the stage are mounted the trapdoors, "escotillones" (112), that give access to the pit, "foso" (107, 108, 129), that is located underneath.

The other branch of the theater paradigm is concerned with the performance that takes place inside the auditorium and with all that that performance entails. There is a theatrical season—"temporada" (53)—and each production involves one "obra" (work) (52), which could be a "tragedia" (124) or a "drama" (53, 110, 117, 124, 128, 131); this in turn possesses a plot—"argumento" or "acción" (51, 53, 125), and is divided into "actos" (118) and "escenas" (112, 113, 115). In the theater, actors and actresses—"intérpretes" (128) perform, that is to say they come out on to the stage—"salir al teatro / [a escena]" (47, 56; also "sacar a escena" and "llevar al escenario" [bring out onstage / take to the stage], 52, 53) in order to create their assigned roles, their characters, "personajes" (50, 126), in front of the audience. The idea of acting and performance, then, is rendered in "representar," "representaciones" (111, 115, 124, 129), and in a number of other expressions: "la comedia de su sufrimiento" (the playacting of his suffering) that the character Romeo plays out (50); Cascabeles's offer to substitute for Pámpanos—"yo haré tu papel" (I will play your role) (65); and Gonzalo's love that, according to the Director, "vive sólo en presencia de testigos" (only lives in the presence of witnesses [that is, an audience]) (91).

In their dressing rooms (not mentioned by name), the actors might well retire behind a folding screen (that is, a "biombo") in order to put on their costume, and the term *traje* appears in precisely this sense of theatrical costume at various junctures in the text (111, 125, 126). Actors also require makeup and frequently use wigs ("pelucas," 48, 97, 116) and false whiskers ("barba," "bigote," 48, 52, 55, 56, 57, 69, 96, 97, 114, 116), and since ancient Greek tragedy onward, they have on occasions employed masks as part of the creation of character onstage. In *El público* the Pastor Bobo has a whole "armario" (cupboard) full of "caretas blancas de diversas expresiones" (white masks with different expressions) (103) to which he alludes repeatedly in his "Solo" (103-4). There is good reason to think that this section, the "Solo del Pastor Bobo," should be placed first and function as a kind of prologue to the play, rather than appearing intercalated between "Cuadro Tercero" and "Quinto" (Monegal's edition) or "Cuadro Quinto" and "Sexto" (Millán's edition). This was, after all, his purpose and that of the *loa* (prologue) in sixteenth-century Spanish drama.[4] The Arlequín Blanco has "una careta amarillo pálido" (a pale yellow mask) (94) and Hombre 3 "una careta de ardiente expresión" (a mask with an ardent expression) (96, 99), while there are several other various references to not only "caretas" (82) but also "máscaras" (90, 91, 97, 112, 123).[5] Onstage the actors use a number of props, including "largas trompetas doradas" (long golden trumpets) (47, 53, 58, 66), "una flauta" (a flute) (59, 61), "un silbato de plata" (a silver whistle) (64), "una espada" (a sword) (79), "una rueda" (a wheel) (84), "largos bastones de laca negra" (long walking sticks of black lacquer) (85), "unos cirios encendidos" (some lit altar candles) (114), "pequeñas linternas eléctricas" (small electric flashlights) (117), "un aristón" (a mechanical organ) (103), "un gran abanico blanco" (a big white fan) (130), and so on. In addition, they make mention of several materials that can serve in the manufacture of these props and the stage decor: "ho-jalata" (tin plate) (52, 115), "yeso" (plaster) (52), "mica" (mica) (52), "cartón" (cardboard) (52, 112, 115, 126), and "sedas" (silks) (112). Finally, seated in the auditorium, watching the spectacle, observing the actors and actresses perform "in character," is of course the audience, which gives its name to Lorca's work. Besides frequent mention of "el público" (45, 48, 51, 53, 90, 108, 110, 111, 117, 125, 126, 132, 133), both "espectadores" (spectators) (52, 117, 126) and sometimes "la gente" (the people) (112, 117, 118) are used as direct synonyms.

While the paradigms of the human body and the theater are, as I have said, the most important, there are several other image clusters readily identifiable in *El público,* though for the most part, these do not manifest the same highly structured concatenation of ideas. For instance, there is a more abstract spatial cluster, which sets notions of "volumen" (volume) (91) and "espesor" (thickness, density) (81) against "forma" (form) (85, 90, 112, 126) and "superficie" (surface) (72, 81, 89, 91). In the first case, substance and depth are stressed, with verbal expressions like "calar hasta lo hondo" (penetrate deep down) (62) and "bajar" (descend) (62), and with prepositions such as "a través" (through) (112), "detrás" (behind) (112, 126), and "(a)dentro" (inside, within) (49, 54, 118, 126). In the second, emphasis is laid rather on what appears on the surface, on the external manifestation of something; thus, "apariencias" (appearances) (110), the idea of "máscara" (90, 112) once again, "la belleza pura de los mármoles" (the pure beauty of the marbles) with their "superficie intachable" (impeccable surface) (72; cf. 81, 125), or a phrase such as "nadar en la superficie" (to swim on the surface) (89).

Two other clusters that parallel one another quite closely are those surrounding the concepts of love and death. While both are on occasions enunciated directly in abstract terms, they are also rendered in a variety of concrete images. Hence, love may be simply denoted by "amor" (62, 68, 79, 82, 83, 84, 85, 88, 92, 93, 97, 99, 100, 118, 120, 127) and by the verbs "amar" (60, 74, 75, 79, 82, 83, 84, 85, 92, 111, 118), "querer" (56, 95), "enamorar(se)" (to fall in love) (48, 119, 124), and "adorar" (56), but it is furthermore suggested by "besar" (to kiss) (56, 60, 68, 91), "corazón" (heart) (64, 75, 82), and "[cantar el] ruiseñor" (nightingale [sing]) (98, 118), and is of course incarnated in the figure of Julieta. Physical passion is conveyed in "deseo(s)" (desire[s]) (72, 82, 90), in such verbs as "desear" (60, 65), "gozar" (to have intercourse) (96), "gustar" (to please, like) (119), "acostar(se)" (to go to bed / to sleep [with]) (87, 88), and "pasar [por tu vientre]" (pass [through your belly]) (86, 88), in the mentions of "cama" and "lecho" (bed) (46, 57, 60, 64, 87), and in the images of "luz," "sol" and "día" (light; sun; day) (81, 82, 84, 86, 88), "llama" (flame) (111), "caracol" and "cuernos" (snail; horns) (83, 84), "caballos" (horses) (46, 81, 82, 84, 86, 87, 94, 100, 108, 110), "semillas" (seeds) (84), "higuera" (fig tree) (88), "manzana" (apple) (59),[6] and "árboles" (trees) (82); elsewhere the image is subverted (46, 84–85).

The cluster of images around the idea of human mortality has at its center the related notions of death, in "morir" (71, 72, 106, 126), "muerte" (72, 77, 105), "muertos" (52, 84, 86, 88, 126), "costar la vida" (to cost the life [of]) (65, 128); of dying, in "agonizar" (126), "moribundo" (128); of killing, "matar" (74, 81), "asesinar"/"asesinato" (95, 104,113, 117, 118, 119, 125), "ahogar" (to drown) (61), "degollar" (to behead) (67, 85), "estrangu-lar" (to strangle) (73), "devorar [el cuello]" (to devour [the neck]) (73, 77), "empujar [. . .] al pozo" (push [. . .] into the well) (78), "usar veneno de rata" (to use rat poison) (81); and finally of committing suicide, in "darme un tiro" (to shoot myself) (50), "clavar[se] [una] espada en el cuello" (to stick a sword in one's neck) (68), "ahogarse" (to drown oneself) (92). The idea is also given concrete form in such transparent symbols as the "sep-ultura" (grave) (49, 89), "sepulcro" (sepulchre) (50, 78, 79, 80, 82, 87, 99, 109, 110, 112, 113, 115, 119, 125), and "tumba" (tomb) (110), the "carnicería" (butcher's shop) (83), or "el que corta las espigas" (he who cuts the ears of wheat) (88), in physical disease—"cáncer" (52, 64), "meningitis" (82), and is of course again incarnated in the figure of the Caballo Negro. Other images and symbols strongly associated with death would include "luna" (moon) (46, 82, 125), "hierba" (grass) (46, 82, 87, 100, 126, 131),[7] "noche" (night) and "lo oscuro" / "oscuridad" (the dark; darkness) (80, 81, 82), "ce-niza" (ash) (84, 85), "asfódelos" (asphodels) (84), "musgo" (moss) (81), and by extension images of emptiness or nothingness—"hueco" (hollow) (104) and "vacío" (empty) (46, 85), "arcos vacíos" (empty arches) (79), "cangrejo devorado" (crab [that has been] devoured) (90).

Finally, mention should also be made here of the opposed concepts of "teatro al aire libre" (theater in the open air) (46, 47, 48, 50, 56, 89), which is theater "out in the open," if not necessarily actually "al fresco"; and in contrast, the "teatro bajo la arena" (theater underneath the sand) (50, 89, 128; cf. 106, 125), which Hombre 1, in particular, thinks it necessary to initiate—"inaugurar" (to inaugurate) (50, 89, 128), "empezar" (to begin) (58), later "dar el primer paso" (to take the first step) (89). The significance of this second kind of theater depends in part on the symbolic burden that we assign to *arena*, a substance that in *El público* is described as Julieta's "medicina para dormir" (medicine to sleep) (95, 99) and which has standard associations of instability (as against rock), sterility and dryness (the desert), and the passing of time (the hourglass), and hence also comes to be intimately connected with death and extinction. The initial indication for the stage set of the "Cuadro Tercero" is of a "muro de arena" (wall of sand) (71); later the wall "se abre y aparece el sepulcro de Julieta en Verona" (opens and the sepulchre of Juliet in Verona appears) (78). The basic meaning of *arena* in Spanish is "sand," but it can also, by extension, denote an arena, or, if you like, an amphitheater, leading us back to the "teatro bajo la arena." Sand was spread on the floors of amphitheaters to absorb the blood of the victims, human and animal. Clearly, then, *muro de arena* could just as well be understood as a wall of sand and as the wall of an arena. (It is probably coincidental that Verona possesses an exceptionally well-preserved Roman amphitheater.) Subsequently, the Director asserts that "el verdadero drama es un circo de arcos" (the true drama is a circus of arches) (128), bringing to mind not the modern tented circus but rather the permanent Roman one, the arena used among other things for gladiatorial combat. If we give priority to the sense of (Roman) arena, amphitheater, or circus, this in turn could suggest the "ruina romana" (Roman ruin) (59) of the "Cuadro Segundo," a "ruina" (62, 63, 66, 68, 73, 74, 76, 91) filled with "columnas" (columns) (67, 69), "capiteles" (capitals) (59, 64, 65, 66), and sand, "arena" (67), and which is precisely the scene of the "lucha" (combat) or "festín [. . .] sangriento" (bloody feast) (71). The ruin, according to the dialogue at the beginning of the "Cuadro Tercero" (esp. 71–76), is not far from this place, with its "muro de arena" (71), where this opening conversation now occurs. Likewise, after the audience's revolt in the theater, "[a Gonzalo] lo están buscando en la ruina" (they're looking [for Gonzalo] in the ruin) (106), while Dama 3 implies that the ruin is somehow actually contained within the theater: "cuando subíamos por el monte de la ruina creímos ver la luz de la aurora, pero tropezamos con los telones" (when we were climbing up the hill of the ruin, we thought we saw the light of dawn, but we bumped into the curtains) (115).

Now, how does all this fit together? Evidently, Lorca has had recourse to the age-old *theatrum mundi* topos, whereby not only the theater is found to reflect the real world but also the real world to mirror the theater.[8] The action of *El público* is located in a nominal city, "ciudad" (city) (51, 83, 88, 124, 125), and there are mentions of a "calle" (street) (91), "callejuela" (alleyway) (107), "esquina" (corner) (121), "edificio" (building) (121), "casa" (house) (60, 64, 82), "terraza" (terrace) (108), "tejado" (roof) (126), "barandas" (railings) (126), "torre" (tower) (107), "café" (café) (74), "taberna" (tavern) (74, 94), "gran almacén" (department store) (76), "mercados" (markets) (129), "farmacias" (pharmacies) (116), "universidad" (university) (105, 121), "catedral" (cathedral) (111), "acuario" (aquarium) (117), "music-hall" (124), "plataformas [de una estación]" (plaforms [of a station]) (116), "trenes" (trains) (116, 121), and "puerto" (port) (74); of the surrounding countryside—"campos" (fields) (124), "prado" (meadow) (87), and "montaña" (mountain) (86, 119); of the inhabitants, "la gente" (the people) (117, 123, 124, 125, 129) (as noted earlier, *gente* is used elsewhere in the text as a synonym for *público* in its meaning of "audience"), "los jóvenes" (the young people) (51); and of various professions, "cocheros" (coachmen) (64, 89), "fogoneros" (boilermen) (64), "médicos" (doctors) (64, 123), "fundidor" (foundry worker) (64), "herradores" (blacksmiths) (89), "obreros" (workmen) (125), and "pescadores" (fishermen) (129). Beyond the buildings of the city, the surrounding natural world is suggested by reference to the sky, "cielo" (71, 79, 86, 104, 132); clouds, "nubes" (81, 85, 132); and the air or wind, "aire" (109, 116, 123, 128).

Following the basic analogy established by this well-known topos, the "equivalent" of the outside world is the whole theatrical space, and in particular the stage with its decor, framed by the proscenium arch. People are actors, and just as actors perform roles and thus create characters, so people have jobs, and they also "act" (create personalities) while interacting with others. People wear clothes ("traje"), cosmetics, have hairstyles, and may sport mustaches or beards; actors wear costumes ("traje" again), put on makeup, and use false whiskers and wigs. When people die, their bodies are reduced to bones ("hueso," "esqueleto"), having been interred in a grave ("sepultura," "sepulcro," "tumba").[9] One further word in Spanish for grave, *fosa*, not used by Lorca in *El público* but surely present at the back of his mind, enables us at once to clinch and round off the set of individual connections within the overall *theatrum mundi* analogy: the "fosa" in the earth corresponds to the "foso" beneath the stage (accessed via the "escotillones") and likewise to the "escena del sepulcro" (sepulchre scene) performed as part of the "teatro al aire libre" and then repeated, with the Director's radical innovations, as part of the "teatro bajo la arena," where "mis personajes [. . .] mueren de verdad" (my characters [. . .] really die) (126).

The articulation and elucidation of this extended analogy also permits us to recognize and appreciate a greater richness of meaning in a further series of related notions that also establish equivalencies between living daily life with acting in a theater. In this way, the terms "ocultar(se)/oculto" (to hide [oneself] / hidden) (57, 89, 125), "mentir/mentira" (to lie / a lie) (57, 110, 125), "falso" (false) (72), "engañar/engaño" (to deceive / deceit) (52, 74, 76, 82), "fingir" (to pretend) (50, 65), and "disfrazar/disfrazado" (to disguise / disguised) (97, 112, 115, 119), all pertain to dissimulation and the concealment of true character, true sexuality, and true emotion in real life and simultaneously evoke the creation of a fictitious persona in a dramatic performance.

This line of analysis leads us to the central concept of the *máscara*, again as it exists both in the real world and the theater. In the theater, it obviously carries the literal sense of the *careta*, an actual mask, as well as referring more broadly to the "mask" of the fictional persona that the actor adopts and projects while "in character." In everyday life, the *máscara* suggests a publicly constructed but false appearance or identity that people utilize in their social interactions—"Mi lucha ha sido con la máscara hasta conseguir verte desnudo" (My struggle has been with the mask until I was able to see you naked) (91); "Ésta no es mi amiga. Ésta es una máscara" (This person is not my friend. She is a mask) (97). However, the *máscara* also comes to symbolize the powerful pressures of a conformist society—public opinion, "decency," prudery even—that induce people to adopt a false outward appearance. Thus, it can stand for a bloodthirsty, out-of-control crowd or a lynch mob—"Yo vi una vez a un hombre devorado por la máscara. [. . .] y en América hubo una vez un muchacho a quien la máscara ahorcó colgado de sus propios intestinos" (Once I saw a man devoured by the mask. [. . .] and in America there was once a boy whom the mask hanged with his own intestines) (51); or an overwhelming principle of propriety and morality—"En medio de la calle, la máscara nos abrocha los botones y evita el rubor imprudente que a veces surge en las mejillas. En la alcoba, cuando [. . .] exploramos delicadamente el trasero, el yeso de la máscara oprime de tal forma nuestra carne que apenas si podemos tendernos en el lecho" (In the middle of the street, the mask fastens our buttons and avoids the imprudent blush that sometimes blooms in our cheeks. In the bedroom, when [. . .] we delicately explore our backside, the plaster of the mask crushes our flesh in such a way that we can scarcely even lie down on the bed) (91).

This complex symbol of the *máscara* pertains directly to one of the major themes of *El público*, the question of identity. Here the imagistic paradigms of both the human body and the theater now link up with the spatial image cluster of "form/surface" versus "substance/volume." In *La zapatera prodigiosa*, the Zapatero, disguised as a "titiritero" (puppeteer), says that in his performances of popular ballads "enseño la vida por dentro" (I show life on the inside) (105). His figurative claim is, in a sense, taken up here and treated concretely and quite literally. Thus, the layers of clothes, cosmetics, and hair under which human beings hide or disguise themselves, corresponding to the costume, makeup, and wigs of the actors who feign to be someone they are not, connect in turn with the notions of external form and superficiality, which are inherently misleading or false. In the "Cuadro Sexto," on the floor of the Director's office, there lies "una gran cabeza de caballo" (a large horse's head) (123; cf. 127, 132). While this abandoned prop suggests the normal way that Bottom would play the ass into which he is transformed in *A Midsummer Night's Dream* (an episode that the Prestidigitador makes much of just a few lines into this last scene [124]), it also establishes the more general idea of an external surface, a disguise, which reminds us that "como los caballos, nadie olvida su máscara" (like the horses, no one forgets their mask) (90). Presumably, this is the way in which Lorca imagined the various Caballos would themselves be performed in *El público*, with this kind of prop—he offers us no hints in the stage directions or elsewhere.

However, the falsity of external appearance and of outwardly projected identity is not, in *El público*, a static concept; rather, the "superficiality" is assured—and at the same time, demonstrated—by an all-pervading inconstancy and a repeated process of chameleonlike metamorphosis. Hence, the layers of costume that are shed, only to reveal another layer underneath, often with the intervention of the *biombo;* the whole "Cuadro Segundo," with the unceasing interplay, based on the verb *convertirse* (to change into), between Cascabeles and Pámpanos, who themselves are "versions" of the Director (Enrique) and Hombre 1 (Gonzalo); the other expressions of transformation: "volverse" (66) (to turn into), "desdoblarse" (to split into two) (69), "[tú] serías" / "[yo] sería" ([you] would be / [I] would be) (76), and so on. The adoption and switching of roles also play their part: Pámpanos commences the "Cuadro Segundo" on the ascendant, with Cascabeles subservient (59–61), but then the roles are reversed with a near repetition of lines in the other character's mouth (62–64). Sexuality, sexual orientation, or sexual identification are also subject to rapid shifts, as depicted, for example, in the changes of male to female costume and in the vacillating attitudes of the Director and Hombres 1, 2, and 3 toward each other and to Elena; the homosexual Hombre 3 even goes so far as to attempt to "play" a mixture of Don Juan and Romeo to Julieta's Juliet (97–98); and Hombre 1 denounces "los falsos deseos" (false desires) (72). Sexual love and physical violence also collapse into one: "HOMBRE 1: (*Luchando.*) Te amo. | DIRECTOR: (*Luchando.*) Te escupo. | JULIETA: ¡Están luchando! | CABALLO NEGRO: Se aman" (HOMBRE 1: (*Wrestling.*) I love you. | DIRECTOR: (*Wrestling.*) I spit on you. | JULIET: They're fighting! | CABALLO NEGRO: They love each other) (92; cf. 71, 76, 78). And by the same token, there are numerous indications of the power struggles and the to-and-fro, sadomasochistic overtones of human, and in particular amorous, relationships, with a vocabulary that includes "látigo" (whip) (46, 57, 62, 74, 89), "azotar/azote" (to lash / lash) (57, 63, 87), "castigar/castigo" (to punish / punishment) (56, 72), "atormentar" (to torture) (60), "golpear" (to beat) (63), "dominar" (to dominate) (62), "obligar" (to compel) (63), "suplicio" (torture) (57), "esclavo" (slave) (77, 78, 88, 93), "arrastrarme" (to drag me) (63), "cadena" (chain) (64, 77), "clavos" (nails) (57), "pinzas" (pincers) (82), "atenazar/tenazas" (to grip tightly / tongs) (57, 89), and "punzones" (hole punches) (88).

In the midst of all this, trying to identify the real self, trying to get down to a bedrock of authentic personality, is very difficult, if not by definition impossible. Hombre 1 claims that "yo no tengo máscara" (I don't have a mask) (90), and his aim has been to "arrancar" (rip) (91) the mask from the Director: "Mi lucha ha sido con la máscara hasta conseguir verte desnudo" (My struggle has been with the mask until I was able to see you naked (91; cf. 93). Carlos Feal casts doubts on Hombre 1's sincerity, contending that any desire, the moment it is expressed in language, is transformed into "un gesto irrisorio" (a ridiculous gesture). The argument, persuasive though perhaps overly subtle, should not divert attention from Hombre 1's largely exemplary—and sacrificial—status.[10] In his search for "uno" (one), the Emperador gives the Centurión the order: "¡Desnúdalos!" (Strip them naked!) (68). By the implacable logic of the paradigms of imagery already established, if and when the layers covering and concealing the body have been peeled away, it follows that what remains—the *desnudo* (the nude)—should become a symbol of the true and the authentic. Indeed, the protagonist of André Gide's novel *L'Immoraliste*, Michel, uses the image of the palimpsest as a model of self or identity ("je me comparais aux palimpsestes" [I compared myself with palimpsests]), with a learned "être secondaire" (secondary being) superimposed over his "être authentique" (authentic being). The stripping away of the burden of the former "laisse voir à nu la chair même" (lets the very flesh be seen naked); sunbathing naked "tout mon être affluait vers ma peau" (all my being was flowing toward my skin); and when he decides to go and get shaved, "sentant sous les ciseaux tomber ma barbe, c'était comme si j'enlevais un masque" (feeling my beard fall under the scissors, it was as if I was taking off a mask).[11]

The discovery or revelation of the *desnudo*, though, if and when feasible, does not in fact represent the end of the journey. Hombre 1, who says that he has rid himself of all masks, is to be found lying—or perhaps better, hanging—on the reverse side of the perpendicular bed on which appears the Desnudo Rojo (105, 116). The identification between them is plain, and we should remember that the Desnudo Rojo, a transposition of Christ on the Cross, is on the point of death (116–17), while Hombre 1 himself expires at the end of this "Cuadro Quinto" (122). Likewise, the Emperador appears to kill the Niño (most probably by strangulation) (66–67): in the manuscript, we find toward the end of the scene in question a crossed-out line that reads: "(por detrás de las columnas sube al cielo el esqueleto de un niño)" ([behind the columns the skeleton of a child goes up to the sky]).[12] The Emperador reminds Cascabeles that "uno es uno y siempre uno. He degollado más de cuarenta muchachos que no lo quisieron decir" (one is one and always one. I have beheaded more than forty boys who would not say it) (67), and Pámpanos promises that "si me besas, yo abriré mi boca para clavarme, después, tu espada en el cuello" (if you kiss me, I will open my mouth to plunge, afterward, your sword down my throat) (68). The process of passing down through the layers, then, does not stop at the epidermis: the *desnudo* is always in danger of becoming an *esqueleto;* the integration of the self ("siendo íntegramente hombres" [being fully men], 72) and the achievement of union are elusive and may well only be possible in death.[13] As Cascabeles defiantly cries: "Llévame al baño y ahógame. Será la única manera de que puedas verme desnudo" (Take me to the bath and drown me. That will be the only way that you can see me naked) (61), to which Pámpanos replies: "Toma un hacha y córtame las piernas. [. . .] Quisiera que tú calaras hasta lo hondo" (Take an axe and cut my legs off. [. . .] I want you to penetrate deep down) (62); or again, as Hombre 1 says to the Director: "Desnudaré tu esqueleto" (I will strip your skeleton naked) (92).

The *desnudo*, therefore, but also the *esqueleto*, as suggested by the X-ray image of the "ventanas [que] son radiografías" (windows that are radiographs) (45), are the principal symbols of what is called repeatedly in *El público la verdad* (the truth). Lorca's model seems to posit that there should exist a core, a kernel, a deep center of truth—"la verdad que me ocultas" (the truth that you are hiding from me) (57), "tenéis miedo de la verdad" (you are afraid of the truth) (89), "yo sé la verdad" (I know the truth) (90). Consequently, most critics to date have adopted what might be called an "essentialist" vision with respect to *El público;* that is, they have assumed that there is indeed a core, an original layer, somewhere deep down waiting to be discovered. However, Honorata Mazzotti Pabello proposes an opposing reading based on an "existentialist" perspective, wherein personality and identity—and for that matter, truth—are only created in the process of living and are therefore in constant flux.[14] In this regard, Feal adduces the Sartrian concept of *être-pour-autrui* from *L'Être et le néant*,[15] in which the subject is partially constituted by its perception by the other and in which one may be tempted to play out the role with which one is labeled or modify one's behavior in order to be seen in some different way. Likewise, André Belamich writes that for Lorca, "el yo es una fábula, una mentira; el yo es un desfile, un carnaval de metamorfosis, de disfraces, de trajes (la palabra traje, en *El público,* simboliza formas fugaces e irreales)" (the self is a fable, a lie; the self is a procession, a carnival of metamorphoses, of disguises, of sets of clothing [the word *traje,* in *El público,* symbolizes fleeting, unreal forms]).[16] Thus, one might conclude that a better model for the self would not in this case be a palimpsest but, rather, something more like an onion, a sum of the parts, an accretion of layers, but with no hidden core or center.[17]

Furthermore, if any truth does exist at all, it may well be that it is, paradoxically, only knowable in death, is actually synonymous with death, or can only be perceived from beyond the grave, from the perspective of the afterlife—the ultimate truth being apprehended at, or even after, the "moment of truth."[18] Indeed, Gerald Brenan reports that in Andalusia "the cemetery was known as the *tierra de la verdad* [the land of truth]."[19] Such a notion would represent a kind of "middle ground" between the proposition that the "true self" is recoverable if enough layers are stripped away and the contention that no stable core exists at all. It might also help us understand the "logic" of the "inmensa hoja verde lanceolada" (immense lance-shaped green leaf) (71) that is part of the decor of the "Cuadro Tercero," as a blade of grass seen from below, from beneath the earth, and which is recalled later by the Prestidigitador's warning to the Director that "si avanzas un escalón más, el hombre te parecerá una brizna de hierba" (if you advance one step more, man will seem like a blade of grass to you) (126). We could view in the same light the more direct references to "la verdad de las sepulturas" (the truth of the graves) (49, 89) and the Caballo Negro's observation that "cuando se hayan quitado el último traje de sangre, la verdad será una ortiga, un cangrejo devorado, o un trozo de cuero detrás de los cristales" (when they have removed the last suit of blood, truth will be a nettle, a devoured crab, or a scrap of hide underneath the glass panes) (90). Consequently, "truth" and identity threaten to dissolve into nothingness, into a void, and to quote the Pastor Bobo, they may be found to be no more than "el hueco de una careta" (the empty hollow of a mask) (104).

A further topic that needs to be acknowledged is the subject of language and its relationship to truth and identity. Although the great majority of lexical items in the play are intelligible, certain utterances in the dialogue— from "Blenamiboá" (47) onward—suggest a shifting interchangeability and arbitrariness that threaten to undermine the link between the sign and its referent. Paul Julian Smith, for instance, finds "a shimmering linguistic surface which conceals no hidden meanings or motives," while Luis Fernández-Cifuentes makes much of this feature, using it to attack Nadal's essentially coherent vision of the play and as a springboard for his own deconstructionist reading.[20] While I find that both Smith and Fernández-Cifuentes in turn overstate their respective cases, the issue of linguistic indeterminacy is undeniably another important facet of *El público*.

The intricate connectedness of things in *El público* does not stop here, however. The theme of identity is closely linked with that of love: if people are difficult or indeed impossible to "know," then it will be commensurately difficult to love them—if real communication is well-nigh impossible, then so inevitably will be amorous communion. In *L'être et le néant*, working from the notions of *être-pour-soi* and *être-pour-autrui*, Jean-Paul Sartre treats at length the particularly acute problems posed by a love relationship. Furthermore, third parties will be denied the ability to judge whether two others might actually, miraculously, have achieved real love: "HOMBRE 1: ¿Usted cree que estaban enamorados? | DIRECTOR: Hombre . . . Yo no estoy dentro" (49) (HOMBRE 1: Do you believe that they were in love? | DIRECTOR: What a question! . . . I'm not inside); "ESTUDIANTE 4: El tumulto comenzó cuando vieron que Romeo y Julieta se amaban de verdad. | ESTUDIANTE 2: Precisamente fue por todo lo contrario. El tumulto comenzó cuando observaron que no se amaban, que no podían amarse nunca" (ESTUDIANTE 4: The uproar began when they saw that Romeo and Juliet really loved each other. | ESTUDIANTE 2: It was for precisely the opposite reason. The uproar began when they observed that they did not love each other, that they could never love each other) (111).

Furthermore, the themes of both identity and love are ultimately related to a third, namely death.[21] The individual self is coterminous with the human body, and when the body dies, so inevitably will the self be extinguished. In addition, as we have just seen, the problem of authenticity in identity as it is depicted in *El público* progresses through a sequence of images to the naked body and thence to the skeleton and the grave. Similarly, but perhaps even to a greater degree, the suggested connections between love and death are multiple. If part of the (mortal) human condition is the imperfection of man, then love will necessarily be imperfect also, an inherent flaw perhaps transcended only in death. Such "subthemes" as the elusiveness, transitoriness, arbitrariness, conflictiveness, and the general unsatisfactoriness of love are prominent in *El público*.

Thus, Romeo and Juliet live out their destiny as star-crossed lovers; Julieta in the crypt is an incarnation of love in death—she refers to her "sepulcro" (sepulchre) as a "camita" (little bed) (79), and her series of exchanges with the Caballo Blanco 1 point up the way love collapses into death (79–83); taking off clothes may be a preliminary to sexual activity, but as we have seen, the naked form (*desnudo*) usually calls to mind the bones beneath; the libidinous Caballos Blancos are offset by a funereal Caballo Negro, with "un penacho de plumas [negras]" (a crest of black feathers) (84) such as might be worn by a horse pulling a hearse; the site of the Desnudo Rojo's "Passion" is a bed (105, 129); in the experimental staging of *Romeo and Juliet*, "se amaban los esqueletos y estaban amarillos de llama" (the skeletons loved each other and were yellow with flame) (111); and the image of the Edenic apple is in most cases subverted, giving "manzanas podridas en la hierba" (rotten apples in the grass) (46) or "bellas manzanas de ceniza" (beautiful apples of ash) (84). It might also be possible to find in the "sepulcro de Julieta en Verona" (sepulchre of Juliet in Verona) (78) a transposition of Christ's tomb: the door that is going to be closed (96, 98) recalls the rock that sealed it up and was subsequently rolled away; the nightingale (or lark) about to sing (98) and then sings (116) is paralleled by the cock crowing; while the three Caballos Blancos assert that "hemos de pasar por tu vientre para encontrar la resurrección de los caballos" (we have to pass through your belly in order to find the resurrection of horses) (86).[22]

In addition, the Emperador's amorous advances are (potentially) deadly. In the figure of the Emperador, Piero Menarini has seen an allusion to Herod, Felicia Hardison Londré has seen Caligula, and Rafael Martínez Nadal has seen Hadrian and also possibly Nero.[23] I would like to suggest a further possibility: Commodus, who has a reputation as one of the worst Roman emperors and who was strangled in his bath by Narcissus, a wrestler: "FIGURA DE PÁMPANOS: Llévame al baño y ahógame" (FIGURA DE PÁMPANOS: Take me to the bath and drown me) (61); "HOMBRE 1: Ahí detrás, en la última parte del festín, está el Emperador. ¿Por qué no sales y lo estrangulas? (HOMBRE 1: Back there, in the last part of the feast, is the Emperor. Why don't you go out and strangle him?) (73).

At this point, we come full circle, back to the theater. The theater serves in *El público* as a complex symbol, as the fundamental generating idea for the paradigms of imagery outlined here, and hence as the concrete medium for the expression of many aspects of precisely those themes of identity, love, and death. However, the theater also functions in the play as a theme in its own right.[24] Lorca comments in *El público* on the state of the contemporary Spanish stage and on the nature of the kind of audience typically in attendance, indicating what is wrong with theater and audience and how they might be "corrected" or improved. If the *teatro al aire libre* represents conventional drama, untroubled and untroubling, designed to engage the spectators' easier sentiments and to enable them to spend two or three hours of diversion in the theater, then clearly the *teatro bajo la arena* points to innovation and experimentation, a concept of drama that will tackle more serious themes and engage and challenge the intellect of the audience. The conventional theater fails to confront reality: instead, it substitutes a false verisimilitude based on actors minimally "in character"— "¿Cuántas veces fingió tirarse de la torre para ser apresado en la comedia de su sufrimiento?" (How many times did he pretend to throw himself off the tower to be snared in the playacting of his suffering) (50); "Sus voces estaban vivas y sus apariencias también" (Their voices were vivid and their outward appearance too) (110); "Romeo y Julieta agonizan y mueren para despertar sonriendo cuando cae el telón" (Romeo and Juliet suffer death throes and die only to wake up smiling when the curtain falls) (126).

Likewise, that thin veneer of verisimilitude depends on other forms of trickery—the decor and props, which are inauthentic in themselves (being two-dimensional) and which may serve to divert attention from the proper objects of interest or concern:

> Hay personas que vomitan cuando se vuelve un pulpo del revés y otras que se ponen pálidas si oyen pronunciar con la debida intención la palabra cáncer pero usted sabe que contra esto existe la hojalata, y el yeso, y la adorable mica, y, en último caso, el cartón, que está al alcance de todas las fortunas como medio expresivo. (52)

There are people who vomit when an octopus is turned inside out and others who turn pale if they hear the word *cancer* spoken with just the right intent, but you know that to combat this, there exists tin plate, and plaster, and the adorable mica, and, as a last resort, cardboard, which is within reach of all budgets as an expressive medium.

The Director later refers again to "los sofás, [. . .] los espejos y [. . .] copas de cartón dorado" (the sofas, [. . .] the mirrors and [. . .] the gilt cardboard goblets) (126). In addition, and here Lorca echoes José Ortega y Gasset's complaints in *La deshumanización del arte,* the conventional theatergoer typically confuses fictional characters with real life—"La gente se olvida de los trajes en las representaciones" (people forget about the costumes in the performances) (111)—and possesses a sensibility that responds more readily to falsity than to truth: lost and wandering in the labyrinth of the darkened theater, nevertheless for Dama 2, "lo que más miedo me ha dado ha sido el lobo de cartón y las cuatro serpientes en el estanque de hojalata" (what scared me the most was the cardboard wolf and the four snakes in the tin plate pond) (115). In her early article, Wilma Newberry was only working with the two published scenes of the play, "Ruina romana" and "Cuadro Quinto"; without access to the rest of the text, and in particular the "Cuadro Sexto," she arrived at a number of erroneous conclusions, but nevertheless, she did bring out several of the striking coincidences with Ortega's thinking.[25]

According to Estudiante 1, who often acts as an authorial mouthpiece, "ahí está la gran equivocación de todos y por eso el teatro agoniza" (there is the big mistake that everyone makes and for that reason the theater is dying) (112). What can be done? The Director provides part of the answer when he explains that "yo hice el túnel para apoderarme de los trajes y, a través de ellos, enseñar el perfil de una fuerza oculta cuando ya el público no tuviera más remedio que atender, lleno de espíritu y subyugado por la acción" (I made the tunnel in order to take control of the costumes and, by means of them, show the profile of a hidden force at a point when the audience could do nothing else but pay attention, with complete mindfulness and captivated by the action) (125). In a dramatic fragment, titled *Teatro de aleluyas,* which forms part of the prehistory of Lorca's *Amor de don Perlimplín con Belisa en su jardín,* we find an early articulation of a broadly similar sentiment: "El personaje no se debe dar cuenta de nada pero sí el público. El drama debe estar en el público no en los personajes. [. . .] [Éstos] son fórmulas matemáticas, frías, y el público lee [en ellos] el problema que llevan dentro" (The character should not realize anything, but the audience should. The drama should be in the audience and not in the characters. [. . .] [The latter] are cold, mathematical formulas, and the audience reads [in them] the problem that they are carrying inside).[26]

The themes that the theater treats must be substantial and serious ones; decor, props, and costume are still crucially important, but the audience members must be educated not to respond to them emotionally or vicariously but, rather, to maintain a certain distance and bring more of their intellect to bear.[27] And in setting the Director against the Prestidigitador in the "Cuadro Sexto," Lorca creates a further, supplementary opposition between the (relative) validity of the scenery and props of the theater and the pure trickery and sleight of hand of a magician's show. Thus, as Estudiante 1 asserts, "el público no debe atravesar las sedas y los cartones que el poeta levanta en su dormitorio" (the audience should not pierce the silks and the cardboards that the poet constructs in his bedroom) (112), and he adduces the analogous example of the aquarium: "Cuando la gente va al acuario no asesina a las serpientes de mar ni a las ratas de agua, ni a los peces cubiertos de lepra, sino que resbala sobre los cristales sus ojos y aprende" (When people go to the aquarium, they don't kill the sea serpents or the water rats nor the fish covered in what looks like leprosy, but rather, they slide their eyes over the glass panels and they learn) (117). It is all a matter of presentation: even the most difficult or provocative subjects can be handled if the technique and the vehicle are adequate to the task—"Es cuestión de forma, de máscara" (It is a question of form, of mask) (112); "un ejemplo [. . .] admitido por todos a pesar de su originalidad" (an example [. . .] accepted by everyone in spite of its unusualness) (124).

Likewise, if this authentic theater ("teatro verdadero") is to deal in basic human truths, then it will necessarily have close connections with mortality—"teatro bajo la arena" (50, 89): "Es a los teatros donde hay que llamar [. . .]. Para que se sepa la verdad de las sepulturas" (You have to call to the theaters [. . .] So that the truth of the graves may be known) (49 and 89); "El Director de escena abrió los escotillones, y la gente pudo ver cómo el veneno de las venas falsas había causado la muerte verdadera de muchos niños" (The director opened the trapdoors, and the people could see how the poison of the fake veins had caused the real death of many children) (112); "Todo teatro sale de las humedades confinadas. Todo teatro verdadero tiene un profundo hedor de luna pasada" (All theater emerges from confined damp spaces. All true theater has a deep stench of moon that's gone bad) (125; and cf. 128); "mis personajes [. . .] mueren de verdad" (my characters [. . .] really die) (126). Or to put the two notions in reverse order: "Sepulturas con focos de gas y anuncios y largas filas de butacas" (Graves with gas spotlights and long rows of theater seats) (49 and 89); "Tendré que darme un tiro para inaugurar [. . .] el teatro bajo la arena" (I shall have to shoot myself in order to inaugurate [. . .] the theater beneath the sand) (50). It will be a theater that does not close itself off from life (and death) but, rather, one open to what is going on in the outside world and one that takes a leading—even revolutionary—role in advances and changes. It will oppose the easy acceptance of the status quo and challenge the *bien-pensant* bourgeois morality, represented in *El público* by "la moral" (moral code), "el estómago de los espectadores" (the spectators' stomachs) (52), "el juez" (the judge) (113), "la letra" (teachings) (118), "la doctrina" (the doctrine) (118), "familias," "sacerdotes," and "la misa" (families; priests; mass) (all 120). Rather, it will lean toward the iconoclastic: "Tendremos necesidad de enterrar el teatro" (We shall have to bury the theater) (50); "La puerta del teatro no se cierra nunca" (The door of the theater is never closed) (96); "Es rompiendo todas las puertas el único modo que tiene el drama de justificarse, viendo, por sus propios ojos, que la ley es un muro que se disuelve en la más pequeña gota de sangre" (Breaking all the doors is the only way that the play has of justifying itself, seeing, through its own eyes, that law is a wall that dissolves in the smallest drop of blood) (128; and cf. 50, 126, 131)—precisely the kind of theater, one imagines, that Lorca wanted to write. His oft-quoted statements concerning the "unperformability" of *El público* should therefore be tempered with data that suggest that there were several separate initiatives made to stage the play within his lifetime.[28]

El público certainly has its loose ends and baffling images, all the more so given the fact that the possibly incomplete first-draft manuscript is our only copy text. However, the great majority of the images, as with the principal paradigms and clusters that I have traced here, are demonstrably open and responsive to rational analysis and traditional interpretative approaches. And if all this is true, if there are significant symbolic structures in the play that serve as a vehicle for major themes, then how can we continue to call *El público,* as so many critics insist on doing, a Surrealist drama?[29] Journalistic responses to the various European premieres of *El público* from 1986 onward are littered with invocations of and appeals to Surrealism, only reinforcing the received idea. Other critics "sit on the fence," denying a direct filiation but still affirming a more or less strong influence.[30]

To date, Carlos Jerez-Farrán is perhaps the critic to have made the strongest and best reasoned attack against the Surrealist label.[31] Fernando Lázaro Carreter agrees that the "apariencia surrealista" (Surrealist appearance) is actually sustained by a "pensamiento racional" (rational thought), but he does not have the space to demonstrate this conviction in detail.[32] Through the tangle and apparent confusion of the fragmented action and the transmogrified characters, there is, in fact, considerable logic to be found here, sometimes admittedly more of a "lógica poética" (poetic logic).[33] Antonio Monegal's fine interpretation of the related symbols of "luna," "pez," and "pez luna" (moon; fish; moonfish) in *El público* (and *Viaje a la luna*) and Piero Menarini's detailed analysis of the organization of the "Cuadro Quinto," in which he finds considerable internal patterning and a structural parallelism with the last four Stations of the Cross, are just two examples of this.[34] Indeed, there is very substantial evidence here of a careful, conscious, controlling hand and mind at work elaborating that "dificilísimo juego poético" that is *El público.*

6

Juliet and the Shifting Sands of *El público*

El público is an unusual and difficult play, posing many and radical problems of interpretation. This condition might perhaps be emblematized by the fact that Rafael Martínez Nadal's first study of the work, published in 1970, appeared six years before the full text of the drama itself first became available and then only in an expensive limited edition.[1] Without the benefit of any prior acquaintance with the actual text, Martínez Nadal's readers encountered a tightly knit and persuasively argued critical commentary, supported only by selective quotation of segments of the dialogue and stage directions (and then not always in their correct textual sequence). As a result, the interpretative act preceded and seemed to be somehow privileged over the diffusion of the very text that it purported to decipher and construe.

Martínez Nadal has been taken to task, most notably by Luis Fernández-Cifuentes, not so much for his part in these strange mechanics of textual transmission, but rather for trying to impose a coherent overall vision on to the work, for "naturalizing" it, and either ignoring or "explaining away" the many loose ends and other indeterminacies that Fernández-Cifuentes identified in it.[2] The play's irresolution and undecidability stem from a whole range of different features, both extrinsic and intrinsic. Among the former, the principal issues are the possibility that the text as we have it may be incomplete; doubt as to the proper order of certain scenes; and the fact that regardless of these two other considerations, the only extant manuscript is unfinished—an unpolished first draft with numerous textual cruces that never went through the different stages of preparation and revision that Lorca's plays would normally follow on their way to a premiere. Among the latter, we encounter within the dialogue the use of opaque or seemingly senseless language; arbitrary lists and series; unsupported or unfulfilled references; the coining of Surrealist-like images; and characters talking at cross-purposes. However, the indeterminacy springs above all from the issue of identity, for in the drama characters appear to be rootless and coreless, undergoing multiple (and potentially open-ended) transformations and repetitions; as a consequence, these metamorphoses and doublings serve to undermine totally our conventional notions and models of human personality.[3]

Without going to either of the extremes represented, respectively, by Martínez Nadal and Fernández-Cifuentes, what I want, rather, to suggest in the present study is that *El público* actually contains a number of messages about its own interpretation, about interpretation in general, and about how making sense of (or giving sense to or finding sense in) something or someone has to do with basic problems of knowing, both heuristic and hermeneutic and both empirical and psychological in nature.

An appropriate starting point for these deliberations is to be found in the "Cuadro Tercero." Some way into the scene, we come across the following stage direction:

El muro [de arena] se abre y aparece el sepulcro de JULIETA *en Verona. Decoración realista. Rosales y yedras. Luna.* JULIETA *está tendida en el sepulcro. Viste un traje blanco de ópera. Lleva al aire sus dos senos de celuloide rosado.* (78)[4]

The wall [of sand] opens, and the sepulchre of JULIET *in Verona appears. Realist scenery. Rosebushes and ivy. Moon.* JULIET *is laid out in her sepulchre. She is clothed in a white opera dress. Her two breasts of pink celluloid are open to the air.*

Julieta, a flesh-and-blood person, is trapped in some kind of "living death" or "life beyond the grave" in the Capulet family vault in Verona. Her opera dress may well bring with it reminiscences of Hector Berlioz's choral work *Roméo et Juliette* (1839), Charles Gounod's opera of the same name (1867), as well as Vincenzo Bellini's opera *I Capuleti e i Montecchi* (1830). The mention of her two exposed "senos de celuloide rosado" raises an interesting but moot question as to her gender (or that of the actor playing her). If, as I would imagine, Lorca did not conceive in 1930 of the possibility of actual onstage nudity, then the effect here may be intended to emphasize her essential femininity. On the other hand, the breasts' very artificiality might point forward to the fifteen-year-old boy who later assumes the role of Juliet. Lorca gives no indication as to his intentions concerning the gender of the actor who is to perform Julieta in the tomb (as he does in some other instances); the action in the remainder of the scene generally tends to favor the former hypothesis.

Julieta springs to her feet from the top slab of her tomb plinth, where she was "sleeping," having been provoked by the sound of "Un tumulto de espadas y voces [que] surge al fondo de la escena" (A commotion of swords and voices [that] emerges from the back of the stage) (79). Elsewhere I have remarked on how these disturbances seem to echo the intermittent "noises off" that punctuate the closing tomb scene (act 5, scene 3) in *Romeo and Juliet*.[5] Paris and his Page, Romeo and Balthasar, Romeo fighting Paris, the three Watchmen, and finally, "the people in the street" are all variously responsible for different kinds of noise and disorder. Julieta now combines a complaint and an assertion: "Cada vez más gente. Acabarán por invadir mi sepulcro y ocupar mi propia camita. A mí no me importan las discusiones sobre el amor ni el teatro. Yo lo que quiero es amar" (Every time [there are] more people. They'll end up invading my sepulchre and occupying my own little bed. I don't care about discussions concerning love or theater. What *I* want to do is [just] love) (79). Perhaps it is no coincidence that this speech appears to have provided Martínez Nadal with components for the title of the first edition of his book (*"El público":* *Amor, teatro y caballos en la obra de Federico García Lorca*), for I think that it goes right to the heart of a number of fundamental issues in the play.

To this initial quotation, we can append three or four more, all drawn from further on in the same scene. Julieta, now fervently courted by Caballo Blanco 1 but herself dissolving with frustration into tears, declares that she has really had more than enough: "Basta. No quiero oírte más. [. . .] Ya estoy cansada. Y me levanto a pedir auxilio para arrojar de mi sepulcro a los que teorizan sobre mi corazón y a los que me abren la boca con pequeñas pinzas de mármol" (That's enough. I don't want to listen to you anymore. [. . .] I'm tired now. And I am getting up to request help to throw out of my sepulchre the people who theorize over my heart and the people who open my mouth with little marble pincers) (82). A little later, though, she seems momentarily to be succumbing to the blandishments of Caballo Blanco 1. Referring to herself, she muses briefly on an attractive possibility: "Sí, un minuto, y Julieta viva, alegrísima, libre del punzante enjambre de lupas. Julieta en el comienzo, Julieta a la orilla de la ciudad" (Yes, a minute, and Juliet alive, joyous, free of the stinging swarm of magnifying glasses. Juliet at the beginning, Juliet at the edge of the city). But her "daydreams" are immediately interrupted by the resurgence of that "tumulto de voces y espadas" (83) already heard once before, and in response she reels off a list of the most recent visitors to the tomb and recounts what some of the more daring of them tried to do:

Ayer eran cuarenta y estaba dormida. Venían las arañas, venían las niñas y la joven violada por el perro tapándose con los geranios, pero yo continuaba tranquila. [. . .] pero ahora son cuatro, son cuatro muchachos los que me han querido poner un falito de barro y estaban decididos a pintarme un bigote de tinta. [. . .]

Cuatro muchachos, caballo. Hacía mucho tiempo que sentía el ruido del juego, pero no he despertado hasta que brillaron los cuchillos. (83–84)

Yesterday there were forty of them, and I was sleeping. The spiders came, the girls came, and the young woman violated by the dog covering herself with the geraniums, but I stayed calm. [. . .] but now there are four of them, there are four boys who have tried to attach a small clay phallus to me and were determined to paint an ink mustache on me. [. . .]

Four boys, horse. I had been hearing the noise of the game for a long time, but I didn't wake up until the knives glinted.

This account seems to echo, in reverse, an earlier mention made by Hombre 2 of "un ángel que se llevaba el sexo de Romeo, mientras dejaba el otro, el suyo, el que le correspondía" (an angel who was taking away Romeo's sex organ while leaving the other one, his one, the one that matched him)

(50). For the clay phallus, Lorca may have had in mind the Egyptian burial practice of sometimes adding them to female mummies,[6] with the possibility even of a very indirect allusion to Cleopatra. (Howard Carter lectured at the Residencia de Estudiantes in 1924 and 1928, and there was considerable interest in the whole subject of ancient Egypt throughout the 1920s in Spain.) The ink mustache is perhaps an echo of Marcel Duchamp's *LHOOQ* (1919), which likewise takes as its starting point yet another icon of Western feminine beauty. Overall, though, this appears to be an attempt to invest Julieta with some (superficially) male attributes, which in turn connects with the gender shifts seen in "Cuadro Primero" and, later, with the doubts cast on the "true" sexual identity of the Caballos Blancos.

At this point, the Caballo Negro comes onstage and offers a wide-reaching rejoinder that brings Julieta's protestations to a temporary halt: "¿Cuatro muchachos? Todo el mundo. Una tierra de asfódelos y otra tierra de semillas. Los muertos siguen discutiendo y los vivos utilizan el bisturí. Todo el mundo" (Four boys? Everyone. A land of asphodels and another land of seeds. The dead carry on arguing, and the living use the scalpel. Everyone) (84). In Greek mythology, the dead in the underworld were thought to eat asphodel tubers, which makes the symbolism clear. However, sometime after the entrance of the other three Caballos Blancos (2, 3, and 4), Julieta returns again and with renewed vigor to her essential theme: "Yo no soy una esclava para que me hinquen punzones de ámbar en los senos, ni un oráculo para los que tiemblan de amor a la salida de las ciudades. Todo mi sueño ha sido con el olor de la higuera y la cintura del que corta las espigas" (I am not a slave so that they can drive amber hole punches into my breasts, nor I am an oracle for those trembling with love at the cities' exits. My whole dream has been of the smell of the fig tree and the waist of he who cuts the ears of wheat) (88).

Before construing in more detail this closely linked sequence of remarks and exchanges, we need to consider the status and purpose of Julieta as she appears in *El público*. It is clear that Shakespeare's characters are invoked in Lorca's play for, among other reasons, their archetypal status, as is evidenced in the discussion between the Director and Prestidigitador in the "Cuadro Sexto" (see especially 124). Nor should we forget that other archetypal woman, Elena, who is, in Lorca's play, both Homer's Helen of Troy (56) and Selene (109), moon goddess, associated by both ancient Greeks and Romans with Hecate.[7] Western culture is replete with pairs of great lovers—Dido and Aeneas, Orpheus and Eurydice, Leander and Hero, Pyramus and Thisbe, Anthony and Cleopatra, Tristan and Iseult, Lancelot and Guinevere, Abelard and Héloïse, Dante and Beatrice, Paolo and Francesca, Petrarch and Laura, to name but a few. Some of these are purely fictional, some may—or may not—have existed, and some are historical. But in all cases, they are transmitted down to us today through written (primarily literary) texts, a process that tends to create a homogenizing effect, blurring the line, in a number of different ways, between legend and history, between mythological or literary characters and real-life personages.

Despite the richness of this tradition, I would still argue that if asked to name just one quintessential pair of lovers, most informants would choose Romeo and Juliet, and it is at least partially in this light that we need to understand the figure of Julieta and what she says here. Martínez Nadal calls her "encarnación de pura feminidad" (the incarnation of pure femininity), "arquetipo" (archetype), and more judgmentally, "perfecta encarnación del amor normal" (the perfect incarnation of normal love).[8] Ana Gómez Torres coincides more exactly with my reading: "Los nombres de Romeo y Julieta simbolizan la expresión más profunda, intensa y concentrada del sentimiento amoroso" (The names of Romeo and Juliet symbolize the most profound, intense, and concentrated expression of the feeling of love); she, in turn, cites Unamuno as a source ("El canto adámico," in *El espejo de la muerte*).[9] Whether a historical model for Juliet ever existed, in Italy or anywhere else, whether "Juliet" is simply an imagined construct communally created and renewed by millions of spectators and readers, is now entirely beside the point:[10] the extraordinary impetus given to the character by Shakespeare's play has bestowed upon her more than four hundred years of intense vitality, and she certainly exists as much more "real" and "alive" to many people than do the great majority of actual human beings, either living or dead. I propose that it is precisely this impetus and this energy that account, through a kind of metaphorical logic, for Juliet/Julieta's continuing life beyond death, the action of *El público's* "Cuadro Tercero" therefore picking up several centuries after where *Romeo and Juliet's* act 5 left off; she lives on in the collective imagination. Here and in what follows, I have tried to maintain as logical a distinction as is possible in the terminology employed, using the name Juliet for the character in Shakespeare's play, Julieta for the character in Lorca's play, Juliet as the female partner in this abstracted and idealized pair of eternal lovers, and Julieta as Lorca's specific depiction of the end result of the "Juliet-archetype."[11]

At the very end of Shakespeare's play, most of the survivors—the Prince of Verona, Capulet and Lady Capulet, Montague, Friar Laurence, Balthasar, and the Page—gather together and engage in a kind of figurative postmortem to try to determine and clarify exactly what has occurred. As the Prince commands, acting in his capacity as chief examiner or magistrate:

> Seal up the mouth of outrage for a while,
> Till we can clear these ambiguities
> And know their spring, their head, their true descent.[12]

As Martínez Nadal rightly notes, these characters in *Romeo and Juliet* stand at the beginning of a very long line of inquirers into what happened, how it could have happened, and why it happened:

> Las subsiguientes explicaciones y discusiones que preside el Príncipe de Verona en la propia cripta de los Capuletos y ante los cadáveres de Romeo, Julieta y París; explicaciones que, para Lorca, parecen anticipar los debates que sobre la verdadera naturaleza del amor ha suscitado la famosa tragedia.[13]

> The ensuing explanations and discussions presided over by the Prince of Verona in the crypt belonging to the Capulets and in the presence of the dead bodies of Romeo, Juliet, and Paris; explanations that, for Lorca, seem to anticipate the debates on the true nature of love that the famous tragedy has provoked.

Taking the Prince's particularly apt word, *ambiguities,* as a starting point, we can imagine an accretion of commentary fanning out in all directions, from these last few pages in the play to Shakespeare's contemporary audiences to latter-day audiences to generation upon generation of exegetes and critics and, finally, to just about anyone who has even vaguely heard of these young, unfortunate lovers. Over time the discussions have inevitably shifted their focus from the mechanics and intricacies of the original tragic plot to more general questions regarding the precise nature and depth of Romeo's and Juliet's reciprocal love, the (adverse) conditions under which it arose, and the hypothetical possibilities of its endurance if, by some impossible but happy chance, their double deaths could somehow have been avoided.

It is this unceasing accumulation, then, of both amateur and professional commentary, together with the accompanying shift of focus, that in all likelihood explains why Julieta is so disgruntled: she is sorely irritated that there are ever more people "poking their noses," as it were, into something that she believes to be uniquely and privately hers, something that is effectively coterminous with her own self and her continuing "existence." As she tells us, these persons to whom she objects are engaged in endless "discusiones sobre el amor [y] el teatro"; she is disturbed by the fact that there are "cada vez más gente"; the final insult, which may only be a matter of time, would be that "acabarán por invadir mi sepulcro y ocupar mi propia camita" (all 79). (The identification of what was supposedly Juliet's tomb in Verona was made at the beginning of the nineteenth century and immediately became a stopping point for literary tourists. The red marble sarcophagus was moved to its modern-day location in 1935.)[14]

The entrance of Caballo Blanco 1 seems to tip the scales, for after rejecting his amorous overtures, Julieta is now to be heard "[pidiendo] auxilio para arrojar de mi sepulcro a los que teorizan sobre mi corazón y a los que me abren la boca con pequeñas pinzas de mármol" (82). In a similar fashion, her expressive, elliptical metaphor, "el punzante enjambre de lupas" (83), from which she longs to be free, can easily be read as a reference to an annoying, jostling crowd ("swarm") of people surrounding her and subjecting her to microscopic scrutiny. The knives that would appear to belong to the "cuatro muchachos" (84) suggest that they, in turn, were to take a further step, from visual examination to bodily intrusion, an inference strengthened in the following speech by the mention of a scalpel. Here the Caballo Negro offers a global generalization that ties several of these threads together: "Los muertos siguen discutiendo y los vivos utilizan el bisturí" (84).[15] Finally, Julieta picks up the images of violence, penetration, and enforced subjugation with her assertion that "yo no soy una esclava para que me hinquen punzones de ámbar en los senos" (88), and she closes with the emphatic rejection of a role that some, perhaps many, would have her play: as an authority on the subject, as an oracle, as a kind of divine or mystical source of often cryptic information, guidance, or wisdom on that ever-mysterious topic—love.

The vocabulary to which Julieta repeatedly has recourse establishes an interconnecting set of scientific or, more precisely, medical or surgical images, a series that has already been anticipated in the "Cuadro Primero" by the Director. There, lamenting his financial losses (which, as a result, now restrict his freedom of action), he asserts: "Pero yo he perdido toda mi fortuna. Si no, yo envenenaría el aire libre. Con una jeringuilla que quite la costra de la herida me basta" (But I have lost all my fortune. If not, I would poison the open air. All I would need would be a syringe that removes the scab from the wound) (46). A syringe would, of course, not be the most appropriate medical instrument for the task at hand—another case of co-herence (the surgical paradigm) partially subverted. However, in terms of the overall figurative language of the play, we can see that his troubled economic situation obliges him to adhere to and maintain a conservative and commercially viable theatrical aesthetic—the "teatro [. . .] al aire libre" (46). The relationship of "costra" to "herida" can, of course, be taken both literally and figuratively—the scab is a cap or cover whose removal would let out all (the blood, the pus) that the wound contains. The consequences of his subsequent decision to risk an experimental performance are later described by Estudiante 4 thus: "El Director de escena abrió los esco-tillones, y la gente pudo ver cómo el veneno de las venas falsas había causado la muerte verdadera de muchos niños" (The director opened the trapdoors, and the people could see how the poison of the fake veins had caused the real death of many children) (112); lifting the scab and opening the trapdoors are, metaphorically speaking, quite closely analogous.

The text of the "Cuadro Primero" is less than clear (possibly deliber-ately so) on what is perhaps an important point. The audience, in the guise of Hombres 1, 2, and 3, comes to see the person identified as "el señor Di-rector del teatro al aire libre" (the director of the theater in the open air) to congratulate him for "su última obra" (his latest work) (48); a little later, he is identified as the "Director del teatro al aire libre, autor de *Romeo y*

Julieta" (director of the theater in the open air, "author" of *Romeo and Juliet*) (50). What are we to make of this? Either they are using *autor* very loosely, as a kind of shorthand for *creator of the production,* or perhaps we should read *autor* historically, in the sense that Hugo Albert Rennert describes: "the earliest theatrical managers in Spain also frequently wrote the pieces played by their companies, hence the name *autor,* which was originally applied to them and which afterward merely designated the chief or director of a company, whether he wrote plays or not."[16] The inference that the Director is only the director and not also the playwright is reinforced in the "Cuadro Quinto," in which Dama 3 talks of the "Director de escena" (director) (109) while the Muchacho refers to a seemingly different person whom he identifies as "el poeta" (the poet) (110).

Later on in the play ("Cuadro Quinto"), we find that the fate of Julieta in the vault (a fate that Julieta herself describes and bemoans) parallels fairly closely that of one of her most recent incarnations, in the person of the actress contracted to play the character of Juliet in the Director's "conventional" production of the play. This personage is provocatively called by Estudiante 4 "la verdadera Julieta" (the true Juliet); at face value, what he means is an ellipsis, for this is the actress who was really supposed to play the character of Juliet until she was forcibly displaced by "un muchacho de quince [años]" (a fifteen-year-old boy) (117). She is discovered, after the first performance of the new "teatro bajo la arena" (theater under the sand), "amordazada debajo de las sillas y cubierta de algodones para que no gritase" (gagged underneath the seats and covered with cotton wool so she would not scream) (111). The actress suffers the same fate at the hands of "la masa de espectadores" (the mass of the spectators) (117) as do the two male actors (aged thirty and fifteen) now actually playing the roles of Romeo and Juliet:

ESTUDIANTE 4: Lo que es inadmisible es que los hayan asesinado.

ESTUDIANTE 1: Y que hayan asesinado también a la verdadera Julieta que gemía debajo de las butacas.

ESTUDIANTE 4: Por pura curiosidad, para ver lo que tenían dentro.

ESTUDIANTE 3: ¿Y qué han sacado en claro? Un racimo de heridas y una desorientación absoluta. (117–18)

ESTUDIANTE 4: What is unacceptable is that they should have killed them.

ESTUDIANTE 1: And that they also killed the true Juliet who was moaning underneath the stall seats.

ESTUDIANTE 4: Out of pure curiosity, to see what they had inside.

ESTUDIANTE 3: And what have they been able to discover? A cluster of wounds and an absolute confusion.

According to the Estudiantes' words, then, the audience's indiscriminate, violent, and almost gratuitous act was intended literally to find out what they were like inside, figuratively to find out "what they were made of," what "made them tick," but it has all been in vain, a total failure, with nothing clearer than before they started this bloody investigation, or "dissection."

Finally, if Julieta is subject to this kind of violence in the vault, as are the actress and the actor playing Juliet in the theater, then so is (the actor playing) Romeo, both directly (at the hands of the audience members) and, in a further doubling, in his guise as the Christlike Desnudo Rojo, who is also stripped naked and then hung on the perpendicular bed for public display, his side pierced:

> Ese Desnudo Rojo que agoniza en el lecho, desdoble de la Figura de Pámpanos, como ésta era desdoble de Gonzalo, el Hombre 1, es también el propio Romeo, desnudado para la representación que precederá a su muerte en el interior del teatro. Vamos, pues, a presenciar al asesinato, la crucifixión del Desnudo Rojo—Romeo, Gonzalo, Hombre 1—malherido por el sueño de completa integración amorosa en el quimérico uno.[17]

> That Desnudo Rojo who is dying on the bed, a double of the Figura de Pámpanos, just as this figure was a double of Gonzalo, Hombre 1, is also Romeo himself, stripped naked for the performance that precedes his death in the interior of the theater. We, therefore, are going to witness the killing, the crucifixion of the Desnudo Rojo—Romeo, Gonzalo, Hombre 1—gravely wounded by the dream of complete amorous assimilation into the chimerical one.

The same chain of imagery permeates the text, from the Director's "jeringuilla" (46) to the Caballo Negro's mention of the "bisturí" (84), through to a later reference to that same surgical instrument made by the Enfermero speaking to the Desnudo Rojo: "a las ocho, vendré con el bisturí para ahondarte la herida del costado" (at eight o'clock, I'll come with the scalpel to deepen your wound in the side) (106). Just as the syringe was the "wrong" implement, there is here an unsettling shift from the traditional version—the wound inflicted by the Roman soldier with his spear (John 19.34).

Set in vivid opposition to this whole vein of probing and inquiry, which ranges from mental conjecture to visual inspection to bodily autopsy, is Julieta's unequivocal expression of her priorities and desires: "A mí no me importan las discusiones sobre el amor ni el teatro. Yo lo que quiero es amar" (79), reinforced by her later explicit, immediate, and total espousal of nature, the sensual, and the erotic: "Todo mi sueño ha sido con el olor de la higuera y la cintura del que corta las espigas" (88). Needless to say, nothing is ever quite this simple or straightforward. The fig tree and the ears of wheat are emblems of nature, and the odor and fruit of the fig tree and the waist of the implied *segador* (reaper) (cf. *La casa de Bernarda Alba*) are overt sexual topoi. However, the appearance of the fig tree in Revelation (6.13) and the profession of the reaper and the cutting of the wheat all bring an inevitable consciousness of the seasonal cycle and of extinction (1 Corinthians 15.36). Ironically, this is something in which she might also like to participate, "trapped" as she is in this perpetual life beyond death, this "mar de sueño" (sea of dream) to which she refers in her opening poem (79).

Once again, Julieta's standpoint is mirrored elsewhere in the play, on this occasion by Estudiantes 1 and 5, who, toward the end of the "Cuadro Quinto," seem spontaneously to fall in love, after which they then resolve to take action:

ESTUDIANTE 1: Y lo destruimos todo.

ESTUDIANTE 5: Los tejados y las familias.

ESTUDIANTE 1: Y donde se hable de amor entraremos con botas de fútbol echando fango por los espejos. (120)

ESTUDIANTE 1: And we'll destroy everything.

ESTUDIANTE 5: The roofs and the families.

ESTUDIANTE 1: And anywhere people are talking about love, we'll go in with football boots spraying mud on the mirrors.

Actions speak louder—perhaps much louder—than words. In the last scene, the Director's exclamatory profession of faith may also be read as a further reformulation of the same basic idea that it is no good just looking on from the sidelines: "¡Hay que destruir el teatro o vivir en el teatro! No vale silbar desde las ventanas" (You have to destroy the theater or live in the theater! It's no good just whistling from the windows) (126), an affirmation that is closely followed by a number of references to "amor" (love) (126–27).

Julieta's pronouncements are therefore to be understood not only as the expression of a personal wish but also, equally, as pointing to a certain line of conduct and a statement of priorities that survivors, witnesses, detectives, magistrates, pathologists, philosophers, spectators, readers, and perhaps above all, literary critics might do well to take to heart: namely, that observation, investigation, speculation, and extrapolation are no substitute for action, for lived experience, for existential assertion. The former are inherently less valuable than the latter, and furthermore, it is implied, the former will never truly achieve their ostensible goal: the elucidation or explanation of the latter. To put it another way, the literary-critical analysis and interpretation of the text should never precede—neither in terms of chronology nor in terms of value—the direct and full experience of the text itself: thus, for example, the huge accretion of studies on Shakespeare's *Romeo and Juliet* should never displace the actual play from the center of our attention and engagement.

At the risk of continuing to defy what I have just established as a basic theme of the play, these preliminary conclusions can be shown to be amply borne out by a more detailed and wide-ranging analysis of *El público*. The starting point for this examination will be those key lexical items already singled out: "discusiones," "teorizan," "me abren la boca," "pequeñas pinzas de mármol," "lupas," "cuchillos," "bisturí," "ver lo que [tiene] dentro," "han sacado en claro," "hin[car] punzones," and "oráculo," to cite them in the order of their textual appearance. If these items are rearranged and thought of as potential "headwords," or category denominators, they suggest the existence of a network of associative chains that extend throughout the play. Using them to orient the search and to highlight certain semantic fields, close textual scrutiny leads to the identification of five or six principal movements, or moments, all related to one another, that may be characterized very roughly, and very abstractly, as follows: (1) an initial or preexisting condition of ignorance or an incomplete, imperfect, or inferior state of informedness; (2) data gathering; (3a) data processing / reflection / conjecture; (3b) intellectual instruction / persuasion; (4) the "breakthrough"; and (5) the resulting or eventual state. In the following paragraphs, I shall illustrate each of these phases in turn.

In the beginning condition, people think, believe, imagine, or assume things to be a certain way. Most often, this subjectivity is implicit in simple statements of apparent objective fact, statements that are actually no more than opinions, formulations of what particular individuals suppose or hold to be true. Occasionally, the use of certain verbs emphasizes the subjective element. Hence, Hombre 1 can ask of the Director: "Y enamorados. ¿Usted cree que estaban enamorados?" (And in love. Do you believe that they were in love?) (49), and the Figura de Cascabeles inquires of the Figura de Pámpanos: "¿Te figuras que tengo miedo a la sangre? [. . .] ¿Crees que no te conozco?" (Do you imagine that I'm afraid of blood? [. . .] Do you believe that I don't know you?) (61–62); or again Estudiante 4, who boasts to the other Estudiantes: "Veréis como tengo razón" (You will see how I am right) (113).

Many of the actions about which Julieta complains so vocally would take their place under the second of the headings I proposed—that of data gathering. These include having her mouth opened "con pequeñas pinzas de mármol," an act of physical examination more appropriate, one might have imagined, for a horse than a human. We should also note that the (veterinary) examination is carried out with this instrument strangely and disturbingly made of marble, a substance much more strongly associated with statues, monuments, crypts, tombs, and headstones than with clinical practice. In addition, she is being peered at through magnifying glasses; being carved open with a knife or scalpel; and admittedly less intelligibly, having "punzones de ámbar" driven into her breasts.[18] Apart from the indignities and persecution to which Julieta is subject, the audience also victimizes the actress who was to have played the part of Juliet, the young woman being killed "para ver lo que tenía[n] dentro"

(118). Estudiante 5 refers to her disparagingly as "aquella muchacha llena de polvo que gemía como una gata debajo de las sillas" (that girl covered in dust that was moaning like a cat underneath the seats) (119)—another animal image.

Analogous actions occur elsewhere and in other contexts. In the "Cuadro Primero," in the original version of the text, when Elena comes onstage and finds the Director transformed, he defends or justifies himself thus: "Prefiero vivir así, que morir bajo [las palabras] el cuchillo de Gonzalo" (I prefer to live like this, over dying under [the words] the knife of Gonzalo). The manuscript shows that the phrase *el cuchillo* replaced *las palabras* before the entire line was discarded by Lorca, perhaps because he recognized that it was too explicit.[19] The "cuchillo" again looms large in the exchanges between the Figura de Pámpanos and the Figura de Cascabeles—particularly in "si tú te convirtieras en pez luna, yo te abriría con un cuchillo" (if you were to change into a moonfish, I would open you up with a knife) (60). Also in the "Ruina romana," the Centurión foresees that "el Emperador adivinará cuál de los dos es uno. Con un cuchillo o con un salivazo" (the Emperor will divine which of you two is one. With a knife or with a gob of spit) (67), and the Emperador issues the command "¡Desnúdalos!" (Strip them!) (68). Hombre 1 urges the Director to scrutinize Hombre 3 (an act that will enable him to recognize him): "Ése es, ¿lo conoces ya? [. . .] Enrique, mira bien sus ojos. Mira qué pequeños racimos de uvas bajan por sus hombros" (That's him, do you recognize him now? [. . .] Enrique, look carefully at his eyes. Look at those small bunches of grapes that hang over his shoulders) (74); and again, Hombre 1 detects latent desires in the Tres Caballos Blancos: "ocultan un deseo que me hiere y que leo en sus ojos" (they are hiding a desire that wounds me and which I read in their eyes) (90). Later, Romeo (the actor playing the character of Romeo) is literally treated by the audience as a specimen for clinical or forensic examination: "DAMA 1: ¿Y Romeo? | DAMA 4. Lo estaban desnudando cuando salimos" (DAMA 1. What about Romeo? | DAMA 4: They were stripping him naked when we left) (109–10). When the Enfermero inquires of the Traspunte: "¿Está preparado el quirófano?" (Is the operating room ready?) (114), we know from an earlier exchange (106–7) that it is the Desnudo Rojo who is going to be—figuratively, if not literally—operated upon or autopsied, the last of several references in this series that are to be added to the chain of

medical-surgical imagery already identified. Finally, and in a quite different context, the Tres Damas and Muchacho 1 are also engaged, as it were,
in an act of searching, of data gathering: they are, quite simply, trying to
find their way out of the building.

Besides all this, the use of a good deal of Freudian symbolism is readily
apparent in the "Cuadro Tercero," in which Caballo Blanco 1 brandishes a
sword (79), the other Tres Caballos Blancos have "largos bastones de laca
negra" (long walking sticks of black lacquer) (85), a later stage direction
indicates: "(Empuñan los bastones y por las conteras de éstos saltan tres
chorros de agua.)" ([They grip the walking sticks, and three jets of water
spurt from their tips]) (88), and the "cuatro muchachos" are equipped with
"cuchillos" (84). These instances, together with the many reverberations
elsewhere of cutting/penetration as not only violent but also (potentially)
sexual (for example, throughout the "Cuadro Segundo"), open up an allied
field of suggestion, albeit indirectly: that of acquiring information/knowl-
edge through sexual intercourse, of knowing someone, as the phrase goes,
in the biblical sense of the word. The verb in Spanish is *conocer,* though
as I will demonstrate, it is not used explicitly in this sense anywhere in
El público.[20]

In the episode in the middle of the "Cuadro Tercero" that has been the
principal focus of our attention, mention is made both of "la joven violada
por el perro" and "cuatro muchachos los que me han querido poner un
falito de barro y estaban decididos a pintarme un bigote de tinta" (83), the
latter phrase establishing the potential reversal or reversibility of percep-
tions of gender, sexual roles, or dominance. Robert Hughes's commentary
on Duchamp's *LHOOQ* is relevant here: "a further level of anxiety reveals
itself, since giving male attributes to the most famous and highly fetishized
female portrait ever painted is also a subtler joke on Leonardo's own homosexuality (then a forbidden subject) and on Duchamp's own interest in
the confusion of sexual roles."[21] As the action evolves, the Caballos Blancos
become increasingly aroused, boasting of their masculinity—"hemos roto
con las vergas la madera de los pesebres" (we have broken with our penises
the wood of the feeding troughs)—and calling to her: "Desnúdate, Julieta,
y deja al aire tu grupa para el azote de nuestras colas" (Take your clothes
off, Juliet, and expose your hindquarters to the air to be whipped by our
tails) (87). The request or injunction to remove her clothes recalls others

that I have already quoted: the Emperador's command to the Centurión and the audience's treatment of Romeo, to say nothing of the Desnudo Rojo's generic state. In these other instances, being stripped naked was chiefly a preliminary to visual examination rather than to sexual activity, though the latent eroticism is never far away. (The state of nakedness is one of the primary components in the paradigm of imagery centered on the human body and discussed in extenso in the previous chapter.)

Julieta, though initially intimidated, soon recovers her sangfroid and indeed mounts a counterattack: "Pues ahora soy yo la que quiere acostarse con vosotros, pero yo mando, yo dirijo, yo os monto, yo os corto las crines con mis tijeras" (Well, now it's me who wants to sleep with you, but I give the orders, I'm in charge, I mount you, I cut your manes with my scissors) (88), the last phrase alluding clearly and significantly to the Old Testament story of Samson and Delilah. On the reverse of page 2 of the manuscript of *El público*, we find the title *Sansón. [Drama] Misterio poético en cuarenta cuadros y un asesinato* and a putative list of characters. Also, a crossed-out line of dialogue in the "Cuadro Primero," in which the Director addresses Hombre 2, runs as follows: "No te pongas bravo que ya sé que tú no eres Sansón" (Don't get boastful; I already know that you aren't Samson).[22] Delilah therefore joins the group of femmes fatales in the play.[23] The Caballo Negro can only comment, perplexed: "¿Quién pasa a través de quién?" (Who is going through whom?), before Julieta delivers her (already quoted) speech: "Yo no soy una esclava . . ." that ends with the exclamations: "¡Nadie a través de mí! ¡Yo a través de vosotros!" (No one through me! Me through you!) (88). These cries, although evidently directed at the libidinous Caballos Blancos, can now also be understood more widely as a rejection of her role as a (passive) subject of intrusive inquiry.

Once in possession of data, irrespective of the techniques employed in their acquisition, people carry out various processes of ratiocination, reflection, and conjecture, both as individuals and groups, both silently and out loud. Thus, during the first visit of the three Hombres to the Director, the latter peremptorily rejects the suggestions of Hombre 1: "Yo no discuto, señor" (I'm not getting into an argument, sir) (52); Julieta protests at "las discusiones sobre el amor" (discussions concerning love) (79), she is fed up with "los que teorizan sobre mi corazón" (the people who theorize over my heart) (82), and in an abandoned variant, she imagines herself "libre de [lupas y meditaciones]" (free of [magnifying glasses and deliberations]),²⁴ while the Caballo Negro ominously adds that "los muertos siguen discutiendo" (the dead carry on arguing) (84). Later one of the stage directions tells us that "Los ESTUDIANTES discuten" (The ESTUDIANTES argue) (109), and this activity is subsequently developed in the fairly lengthy and heated debates in which the Estudiantes do indeed engage (111–13, 117–20). Estudiante 1 likewise makes seemingly scornful mention of "donde se hable de amor" (anywhere people are talking about love) (120). Needless to say, people do not appear to be in possession of sufficient or of the right data, the data suggest different things to different people at different times, and people are unable to agree on a common conclusion to be drawn from them. This is also exemplified in the "Cuadro Sexto," in which the conversation between the Director and the Prestidigitador is in fact another long, tense discussion. During its course, the Director explains his motives: "Yo hice el túnel para apoderarme de los trajes y, a través de ellos, haber enseñado el perfil de una fuerza oculta" (I made the tunnel in order to take control of the costumes and, by means of them, show the profile of a hidden force) (125). What is particularly interesting to note here is that in the original version of the text, Lorca first wrote "y a través de ellos haber demostrado mi tesis" (and by means of them to have demonstrated my thesis)²⁵—a thesis, a speculative proposition, possibly concerning Romeo and Juliet, that he had hoped to demonstrate, and thereby prove, in and through the medium of the experimental performance.

Alongside individual reflection and group discussion, we also find acts of instruction and persuasion, which likewise bear on those intermediate mental processes of moving from raw data to some kind of extrapolated result. Again, we should first note that Julieta disclaims any role as an oracle (88), as a source of information, guidance, or wisdom, especially for those less skilled in or knowledgeable about love than herself. She also denounces the wheedling Caballo Blanco 1 for engaging in what she sees as blatant sophistry:

Basta. No quiero oírte más. ¿Para qué quieres llevarme? Es el engaño la palabra del amor, el espejo roto, el paso en el agua. Después me dejarías en el sepulcro otra vez, como todos hacen, tratando de convencer a los que escuchan de que el verdadero amor es imposible. (82)

141

That's enough. I don't want to listen to you anymore. Why do you want to take me? The word *love* is deceit, a broken mirror, stepping into water. Afterward you would leave me in the sepulchre again, as they all do, trying to convince those who are listening that true love is impossible.

The Estudiantes discuss whether Romeo and Juliet necessarily have to be a man and a woman, and Estudiante 1 argues: "No es necesario, y esto era lo que se propuso demostrar con genio el Director de escena" (It is not necessary, and this was what the director decided to demonstrate in a stroke of genius) (113). The Director's own initial use of the verb *demostrar,* and its replacement with *enseñar* (125) (in its sense of "to show") have just been noted, and a few lines later on in the same scene he returns to spelling out the aims of his endeavor: "Y demostrar que si Romeo y Julieta agonizan y mueren para despertar sonriendo cuando cae el telón, mis personajes, en cambio, queman la cortina y mueren de verdad [en] presencia de los espectadores" (And to demonstrate that if Romeo and Juliet suffer death throes and die only to wake up smiling when the curtain falls, my characters, in contrast, burn the curtain and really die in the presence of the spectators) (126).

In the tomb scene, Julieta, rebuffing Caballo Blanco 1's advances, uses the verb *enseñar* in such a way that it could be translated either as "to show" or as "to teach": "¿Eras tú el que ibas a enseñarme la perfección de un día?" (Were you the one who was going to reveal to me the perfection of a day?) (81); "¡Lo de todos! Lo de los hombres, lo de los árboles, lo de los caballos. Todo lo que quieres enseñarme lo conozco perfectamente" (It's the same thing with everyone! The thing with men, the thing with trees, the thing with horses. Everything that you want to reveal to me I [already] know perfectly) (82). Lines earlier, she had angrily—and self-confidently— asserted her own wealth of experience and lack of need for any further instruction: "¿Y qué tengo yo, caballo idiota, que ver con la noche? ¿Qué tengo yo que aprender de sus nubes o de sus borrachos?" (And what have I, stupid horse, got to do with night? What do I need to learn from its clouds or its drunks?) (81). The verb *aprender* also appears in Estudiante 1's mouth, as he opines on the proper role of the audience in a theater:

Un espectador no debe formar nunca parte del drama. Cuando la gente va al acuario no asesina a las serpientes de mar ni a las ratas de agua, ni a

los peces cubiertos de lepra, sino que resbala sobre los cristales sus ojos
y aprende. (117)

A spectator should never form part of the drama. When people go to the
aquarium, they don't kill the sea serpents or the water rats, nor the fish
covered in what looks like leprosy, but rather, they slide their eyes over the
glass panels and they learn.

However, as far as teaching and learning are concerned, it is the aca-
deme itself that is the principal focus for attention and, I think, for a certain amount of irony. The stage directions at the beginning of the "Cuadro
Quinto" call for "A la derecha la portada de una universidad" (On the right-
hand side the facade of a university) (105), and under the circumstances, it
is hard not to be put in mind of the University of Salamanca, one of Spain's
oldest, especially famous for its resplendent, sixteenth-century Plateresque
doorway facade. In the same scene, mention is made of a "profesor de
retórica" (professor of rhetoric) (in Lorca's day perceived as a particularly
stuffy subject) who was killed at the outbreak of the "revolution" and whose
lascivious wife (perhaps the same Elena from the "Cuadro Primero") had,
it seems, already been cuckolding him with a horse (108). Another professor is implied at the end of the scene, when the Traspunte appears, temporarily assuming the role of a beadle, reminding the Estudiantes that it is
time for a "clase de geometría descriptiva" (class of descriptive geometry)
(120), again hardly the most scintillating of disciplines. The Estudiantes
themselves, four of them at first, are clad in full ceremonial academic garb:
"Aparecen los ESTUDIANTES: Visten mantos negros y becas rojas" (The ES-
TUDIANTES come onstage. They are wearing black gowns and red hoods)
(107), and when a fifth comes onstage, he likewise talks of "mis estudios"
(my studies) (119). As already noted, the Estudiantes are prone to engage
in discussion, and coherent and consistent shades of opinion emerge from
these debates (the individual characters being relatively "stable" in this
regard and fairly well delineated and differentiated one from another).
While the group as a whole certainly tends to express what one might call a
"liberal" or "progressive" point of view (as compared, say, with the attitude
attributed to the audience, whose values are distinctly more conservative),
it is also true that they can never manage to agree among themselves.

Reaching agreement, or arriving at a conclusion, is immediately preceded by what was earlier termed the "breakthrough," that brief moment of perception or illumination that bridges the processes of reflection and conjecture with the possession of an "end result." Intuition seems to play some role in this: as noted, the Centurion states that "el Emperador adivinará cuál de los dos es uno" (the Emperor will divine which of you two is one) (67). However, the more usual act of recognizing someone—the moment of recognition—implies the use of memory and of recollected data. Thus Hombre 1, replying to Hombre 2, but referring to, and only at the end directly addressing, the Director, says:

> Lo reconozco todavía y me parece estarlo viendo aquella mañana que encerró una liebre que era un prodigio de velocidad en una pequeña cartera de libros. Y otra vez, que se puso dos rosas en las orejas el primer día que descubrió el peinado con la raya en medio. ¿Y tú me reconoces? (53)

> I recognize him still, and it seems like I'm seeing him that morning when he shut a hare, which was a prodigy of speed, in a small bag of books. And another time, when he put a rose behind each ear that first day when he discovered the hairstyle with a parting in the middle. And you, do you recognize me?

As already quoted, *conocer* can also serve at times as a synonym of *reconocer*.

Beyond occasional instances of intuitive or visual recognition, the stress generally falls on intellection, whether active or passive, and a fair number of different verbs describe this event. Hombre 1, referring to the Director, recalls "el primer día que descubrió el peinado con la raya en medio" (53); Hombre 3 vaunts the fact that "yo he descubierto una bebida maravillosa" (I have discovered a marvelous drink) (74–75); the Muchacho boasts that "yo descubrí la mentira cuando vi los pies de Julieta" (I discovered the lie when I saw Juliet's feet) (110), and Estudiante 4 affirms that "el público tiene sagacidad para descubrirlo todo" (the audience has the sagacity to discover it all) (111). Estudiante 2 praises the Director, who "evitó de manera genial que la masa de espectadores se enterase de esto" (prevented in a brilliant way the mass of spectators from finding out about this), while after Estudiante 4's line—"Lo que es inadmisible es que los hayan asesinado" (What is unacceptable is that they should have killed them) (117)—the manuscript shows that Lorca had originally planned to continue the sentence with *para enterarse* (in order to find out).[26]

Caballo Blanco 1 chides Julieta: "Sigues tan loca como siempre. Julieta, ¿cuándo podrás darte cuenta de la perfección de un día?" (You're just as crazy as ever. Juliet, when are you going to realize the perfection of a day?) (80); Estudiante 4 incredulously inquires of Estudiante 5: "¿Pero no te has dado cuenta de que la Julieta que estaba en el sepulcro era un joven disfrazado [. . .]?" (But haven't you realized that the Juliet who was in the sepulchre was a disguised young man [. . .]?) (119) (again, Lorca had originally written *enterado* before replacing it with *dado cuenta*); and the Prestidigitador, in another passage also later crossed out, tries to soothe the Director: "Usted llora porque todavía no se ha dado cuenta de que no [hay] existe diferencia alguna entre una persona y un traje" (You are weeping because you still haven't realized that there does not exist any difference between a person and a costume).[27] Verbs for "to see" are also used in their extended, figurative sense of "to realize," "to gain insight":

ESTUDIANTE 4: El tumulto comenzó cuando vieron que Romeo y Julieta se amaban de verdad.

ESTUDIANTE 2: Precisamente fue por todo lo contrario. El tumulto comenzó cuando observaron que no se amaban, que no podían amarse nunca. (111)

ESTUDIANTE 4: Vamos. Veréis cómo tengo razón. (113)

ESTUDIANTE 5: [. . .] no me queda tiempo para pensar si es hombre o mujer o niño, sino para ver que me gusta con un alegrísimo deseo. (119)

ESTUDIANTE 4: The uproar began when they saw that Romeo and Juliet really loved each other.

ESTUDIANTE 2: It was for precisely the opposite reason. The uproar began when they observed that they did not love each other, that they could never love each other.

ESTUDIANTE 4: Let's go. You will see that I am right.

ESTUDIANTE 5: [. . .] I don't have time to think about whether it's a man or a woman or a child but only to see that I like them with the most joyous of desires.

In the course of the overall sequence that I have been describing, it is normally presupposed that the resulting or eventual state will leave the person or people involved in possession of information, familiarity, understanding, insight, knowledge, or a truth that was not previously at their disposal. Predictably, the two verbs *conocer* and *saber* are well to the fore in assertions of this sort. Bertrand Russell reminds us that

[it] is in fact false, that we cannot know that anything exists which we do not know. The word "know" is here used in two different senses. (1) In its first use it is applicable to the sort of knowledge which is opposed to error, the sense in which what we know is true, the sense which applies to our beliefs and convictions, i.e. to what are called judgements. In this sense of the word we know that something is the case. This sort of knowledge may be described as knowledge of truths. (2) In the second use of the word "know" above, the word applies to our knowledge of things, which we may call acquaintance. This is the sense in which we know sense-data. (The distinction involved is roughly that between *savoir* and *connaître* in French, or between *wissen* and *kennen* in German.)[28]

Thus, the Figura de Cascabeles asks the Figura de Pámpanos: "¿Crees que no te conozco?" (Do you believe that I don't know you?) (62), and the Figura de Pámpanos jogs the Emperador's memory: "Tú me conoces" (You know me) (68); Hombre 3 boasts to his companions of "una bebida maravillosa que solamente conocen algunos negros de Honduras" (a marvelous drink that is only known by some Black people from Honduras) (74–75); Julieta scolds Caballo Blanco 1: "Todo lo que quieres enseñarme lo conozco perfectamente" (Everything that you want to reveal to me I [already] know perfectly), and a little later she reprimands him: "No me mires, caballo, con ese deseo que tan bien conozco" (Don't look at me, horse, with that desire that I know so well) (82).

Hombre 1 describes the Director as someone experienced in decor and stage design: "pero usted sabe que contra esto existe la hojalata" (but you know that to combat this there exists tin plate) (52); and there is a whole series of examples in which one character claims superior or greater knowledge than someone else. Hence, the Figura de Cascabeles to the Figura de Pámpanos: "Sé la manera de dominarte" (I know how to dominate you) (62), and later: "Ya sé lo que deseas" (I already know what you want) (65); the Figura de Pámpanos to the Emperador: "Tú sabes quién soy" (You know who I am) (68); Hombre 1 to Hombre 3: "Sabes que no te resisto" (You know that I can't hold out against you) (74); Hombre 3 to Hombre 1 and the Director: "Vosotros no sabéis que yo he descubierto una bebida maravillosa" (You don't know that I have discovered a marvelous drink) (74–75); the Director to Hombre 1: "Pero tú no sabes que Elena puede pulir sus manos dentro del fósforo y la cal viva" (But you don't know that Elena can buff her hands in phosphorus and quicklime) (75); Caballo Blanco 1 to Julieta and the other Caballos: "Yo estaba en el sepulcro la última noche y sé todo lo que pasó" (I was in the sepulchre this last night, and I know everything that happened) (87); and Hombre 1 to the Tres Caballos Blancos: "Pero yo sé positivamente que tres de vosotros se ocultan [. . .]. Yo sé la verdad, yo sé que no buscan a Julieta" (But I know for sure that three of you are hiding [your true nature] [. . .] I know the truth, I know that you are not interested in Juliet) (89–90). Furthermore, the Figura de Pámpanos attributes "sagacidad" (astuteness) to the Figura de Cascabeles (60) and Estudiante 4 the same quality to the audience (111).

Both main verbs (*conocer, saber*) lead naturally enough to the noun-adjective pair *verdad, verdadero* (truth, true), a lexical item that occurs with notable frequency throughout the text. I have already dwelled at some length on the notion of truth in the play in the previous chapter, so suffice it to say here that *verdad* appears on ten occasions (49, 57, 89 [two times], 90 [two times], 111, 118, 124, 126); *verdadero* on twelve (50, 82, 87, 89, 101, 112, 113, 119, 121, 125, 128 [two times]); and on one occasion each, the related notions of "seguro" (certain) (115), "indudablemente" (undoubtedly) (118), and "auténtico" (authentic) (128).

From this survey just completed, it can be seen that *El público* both alludes to and dramatizes the various stages in a general process of "finding things out," in that endeavor to move from a relative state of ignorance, uncertainty, or supposition to a relative state of familiarity, knowledge, or certainty. However, and even more importantly, the action and text of

El público also both refer to and indeed enact the breakdown and failure of that very same process:

> Pero el caso más elaborado de este tipo de desorden lo presenta la "verdad." No se trata ya de una presencia aislada sino de la recurrencia de un término especialmente marcado que, en cada una de sus reapariciones, parece remitir a un contexto distinto, a veces identificable, a veces no. Así, la "verdad"—transparente o irrecuperable—no sólo se incorpora al conjunto de los otros fragmentos sino que comporta en sí misma la fragmentación, la diferencia y el vacío.[29]

> But the most developed instance of this kind of disorder is presented by "truth." Now it is not a question of an isolated presence but, rather, of the recurrence of a specially marked term that, in each one of its reappearances, seems to allude to a different context, sometimes identifiable, sometimes not. Thus, "truth"—be it transparent or unrecoverable—not only joins the group of the other fragments but also entails in and of itself fragmentation, difference, and emptiness.

Against the ideas of ascertaining, construing, knowing, and truth are ranged a wide variety of lexical items that denote concealment, deception, falsehood, error, uncertainty, confusion, and ignorance. Some of them, such as *engañar/engaño, ocultar/oculto, mentir/mentira, fingir,* and *falso* (deceive/deceit; to hide / hidden; to lie / falsehood; to pretend; false), are all actions or states that can disrupt the process or bring about that breakdown of understanding, that induce doubt and confusion; others are terms that denote this resulting state. (Again, in the previous chapter, I devote a paragraph to the members of this first group that "all pertain to dissimulation and the concealment of true character, true sexuality, and true emotion in real life.")

That the process of finding things out is both fraught with difficulty and yet at the same time absolutely crucial is established early on in *El público,* when Hombre 2 presents the Director with a whole series of highly provocative questions about Romeo. Clearly shaken by this verbal "attack" and at something of a loss, the Director tries to avoid even making an attempt at an answer and so responds: "Señores, no es ése el problema" (Gentlemen, that is not the problem), but Hombre 1 immediately interrupts with the rejoinder: "No hay otro" (There is no other) (50). That knowledge is often lacking and that it is hard, if not impossible, to acquire are dramatized in the same scene, in which the Director and Hombres 1, 2, and 3 discuss Shakespeare's *Romeo and Juliet:*

DIRECTOR: Un hombre y una mujer que se enamoran. [. . .]

DIRECTOR: Pero nunca dejarán de ser Romeo y Julieta.

HOMBRE 1: Y enamorados. ¿Usted cree que estaban enamorados?

DIRECTOR: Hombre . . . Yo no estoy dentro . . .

HOMBRE 1: ¡Basta! ¡Basta! Usted mismo se denuncia. (48–49)

DIRECTOR: A man and a woman who fall in love. [. . .]

DIRECTOR: But they will never cease being Romeo and Juliet.

HOMBRE 1: And in love. Do you believe that they were in love?

DIRECTOR: What a question . . . I'm not inside . . .

HOMBRE 1: That's enough! That's enough! You're revealing yourself for what you are.

In a parallel fashion, Estudiante 4 points out that there is much still not known about the natural world: "Lo que pasa es que se sabe lo que alimenta un grano de trigo y se ignora lo que alimenta un hongo" (What happens is that we know how much a grain of wheat nourishes, and we don't know how much a mushroom nourishes) (113). People are also likely to commit oversights and to make errors in arriving at conclusions. Thus, the Ladrones turn up at the wrong time because, as they say, "se ha equivocado el traspunte" (the prompter made a mistake) (114), while Estudiante 1 puts his finger on what he considers a much more serious mistake: "Aquí está la gran equivocación de todos y por eso el teatro agoniza: el público no debe atravesar las sedas y los cartones que el poeta levanta en su dormitorio" (Here is the major mistake that everyone makes, and it's for this reason that the theater is in its death throes: the audience should not pierce the silks and the cardboards that the poet constructs in his bedroom) (112).[30]

(The last assertion can also be read as an attack on the biographical approach to the interpretation of literary texts and a reaffirmation of the author's necessary privacy.)

During the "Cuadro Quinto," Damas 1, 2, and 3 and the Muchacho repeatedly cross the stage, lost in the theater and trying desperately to find their way out, a goal that seems to be extremely difficult, if not, simply but significantly, impossible:

> DAMA 3: ¿No podremos salir?
> MUCHACHO 1: En este momento llega la revolución a la catedral. Vamos por la escalera. (*Salen.*) (111)

> MUCHACHO 1: (*Aparece con las* DAMAS.) ¡Por favor! No se dejen ustedes dominar por el pánico.
> DAMA 1: Es horrible perderse en un teatro y no encontrar la salida. [. . .]
> DAMA 3: Cuando subíamos por el monte de la ruina creímos ver la luz de la aurora, pero tropezamos con los telones [. . .]
> MUCHACHO 1: Por las ramas de aquel árbol podemos alcanzar uno de los balcones y desde allí pediremos auxilio. (115)

> DAMA 1: (*Por las escaleras.*) ¿Otra vez la misma decoración? ¡Es horrible!
> MUCHACHO 1: ¡Alguna puerta será la verdadera!
> DAMA 2: ¡Por favor! ¡No me suelte usted de la mano!
> MUCHACHO 1: Cuando amanezca nos guiaremos por las claraboyas. (121)

> DAMA 3: Won't we be able to get out?
> MUCHACHO 1: Just at this moment the revolution is reaching the cathedral. Let's go by the stairs. (*They exit.*)

> MUCHACHO 1: (*He appears with the* DAMAS.) Please! Don't give way to panic.
> DAMA 1: It's horrible getting lost in a theater and not finding the exit. [. . .]
> DAMA 3: When we were climbing up the hill of the ruin, we thought we saw the light of dawn, but we bumped into the curtains. [. . .]
> MUCHACHO 1: Over the branches of that tree, we'll be able to reach one of the balconies, and from there we'll ask for help.

> DAMA 1: (*From the staircase.*) The same scenery again? It's horrible!
> MUCHACHO 1: One of the doors will be the right one!

DAMA 2: Please! Don't let go of my hand!

MUCHACHO 1: When dawn breaks, we'll guide ourselves by the skylights.

To their fate we might compare that of the Señora (the mother of Gonzalo) in the "Cuadro Sexto," who cannot leave by any of the doors (130). All in all, then, there is a clear tendency to end up confused, one's bearings lost. As we have seen, there is much debate during the tomb scene ("Cuadro Tercero"), and in a speech again subsequently crossed out, Julieta pondered the rhetorical question: "¿Está bien que yo me encuentre ahora entre caballos sucios y más desorientada [de lo] que estaba?" (Is it acceptable that I should find myself now surrounded by dirty horses and more disoriented than I was?).[31] To conclude, it is worthwhile quoting once more Estudiante 3's summation of the results of the spectators' violent intervention: "¿Y qué han sacado en claro? Un racimo de heridas y una desorientación absoluta" (And what have they been able to discover? A cluster of wounds and an absolute confusion) (118).

Una desorientación absoluta, a phrase that seems to go well beyond the Prince of Verona's reference to "these ambiguities"—the Prince himself finding an analogue in *El público* in the figure of the "juez," the investigating magistrate who arrives on the scene to take charge of the criminal inquiries (113). Indeed, in the latter play, just about everything is thrown into doubt. The atmosphere of all-pervasive uncertainty is enhanced by the large number of questions contained in the dialogue. In a total of 623 individual speeches that I have counted, there were 166 interrogations (some single speeches obviously containing two or more questions), which works out at an incidence of something like 27 percent. The different Cuadros show quite a range of variation: "Cuadro Primero," 44 percent; "Cuadro Segundo," 38 percent; "Cuadro Tercero," 16 percent; "Cuadro Quinto," 26 percent; "Cuadro Sexto," 24 percent. The atmosphere of uncertainty is thus established particularly strongly at the start and then is maintained at a more moderate level throughout the rest of the play.

Clearly, then, there are more questions posed than answers offered here. When and if they stop to reflect, on Juliet/Julieta, on any and all of the aspects of love, on many other issues of identity, psychology, and motivation, on life and death themselves, all of the characters find themselves on distinctly shaky ground. As a kind of countermeasure against these dangerously shifting sands, Julieta, seconded by the Hombre 1 and Estudiantes 1 and 5, proclaims the simple desire to live and love, actively and in the here and now, a desire, however, far from completely fulfilled. Julieta is of course dead, trapped in her tomb, courted by insincere and devious suitors, and besieged by the inquisitive. The Hombre 1 ends up as the assassinated Romeo, the crucified Desnudo Rojo, and finally as "un enorme pez luna pálido, descompuesto" (an enormous pale moonfish, decomposed) (129). We do not know what becomes of the "ESTUDIANTE 5: (Huyendo por los arcos con el ESTUDIANTE 1.)" (ESTUDIANTE 5: [Fleeing through the arches with ESTUDIANTE 1.]) (121).

The characters' predicament within the play is paralleled by our own dilemmas in relation to it. Despite its overall somewhat allegorical flavor that on initial acquaintance seems to hold out the chimerical promise of a stable, recuperable "meaning," *El público* remains stubbornly enigmatic and is, in the last instance, radically self-reflexive. Given its formal, structural, and verbal complexities, first-time readers or spectators are very likely to come away feeling pretty baffled, but then with repeated readings and study, with the identification of patterns and the making of connections, things (some things at least) begin to fall into place. However, what we actually encounter, when and if this enterprise of "recognition" and "ordering" is undertaken, are mainly subversive messages in the text about its own reading and interpretation, messages that call into question the endeavor of interpretation itself and threaten the very foundations of conventional epistemology. Gómez Torres describes the play as "una historia que se disfraza y cambia en un mundo de espejos, un universo deslizante y resbaladizo donde el ser es inaprensible y el conocimiento humano está sujeto al engaño de las máscaras" (a story that disguises itself and changes in a world of mirrors, a sliding and slippery universe in which beings are incomprehensible and human knowledge is subject to the deceit of masks) and speaks of "una oleada de inquietud" (a wave of disquiet) that, as a result, overcomes the audience members.[32] Monegal, in a slightly different vein, calls *El público* "an illusion of a play that plays with illusions and uses undecidability to its advantage, to the extent that it can be seen as a necessary condition for the delivery of its message," and later points to "the impossibility of achieving a solution to the problem the play as such poses."[33]

El público does seem at moments to be on the brink of solipsism or aporia, flirting with the theatrical equivalent of "All I know is that I know nothing" or even approaching the nihilistic critical notion that "All interpretation is misinterpretation." As Derek Harris contends in the introduction to his edition: "En el fondo de la obra yace una amarga burla: el tema fundamental es la imposibilidad de representar el tema fundamental" (At the core of the work lies a bitter taunt: the fundamental theme is the impossibility of representing the fundamental theme).[34] Monegal likewise writes of "the attempt to represent a truth that escapes representation" and "the tension that underlies the effort to say by poetic means what cannot be said."[35] However, I believe (though I cannot, by definition, prove) that there are nevertheless substantive comments to be made about the play and very important things to be learned from it, as I have tried to illustrate in the preceding paragraphs.

El público emerges from this scrutiny clearly as Lorca's most adventurous, daring, exploratory, disconcerting, edgy, and forward-looking play, one that dramatizes the superiority of pure, direct, firsthand (literary or poetic) experience over mediated, secondhand (critical) cognition, even though it is much less confident as to the feasibility of achieving or sustaining that preferred kind of experience. Furthermore, and despite this precedence just mentioned, it is a play that, in literary-critical terms, still just responds to standard approaches and conventional modes of analysis. At the same time, however, *El público,* conceived in 1930, seems to be anticipating the more contemporary period and calling for other kinds of what, for want of a better word, we might provisionally call "metacriticism." It is in this, in part, that resides its striking modernity.

7

Destiny and Denial in
Así que pasen cinco años

The history of criticism concerned with *Así que pasen cinco años* is rather strange and surprising. The authors of some of the very early studies from the 1940s and 1950s professed to be baffled or to find the play deeply flawed, yet at the same time, several others displayed remarkable insight into its workings and themes. Indeed, I would venture to say that at the time, the latter group established a more solid interpretative framework for *Así que pasen* than had been achieved for Lorca's better-known plays. However, in subsequent decades, from about the mid-1960s onward, these pioneering books and articles were almost always overlooked or neglected, and an increasing number of commentators, having failed to perform more than a minimal amount of bibliographical research, tended to "reinvent the wheel," with the consequent result being that the same few basic ideas were repeated time and again with only minor variations. These ideas rapidly coalesced into a mainstream of closely aligned readings (from which, broadly speaking, I do not dissent); subsequently, interpretative advances were occasionally made in respect to one or other aspect of the play, and only a few truly divergent voices emerged. In this chapter, I shall comment briefly on the main landmarks and highlights of this uneven critical tradition and then move on to a consideration of various, more detailed aspects of the text that—in light of my examination of this body of secondary material—I have found to have received little or no attention, aspects that are closely connected with the two concepts in my title, of destiny and denial.[1]

For Edwin Honig, *Así que pasen* was "the [. . .] most difficult of Lorca's plays. Its unrealized possibilities become evident as the poet's brusque inventiveness outspeeds the progress of the slight dramatic theme."² Roberto Sánchez devotes less than three pages to it, finding a "raro estado de ánimo que domina la obra" (strange state of mind that dominates the work) obscured by "un velo de superrealismo" (a veil of Surrealism).³ François Nourissier was even more damning: "Peut-être d'ailleurs gêne-t-il aussi comme un échec? La tentative théâtrale de Lorca dans le sens surréaliste échoue" (Perhaps, in addition, it is bothersome like a failure? Lorca's theatrical attempt in the Surrealist vein fails).⁴

However, before any of these early studies were published, in Buenos Aires in 1941 Alfredo de la Guardia had essentially laid out the ground plan for approaching the play. With a remarkably cosmopolitan and comparativist vision, he identified a wide range of contemporary plays that displayed some parallel or coincidence with Lorca's (the playwrights whom he names are Lenormard, Strindberg, Maeterlinck, Kaiser, Luigi Antonelli, Sutton Vane, John L. Balderston, and Eugene O'Neill, to say nothing of Claudio de la Torre [*Tic-tac,* 1926]).⁵ As for the action of *Así que pasen,* he proposes that the protagonist falls asleep at the end of act 1 and wakes up at the end of act 3, scene 1, while adding that act 1 takes place "outside time."⁶ Ofelia Machado Bonet had read de la Guardia and for her part sees in the Joven a person who "vive una realidad de ensueño, como una emanación difuminada de su subconsciente" (lives a reality of daydreams, like an indistinct emanation from his subconscious).⁷ He and the Viejo are "las dos faces separadas del mismo ser dividido" (the two separated faces of the same divided self), and the Amigo 2° is "otra faz del joven" (another face of the Joven) while the Mecanógrafa and Amigo 1° manifest more "rotunda solidez" (decisive solidity).⁸ Still, she comes to conclude that "todos los personajes de esta obra son como aspectos diferentes del mismo, del principal, el joven" (all the characters in this work are like different aspects of the same one, the main one, the Joven) and that the play depicts "el mundo arcano de lo subconsciente, con su incoherencia aparente y su intemporalidad" (the arcane world of the subconscious, with its apparent incoherence and its timelessness).⁹ Ramón Xirau goes one better, claiming that as act 1 opens, we are at "la entrada de un mundo de sueños" (the entrance to a world of dreams); he wrestles with the conflicting chronological indications, wondering "el tiempo (¿pasa a lo largo de toda la obra?)" (time [does it pass over the course of the work?]) and as a result finds that "hay que tratarlo [el drama] como trataríamos un sueño" (it is necessarily to treat it [the drama] as we would treat a dream).[10] Still, his main emphasis is on what he conceives of as its strongly existentialist themes.

It was thus, as far as I am aware, Margot Arce and Eugenio Granell who, in a special number of the journal *La Torre* and on the occasion of a production of the play, pursued these early readings to their logical conclusion. Arce writes:

> Obra de carácter psicológico, la acción externa se presenta como simbólica de los estados mentales del Joven, del protagonista. Los otros personajes, casi todos proyecciones, alter egos suyos, sirven para comunicar movimiento y visualidad exterior al drama que se desarrolla en la honda intimidad de su conciencia.[11]

> A work of a psychological nature, its external action is presented as symbolic of the mental states of the Joven, the protagonist. The other characters, almost all projections, alter egos of him, serve to communicate movement and outward visuality in the work that develops in the deep intimacy of his consciousness.

Granell, for his part, perceives "un ser humano en trance de discurrir para sus adentros" (a human being on the path of thinking inwardly). He states directly that "los interlocutores de un coloquio mental son los desdoblamientos del sujeto" (the interlocutors of a mental conversation are the doublings of the subject) and that "el drama sucede en la mente del Joven" (the drama takes place in the mind of the Joven.)[12]

Ofelia Kovacci and Nélida Salvador (who do not cite any of the previously mentioned critics but do allude to others) take a step back from this position. For them, "el primer acto y el segundo cuadro del tercero parecen formar un marco dentro del cual se proyectan el segundo acto y el primer cuadro del tercero con un grado mayor de abstracción, ya que se trataría de una proyección de la mente del Joven" (the first act and the second scene of the third seem to form a frame within which the second act and the first scene of the third are projected with a greater degree of abstraction, since [here] it would be a question of a projection of the mind of the Joven). However, later on they hedge their bets by writing that "el Joven aparece en el segundo cuadro del último acto como volviendo de un viaje (era la Novia quien viajaba), lo que sugiere que todo el conflicto no es más que la ambigüedad interior del personaje mismo" (the Joven appears in the second scene of the last act as if returning from a journey [it was the Novia who was traveling], which suggests that the whole conflict is no more than the internal ambiguity of the selfsame character).[13] It fell to Robert Lima to restate as plainly as possible, and for the first time in English, the viewpoint proposed by Arce and Granell: "The 'reality' of the action takes place in the amorphous mind of El Joven. He is the only real person in the play. All the personages are no more than physical representations of his varied thoughts, his personalities, his desires."[14]

We thus arrive at R. G. Knight's rightly influential article. He does not appear to have consulted de la Guardia, Machado Bonet, Xirau, Arce, Granell, Kovacci and Salvador, or Lima, but nonetheless, he does pull together the various interpretative strands that I have been tracing and proposes the most consistent and comprehensive reading to date. Specifically, he contends that "the play is in fact a daydream; that is, the only action is that which occurs in the Joven's mind," and hence "there is only one real person in the whole play, the Joven. All the others either represent the different elements in the spiritual struggle or are projections from the nonhuman sphere."[15] From there, it is but a short step for us to see the whole action of the play not necessarily as a daydream but as the enacted representation of a sleeping dream, a nightmare, or a feverish hallucination. At the time no one knew the article by Valentín de Pedro in which Margarita Xirgu recounted Lorca's own explanation of his work to her: "*Así que pasen cinco años* es una obra que se desarrolla fuera del tiempo y de la realidad, en la cabeza del protagonista: son presentimientos, sueños . . . , todo lo que se agita en el subconsciente" (*Así que pasen cinco años* is a work that unfolds outside time and reality, in the head of the protagonist: they are premonitions, dreams . . . , everything that is churning in the subconscious).[16]

From 1966 onward, therefore, this has remained the mainstream reading of the play, to which other elements were sometimes grafted and, more rarely, against which an alternative vision was offered. Thus, Victor

Sapojnikoff was the first to see the Joven as a homosexual figure, a proposal echoed later by several others,[17] while Rupert Allen argued that "the protagonist's condition accumulates psychotic proportions" and finds in the play a portrayal of "a schizophrenic process leading to catatonia,"[18] a perspective taken up later by Farris Anderson.[19] Eutimio Martín identified an important source in Victor Hugo's *Légende du beau Pécopin et de la belle Bauldour* (from *Le Rhin*).[20] Luis Fernández-Cifuentes was the first to connect the play's theme of the passage of time with contemporary theories associated with Henri Bergson and Einstein.[21] More radically, C. Christopher Soufas hypothesizes a "mature adult" as protagonist, in whose dream the Joven embodies the past and the Viejo the present and future.[22]

The theme of time and the Joven's changing attitudes toward temporality have also been discussed very extensively. In act 1 his retreat into his house, and more particularly into his library or den within the house (191, 216), and in parallel his retreat into the world of the mind or the imagination, represent an attempt to shut himself away from visible reminders of passing time and almost to deny temporality itself,[23] aiming thus for a kind of (illusory) fixity or immutability, one that can only exist inside the mind ("debajo de la frente"; "lo de adentro" [under the forehead; what goes on inside], 202–3). In contrast, to engage with the present and the outside world implies dealing with the here and now: "¿No le angustia la hora de la partida, los acontecimientos, lo que ha de llegar ahora mismo?" (Don't you find distressing the time for departure, events, what is going to come about right now?) (197). Furthermore, to enter and be immersed in the flow of time also immediately obliges one to look toward the future, a consequence that he seeks to avoid by limiting himself to a kind of abstracted or idealized love:[24]

Mire usted, la última vez que la [la Novia] vi no podía mirarla muy de cerca porque tenía dos arruguitas en la frente que, como me descuidara . . . ¿entiende usted? le llenaban todo el rostro y la ponían ajada, vieja, como si hubiera sufrido mucho. Tenía necesidad de separarme para . . . ¡enfocarla!, ésta es la palabra, en mi corazón. (203)[25]

Consider this: the last time that I saw her [the Novia] I couldn't look at her close up because she had two tiny wrinkles in her forehead that, if I weren't careful . . . do you understand? filled her whole face and turned her haggard, old, as if she had suffered a lot. I needed to separate myself in order to . . . focus her! that's the word, in my heart.

Here *enfocarla* implies holding her (his perception of her) steady in his mind in one fixed moment of time. In adopting this stance, the Joven finds himself closest to the Viejo among the three figures arrayed around him, but it is important to note that they are not fully aligned. Furthermore, when we reach act 2, the Joven has moved closer to Amigo 1° ("ahora gano mi sueño" [now I am achieving my dream], 268), while in act 3, scene 1, the Joven tries to turn back the clock to rekindle the relationship with the Mecanógrafa, and in scene 2 he reminisces about his childhood, both of which place him closer to Amigo 2° (335–37).

In act 1, on the one hand, the Joven and the Viejo agree with regard to the postponement of pleasure ("Yo guardaba los dulces para comerlos después" [I used to keep the candies to eat them later] [192]) and on the benefits of waiting: "JOVEN: Esperando, el nudo se deshace y la fruta madura" (JOVEN: By waiting, the knot comes undone and fruit ripens) (234); "VIEJO: Esperar es creer y vivir" (VIEJO: Waiting is believing and living) (207). On the other, the Joven's withdrawal into himself is signaled by the verb *pensar:* "JOVEN: (*Se levanta.*) ¡Pienso tanto! | VIEJO: ¡Sueña tanto! | JOVEN: ¿Cómo? | VIEJO: Piensa tanto que . . ." (JOVEN: [*Getting up.*] I think so much! | VIEJO: You dream so much! | JOVEN: What? | VIEJO: You think so much that . . .) (200–201; and cf. 212), while the Viejo is associated with living in the future via the disconcerting idea of "recordar antes" or "recordar hacia mañana" (remembering before; remembering toward tomorrow) (194), and later he distances himself completely from the act of recalling the past: "No recuerdo nada" (I don't remember anything) (235); "JOVEN: Usted la vio en mi casa, ¿no recuerda? | VIEJO: "No recuerdo" (JOVEN: You saw her in my house, don't you remember? | VIEJO: I don't remember) (289).

Needless to say, neither the Joven nor his three interlocutors in act 1 are fully successful in their respective denials. Dents in walls, weeds, and broken pieces of furniture penetrate the Joven's defenses, and he can only aspire to keep "todos sus perfiles intactos" (all their profiles intact) (193). The Viejo acknowledges that the lifestyle he proposes—"volar de una cosa a otra hasta perderse" (to fly from one thing to another until you lose your-self)—is only a form of avoidance: "es más hermoso pensar que todavía mañana, veremos los cien cuernos de oro con que levanta a las nubes el sol" (it is more pleasant to think that still tomorrow, we shall see the hundred golden horns with which the sun lifts the clouds) (205–6), and grudgingly, he is obliged to use the past tense (215). Amigo 1°'s extreme implementation of carpe diem ends up with the result "que me quedo sin ninguna [conquista] porque no tengo tiempo" (that I've been left with none [no conquest] because I don't have time) (211), while Amigo 2° is forced to admit that despite his best efforts to remain young or indeed to turn back the clock, "quiero vivir lo mío y me lo quitan" (I want to live what belongs to me, and it is taken away from me) (237).

Now, the closest corollaries of temporality are mutability, decay, and mortality. Thus, interwoven with the delineation of the four existential attitudes of the Joven, Viejo, Amigo 1°, and Amigo 2° and some suggestions of the limitations of each, we encounter a number of explicit reminders of the human condition. The Viejo indirectly quotes Heraclitus: "El agua que viene por el río es completamente distinta de la que se va" (The water that comes with the river is completely different from that which goes) (202) and later states sententiously: "Los trajes se rompen, las anclas se oxidan" (Clothes rip and tear, anchors rust) and "Se hunden las casas" (Houses fall down) (238). Amigo 2° expresses his fear of aging—"no quiero estar lleno de arrugas y dolores como usted" (I don't want to be covered with wrinkles and full of aches and pains like you) (237)—and his extreme disinclination to enter into adulthood (238). Death is mentioned on a number of occasions: directly by Amigo 1°: "Todo eso no es más que miedo a la muerte" (All that is nothing more than fear of death) (237), and metaphorically by the Viejo: "Se apagan los ojos y una hoz muy afilada siega los juncos de las orillas" (The eyes are extinguished and a very sharp sickle reaps the reeds of the riverbanks) (240). The long conversation in act 1 is interrupted by the doubly unreal scene of the Niño and Gato/Gata (217–30), who find themselves in a kind of limbo prior to interment. Further mentions of them reverberate through all three acts (231–32, 238, 265, 270, 293, 301, 304–6, 319–20, 322–23, 332–34), and as becomes increasingly clear as the play progresses, the dead child represents not only a tragic case of infant mortality but also, as Gérard Lavergne and José Ángel Valente point out,[26] the Joven's lost childhood (the child in him that "died" in order for him to become the adult that he is today) as well as the child of his own that he desires (as he comes to realize in the dialogue with the Maniquí [282–86]), a child that is never to be engendered but if born would have constituted a kind of Unamunian immortality for him.[27] Arguing with the Novia, the Joven insists that she has to go with him "para que no muera. ¿Lo oyes? Para que no muera" (so that I don't die. Do you hear me? So that I don't die) (272); later he tells the Mecanógrafa, "me parece que agonizo sin ti" (it seems to me that I am dying without you) (321), and shortly afterward the dead child silently crosses the stage (322).

Perhaps the most ominous reference of all comes from an unlikely source, Amigo 2°: "dentro de cuatro o cinco años existe un pozo en el que caeremos todos" (within four or five years, there exists a well into which we will all fall) (240).[28] This notion, of future inevitability coupled with a specific time frame, leads us to that of the *emplazado,*[29] a topic already treated by Lorca in the ballad of that same name, the "Romance del emplazado" (*Romancero gitano*). Broadly speaking, *emplazado* refers to someone summoned by an authority to appear before them at a certain point in the future; the *plazo* is the intervening period of time between the receipt of the order and the appointed date. While the authority can be a magistrate, a king, or some such, often the idea is that the person is summoned by God. However long the *plazo* is, the time will ebb away, the date fixed will be reached, and the future will become the present. Of course, Amigo 2°'s lapidary statement closely echoes the title of the play that enshrines the other *plazo,* the one that is supposed to be nuptial in nature: "JOVEN: Yo no me casaré con ella . . . hasta que pasen cinco años" (JOVEN: I will not marry her . . . until five years have passed) (196), and both periods of time coincide in Victor Hugo's *Légende.*[30] There Pécopin leaves Bauldour when she is fifteen, is away on his travels for five years, but is possessed of a talisman given to him by a sultana that prevents him from aging. One day he stumbles into the "bois des pas perdus" (forest of lost steps) from which supposedly there is no escape, but he encounters a gentleman (the devil) who promises to return him to Bauldour if he will only spend one night of hunting with him. At daybreak he finds himself back at the castle but discovers that in his absence, Bauldour has aged not five years but is now almost one hundred, while he is still his youthful self. Curiously, in one of the dreams recounted by Freud in *The Interpretation of Dreams*, we find this: "*Four or five years*—that is [. . .] the time during which I kept my bride waiting before I married her; [. . .]. '*What are five years?*' ask the dream thoughts. '*That is no time at all for me*'" (344).

Another significant thread in existing criticism on *Así que pasen* is focused on the *auto sacramental* and Calderón. In a fine but largely overlooked essay of 1972, Simone Saillard takes a cue from comments in an interview given in the 1930s—Lorca described *Así que pasen* as "un misterio, dentro de las características de este género, un misterio sobre el tiempo" (a mystery play, within the characteristics of that genre, a mystery play about time)[31]—and proposes that the debate in act 1 between the four individuals be seen as an extended allegory reminiscent of an *auto sacramental*.[32] Margarita Ucelay, Nadine Ly, and Gérard Lavergne concur.[33] Also relevant here is one of Lorca's earliest plays, *Teatro de almas* (1917, unfinished), in which the opening stage direction reads, "La escena en el teatro maravilloso de nuestro mundo interior" (The setting in the marvelous theater of our internal world), and in which the dramatis personae was to include Los Sueños, La Lujuria, El Amor, El Bien, El Mal, Un Hombre, Una Estrella, La Sombra de Cristo, La Muerte, and Voces (92).[34]

The genre of the *auto sacramental* leads us directly to Calderón, and we know that Lorca engaged with that playwright in a number of ways.[35] In a 1935 interview, he said of his own characters, "Son reales, desde luego. Pero, todo tipo real encarna un símbolo" (They are real, of course. But every real type embodies a symbol), and he went on to state that "la raíz de mi teatro es calderoniana. Teatro de magia [. . .] salto de lo real a lo real simbólico, en el sentido poético de obtener ideas vestidas, no puros símbolos" (the root of my theater is Calderonian. Theater of magic [. . .] I jump from the real to the symbolically real, in the poetic sense of obtaining clothed ideas, not pure symbols).[36] Calderón's *auto sacramental El gran teatro del mundo* was staged in Granada in 1927, with Lorca's brother Francisco in the role of El Mundo and with the direction, set and costume design, music, and orchestral direction undertaken by four friends of his, Antonio Gallego Burín, Hermenegildo Lanz, Manuel de Falla, and Ángel Barrios.[37] La Barraca's production of *La vida es sueño (auto sacramental)* was first given in Soria in July 1932, with Lorca in the role of La Sombra.

We have the text of Lorca's presentation of the play, and here he asserted that in Calderón's "teatro religioso" (religious theater), "el drama lo llevan los símbolos, lo llevan los elementos de la naturaleza" (the drama is carried along by symbols, it is carried along by the elements of nature) and also that "los símbolos siguen [siendo] símbolos, dentro de la más estricta disciplina, los pensamientos se enlazan con rigor dogmático, y la escapada al misterio va provista de telescopios seguros y divinos reflectores" (the symbols continue to be symbols, within the strictest discipline, thoughts are connected to each other with dogmatic rigor, and the escape to mystery is equipped with reliable telescopes and divine spotlights).[38] In 1936 a newspaper reported on a brand-new play that Lorca was working on:

—Que la obra no tiene título aún, pero que el que más le cuadraría hubiese sido *La vida es sueño.*
—Que ese título ya lo "utilizó" Calderón . . .
—Que, de todas formas, el título será parecido a ese.[39]

—That the work still has no title, but that the one that would fit it best would have been *La vida es sueño.*
—That that title was already "used" by Calderón . . .
—That, in any event, the title will be similar to that one.

True to this "rumor," the title that Lorca eventually settled on was *El sueño de la vida.*[40]

If we consult the text of *La vida es sueño (auto sacramental)*, we find a number of passages that seem to connect in some way with *Así que pasen*, a case of intertextuality largely overlooked by previous commentators. The character Sabiduría (representative of Christ in the Trinity) introduces himself thus:

yo, para quien el presente
tiempo solamente es fijo,
pues si miro hacia el pasado,
y si hacia el futuro miro,   335
es tiempo presente todo,

futuro o pasado siglo;
habiendo con mi presencia
en ese dorado libro
de once hojas de cristal⁴¹   340
previsto al hombre (139)⁴²

I for whom only the present
time is fixed,
for if I look toward the past,
and if I look toward the future,
everything is present time,
[both] future or past century;
having with my presence
in that gilded book
of eleven leaves of crystal
foreseen man

He foresees that, if created, humankind will commit original sin and bring
death into the world:

Pero ¿qué mucho, si habiendo   362
una vez introducido
la palidez de la muerte
sus últimos parasismos,   365
será tan universal
el morir? (139–40)

But how overwhelming [would it be] if,
the pallor of death
having once ushered in
its last paroxysms,
dying will be so universal?

When Hombre is freed from the rock, El Príncipe de las Tinieblas and Sombra
are angered and envious, since so much has been given to him and yet he is
only "sujeto / a más que a un leve preceto!" (subject to no more than a mild

precept) (153). This precept, of course, is to follow Luz/Gracia and to exercise his free will for good. Sombra outlines a plan to El Príncipe to bring about Hombre's downfall:

La Culpa, si introducida
se ve, ¿que será, no advierte,
otra imagen de la muerte?
[. . .] Mientras la vida   770
durare, también el sueño
¿de la muerte no será
otra imagen? [. . .]
Luego posible es mi empeño,
si al hombre en su paz le asombra,   775
sueño que de muerte es
imagen, muerte después
que es culpa, y culpa que es sombra; (153–54)

Sin, if once introduced,
do you not realize that it will be
another image of death?
[. . .] While life lasts,
will not dream also
be another image of death?
[. . .] Then my undertaking is possible,
if man asleep is amazed
by a dream that is an image
of death, death afterward
that is sin, and sin that is darkness;

And he proposes that together they prepare a sleeping draft.

Later Sombra offers Hombre a "dorada poma" (gilded apple) (167), prompting a warning from Entendimiento:

Mira
que quizá en el Aire fundas
altas torres, y que suelen

ser soñadas las venturas;
y podrá ser, si despiertas,   1185
que entre fantasmas confusas
todo esto vuelva a la nada. (167–68)

Watch out,
for perhaps you are building
tall towers in the air,
and happiness and good fortune are usually dreamed;
and it could be, if you awake,
that all this might return to nothingness
among indistinct phantoms.

As soon as he eats the "vedada fruta" (forbidden fruit) (169), the Fall is rendered as an earthquake and the extinguishing of light, he is shunned by all the other characters, and he falls into a profound sleep:

¿Qué mucho, pues, ¡ay de mí!
si todos me desahucian,
que en brazos de letal sueño,
negra Sombra de la Culpa,   1280
pues dejó a la muerte viva,
deje a la vida difunta? (171)

So, how overwhelming, woe is me!
if everyone and everything give up on me as a lost cause,
[and] that in the arms of a mortal dream,
the black Shadow of Sin,
since it left death alive,
should [now] leave life dead?

He talks in his sleep, dreaming that he "competir puedo a mi padre" (can rival my father) and that he is an "inmortal príncipe soy del orbe" (immortal prince of the world) (175). On awakening, he is astounded by what he dreamed and initially wonders how much confidence he should have in it:

> ¡Válgame el cielo,
> qué de cosas he soñado! . . .
> Pero ¿qué me desconfía
> presumir que sueño fue,   1405
> si por lo menos saqué
> de él, según mi fantasía,
> saber quién soy? (175–76)

> Oh my God,
> what things I have dreamed! . . .
> But, why does assuming
> that it was a dream
> make me have doubts,
> if at least I got from it,
> according to my imaginings,
> finding out who I am?

Later, though, he comes to question everything:

> ¿Quién me dirá cuál ha sido   1440
> en mis mudanzas más cierto,
> lo que allá soñé despierto,
> o lo que aquí veo dormido? (177)

> Who can tell me which has been
> more true in my inconstancy,
> what I dreamed there awake,
> or what I see here asleep?

In dialogue with Sombra, Hombre wonders if the time in Paradise was only imagined, but Sombra corrects him:

> HOMBRE: ¿Luego no fué
>   sueño?
> SOMBRA: Sí fué; que, pasada,
>   ¿qué ventura no es soñada? (178)

HOMBRE: So then, it wasn't a
   dream?
SOMBRA: Yes it was; for, once in the past,
   what joy or good fortune is not dreamed?

Nonetheless, Hombre still harbors delusions of grandeur, which obliges Sombra to disabuse him further:

HOMBRE: Príncipe heredero soy,
   y que aquella majestad
   no fué sueño, iré a cobralla.
SOMBRA: Sueño fue para ese empeño,   1485
   que toda la *vida es sueño.* (178)

HOMBRE: I am a hereditary prince,
   and since that majesty
   was not a dream, I shall go and claim it.
SOMBRA: As regards this resolve of yours, it was a dream,
   since all *life is a dream.*

Hombre realizes his mistake, and the process of redemption follows, culminating in the crucifixion of Christ (Sabiduría) and His resurrection. For theatrical purposes, the period of three days is rendered as a single moment, as explained by Sombra:

Ya que sincopado el tiempo,   1760
en representable escena,
el término de tres días
a sólo un instante abrevias,
volviendo de mí triunfante
a segunda vida, (188)   1765

Since time is shortened
into a performable scene,
you compress the lapse of three days

into only a single instant,
returning triumphant from me [darkness]
to a second life,

Finally, as the play ends, Poder (God the Father) drives the point home: "cuanto vives sueñas / porque al fin la *vida es sueño*" (whatever you live through you dream, / because in the end *life is a dream*) (194).

Here, then, the idea of the temporal coincidence of past, present, and future is mentioned at the beginning of the *auto sacramental,* and at the end, the compression of time for theatrical purposes is explained. In *The Interpretation of Dreams,* Freud critiques certain contemporary theories concerning dream life, namely that it "can regard itself supreme in reference to distance of time and space" and also "that the dream can crowd together more perception content in a very short space of time than can be controlled by our psychic activity in the waking mind" (53). Still, Calderón's three days in an instant is analogous to Lorca's five years in some three hours (the approximate running time of the play) or indeed five years in a few moments (the likely duration of the Joven's dream).[43]

Thematically, the *auto* presents a number of clearly relevant ideas: the notion of original sin and the introduction of human mortality into the world, the difficulty of distinguishing between a dream state and waking reality, the problematic consequences of confusing one with the other, the insubstantiality of human fantasies, the fleetingness of human happiness, and hence the final morality lesson that "toda la *vida es sueño.*"

One other passage of the text remains to be commented on, and it, like several others, connects the *auto* with the *comedia* of the same title on which it is based:

SABIDURÍA: Yo, que sé todas las ciencias,   324
            de que son fieles testigos
            los astros (pues que no hay
            en todo ese azul zafiro,
            encuadernado volumen
            de quien el sol es registro,
            ninguno que por su nombre330
            no llame, adverso o propicio). (138–39)

SABIDURÍA: I who have knowledge of all the sciences,
of which the stars are faithful witnesses
(for there is not
in all that sapphire blue [sky],
a bound volume
of which the sun is the clasp,
any [star] that by its name
I do not call adverse or propitious).

Likewise, in *La vida es sueño (comedia)*, King Basilio gives a lengthy speech, which starts by laying out his studies in astrology and his abilities in predicting the future (act 1, lines 612–43), a skill that in a sense sets him above time (615–17, 622–23).[44] However, he has experienced great sadness at having read his own tragedy in the stars (644–59). He recounts the details of his wife's pregnancy and his son's birth (660–79), the doom-laden auguries that accompanied it (680–707), and his own dire astrological predictions (708–29), which resulted in him locking Segismundo away in an isolated tower (730–51). Not only did Clorilene die in childbirth, but Segismundo:

nació en horóscopo tal	680
que el sol, en su sangre tinto,	
entraba sañudamente	
con la luna en desafío;	
y, siendo valla la tierra,	
los dos faroles divinos	685
a luz entera luchaban,	
ya que no a brazo partido.	
El mayor, el más horrendo	
eclipse que ha padecido	
el sol, después que con sangre	690
lloró la muerte de Cristo,	
éste fue, porque anegado	
el orbe, entre incendios vivos,	
presumió que padecía	
el último parasismo:	695

los cielos se escurecieron,
temblaron los edificios,
llovieron piedras las nubes,
corrieron sangre los ríos. (152–53)[45]

was born under such a horoscope
that the sun, stained red in its blood,
entered furiously
into [a jousting] combat with the moon;
and, with the earth as the [tilt] barrier [between them]
the two divine lamps
fought full light against light,
but not arm to arm [tooth and nail].
This was the greatest, the most horrendous
eclipse that the sun has endured,
which afterward wept
with blood for the death of Christ,
because, with the world engulfed
by intense fires,
it assumed that it was suffering
its last death throes:
the skies darkened,
the buildings shook,
the clouds rained hailstones,
the rivers ran as blood.

Returning now to *Así que pasen,* the aforementioned idea of a person being *emplazado* brings with it the closely associated concept of destiny, and specifically of a destiny known in advance. If at the same time we remember that the Padre's hobby is astronomy and that in act 2 he hopes to observe an eclipse of the moon—both details that have received little attention from critics of the play[46]—we can see that there is another connection with Calderón here, one that provides a set of ideas and a vein of imagery that Lorca capitalizes upon in important ways.

The Viejo, who claims to be a good friend of the family, nonetheless mocks the Padre's amateur pursuit when it is first mentioned (195), an attitude seemingly justified when the Novia's father first comes onstage: "(Entra EL PADRE DE LA NOVIA. Es un viejo distraído. Lleva unos prismáticos colgados al cuello. Peluca blanca. Cara rosa. Lleva guantes blancos y traje negro. Tiene detalles de una delicada miopía.)" (EL PADRE DE LA NOVIA enters. He is an absent-minded old man. He has some binoculars hanging around his neck. White wig. Pink face. He wears white gloves and a black suit. He shows signs of a mild shortsightedness.) (260). Technically, shortsightedness should not necessarily be a hindrance for an astronomer, but it does speak to his overall characterization, and a pair of binoculars is a poor substitute for a large and powerful telescope. Furthermore, the Padre is no Basilio, and while he did take the Novia on a five-year cruise around the world, during which time she reportedly did not socialize and remained isolated in her cabin (261), at home he is unable to exercise any paternal authority over her (262–63).

Stars are only mentioned explicitly twice in the text, but on both occasions, they are charged with significance. In Calderón's *comedia,* it is no coincidence that the woman who aspires to the throne of Poland is called Estrella and that Rosaura, in her second disguise, adopts the name of Astrea. At the beginning of the scene between Niño and Gato, "Los tres personajes se ocultan detrás de un biombo negro bordado con estrellas" (The three characters hide behind a black folding screen covered with embroidered stars) (217), and during that dialogue, the Niño recounts details of the preparations for his burial: "un hombre con martillo iba clavando / estrellas de papel sobre mi caja" (a man with a hammer was nailing / paper stars on to my box) (219). While an ominous darkening of the sky has been caused by the approaching summer storm—"La luz desciende y una luminosidad azulada de tormenta invade la escena" (The light dims and the bluish luminosity of a storm fills the stage) (217), it is still only early evening in the summertime (195). The black folding screen decorated with stars therefore represents the night sky and—literally and figuratively— serves as the backdrop for the scene between the dead cat and the dead child in the intermediate limbo that they temporarily occupy. The same imagery is picked up by the decorative paper stars affixed to his coffin. The Niño shares with the Gato his fears of what awaits them in the grave, since "no es el cielo" (it's not heaven) (226) (*cielo* is to be taken primarily in its sense of heaven, as earlier he commented that "no vinieron los ángeles. No" [the angels didn't come. No] [219]). Furthermore "nunca veremos la luz" (we'll never see the light) (227), and the sun "apagado va por el cielo" (extinguished goes across the sky) (228).

Lighting effects are important throughout the play, and a bluish tone is first called for in act 1, as we just saw: "La luz desciende y una luminosidad azulada de tormenta invade la escena" (217). It appears again in act 3: "El efecto de este personaje debe ser el de una llamarada sobre el fondo de azules lunares y troncos nocturnos" (The effect of this character should be that of a flash against the background of lunar blues and nocturnal trunks) (303). However, it predominates in act 2, in which (as in the last example) it is largely, but not exclusively, attributed to moonlight. Leaving aside the monochromes of white, gray, and black, blue is also the most dominant color of characters' costumes and props. Its strongest association is with the Joven (191, 230, 273, 308).[47] As the act 2 scene opens, "Los balcones están abiertos y por ellos entra la luna" (The balconies are open, and through them the moon enters) (245), and later the Novia "Enciende la luz del techo. Una luz más azulada que la que entra por los balcones" (Turns on the ceiling light. A more bluish light than that which enters through the balconies) (248). Just as in act 1 "la luz desciende" (the light dims) (217) immediately before the appearance of the Niño and Gato, so here, at the moment of the transition to the sequence involving the Joven and the Maniquí, "La luz de la escena se oscurece. Las bombillas de los ángeles toman una luz azul. Por los balcones vuelve a entrar una luz de luna que irá en aumento hasta el final" (The stage lighting gets dark. The light bulbs held by the angels take on a blue light. Through the balconies, moonlight again enters, and it will gradually increase up to the end [of the scene]) (276). By the end, "La luz es de un azul intenso" (The light is an intense blue). When the Criada enters, the Maniquí freezes, and the main lighting changes back: "Entra la CRIADA por la izquierda con un candelabro y la escena toma suavemente su luz normal, sin descuidar la luz azul de los balcones abiertos de par en par que hay en el fondo" (The CRIADA enters from the left with a candelabra, and the stage smoothly takes on its normal light, without forgetting the blue light from the wide-open balconies that are in the background) (287). Just before the curtain falls, when everybody else has left, the Maniquí is reanimated, and again "Queda la escena azul y el MANIQUÍ avanza dolorido" (The stage turns blue, and the MANIQUÍ comes forward, sorrowful) (291).

The balconies that are open to the moonlight are those of the Novia's boudoir; through them her paramour, the Jugador de Rugby, makes his clandestine entrance and exit (a distant echo of Romeo and Juliet?), and from them the Padre plans to observe the eclipse. The moon first becomes a point of conversation between the Novia and the Criada, who seems to think of the Joven as a romantic:

> CRIADA: Su novio busca otra cosa. En mi pueblo había un muchacho que subía a la torre de la iglesia para mirar más de cerca la luna, y su novia lo despidió.
>
> NOVIA: ¡Hizo bien!
>
> CRIADA: Decía que veía en la luna el retrato de su novia. (257)

> CRIADA: Your fiancé is looking for something else. In my village there was a boy who used to go up to the church tower to see the moon more closely, and his girlfriend broke it off with him.
>
> NOVIA: She did the right thing!
>
> CRIADA: He said he saw the portrait of his girlfriend in the moon.

In trying to observe the moon more closely by climbing the tower, the young man from the village was acting, in a sense, as the most rudimentary of astronomers in his attempt to compensate for the lack of any device of optical magnification. Pertinent here, too, would be the Joven's childhood memory: "La [cama] de nogal tallado. ¡Qué bien se dormía en ella! Recuerdo que, siendo niño, vi nacer una luna enorme detrás de la barandilla de sus pies. . . . ¿O fue por los hierros del balcón?" (The carved walnut bed. How well one slept in it! I remember that when I was a child, I saw an enormous moon rising behind the spindles of its footboard. . . . Or was it through the wrought-iron railings of the balcony?) (337).

The moon looms largest, however, in the poetic dialogue between the Joven and the Maniquí. The mannequin wearing the wedding dress tearfully laments the fact that the bridal garland of white orange blossom will not be used and now appears to be a halo (?) around the moon:

¿Quién usará la plata buena
de la novia chiquita y morena?
Mi cola se pierde por el mar
y la luna lleva puesta mi corona de azahar. (277)

Who will use the good silver
of the little dark-haired bride?
The train of my dress is lost in the sea
and the moon is wearing my orange blossom garland.

The many images of whiteness—"azahar," "traje," "velo," "ropa interior,"
"nieve," "encajes," "espumas," "escarcha," "camisa," "nardo," "blanca seda"
(orange blossom; [wedding] dress; veil; underwear; snow; lace; foam;
frost; chemise; spikenard; white silk) (277–81)—point to the disjunction
between the traditional symbolism of the purity of a bride about to marry
and the coldness and sterility of the unused and abandoned. Answering
the Maniquí's question, "¿Quién usará la ropa buena [. . .]? (Who will use
the good clothes [. . .]?)" (278), the Joven, apparently resigned to his failure, first echoes her with similar ideas:

Se la pondrá el aire oscuro
jugando al alba en su gruta,
ligas de raso los juncos,
medias de seda la luna. (278)

The dark wind will put them on,
pretending to be dawn in its cavern,
the reeds will put on the satin garters,
and the moon the silk stockings.

And likewise: "Y la luna lleva en vilo tu corona de azahar" (And the moon
carries off into the air your garland of orange blossom) (280).

However, after the Maniquí manages to change the Joven's mind by
showing him the pink baby outfit (282)—and in this section of the dialogue, there are more ambivalent images of both fertility and sterility:
"leche blanca," "dolor blanco," "jazmines de cordura," "niño de nieve"

(white milk; white sorrow; jasmines of good sense; child of snow) (282–85)—he resolves to go immediately and seek out the Mecanógrafa, who can give him the longed-for child:

> Antes que la roja luna
> limpie con sangre de eclipse
> la perfección de su curva,
> traeré temblando de amor
> mi propia mujer, desnuda. (286)

> Before the red moon
> wipes with the blood of an eclipse
> the perfection of its curve,
> I will bring trembling with love
> my own wife, naked.

Basilio recounts a solar eclipse that took place years ago (when the moon passes between the sun and the Earth), while here what is expected, and what the Joven sets at a point of time in the near future, is a lunar eclipse (when the Earth passes between the sun and the moon, covering it with its shadow). Nevertheless, blood accompanies them both, the biblical rivers of blood in *La vida es sueño* (Exodus 7:20–21; Revelation 16:3–4), and the so-called blood moon that occurs every time there is a total lunar eclipse. In the context of the passage just quoted, blood points to the association of the moon with menstruation and, specifically, to defloration,[48] as the Maniquí articulates quite explicitly:

> Tu niño canta en su cuna
> y como es niño de nieve
> espera la sangre tuya.
> Corre, a buscarla, ¡deprisa!
> y entrégamela, desnuda,
> para que mis sedas puedan,
> hilo a hilo y una a una,
> abrir la rosa que cubre
> su vientre de carne rubia. (285)

Your child sings in his cradle,
and as he is a child of snow,
he awaits your blood.
Run, go and look for her, quickly!
bring her back and give her to me, naked,
so that my silks can,
thread by thread and one by one,
open the rose concealed
by her belly of blonde flesh.

A childhood memory of the Mecanógrafa connects her love for the Joven with balconies and also with blood: "¡que te quiero! Desde siempre. [. . .] Cuando pequeñito yo lo veía jugar desde mi balcón. Un día se cayó y sangraba por la rodilla ¿te acuerdas? Todavía tengo aquella sangre viva como una sierpe roja temblando entre mis pechos" (I love you! Since forever. [. . .] When you were very little, I used to watch you playing from my balcony. One day you fell over and were bleeding from your knee, do you remember? I still have that blood alive like a red snake trembling between my breasts) (208).

The moon, eclipse, and blood are also connected via the figure of the Padre, and the negativity that he expresses has to do, in turn, with the Novia's rejection of the Joven. Indeed, the Padre's annoyance at his inability to observe the upcoming astronomical phenomenon is directly linked to his anger at his daughter's sudden change of heart: "¿Es que no tengo derecho a descansar? Esta noche hay un eclipse de luna. Ya no podré mirarlo desde la terraza. En cuanto paso una irritación se me sube la sangre a los ojos y no veo. ¿Qué hacemos con este hombre?" (Don't I have a right to some peace and quiet? Tonight there is a lunar eclipse. No longer will I be able to observe it from the terrace. As soon as I get irritated, the blood wells up in my eyes and I can't see. What are we going to do with this man?) (262). When she resists his sternest remonstrations, he becomes deflated: "Todos contra mí. (*Mira al cielo por el balcón abierto.*) Ahora empezará el eclipse. (*Se dirige al balcón.*) Ya han apagado las lámparas. (*Con angustia.*) ¡Será hermoso! Lo he estado esperando mucho tiempo. Y ahora ya no lo veo. ¿Por qué lo has engañado?" (Everyone against me. [*He looks at the sky through the open balcony.*] The eclipse will begin anytime now. [*He goes to the balcony.*] They've already extinguished the lamps. [*Anguished.*] It will be beautiful! I've been waiting for it a long time. And now I can no longer see it. Why did you deceive him?) (263). The Padre's situation parallels that of the Joven: having waited a long time for a much-anticipated event, its fruition is frustrated. Indeed, when he laments the state of affairs: "Cinco años, día por día. ¡Ay Dios mío!" (Five years, day by day. Good God!) (264), it is not clear to whom he refers, himself or the jilted fiancé.

There may, however, be a more fundamental problem here, not stated openly but subtly hinted at. In act 2 moonlight is called for in the first stage direction (245), and as we have seen, this is often evoked by its bluish color. Two-thirds of the way through the act, when the Maniquí sequence begins, Lorca calls for "una luz de luna que irá en aumento hasta el final" (moonlight that will gradually increase up to the end of the scene), and in the same stage direction, Lorca also instructs that "Las bombillas de los ángeles toman una luz azul" (The light bulbs held by the angels take on a blue light) (276). Furthermore, it would not be too far-fetched to see the equipment that illuminates the Novia's art nouveau–style dressing table—"un tocador sostenido por ángeles con ramos de luces eléctricas en las manos" (a dressing table held up by angels with bunches of electric lights in their hands) (245)—as a version of artificial stars.[49] By the end of this sequence, "la luz es de un azul intenso" (the light is an intense blue), and even when the Criada enters with the candelabra, still visible is "la luz azul de los balcones abiertos de par en par que hay en el fondo" (the blue light from the wide-open balconies that are in the background) (287).

The Padre stands at the balcony using his binoculars: "EL PADRE se asoma a los balcones y mira con los prismáticos" (EL PADRE leans out of the balconies and looks through his binoculars) (266), and then the last we see of him is when he is looking longingly at the balcony. He conjectures that "debe estar ya en el comienzo" (it must already be beginning) (275), but his excitement may well be misplaced because the lighting effects indicate that the moonlight stays constant, if not indeed increasing, which would suggest that in fact the eclipse never takes place. The blue light remains, it is never extinguished and never turns a shade of red, and while this may point to the Padre's astronomical incompetence and later, as we discover, to the Joven's inability to fulfill his parting promise to the

Maniquí, the other more important meaning of this nonevent is that the moon's influence is never—figuratively—eclipsed. In advancing this interpretation, I disagree with Ricardo Doménech, who posits that in a kind of pathetic fallacy, the elopement of the Novia and the Jugador in the car coincides with the eclipse; likewise, I diverge from Michèle Ramond, who sees the eclipse as a symbol of the Joven's failure and indeed of much else in act 2.[50] Inés Marful Amor is the only other critic I am aware of who points out that the event does not actually occur, though most other elements of her interpretation I find unconvincing.[51]

The association of the moon with death is a cliché of Lorca criticism, but in *Así que pasen*—two years before *Bodas de sangre*—it nevertheless holds true.[52] The Joven's fate is predetermined—his destiny is written in the stars, he is an *emplazado,* he is betrothed to the moon (she now wears the wedding garland [280]), the three Jugadores have a prearranged time to call at his house (339, 343)—all this because the dream or hallucination that constitutes the action of the whole play is taking place in his mind just moments before his demise,[53] so that everything that happens has in fact already happened. If *Así que pasen* stages a kind of mental struggle or conflict—"la obra teatral desarrolla, bajo un sutil entramado de naturaleza onírica, una *psicomaquia*" (the play unfolds, under a subtle network of an oneiric nature, a *psychomaquia*)[54]—then the protagonist's defeat is already known to him from the very start. Any attempt by the Joven to stop the passage of time or to take refuge in some invented alternative reality is inevitably doomed to failure, as temporality is relentless.[55] As for the connection with Calderón, Stefano Afata conjectures the following:

> Intuimos quizá que Lorca, ya en los años 30, se acercaba a una interpretación que ve en los cimientos del universo calderoniano no la fuerza de un destino providencial, sino todo lo contrario: el silencio de la divinidad, que deja al hombre desnudo y solo en la tierra en busca de un padre ausente; un teatro en el que al anhelo amoroso de los hijos le corresponde el radical fracaso de la instancia paterna.[56]

> Perhaps we intuit that Lorca, once in the 1930s, was getting close to an interpretation that sees in the underpinnings of the Calderonian universe not the force of a providential destiny but, rather, the exact opposite: the

silence of the divinity, who leaves mankind naked and alone on the earth searching for an absent father; a theater in which the loving yearning of the offspring is matched by the radical failure of the paternal authority.

I would go one further: it is not just a question of the lack of divine providence or the emptiness of a godless universe but the fundamental existential dilemma of trying to deal with the knowledge that mortality *is* destiny and the eventual ineffectiveness of denial as a coping mechanism.[57]

8

Así que pasen cinco años, Act 3, Scene 1
A Reading

In acts 1 and 2 of *Así que pasen cinco años,* the audience has already witnessed a number of distinctly disconcerting events, notably the appearance onstage of a dead child and a dead cat and the conversation between them (act 1, 217–30) and the coming to life of a mannequin and the conversation between her and the Joven (act 2, 276–87).[1] However, the first part of act 3 takes this tendency to a whole new level, which is why I have chosen to focus on it here. In what follows, I will be using *Cuadro* to refer to this part of the play, rather than the more familiar English *scene,* which will be reserved for distinct sections within the Cuadro. Unlike English, Spanish identifies three different divisions within a play, *acto, cuadro,* and *escena:* a *cuadro* is a major division within an *acto,* with a brief pause (but no intermission) for a change of set, while *escenas* are marked simply by the entrance or exit of one or more characters with no interruption of the action.

After the curtain goes up, the audience encounters here not only a seamless succession of perplexing episodes but also a stage set radically different from those in acts 1 and 2: now we are not in a house but, rather, outside, in a dark forest (292), though later we discover it is actually a thickly wooded urban park (309), and the time of day, or night, is not specified (though subsequently, it becomes evident that it is nighttime). Disconcertingly, two figures dressed in black, with blank white faces and hands, flit among the trees, and there is music in the distance (292); shortly afterward, far-off hunting horns are heard, which sound at intervals throughout the whole of the Cuadro (294, 303, 308). The wood, the hunting horns, and later the notion of encirclement and enclosure that is introduced (309) certainly seem to anticipate the location and atmosphere of act 3, Cuadro Primero, of Lorca's own *Bodas de sangre*. At the same time, the setting brings to mind a host of folk tales, fairy tales, and many other literary antecedents, including Maurice Maeterlinck and Shakespeare. Here there may be a special debt to Victor Hugo's *Légende du beau Pécopin et de la belle Bauldour* (from *Le Rhin*) and the "bois des pas perdus" (forest of lost steps), where the protagonist finds himself at the climax of the story.[2] Other critics have related it to the dark wood of canto 1 of Dante's *Inferno*,[3] which opens with the well-known lines:

Nel mezzo del cammin di nostra vita
mi ritrovai per una selva oscura,
ché la diritta via era smarrita. (11.1–3)

In the middle of the journey of our life
I found myself in a dark wood
because the straight way was lost.

Dante then develops on the idea, describing it as "esta selva selvaggia e aspra e forte" (this wild and harsh and dense forest) (1.5) and offering this comparison: "Tant' è amara che poco è più morte" (So bitter is it, that death is little more) (1.7).

One other principal feature, which is particularly jarring and which at the same time marks out the space as primarily symbolic, is the presence of a small theater in the middle of the stage, surrounded, as it were, by the forest: "En el centro un teatro rodeado de cortinas barrocas con el telón echado. Una escalera une el tabladillo con el escenario" (In the center, a theater covered on all sides by Baroque curtains and with the stage curtain lowered. Stairs join the miniature stage with the main acting space) (292). Later, when the curtains are drawn, it is referred to, appropriately enough, as a "teatrito" (little theater) (319) that houses an "escenita" (little stage) (319, 320, 322), but for the moment, it just stands there, enigmatically.

From the point of view of the action and the number of characters who participate in it, the first Cuadro of act 3 is the most complex part of the entire play. There are seven characters with speaking roles, four of whom are newly introduced here, while the other three (including the protagonist) have been onstage previously; there are two nonspeaking characters already known to us who make brief appearances here; and six other silent and very much subsidiary figures. The action is articulated in a series of four segments, the first anchored by the Arlequín, who is later joined by the Muchacha and the Payaso (292–302), the second is a dialogue between the Mecanógrafa and the Máscara Amarilla (303–8), the third involves the interaction between the Joven and the Arlequín, later joined by the Payaso (309–13), and the fourth—by some margin the longest and most intricate—revolves around the dialogue between the Joven and the Mecanógrafa, both on the main stage and on the miniature stage, but with various interjections also from the Máscara Amarilla, the Viejo, the Arlequín, and the Payaso (309–31).

As the Cuadro begins, the Arlequín is alone onstage, and this initial sequence is composed of his recitation of a poem, with assonantal *romance* meter for the stanzas and contrasting rhyming hendecasyllabics for the refrain. Lorca simply specifies that he be dressed in black and green (292), which we assume are the two colors of the lozenge shapes that typically characterize a Harlequin's costume. These are not the traditional colors— normally his suit is multicolored, with neither black nor green predominating—and some have seen in this choice the mixed symbolism of death (black) and hope (green, associated in Spanish culture with hope and not with envy). The Harlequin figure appears first in the commedia dell'arte and is the best known of the Zanni, the comic servant characters. Most typically, he is paired with the sad clown Pierrot (who in this play has morphed into the rather different Payaso). Relevant here might well be the figure of Brighella, another of the Zanni, who is strongly associated with the color green (mask and costume trim).[4] He is as clever and cunning as Arlecchino, and furthermore, Brighella is characterized by his musical ability and, in traditional commedia, normally carries a stringed instrument.

The poetic imagery and symbolism that suffuses Arlequín's poem has made it susceptible to a number of different readings by critics, but that offered by Julio Huélamo Kosma is by far the most compelling. He argues that the poem, via the figurative language employed, summarizes the plot so far, looks forward to the denouement, and expounds on the key thematic material treated in the play, which obviously revolves around the binary of dream and time.⁵ In stanza 1, then, dream is likened to a sailing ship, which floats on or over time, thus expressing how dream seems to be "outside" the passage of chronological time. However, it also reminds us that a retreat into the world of dream is sterile because of its lack of contact with reality. In the first refrain, dawn, song, and the color blue should have positive connotations, the dawn specifically of hope, but the coldness and inertness of ice predominate (292–93). Stanza 1 and the first refrain, therefore, may be seen to correspond to the Joven's attitude in act 1 and to its fundamental, inherent flaws.⁶ Stanza 2 depicts the weight of time nearly sinking the sailing ship of dream. The notions of both temporal past (memory, a lost ideal) and future (hopeful anticipation) bring with them the inevitability of negation and mortality ("comen," "duelo" [eat, mourning]) (293). Ucelay reminds us that the Greeks believed that the dead sustained themselves in the afterlife by eating asphodel tubers.⁷ Extending the contrastive pattern, the second refrain foregrounds night (and hence the eternal cycle of time), and the flowers that sprout up in thick bunches are anemones. Anemones are toxic—the name, deriving from the Greek, means "the wind's daughter"—while in Ovid's *Metamorphoses,* Venus, in her grief at Adonis's mortal wounding by the wild boar, transforms his blood into that flower. Wind symbolism, of insubstantiality and impermanence, returns later in this Cuadro, so again the combined connotations are distinctly negative, despite the anemone's outward, if fragile, beauty. Stanza 2 and the second refrain thus encapsulate the reasons underlying the failure of the Joven's original plan that occurs in act 2.⁸

Stanza 3 suggests that while the passage of time and the act of dreaming may coincide in the overall experience of life, the former will always prevail, and in terms redolent of Baroque *desengaño,* the lines stress the fugacity and brevity of life in the conjunction of "el gemido del niño" (the wail of the child) and "la lengua rota del viejo" (the broken tongue of the old man) (293), phrases that are themselves reminiscent of the Niño Muerto and the Viejo of act 1.⁹ Stanza 4 returns to the superior power of time but now viewed from a different perspective. Time is imagined as a never-ending continuum—the "llanura" (plain); dream may give the dreamer the impression that divisions or limits or fixed points ("muros" [walls]) can somehow be established in the flux of time, either looking back toward the past or forward toward the future, but this is completely illusory. However much they might think they do, human beings do not have the measure of time.[10] The second two lines—"el Tiempo le hace creer / que nace en aquel momento" (Time makes him believe / that he is born at that moment) (294)—pertain directly to the end of act 2 and beginning of act 3: the Joven has adopted this new hope that he projects on both the past and the future. For the moment, until his final, definitive disillusionment, he believes that he can turn the clock back to recover the Mecanógrafa's love and hence achieve in short order his new objective, that she should be the future mother of his child.[11]

The Arlequín's deployment of two masks is somewhat disconcerting. With a nod to Melpomene and Thalia, his are different, one with an "alegrísima expresión" (most joyful expression) and the other with an "expresión dormida" (sleepy expression) (293). He puts on the "happy" mask for the refrain accompanying stanza 1 and the "asleep" mask for the refrain accompanying stanza 2. Although dream might seem to correlate more obviously with sleep, the Arlequín first dons the happy mask because it is dream that brings the Joven (temporary) happiness, while at the same time this lulls him into forgetfulness ("asleep") of the ineluctable passage of time. Things soon begin to blend together and merge, as the two masks are used to deliver the two lines of stanza 3's refrain (293) and are then abandoned for stanza 4.[12]

When the Arlequín's poem ends, this is the first moment at which the hunting horns are heard, and immediately thereafter, the Muchacha comes onstage, ushering in the remainder of this first segment of the Cuadro. Lorca's stage direction reads: "Aparece una MUCHACHA vestida de negro, con túnica griega. Viene saltando con una guirnalda" (A MUCHACHA appears dressed in black, with a Greek tunic. She enters skipping with a garland) (294). The Greek tunic constitutes another echo of classical theater, while the color black could well indicate mourning for her lost, and apparently dead, lover.[13] These overtones contrast sharply with the gaiety of her skipping ("saltando") and the garland, presumably of flowers and worn on her head. Ucelay reveals that in rehearsal the actress cast in the role was actually skipping rope and barefoot so that as she skipped she would not cause excessive noise landing on the stage floor.[14] All this suggests a young girl with, perhaps, conflicted emotions.

After the Arlequín's solo recitation of the poem comes to a close, the dialogue commences and continues in irregular, short-line verse. For this sequence, Lorca adapts to his own purposes the brief lyrics that are part of three childhood games.[15] The first is known as "Tira y afloja," or alternatively "Estira y encoge," and takes various forms. It can be played with a handkerchief, ribbon, string, rope, or a similar material and in some versions comes close to a "tug-of-war." Most importantly, the verses that accompany it are

Al tira y afloja
perdí mi caudal
y al tira y afloja [*estira y encoge* can be substituted for *tira y afloja*]
lo volví a ganar.

While pulling and slackening
I lost my fortune
and while pulling and slackening
I got it back again.[16]

The second is "La gallina ciega," a version of blindman's buff. The person who is "it" is blindfolded, and then he or she has to pursue the other players within a demarcated area. Before the chase begins, the group sings, "Gallinita ciega, ¿qué se te ha perdido?" (Little blind hen, what have you lost?); "it"—the "gallina"—responds: "Una aguja y un dedal" (a needle and a thimble), to which the group replies: "Pues da la media vuelta y lo encontrarás" (Well, turn halfway around, and you'll find it).[17]

Third, there is "La pájara pinta," which is a kind of kissing game involving a group of girls. "It"—the "pájara pinta"—stands in the middle of a circle, the song begins, "it" chooses one of the girls in the circle by kneeling before her, she takes her hands, together they perform several steps and movements dictated by the lyrics, then "it" is initially ashamed to give the other girl a kiss but eventually does so.[18] There are many variations of the accompanying text, which is longer than that of the other two games, but this version is representative and follows the stages of the action just described:

Estaba la pájara pinta
sentada en su verde limón;
con el pico recoge la rama,
con la rama cortaba la flor.
¡Ay, ay, ay! ¿cuándo vendrá mi amor?
¡Ay, ay, ay! ¿cuándo vendrá mi amor?
Daré la media vuelta,
daré la vuelta entera,
daré un pasito atrás haciendo la reverencia.
Pero no, pero no, porque me da vergüenza.
Pero sí, pero sí, porque te quiero a ti.[19]

The piebald bird
was perched in its green lemon tree;
with its beak it collects the sprig,
with the sprig it was cutting the flower.
Oh, oh, oh! when will my love come?
Oh, oh, oh! when will my love come?
I will turn halfway around,
I will turn completely around,
I will take a small step backward, curtseying.
But no, but no, because it makes me embarrassed.
But yes, but yes, because I love you.

Finally, in conjunction with the sung texts of these three games, Lorca may well be working into this sequence some additional material that derives indirectly from Rafael Alberti's *Marinero en tierra*, much of which is itself based on traditional lyrics and children's games, and in particular several poems that imagine a fantasy life under the waves and at the bottom of the sea.[20]

All three games are relevant to this particular juncture in *Así que pasen cinco años*. The first and second have to do with loss and recovery, while the third involves choosing a partner and kissing. The Muchacha states first that her lover is waiting for her but at the bottom of the sea, strongly implying that he has in fact drowned.[21] She insists that although she has experienced the loss of two quite different items ("deseo," "dedal" [(object of my) desire; thimble]), "en los troncos grandes / los volví a encontrar" (among the big tree trunks / I found them again) (295). The tree trunks must refer to the location where the whole Cuadro is set, and although we do not really know it yet, the wood is actually a very menacing place—if not the domain of death itself, then at the very least in close proximity to it. This recovery claimed by the Muchacha is evidently more fantasized than real, and so the Arlequín calls for a very long rope—her skipping rope will not suffice, presumably so that she can be lowered down to visit her lover. She temporizes, imagining him as a captain of the depths, but then becomes afraid when the Arlequín starts to puncture her fantasy by suggesting that she will indeed be able to see her lover "Ahora mismo" (Right now) (296). She opposes the idea of seizing the present just as the Joven did in act 1; instead, she attempts to counter the Arlequín by stating that "No se llega nunca / al fondo del mar" (You can never reach / the bottom of the sea) (297), an assertion that, if it were true, would somehow safeguard her status quo.

This resistance on her part causes the Arlequín to call for reinforcements, and onstage comes "un espléndido PAYASO lleno de lentejuelas. Su cabeza empolvada dará sensación de calavera" (a resplendent PAYASO covered in sequins. His powdered head suggests a skull) (297). While the Arlequín comes directly from commedia dell'arte and is most frequently accompanied by the melancholy Pierrot, a clown is most obviously connected to a different genre, the circus, which plays a major role here too. The clown (Pagliaccio) is the central character in Ruggero Leoncavallo's opera, and Pagliaccio and Pierrot are both variants of the original Pedrolino figure (another of the Zanni); here Pierrot's white face may be echoed in the Payaso's bald pate. However, the Payaso's costume is quite different and much showier, and above all, the Payaso here is anything but sad.

Performing as if this were a circus skit,[22] the Payaso wants to substitute a ladder for the long rope, so that the Muchacha can go down and see her lover. The Payaso underlines the humor in the impracticality of the suggestion by acknowledging the presence of the audience to which he is playing, but the Muchacha is nonetheless scared. He and Arlequín continue to torment her, by pretending to be the lover singing about his life on the ocean floor. In the stage direction, "asustada de la realidad" (frightened by reality) (299), Lorca makes it clear that the Muchacha is not just unwilling but afraid of leaving her more comfortable fantasy world, and as she exits, she announces her next delaying tactic:

> Me voy a saltar
> por las hierbas altas.
> Luego nos iremos
> al agua del mar. (300)

> I'm going to skip
> through the long grass.
> Then we shall go
> to the water of the sea.

"Luego" (Then [as in *later*]) rather than "Ahora mismo" (Right now) (296).

The Arlequín and Payaso are briefly left alone, and the latter commands the former "A representar" (Begin your performance), underlining the doubly metatheatrical nature of their action onstage.[23] The Payaso recites the lines

> Un niño pequeño
> que quiere cambiar
> en flores de acero
> su trozo de pan. (301)

> A small child
> who wants to turn
> his piece of bread
> into flowers of steel.

This may recall the Niño Muerto in act 1, striving for a strange kind of permanence in the unnatural and paradoxical "flores de acero," possibly an enduring decoration for a tomb.[24] He continues with another verse that contains some echoes of the Muchacha's lines,

Perdí rosa y curva,
perdí mi collar,
y en marfil reciente
los volví a encontrar. (301)

I lost a rose and a curve,
I lost my necklace,
and in fresh ivory
I found them again.

Several elements here are very ambiguous: "rosa y curva," which could be interpreted in any number of ways, and "marfil reciente," which could just as easily refer to a newborn as to the bone of a skull, connecting back to that "sensación de calavera." This is reminiscent of the lines from "Cielo vivo" (*Poeta en Nueva York*): "ni puedes acariciar la fugaz hoja del helecho / sin sentir el asombro definitivo del marfil" (nor can you caress the fleeting leaf of the fern / without experiencing the definitive shock of ivory), lines that in turn are echoed by those of "Gacela de la huida" (*Diván del Tamarit*):

No hay nadie que, al dar un beso,
no sienta la sonrisa de las gentes sin rostro,
ni hay nadie que, al tocar un recién nacido,
olvide las inmóviles calaveras de caballo.

There is no one who, on giving a kiss,
does not sense the smile of the people without a face,
nor is there anybody who, on touching a newborn baby,
forgets the motionless horse skulls.

As the pair begins to exit, the Payaso again addresses an imaginary audience, repeating twice the phrase "voy a demostrar" (I am going to demonstrate) (302). Arlequín finishes his thought, first with a repetition of the last two cited lines and then with two new ones: "La rueda que gira / del viento y el mar" (The wheel that revolves / of the wind and the sea) (303). The symbolism here is easier to grasp. The wheel turning is a classic emblem of the cyclical nature of existence, of birth, death, and rebirth; the wind brings notions of insubstantiality, of fugacity, of things being swept away, and the sea related ones of the ever-changing tides, eternal motion, and almost infinite immensity.

None of these three characters formed part of the action of acts 1 and 2, and one might well wonder why this disparate and strange group now opens act 3. The simplest answer would be that as the whole play is the projection of the dream or hallucination experienced by the Joven, then any new characters can in theory appear onstage at any time as the product of his unconscious. Beyond Lorca's own predilection for both harlequin and clown figures in his drawings, the associations of performativity and metatheatricality that they bring, both in their costume, masks, or heavy makeup and in how they comport themselves during this segment of the Cuadro, contribute to the idea of the enactment, onstage, of a kind of *psychomaquia* that is expressed, for the moment indirectly, through these fantastic figures. In addition, the Arlequín, as one of the Zanni, represents a form of doubling of Juan, the astute and knowing Criado in the employ of the Joven, while the Payaso can obviously be connected directly with the circus that will become one of the major symbols in this Cuadro.

Different critics have seen different things in the Muchacha, as a version or projection or doubling of one or other of the previously established characters. For Lucette-Élyane Roux, she incarnates the development of the Mecanógrafa's psychological state since she left the Joven's house, veiling her certainty of their never being together under the pretext of waiting and foreshadowing the Mecanógrafa's response later on to the Joven's entreaties;[25] Edgard Samper simply calls her "el avatar onírico" (the dreamworld avatar) of the Mecanógrafa, and Gérard Lavergne makes a similar point.[26] Rupert Allen, on the other hand, sees a similarity between the Muchacha and the Joven, both dreamers, both looking to recover a "treasure" that is irremediably lost,[27] and he in turn is echoed by Margarita Ucelay and Lavergne.[28] For her part, Nadine Ly argues that the Muchacha functions as a kind of "replacement" in act 3 for the Novia but now a widow (or at least a grieving fiancée), though strangely she is also, somehow, simultaneously, "un avatar de Joven" (138). Fernando Lázaro Carreter proposes a more radical reading wherein the Muchacha is already dead, just like her lover at the bottom of the sea, and she struggles in vain to avoid her mortal fate.[29] Evidently, she is a somewhat amorphous figure upon whom, thanks to the lack of specificity of her poetic exchanges with the Arlequín and Payaso, various roles or identities can be projected, though to my mind her situation and attitude are most strongly reminiscent of the Joven, thus providing a different kind of recapitulation that pairs with the Arlequín's opening poem.

The stage stands vacant for a moment, the distant hunting horns sound ominously, and the Mecanógrafa and the Máscara enter, marking the beginning of the second substantial segment within this Cuadro. Since we last saw her in act 1, the Mecanógrafa has changed. She is not quite transformed into a flapper, but the tennis outfit, together with the beret, indicate a turn toward sporty modernity (303). Jean Borotra, a French tennis player nicknamed the "bounding Basque," popularized the use of the beret as tennis attire in the 1920s. As for the Máscara, some of the details that she discloses to the Mecanógrafa in the course of their conversation lead us to suspicions about her identity, but these are not fully confirmed until the next and final Cuadro, which starts in media res with the Criado and the Criada gossiping about the mother of the Niño Muerto:

CRIADO: Ahora está de portera, pero antes fue una gran señora. Vivió mucho tiempo con un conde italiano riquísimo, padre del niño que acaban de enterrar. [. . .]

CRIADO: De esta época le viene su manía de grandezas. Por eso ha gastado todo lo que tenía en la ropa del niño y en la caja. (332–34)

CRIADO: Now she's working as a doorkeeper, but before that, she was a great lady. She lived for a long time with an extremely rich Italian count, the father of the child that they have just buried. [. . .]

CRIADO: Her delusions of grandeur come from that period. This is why she has spent all that she had on the clothes for the child and the coffin.

Here she is wearing a costume and offers an overall appearance that evoke a kind of distorted version of the person that she once seems to have been (303). The matte white mask points directly to the fact that the individual is performing a role that hides her true—or at least present—nature. Her over-the-top garb—yellow hat, long and silky yellow hair, and a bright-yellow turn-of-the-century style dress with an empire waist, golden sequins all over the front, and a long train—combines with the slight Italian accent and her unfolding backstory to paint a character who has stepped directly out of a particularly gaudy and melodramatic Italian opera.[30]

The conversation between the Mecanógrafa and the Máscara has already started offstage, and as they enter, they continue recounting to each other their personal histories, focused on their respective love stories. We hear from the Mecanógrafa first and immediately realize that this is a fantasized, inverted, or "through-the-looking-glass" version of events that we witnessed in act 1. Some details are the same—the Mecanógrafa's departure from the Joven's house, the summer storm, the death of the doorkeeper's young child, the library as the locale of their last conversation—but the roles are now reversed, and the Mecanógrafa attributes to herself the exact last words spoken to her by the Joven, and vice versa, as if she were spurning him (242–43, 303–4). The other important plot point—that the Mecanógrafa has been in love with him for many years: "¡que te quiero! Desde siempre. [. . .] Cuando pequeñito yo lo veía jugar desde mi balcón" (I love you! Since forever. [. . .] When you were very little, I used to watch you playing from my balcony) (208)—is also turned on its head, but the precise details are now changed:

MECANÓGRAFA: [Él] Esperaba siempre de pie toda la noche hasta que yo me asomaba a la ventana. [. . .]

MECANÓGRAFA: [Yo] No me asomaba. Pero . . . lo veía por las rendijas . . . ¡quieto! (*saca un pañuelo*) ¡con unos ojos! Entraba el aire como un cuchillo pero yo no le podía hablar. [. . .]

MECANÓGRAFA: Porque me amaba demasiado. (304–5)

MECANÓGRAFA: He used to stand waiting for the whole night until I appeared at the window. [. . .]

MECANÓGRAFA: I didn't appear. But . . . I saw him through the cracks . . . standing still! (*she takes out a handkerchief*) with what eyes! The draft entered like a knife, but I could not speak to him. [. . .]

MECANÓGRAFA: Because he loved me too much.

Although in this new version, she is not the instigator of the observation nor the person hopelessly in love, at least she admits that she spied on him back.

The Máscara, in turn, recounts to the Mecanógrafa her story, the dynamics of which she claims run parallel to those of the Mecanógrafa. Her past love was "el conde Arturo de Italia" (Count Arturo from Italy) (305), and for a brief while at least, they lived a luxurious life of the high aristocracy. But soon, according to the Máscara, she rejected and abandoned him along with the small child they had together, and she continued to enjoy the high life, centered on the Paris Opera (the sumptuous building of the Palais Garnier is held by many to be the most famous opera house in the world). The count was much affected by her attitude, weeping over his lost love; she scornfully tossed him a diamond, but he and the child still had to sleep rough and go hungry (305–6). But the Máscara is unable to control her own emotions for very long and to stick to what is, as soon becomes clear, a fictitious and completely reversed version of what actually happened. The truth breaks through: she was the one who was abandoned with her child; they were the ones who went hungry, and the child died; Arturo married a "gran dama romana" (great Roman lady), while she was reduced to begging and sleeping with dockworkers who unloaded coal; and the scar from a dagger that she first says Arturo got fighting over her is actually on her body (305–6, 307). Thus, not only does her tale contain striking inaccuracies and improbabilities (in particular, her assertion that the balconies of the Paris Opera overlook the sea), but also the thin veneer of plausibility is punctured by her own self-contradiction. The only way to inject some semblance of realism into it is to explain its nature by proposing that it is the product of a mother nearly deranged by grief at the loss of her child (an event that in her account took place in the past but which, according to the rest of the play, is extremely recent).

Nonetheless, the Mecanógrafa seems predisposed to go along with the pretense: just as the Máscara pronounces the Mecanógrafa's tale "¡Precioso!" (Beautiful!) (304), so the Mecanógrafa finds the Máscara's "Delicioso" (Delightful). The only hint of needling between them comes when they ask each other when they expect that their respective lovers will arrive (306). In both cases, as one might well expect under the circumstances, the reply is that both will be some time yet (306–7). This, in turn, ushers in the key topic of waiting, which the Mecanógrafa extols: "Hace cinco años que me está esperando, pero . . . ¡Qué hermoso es esperar con seguridad el momento de ser amada!" (It's been five years that he has been waiting for me, but . . . How lovely it is to wait with [absolute] certainty for the moment of being loved!) (307), an attitude that the Máscara approvingly endorses: "¡Y es seguro!" (And it's certain!) (308). Of course, what the Mecanógrafa has just said closely echoes the Joven's initial standpoint, speaking of his feelings toward not her but the Novia: "Pero es que yo estoy enamorado como ella lo está de mí y por eso puedo aguardar cinco años" (But the thing is that I am in love just as she is in love with me, and because of this, I can wait five years) (199); "Pero tú no puedes comprender que se espere a una mujer cinco años colmado y quemado por el amor que crece cada día" (But you cannot understand that one might wait five years for a woman, full and burning with the love that grows every day) (233). The Mecanógrafa then goes on to add, in regard to waiting and anticipation, that "De pequeña, yo guardaba los dulces para comerlos después" (When I was little, I used to keep the candies to eat them later), a practice that the Máscara endorses: "¡Ja, ja, ja! ¿Verdad? ¡Saben mejor!" (Ha, ha, ha! Isn't that true? They taste better!) (308), an exchange that reproduces almost verbatim one between the Joven and the Viejo in act 1 (192). Not only does this reinforce the notion of the reversal of roles between the Joven and the Mecanógrafa, but we can also now appreciate how in a sense the Máscara plays a role vis-à-vis the Mecanógrafa somewhat analogous to that between the Viejo and the Joven.[31] Another reason why the Máscara appears here accompanying the Mecanógrafa has to do with her "other" identity as the doorkeeper and the tragedy that has befallen her. If, as we shall witness shortly, the Joven is inspired to seek out the Mecanógrafa, who he now believes is the only viable possibility as the future mother for the child that he desperately wants to have, then the Máscara qua doorkeeper represents the other side of the coin, as an anguished mother who has just lost a young child.

The two women exit, leaving the stage clear for the entrance of the Joven, which marks the beginning of the third segment of the Cuadro. Just as with the Mecanógrafa, his clothing indicates a significant change in him and an espousal of modernity. While in act 2, he simply "viene vestido de calle" (is dressed in street clothes) (264), he is now wearing gray knickerbockers (308), fashionable in the United States in the early decades of the twentieth century. And the fact that these are combined with argyle socks suggests further that they might well be identified as plus fours (four inches longer than the original knickerbockers) and strongly associated with golf attire of the period, answering the tennis outfit of the Mecanógrafa. If not at the level of the stereotypical image of physical prowess exemplified by the American football player, the Jugador de Rugby, with whom the Novia has become besotted, then the Joven has nonetheless moved quite significantly in that direction. He is immediately joined by the Arlequín (309), and later by the Payaso, mirroring the earlier sequence involving the Muchacha.

Just as the Arlequín did with the Muchacha, he now toys with him, though the Joven is for the moment unaware of the predicament in which he finds himself. When first approached, the Joven seems to give the knee-jerk response that he is headed home (309), though we know that after the conversation with the Maniquí, he is actually looking for the Mecanógrafa, and he later corrects his destination as "otra casa" (another house) (312). The tree trunks of the initial stage direction are those, it transpires, of a thickly wooded urban park (292, 309), and at least some of the exits are cut off by the arrival of a traveling circus that has set up in this space (309–10). Ominously, the Arlequín invites the Joven to enter this circus (the big top), which he describes as "lleno de espectadores definitivamente quietos" (full of spectators who are permanently still). The Joven captures at least some of the menacing implications of this description, as the stage directions call for the Joven in his reaction to be "Estremecido" (Shuddering) and "No queriendo oír" (Trying not to hear) (310). The phrase *definitivamente quietos* can only refer to people who are dead, so this unreal circus becomes a new version of the afterlife or the underworld, immediately contiguous to where they now stand. The Joven is urged to go in—as he will inevitably have to do at the end of Cuadro 2—but for the moment he resists and attempts to find alternative ways out.

Another of the park's avenues, the Arlequín informs him, is blocked by the caravans of the circus people and the cages of the wild animals (though snakes are an improbable species to train to perform in a circus, and cages do not seem the best method of containing them), so the Joven decides to retrace his steps, following the same route that he presumably used to enter the park (310). But now, rather than the big top or the parked trailers, it is a performer—the Payaso—who stands in his way, mocking him for thinking that this was still a possible way out: "¿Pero dónde va? ¡Ja, ja, ja!" (But where are you going? Ha, ha, ha!) (312). The Payaso seemingly asserts his authority, delivering a slapstick blow to the Arlequín, and the Joven begins to lose his patience with these two jokesters. In an implicit plea for a moment of seriousness, he explains that he was just returning home—or rather, going to someone else's house (the Mecanógrafa's)—but these two beings already know that: he was going "a buscar" (to seek) (312), with another direct echo of a line from the end of act 2 (289). Unmoved, the Payaso repeats nearly identically a line of the Muchacha's verse, "Da la media vuelta y lo encontrarás" (Turn halfway around, and you will find it) (313), one that suggests that by turning halfway around (that is, 180 degrees), the Joven will find—as promised by the lyrics of "La pájara pinta"—the person he is looking for.

Instead of a clear demarcation, signaled by a momentarily empty stage before the new characters make their entrance, this segment—the third—blends seamlessly into the fourth and last, which will also be the longest and structurally most complicated. Before the Arlequín and the Payaso have left, the Mecanógrafa is already heard singing, offstage:

¿Dónde vas, amor mío,
¡amor mío!
con el aire en un vaso
y el mar en un vidrio? (313)

Where are you going, my love,
my love!
with the wind in a glass
and the sea in a glass container?

The lines represent a significant variation and development on some of the verses recited by the Arlequín during his interaction with the Muchacha:

Tu amante verás
a la media vuelta
del viento y el mar. (296)

You will see your lover
turned halfway around
from the wind and the sea.

And "La rueda que gira / del viento y el mar" (The wheel that revolves / of the wind and the sea) (303). The symbols of incommensurate nature from earlier on are now contained—literally, bottled up—by the Joven, as if by seizing the moment, coming here, and seeking out the Mecanógrafa, he had somehow brought them under control.

The Arlequín and Payaso discreetly tiptoe offstage, with an ironic finger held to their lips, while the Joven responds in kind to the song. The Mecanógrafa enters, "llena de júbilo" (full of joy) (314), and they passionately embrace each other. An important exchange in verse dialogue ensues, with telling echoes of the earlier scene between the Joven and the Maniquí. While the verbatim repetition of specific words or phrases is quite rare ("juncos," "sedas," "calor," "desnuda," "sangre," "antes que," "temblando" [reeds, silks, heat, naked, blood, before, trembling], 278, 280, 281, 285, 286), the same sense of how the Maniquí urges the Joven to act and what he resolves to do is very much present here, too, as he strives to put his new plan into practice. He wants the Mecanógrafa to go with him, so they can physically consummate their love, and he wants this to happen straightaway, that very night, before sunrise: "Antes que las ramas giman / ruiseñores amarillos" (Before the branches moan / yellow nightingales) (314).

At first sight, the Mecanógrafa's response seems disconcertingly tangential to the Joven's passionate entreaty:

Sí; que el sol es un milano.
Mejor: un halcón de vidrio.
No: que el sol es un gran tronco,
y tú la sombra de un río. (314–15)

Yes; for the sun is a kite [hawk].
Better: a falcon of glass.
No: for the sun is a great trunk,
and you the shadow of a river.

But then gradually her pattern of thought becomes clearer. The Joven's temporal reference involves nightingales, strongly associated with romance and the night, and the sun of dawn would "prey" on the darkness in the same way as a hawk might on a nightingale illuminated (turned yellow) by the rays of sun at dawn. But then she changes direction, likening the sun to a sturdy tree trunk, beside which the Joven now pales into insignificance, as he is not a river but merely the shadow of one. The next four lines elaborate on this trope. If he is the shadow of a river, then he will not have arms but, rather, waves or ripples, but when he embraces her, the Mecanógrafa finds that the effect on her is disappointingly tepid:

> ¿Cómo, si me abrazan, di,
> no nacen juncos y lirios
> y no destiñen tus ondas
> el color de mi vestido? (315)

> If your waves embrace me,
> tell me how reeds and lilies don't sprout up
> and they don't make
> the color of my dress fade?

Here she now seems to be channeling the Novia, who, when encountering the Joven in act 2, asked a series of questions whose implications were similar: wasn't he taller, didn't he have a "violent smile," didn't he play rugby, and didn't he ride bareback and kill three thousand pheasants in a day? (266–67). Apparently as a consequence of her disappointment, she asks to be left alone in an isolated place so that she can imagine him more fondly from a distance, a perspective that will transform her perception of him:

> Amor, déjame en el monte
> harta de nube y rocío,
> para verte grande y triste
> cubrir un cielo dormido. (315)

> Love, leave me on the mountainside
> replete with cloud and dew,

in order to see you big and sad
cover a sleeping sky.

Impatiently, the Joven rejects any such delay and tries to get her to share in his new attitude of carpe diem. But somehow she does not quite seem to hear him and rather dreamily focuses instead on some far-off sound that the Joven identifies as that of "el día que vuelve" (the day that's returning). Picking up on the Joven's earlier poetic circumlocution, the Mecanógrafa seems to identify the sound she hears not as that of the approach of daybreak—or for that matter, the distant hunting horns—but, rather, as a nightingale's beautiful song. Strangely, this is not the nightingale of night or dawn but, according to her, "de la tarde" (of the afternoon), she describes it as gray rather than its actual brown color, and it is hard to know why she associates it with the maple tree. But she says she has received its message, and so now exclaims, directly echoing the Joven, "¡Quiero vivir!" (I want to live!). It is hard to avoid the suspicion of some vague resonance with the scene from *Romeo and Juliet* when the young lovers debate whether what they have heard is the nightingale (night) or the lark (dawn) (act 3, sc. 5), a scene already alluded to specifically in *El público*. In turn, the Joven echoes the Mecanógrafa, "¿Con quién?" (With whom?), but instead of the anticipated reply, "Contigo" (With you), she reverts to her previous characterization of him: "Con la sombra de un río" (With the shadow of a river) (316).

For a moment, it seems as if the Joven may have convinced her: the stage directions have her "refugiándose en el pecho de EL JOVEN" (taking shelter against the JOVEN's chest) (316), but at the same time, she is still "angustiada" (distressed) by those distant and difficult-to-identify sounds. Instead of the return of day, he now tells her that they are rather those of "¡La sangre en mi garganta[!]" (The blood in my throat[!]), and in response, the Mecanógrafa calls for them to eternalize this moment of togetherness: "Siempre así, siempre, siempre, / despiertos o dormidos" (Always like this, always, always, / awake or asleep). However, the Joven understands what might otherwise be taken as a rather trite expression of commitment as a desire to stay exactly where they are and not to change anything: "Nunca así, ¡nunca! ¡nunca! / Vámonos de este sitio" (Never like this, never! never! / Let's get away from this place). And with this now comes the denouement of the first sequence between the two of them:

the Mecanógrafa calls for him to wait, he responds urgently "¡Amor no espera!" (Love does not wait!) (318), but she extricates herself from his embrace and again sings the lines (313, 318) with which she first announced her presence. The Joven has failed to convince her and to win her over, and there is a pause in the dialogue.

The next section of this segment now commences as she moves toward the short flight of steps that connect the main stage with the raised platform of the small theater that stands within it. The curtains are drawn back, and the set that is revealed is "la biblioteca del primer acto, reducida y con los tonos muy pálidos" (the library of the first act, reduced in size and with very pale tones) (319). The decrease in size and the fading of colors both point to the effects of the passage of time and of memory,[32] and indeed, if we remember that in this representation of the Joven's psychic processes he is going, one might almost say, *à la recherche du temps perdu,* then this miniaturized stage decor is entirely fitting. The Joven's new outlook is, as we have seen, one of carpe diem, but in order to achieve that goal, he is trying to turn back the clock, to when the Mecanógrafa was in his house—his library—and she was openly declaring her love for him. Fernández-Cifuentes points out that here the Joven's new attitude echoes, in part, that of the Amigo 2° in act 1, a link strengthened by the fact that the Mecanógrafa was in love with the Joven when they both were children.[33] In fact, combining all three temporal stances from act 1, the Joven needs to go back in time in order to seize the day and find the person with whom he now wants to live and with whom, in the future, he wants to have a child, which is his ultimate goal (cf. 284–85).

At this point the presence of characters on either of these two performing spaces or their movement from one to another becomes highly significant. For the moment, the only person actually on the small stage is the Máscara. A handkerchief and smelling salts indicate the degree of her emotional distress (319) and connect her again with the Viejo (288, 322). In a kind of chronological flashback, she claims to have just abandoned the count and their child (319), though of course, we know that inasmuch as we can talk at all of any "real world," she has been working as a doorkeeper and has just lost her young son. She descends to the main stage and continues to refer to this episode (that she has completely rewritten) and what she expected to happen subsequently, all the while expressing herself

LORCA'S EXPERIMENTAL THEATER

in plainly inverted terms, remarking at how happy she is as she weeps. Likewise, she shouts, so she says, so that Arturo cannot hear her and find her, and she exits, repeating her refrain in reverse: "no te quiero" (I don't love you) (319–20). This brief recapitulation does not really advance the action of act 3 but does remind us of the impossibility of recovering the past, the depths of denial that people can engage in, and the loss of future potential associated with the death of a child.

Next, two self-effacing servants bring two stools onstage and leave them on the left, seating that somewhat later the Arlequín and Payaso will occupy. Up on the small stage, Juan, the servant from act 1, silently crosses from one side to another, reinforcing the connection of the set with the Joven's home. Now the Mecanógrafa slowly climbs the steps to the small stage from which the Máscara recently descended and, speaking to Juan as if she were master of the house, tells him to let in "el señor" (the gentleman)—one assumes the Viejo—should he come, though it will be a while (320). At this point, the Mecanógrafa has not only inverted the dynamic that existed between her and the Joven in act 1 (with her now scorning him) but also, in a full reversal of the situation, has actually adopted the Joven's role, giving instructions to the servant.

The Joven slowly—and perhaps reluctantly—joins her on the small stage. In a sense, this ensuing scene in the theater inside the theater, and within the faded version of his den, will repeat, but now in prose and more pointedly, the lack of connection and differing attitudes that we just saw, poetically, in the wood. In response to his question as to whether she is happy here back in the library, she replies in role reversal character, asking, as he did in act 1, if he has typed the letters (cf. 206). They carry on talking at cross-purposes. The Joven urges her to come with him: "Arriba se está mejor" (It's better upstairs) (321), possibly alluding to his bedroom that is on the upper floor (cf. 336), as he has just been described as "apasionado" (passionate) (320), but the Mecanógrafa continues on her own tack. She displaces her love for the Joven first to the past (as in act 1) and then to the future—"¡Espera!" (Wait!) (318)—but not the present, which is, of course, what he now desires. He reiterates his commitment to her, recalling to some degree his reaction when the Novia announced her intention of breaking with him (270–72). When he insists that their relationship should start that very instant—"Ahora . . ." (Now . . .) (321)—this brings to mind his deep resistance to that very word in act 1 (196, 216), an aversion that the Mecanógrafa has adopted as her own, and it follows that precisely the person most sympathetic to the Joven's stance in act 1, the Viejo, should now reappear. He has swapped his "chaqué gris" (gray morning coat) (191) for a blue suit ("vestido de azul," 322), which picks up the Joven's "pijama azul" (blue pajamas) (191) of act 1, and the handkerchief that he was clutching at the end of act 2 is now bloodstained (322), indicating literally that the radical change that has come over the Joven has "wounded" him deeply.

The conversation between the Mecanógrafa and the Joven now continues, witnessed by the Viejo standing on the main stage, almost as if he were the member of an audience, and he is later joined by other "spectators." The Joven expresses in a nutshell the mistaken standpoint that he had adopted in the past: he did not realize the real effects of the passage of time as he tried to take refuge in years of deferral—"Yo esperaba y moría" (I was waiting and dying), to which the Mecanógrada neatly counters: "Yo moría por esperar" (I was dying on account of waiting) (323). She kept on waiting for him to change his mind about her, she suffered terribly over those years because of her unrequited love, and simultaneously, time was passing for her too. But the Joven has now changed, and he claims to be newly vitalized—"la sangre golpea en mis sienes con sus nudillos de fuego" (the blood is knocking in my temples with its knuckles of fire) (322)—the mention of blood recalling several previous instances in which it was repeatedly connected with passion or procreation (208, 268, 285, 290). On cue, we hear the Máscara crying out for "¡Mi hijo!" (My son!), and to underline the point, the Niño Muerto flits across the stage (322). As has been pointed out by José Ángel Valente and others, the dead child is an avatar of an (as yet) unborn child. These aural and visual prompts immediately focus the Joven's attention on the principal reason why he has sought out the Mecanógrafa: not because he has realized that he genuinely loves her but, rather, because he knows that she loves him, and so she will make the perfect mother for the child that he now longs for: "¡Sí, mi hijo!" (Yes, my son!) (322). Of course, this misguided motivation is what, unbeknownst to the Joven, has from the start condemned this quest of his to failure.

The Máscara now returns, and she is joined by two more rather mysterious "máscaras" on the main stage (323)—the text does not say anything more about them. One might presume that they could be individuals in situations similar to the Máscara. The "audience" swells to four. The Mecanógrafa reacts severely to the Joven, first repeating her recent question mimicking from act 1 his inquiry about the letters being typed (206), but then returning to the present and confronting the Joven with his basic error: "No es tu hijo, soy yo" (It's not your son, it's me). She continues, showing considerable insight concerning past events: the Joven held out those five years for the Novia, and in the meantime, he was quite prepared to let the Mecanógrafa slip through his fingers and leave (as we saw in act 1), but after her declaration of love, he always knew that he was loved, which, she implies, was a consoling thought and, when he was finally jilted by the Novia, was a kind of fallback position for him. The Mecanógrafa knew, back then and as she does now, that he would never really love her, that he is incapable of doing so (as he says to the Viejo, "Yo quisiera quererla como quisiera tener sed delante de las fuentes" [I wish I could love her just as I wish I could feel thirst when standing in front of fountains], 209), but nonetheless, since she left, she has maintained her love for him and perhaps also idealized him: "yo he levantado mi amor y te he cambiado y te he visto por los rincones de mi casa" (I have raised up my love, and I have changed you, and I have seen you in the corners of my house) (323).[34]

But that is the problem. The transformation that her love has undergone over the intervening years(?) means that it is now similar, if not identical, to the love that the Joven professed for the Novia in act 1: "¡Te quiero, pero más lejos de ti! He huido tanto, que necesito contemplar el mar para poder evocar el temblor de tu boca" (I love you, but farther away from you! I've run away so far, that I need to contemplate the sea in order to bring to mind the trembling of your mouth) (323). As he said back then, "Tenía necesidad de separarme para . . . ¡enfocarla!, ésta es la palabra, en mi corazón" (I needed to separate myself in order to . . . focus her! that's the word, in my heart) (203). And immediately after, it is no coincidence that the Viejo starts to riff again on the nomenclature of measures of time. In act 1:

> VIEJO: ¿Pero por qué no decir tiene quince nieves, quince aires, quince crepúsculos? ¿No se atreve usted a huir? ¿a volar? ¿a ensanchar su amor por todo el cielo? [. . .]

VIEJO: (*De pie y con energía.*) O bien decir tiene quince rosas, quince alas, quince granitos de arena. (198–99)

VIEJO: But why not say she's fifteen snows old, fifteen winds, fifteen sunsets? Don't you dare to run away? To fly away? To extend your love over all the sky? [. . .]

VIEJO: (*Standing and forcefully.*) Or else say that she's fifteen roses old, fifteen wings, fifteen grains of sand.

And here in act 3: "VIEJO: Porque si él tiene veinte años puede tener veinte lunas" (VIEJO: Because if he is twenty years old, he can be twenty moons old), to which the Mecanógrafa herself adds: "(*Lírica.*) Veinte rocas, veinte nortes de nieve" ([*Lyrically.*] Twenty rocks old, twenty snowy norths old).

The Joven insistently reasserts his overriding goal: "Tú vendrás, conmigo. Porque me quieres y porque es necesario que yo viva" (You will come with me. Because you love me and because it is necessary that I live), noticeably not because he loves her but, rather, because she loves him and he needs to "live" (that is, live on in a child). The Mecanógrafa will have none of it, and she counters with these arguments underlining the lack of true reciprocity in the relationship: "Sí, te quiero, pero ¡mucho más! No tienes tú ojos para verme desnuda, ni boca para besar mi cuerpo que nunca se acaba. Déjame. ¡Te quiero demasiado para poder contemplarte!" (Yes, I love you, but much more! You don't have eyes to see me naked nor a mouth to kiss my body that never ends. Leave me alone. I love you too much to bear looking at you!) (324). Again, there are echoes here of the Joven in act 1: back then, the Joven had explained to the Viejo, in regard to the Novia, "¡La quiero demasiado!" (I love her too much!) (198), and "la última vez que la vi no podía mirarla muy de cerca" (the last time I saw her, I couldn't look at her very close-up) (203).

Increasingly frustrated by the way in which the Mecanógrafa evasively deflects his urgings and continues to prevaricate, the Joven becomes physical, grabbing her by the wrists to pull her along with him. To her cry of pain, the Joven simply replies: "¡Así me sientes!" (This way you'll feel me) (324). Once more, the brief exchange takes us back to act 2, first to the Novia's Criada, "Tuve un novio soldado que me clavaba los anillos y me hacía sangre" (I had a soldier boyfriend who squeezed my rings so hard that it made me bleed) (255), and then the Novia herself: "Tenía las manos llenas de anillos. ¿Dónde hay una gota de sangre?" (I had my hands covered in rings. Where is there a single drop of blood?) (267). In a way, then, the Joven attempts to treat the Mecanógrafa in a manner that the Novia implied he had failed to do with her (unlike the taciturn, "macho" Jugador de Rugby).

At this moment, however, the Mecanógrafa tries to defuse the situation, with her tone of voice, "Dulce" (Sweetly), and her action, "Lo abraza" (She embraces him). Still, what she says at the same time does not bode well because on each side of the seemingly promising phrase "Yo iré" (I will go), she utters two other words that the Joven does not want to hear: "Espera" (Wait) and "Siempre" (Always) (325). In different ways, they both negate the Joven's new watchword, "Ahora" (Now) (314, 321, 322). Of course, the Viejo endorses the Mecanógrafa's intentions, and despite the Joven's anguished "NO," while she is still embracing him, she seems to drift away almost in a semi-trance or dream: "Estoy muy alta. ¿Por qué me dejaste? Iba a morir de frío y tuve que buscar tu amor por donde no hay gente. Pero estaré contigo. Déjame bajar poco o poco hasta ti" (I am very high up. Why did you leave me? I was going to die of cold, and I had to look for your love where there aren't any people. But I will be with you. Let me come down little by little toward you) (325). She implies that although she is physically in his arms, she is psychically a long way distant from him, as a result of having to save herself from the torment that she was experiencing in act 1, and that she will now need a good deal of time to get closer to him. This idea recalls things that she said earlier, not only "He huido tanto, que necesito contemplar el mar para poder evocar el temblor de tu boca" (I've run away so far that I need to contemplate the sea in order to bring to mind the trembling of your mouth) (323) but also and more particularly:

Amor, déjame en el monte
harta de nube y rocío,
para verte grande y triste
cubrir un cielo dormido. (315)

Love, leave me on the mountainside
replete with cloud and dew,

in order to see you big and sad
cover a sleeping sky.

Before the Joven can respond to the last utterance, this section of the segment ends and the very last one begins, marked by the return of the Payaso and the Arlequín, who enter and sit on the two stools. They are ironic observers of what is happening on the small stage, joining the four others who are already part of the "audience." The Arlequín brings his white violin with two golden strings, while the Payaso now has a concertina, and together they start to recite some lines of verse or a lyric, divided between the two of them. The song is related to time—"Una música. | De años" (A piece of music. | Of years) (325–26), and the imagery connects back with the lunar eclipse of act 2 and the sequence with the Muchacha earlier in this Cuadro. The line "Lunas y mares sin abrir" (Unopened moons and seas) appears to be calqued on the more common phrase *flores sin abrir* (unopened flowers) and so might look to a future of possibility and potential—the moment of blooming, though it could also refer to the loss of those qualities if the moons/seas/flowers remain closed and never open. The second two lines look back to the past: "¿Queda atrás?" (Was it left behind?), and the reply is that what remains there is primarily connected with death: "La mortaja del aire. | Y la música de tu violín" (The shroud of the wind. | And the music of your violin) (326). Then they play some music.

The next stage direction for the Joven is "Saliendo de un sueño" (Emerging from a dream) (326). This whole Cuadro is, of course, part of his dream, but here the implication is that he has briefly fallen into a kind of deeply reflective or trancelike state, perhaps brought on by the Mecanógrafa's last response to him or by the song and music from the Payaso and Arlequín. At all events, once more he tries to spur her into immediate action, echoing his previous exhortations ("¡Vente!" 321; "¡Vamos!" 324 [Come on!; Let's go!]). And as before, the Mecanógrafa does not respond to him directly but, rather, marvels that this is the same Joven whom she knew in act 1, "¿Será posible que seas tú?" (Can it be possible that it's you?), and then proposes a further delay so that he can properly savor the moment: "¡Así de pronto! . . . Sin haber probado lentamente esta hermosa idea: mañana será" (So suddenly! . . . Without having slowly sampled this lovely idea: it'll be tomorrow). In turn, the Joven's reply to this is hardly straightforward. He mentions a nest—"Arriba hay como un nido" (Upstairs there's something like a nest) (326)—which could be a symbol of his desire to form a family with the Mecanógrafa or, more speculatively, an allusion to his bed (cf. 321). He also refers to the nightingale's song, previously mentioned by both him and her (314, 316) and which here seems to bring its traditional associations of romance and love and also, in conjunction with the nest, procreation. But then he goes further, invoking a very different—and for many, repulsive—flying creature of the night, the bat. The implied message would be that he wants them to be together, and while favorable conditions would be preferred, he is prepared to face unfavorable or even threatening ones: "¡aunque el murciélago golpee los cristales!" (even though the bat might beat at the windowpanes) (326). The creature is quite unlike Bécquer's Romantic swallows:

> Volverán las oscuras golondrinas
> en tu balcón sus nidos a colgar,
> y otra vez con el ala a sus cristales
> jugando llamarán.

> The dark swallows will return
> and again hang their nests at your balcony,
> and once more with their wings
> will playfully knock at your windowpanes.

We are now approaching the last repetition of a well-established pattern. The Mecanógrafa agrees with him but then indicates a hesitation or reservation: "Sí. Sí, pero . . ." (Yes. Yes, but . . .) (327). By way of reply, and having previously embraced her (314, 325), the Joven simply kisses her. Now, in a rapid-fire exchange, during which the Joven still does not fully realize just how hopeless the situation is, he continues pushing her to go with him, while she keeps on delaying (327–28). The phrase that she utters, "¡Yo me iré!" (I'll go), and then twice "¡Me iré contigo!" (I'll go with you), is finally completed by her with the crushing proviso: "¡Así que pasen cinco años!" (When five years have passed!), bringing to a close this extended and reiterative playing out of the inversion of roles. The

Payaso's words to the Joven just before the Mecanógrafa appeared—"Da la media vuelta y lo encontrarás" (Turn halfway around, and you will find it) (313)—now acquire a new meaning that the Joven had not suspected at the time: he did in a sense win over the Mecanógrafa, but everything has literally been turned around 180 degrees.[35] Underlining the metatheatrical dimension of this whole dialogue on the small stage, the Viejo cheers the Mecanógrafa's "performance" with a sotto voce "Bravo" (328).

The Joven now finally admits defeat, this change being marked by his descent from the faded library back to the main stage. At the same time, the Mecanógrafa "freezes" in place on the small stage, and the Criado comes out and drapes a large white cloak over her (328), clearly indicating that the episode is over and also that the Mecanógrafa was not real and nothing more than a kind of projection, not entirely dissimilar to the Maniquí in act 2 who, whenever anyone else is onstage, "queda rígido" (goes rigid) (287) and who, at the end of the act, "Se desmaya y queda tendido en el sofá" (Faints and ends up stretched out on the sofa) (291). The curtains remain open.

The Payaso and the Arlequín repeat (329), word for word, their brief lines of verse and music (325–26), perhaps suggesting that nothing fundamental has changed now that the Joven has recognized his defeat. Two other characters react in dissimilar ways: the Máscara fantasizes that the Count kisses her photograph, while the Viejo, recalling something he said in act 1 ("Por eso vamos a . . . a no . . . ir . . . o a esperar" [For that reason we are going to . . . to not . . . go . . . or else to wait], 205), restates his philosophy of life: "Vamos a no llegar, pero vamos a ir" (We are not going to arrive, but we are going to go) (329), always moving forward but carefully avoiding ever arriving.

Meanwhile, having reached this juncture, the crestfallen Joven just wants to find his way out of the park. This final exchange with the Payaso and the Arlequín mirrors his first interaction with them, in which they also gave him deliberately confusing and obstructive directions (309–13). Now they are more openly having fun at his expense, pointing him this way and that, while he becomes increasingly desperate (330–31). The Mecanógrafa, from under the cape and standing "en actitud extática" (in an enraptured pose), calls to him, promising to wait for his return, but he pays her no heed. The Cuadro ends with his words—"¡Quiero volver! Dejarme"

(I want to go back! Let me go) (331)—that are somewhat reminiscent of the Muchacha's conflictive exchanges with the Arlequín and Payaso but which are actually closest to something said by the Amigo 2°: "dejadme volver" (let me go back) (236), as he longs to turn back time.

Act 3, Cuadro 1, is in many ways recapitulatory, from the Arlequín's opening verses onward. There are also many effects of echoing and repetition, and as has been noted, it does often feel as if the successive segments or scenes of the Cuadro are going round in circles—which is surely part of the point. The action of the play only progresses a little over how it was left at the end of act 2: on the literal level of what is performed onstage, we see the Joven eventually find the Mecanógrafa, but he fails in achieving what he had resolved to do after the dialogue with the Maniquí.

There are at least two reasons for this. One very important factor here is that all of the Cuadro is the representation onstage of the Joven's dream or feverish hallucination. The fantastic elements, the appearance of strange characters not heard from previously, and the repetitive structure can all be attributed to this fact. Furthermore, what the Joven's psyche portrays here is his own failure. On one level, it could seem as if the Mecanógrafa were taking a particularly appropriate revenge on him, turning him now into the recipient of the near-endless postponement that characterized his attitude toward the Novia in act 1 and which consequently also motivated his spurning of the Mecanógrafa back then. But as she is ultimately a figment animated by the Joven's mind, what we have here is either an example of self-knowledge or self-insight or, alternatively, one of self-recrimination or self-punishment. The right moment to respond to the Mecanógrafa was back in act 1, before he let her leave his house.[36] Although the Joven wants to turn back the clock, part of him already knows that this is not possible, that the opportunity is irremediably lost in the past and therefore cannot be recouped. Thus, the Cuadro portrays the Joven's explicit realization of this fact and perhaps, too, the Joven reproaching or castigating himself by having the Mecanógrafa now insist on the very same postponement—five years—as he had embraced in act 1 but which backfired on him in act 2.[37]

The other principal factor is that already in this Cuadro, the Joven is close to death, an event consummated in the final Cuadro, in which the three Jugadores, as modern-day Fates, come to collect his heart. Therefore, as Martínez Nadal and Lázaro Carreter argue, here we are already in the "antesala de la muerte" or the "antesala del Hades" (antechamber of death/ Hades),[38] represented by the almost archetypal dark and mysterious wood where hunting horns are to be heard.[39] In conventional mythology, Charon is the ferryman of the underworld, and its gates are guarded by the dog Cerberus, but here they are replaced by the Arlequín and the Payaso.[40] Hence the overall impression that they are always in control, although they choose to exercise that power in different and often unkind, teasing, mocking, and taunting ways.[41] And hence, more specifically, their scene with the Muchacha, who is (rightly) afraid of being given the opportunity to see her dead lover, the reference to the "circo [. . .] lleno de espectadores definitivamente quietos" (310), the music that they play as a kind of parodic dance of death,[42] the brief presence of the Niño Muerto who crosses the stage, their increasingly cruel treatment of the Joven at the end of the Cuadro, and his desire not so much to get out of there as to go back ("¡Quiero volver!" 331).

After all this, the relatively brief Cuadro 2 is largely a coda, fulfilling events already announced. Its opening scenes give the impression of a return to something approaching a realistic presentation—we are back in the full-sized library, we eavesdrop on two servants gossiping, then the Joven gives a series of instructions to his manservant. However, the temporal indicators in the dialogue immediately indicate that normalcy has in fact not been restored: the doorkeeper's child's funeral has just taken place (334), while long ago—the Joven does not remember the detail—he gave his old walnut bed to his "antigua mecanógrafa" (former typist) (337). The open suitcases in the initial stage direction (332) establish the idea of a recent return from a journey, which is then confirmed by Juan (336). This harks back to the five-year trip taken by the Padre and the Novia around the world (261), but up to this point, there has been no suggestion of the Joven having undertaken anything like this. The circularity of the stage sets suggests that the journey is to be understood as psychic rather than physical and that it is at its end. The Joven somehow knows that he cannot avoid playing cards with the three Jugadores, a transparent reincarnation of the Fates. Despite some ineffectual attempts at delay, he must eventually lay his ace of hearts on the table, and as he exits, the Jugador 3° utters his final recommendation: "No hay que esperar nunca. Hay que vivir" (One must never wait. One must live) (351).

9

Social Concern, Metatheater, and the Audience's Experience in *El sueño de la vida*

The single extant act 1 of *El sueño de la vida* (1935–36) combines sociopolitical concerns, expressed more explicitly here than Lorca had ever done before, with experiments in metatheater that are in some senses more extreme than those found in any of his previous plays. Metatheatrical elements include a broken fourth wall, "plants" in the audience, actors who lapse in and out of character or change character, powerful sound effects emanating from outside the auditorium, and reported events occurring offstage that finally engulf the theater at the end of the act. At the same time, the work's themes involve, among other things, social inequality and injustice, radical politics (Left and Right), religion, and the pressing need for major economic and cultural change. These two distinct threads intertwine in the idea of revolution and in the relation of the theater with, and impact on, real life that is envisaged and advocated by the text. Furthermore, while previous criticism has rightly stressed the play's many striking and unusual features, it has not fully recognized the numerous odd occurrences, uncertainties, and internal inconsistencies that permeate the script and hence serve to subvert any simple, univocal interpretations.[1] This underlying and pervasive ambiguity creates in turn an unsettling effect that is ultimately disruptive of the status quo.

The action takes place inside a theater, extending to both the stage and the auditorium, meaning that in any given production, the designated performance space as well as the area where the audience is seated function simultaneously as the overall setting where the scenes of the play unfold. This fact alone blurs, indeed almost obliterates, the distinction between the real and the fictional, creating an effect reminiscent of Manuel Tamayo y Baus's *Un drama nuevo.* There, similarly, in the second part of act 3, the nineteenth-century Madrid theater serves imaginatively as the space where the Elizabethan-era tragedy is performed, and the Spanish audience passively plays the part of the groundlings watching it, creating a confusion that is only partly clarified by the character of Shakespeare in his closing speech.

In the case of *El sueño de la vida,* the basic circumstances surrounding the action are even less clear. There are two plausible possibilities, though neither serves to integrate and explain all the details that we eventually encounter. The first scenario that can be imagined is that the audience has gone to see a performance of a more or less conventional play, one whose title is never revealed. A number of critics claim that the audience expects to see a production of *A Midsummer Night's Dream,* but nothing in the text supports this; it is quite clear that what has been scheduled is a *rehearsal* of that play elsewhere in the theater (149).[2] However, the Autor hijacks that day's performance of the unnamed play and, improvising, turns it into something completely different. Consequently, the audience's expectations are unfulfilled, as is conveyed in some of the comments made early on by the married couple Espectador 1.° and Espectadora 1.ª (139–43). The second possibility is that this would be the opening night of a new play about which very little is known in advance. Again, the audience members attend the premiere with their usual expectations of being entertained, given the standard dramatic fare of the time, but are confounded when they encounter an entirely disconcerting presentation that breaks almost all the prevailing theatrical norms and which has been carefully planned out in advance by the Autor.

No curtain rises at the beginning of the play. Rather, the Autor comes out onstage with a "Telón gris" (Gray curtain) behind him. One might reasonably assume that this was the front or house curtain—as is implied by the phrase "No voy a levantar el telón" (I'm not going to raise the curtain) (137), but subsequent stage directions cast doubt on this. At different points, three painted curtains are lowered; all of them appear to be backdrops, and the third is specifically identified as such (139; 149; "telón de fondo," 153; cf. also the reference to "telones pintados" [painted curtains], 149). Either the draft manuscript is lacking the indication for the gray curtain to be raised (though it is unclear what would be the appropriate moment for this to happen), or else it needs to be imagined as situated considerably farther back in the stage space, to allow for these three curtains to cover it and each other in turn.

The Autor is never addressed by this title; rather, the Traspunte calls him "señor director" (149), and the Actriz uses his name, Lorenzo (151). As the Autor himself refers to someone else as "el autor" (139), we can conclude that Lorca is using the term in its Golden Age sense as the director of a company (much as Shakespeare is the head of the troupe of players in *Un drama nuevo*).[3]

Most plays in Lorca's time did not commence with a spoken prologue, but it would not have been completely unheard of, and he also used prologues for a variety of experimental effects in other plays, notably the two works for puppets as well as *La zapatera prodigiosa* (1930) and the fragment of *Dragón* (ca. 1929), in which we also find a blurring of levels of reality.[4] Here, in *El sueño de la vida,* the Autor informs the audience members that he is not going to give them what they have come for, namely two or three hours of escapist entertainment and mindless distraction in the form of the *género chico* ("un juego de palabras" [a pun on words]) or the so-called *alta comedia* ("un panorama donde se vea una casa en la que nada ocurre y adonde dirige el teatro sus luces para entretener" [a panorama where a house can be seen in which nothing happens and on which the theater trains its lights in order to entertain]) (137). Lorca's own comments referring to run-of-the-mill bourgeois drama are in a similar vein: "Eso no es teatro, no es nada" (That is not theater; it is not anything).[5] His criticism of the commercialism and the superficiality of conventional theater runs through many of his newspaper interviews and becomes more intense from December 1934 onward.[6]

The Autor's purpose is very different, as he aspires to "conmover vuestros corazones enseñándoos las cosas que no queréis ver, gritando las simplísimas verdades que no queréis oír" (touch your hearts by showing you things that you don't want to see, by shouting the simplest truths that you don't want to hear). At the same time, he readily acknowledges that "ver la realidad es difícil. Y enseñarla, mucho más" (to see reality is difficult. And to show it, much more so) (138). To this end, the Autor (director) seems to have entered into some form of understanding or collaboration with the "autor" (playwright): "El autor [. . .] ayer me dijo que en todo arte había una mitad de artificio que por ahora le molestaba" (Yesterday the author [. . .] told me that half of all art was artifice, which for the moment was bothering him) (139).

Here the Autor, and Lorca behind him, wrestles with one of the fundamental paradoxes of theater and, indeed, all literature: a play depends on theatrical illusion, on actors pretending to be people that they are not, yet—in theory at least—it is supposed to be a vehicle for truths, truths that an audience is generally more likely to be receptive to and absorb through this fictional medium rather than from a more direct or confrontational one (such, precisely, as listening to a preacher in a church). As the Autor says, he turns the prologue into a sermon (138) because of his concerns that the theater has lost much of its purpose ("Venís al teatro con el afán único de divertiros y tenéis autores a los que pagáis" [You come to the theater with the sole desire to have a good time, and you have authors whom you pay], 137), and because that "mitad de artificio" (139) is threatening to swamp any truth-telling function.

To remedy this and redress the imbalance, the director and playwright have come up with the idea of turning the tables on the audience member:

¿Por qué hemos de ir siempre al teatro para ver lo que pasa y no lo que nos pasa? El espectador está tranquilo porque sabe que la comedia no se va a fijar en él, ¡pero qué hermoso sería que de pronto lo llamaran de las tablas y le hicieran hablar, y el sol de la escena quemara su pálido rostro de emboscado! (138)

Why have we always got to go to the theater to see what happens and not what happens to us? The spectator is calm because he knows that the play is not going to fix its attention on him, but how lovely it would be if suddenly he were to be called on from the stage and made to talk, and if the stage's sun were to burn his pale face of someone lying in ambush!

Their goal is to take the audience members out of their comfort zone; if the theater has become complicit in the escape into fantasy and deliberate forgetfulness (137–38), then literally or figuratively, the audience will somehow have to be forced outside to perceive and confront the truths that it would rather ignore: "La realidad empieza porque el autor no quiere que os sintáis en el teatro sino en mitad de la calle y no quiere, por tanto, hacer poesía, ritmo, literatura, quiere dar una pequeña lección a vuestros corazones" (Reality is making a start because the author does not want you to feel that you are in a theater but rather in the middle of the street, and hence, he does not want to create poetry, rhythm, literature; he wants to give a small lesson to your hearts) (138–39); "Hay que despertarlos y abrirles los ojos aunque no quieran" (It is necessary to wake them up and open their eyes even though they might not want to) (147). This is no easy task, however, and the prologue ends with the Autor posing a rhetorical question as to how to bring that "outside" inside: "¿Pero cómo se llevaría el olor del mar a una sala de teatro o cómo se inunda de estrellas el patio de butacas?" (But how can the smell of the sea be brought into a theater's auditorium, or how can the stalls be flooded with stars?) (139).

In the event, before the Autor can pick out an audience member by aiming a spotlight ("el sol de la escena," 138) on her or him, a spectator interjects himself by interrupting him. A conventional spoken prologue stands apart from the play proper and therefore technically does not break the fourth wall. Here, however, the prologue blends seamlessly into the action of the play when someone from the auditorium begins to interact with someone onstage and all notions of the dividing line between the two are left far behind. (Curiously, none of the other characters who subsequently appear onstage interacts in any way with the audience or even acknowledges its existence, thus conferring some sort of special status on the Autor.) Of course, the Espectador 1.° and later the Espectadora 1.ª, Joven, Espectador 2.°, Espectadora 2.ª, and Obrero are all actors planted among the audience. This device has been used, occasionally, over the centuries, but in modern times, critics tend to trace it back to Pirandello's *Tonight We Improvise* (*Questa sera si recita a soggetto*, 1930). It had already been used by Roger Vitrac in *Les Mystères de l'amour* (1924)[7] and would be employed, shortly after Pirandello's play, by W. H. Auden (*The Dance of Death*, 1933), Clifford Odets (*Waiting for Lefty*, 1935), Ayn Rand (*Night of Janu-

ary 16th, 1935), Jean Cocteau (*L'Impromptu d'Alice,* 1937), and Thorton Wilder (*Our Town,* 1938). Of all these, because of their date or where they were published and/or performed, it is only really plausible that Lorca could have known Pirandello's work.[8] By now real audience members who were unfamiliar with Lorca's play would be asking themselves what was happening: after being sternly lectured by this person (who at this point remains unidentified by the script), someone in their midst argues with him, with both of them becoming increasingly confrontational over quite a long series of exchanges (139–43).

This strikingly unusual beginning of the act invites us to consider its overall structure as well as the major and minor disconcerting features and inconsistencies that run through it. Broadly speaking, the action breaks down into two roughly equal halves, with the pivotal point coming when the sounds of the violence outside are initially heard (154). The first half falls into five sequences: the prologue (137–39); the argument between the Autor and Espectador 1.º (139–44); the dialogue between the Autor, Joven, and Criado (144–49); the conversation between the Autor and the Traspunte (149–51); and the interaction between the Autor and the Actriz (151–54). This kind of segmented organizational pattern disappears completely from the second half, in which, appropriately enough, confusion reigns, multiple characters enter and exit repeatedly, and no single dialogue is sustained for any substantial period of time.

While this structure seems reasonable and straightforward enough, it soon becomes impossible for anyone viewing the performance to integrate into a logical and coherent whole all the elements that appear or are mentioned. Beyond our initial uncertainty as to exactly what play the audience has come to see, much else is perplexing or disturbing. Toward the end of his opening harangue, the Autor suddenly stops, claps his hands, and requests that he be brought a cup of coffee, before continuing on with his train of thought, a banal yet very strange act under the circumstances. After he adds that he wants the beverage good and strong, he sits down, something that people delivering a speech of this sort rarely do, and then totally unexplained violin music is heard (139), never to return. Moments after the exchange between the Autor and Espectador 1.º begins, the audience receives another surprise: "Aparece corriendo por la escena un hombre vestido de mallas rojas. Lleva una cabeza de lobo. Da dos saltos y cae en medio de la escena" (There appears running across the stage a man dressed in red tights. He is carrying a wolf's head. He jumps twice and falls over in the middle of the stage) (140). While somewhat reminiscent of Bottom, who appears with his ass's head later on (155), there is of course no wolf-man in *A Midsummer Night's Dream*. The Autor checks that the individual is not hurt—no explanation is offered of who he is or why he is there—and then we also hear the first instance of the offstage (female) voice crying out for Lorenzo, two unconcatenated and unexplained events that nevertheless do not perturb the Autor in any way, and he simply returns to his increasingly heated dispute.

As the invective mounts, the coffee arrives, brought by a Criado (141) who is not a stagehand but, rather, a waiter from a small nearby café (145). The Criado stands there holding the cup for quite a while, beyond the end of the argument—the spectator and his wife eventually leave (144)—and into the next sequence, and only then does the Autor take the cup and complain about the lack of coffee in it, which has been spilled (144). At that point, the Criado becomes the third participant in the three-way conversation that ensues (144–49). Furthermore, the Criado's account of his misadventures while carrying out his errand is decidedly odd and cannot be explained naturalistically: "tropecé con unos pescadores que cantaban con unos peces de plomo en la cabeza" (I bumped into some fishermen who were singing with lead fishes on their heads) (144–45).

The next disruptive jolt comes after the Criado exits and immediately after the Traspunte appears and asks the Autor: "Señor director, ¿no acude al ensayo?" (Mr. Director, aren't you coming to the rehearsal?) (149). We are in the middle of some kind of live performance, either planned or hijacked, yet the Traspunte (a kind of stage manager–prompter, different from the script prompter—*apuntador*) somehow expects the Autor to attend a scheduled rehearsal in the theater's "salón de ensayos" (rehearsal room) elsewhere in the theater building (148) and does not seem to find it at all peculiar that the Autor is out there onstage in front of an audience that fills the auditorium. Equally strangely, the Autor does not appear to know what play is to be rehearsed, even though he must be its director; when informed that it is Shakespeare's *A Midsummer Night's Dream*, this provides him with the pretext to launch into his own interpretation of the work (150). However, the new backdrop that is lowered at the moment of the Traspunte's entrance—of a "palacio inverosímil" (wildly unrealistic palace) (149)—matches the play referred to and hence somehow seems to be synchronized. Soon the first of several actors in costume appears: the Actriz, who turns out to be the source of that Voz already heard twice previously (140, 144), is dressed as Titania (151)—precisely the character who was the central focus of the Autor's seemingly impromptu analysis. After a fairly lengthy exchange, the Actriz concludes that she would have more success in convincing her erstwhile lover if she were Lady Macbeth, and so she immediately sheds her blonde wig and white cloak to appear now as this new character, with black hair and a bright-red dress underneath—yet another detail that lacks all verisimilitude. Again, the next change of backdrop—to a "claustro de piedra" (stone cloister) (153)—matches the shift onstage.

Lady Macbeth has little time to try to win over the Autor, though her request for "luz roja" (red light) is immediately fulfilled by an unseen and attentive lighting technician. Her impassioned speech, in line with the single-minded fanaticism of Shakespeare's character—"Qué me importa a mí que mueran los soldados" (What does it matter to me if soldiers were to die)—is interrupted, and with this we arrive at the turning point in the action, when the first gunshots are heard, momentarily creating a juxtaposition bordering on pathetic fallacy (154).

These sound effects will become louder and more menacing, incrementally, over the second half of the act, as confusion, fear, and revolutionary fervor escalate. The shots are heard nearer (155), then there is cannon fire (159), then four airplanes approach (160), an aerial bombardment is announced (161), it begins (163), it intensifies (164, 166, 166), and finally, fire breaks out (169). Curiously, amid all this hubbub, various characters still have time for less-than-pressing conversations, though each is admittedly quite short: the Autor questions the Traspunte's invocation of "la economía" (the economy), of which he has no understanding (156), the Leñador expresses his commitment to his role and recites snippets of the text in verse (158–59, 159–60), the Autor and Espectador 2.° argue about the reliability or unreliability of what today we can easily identify as disinformation—a supposed worker massacre of children (160–61)—and Espectador 2.° and Joven have an exchange on the subject of religion, Espectador 2.°'s exclusive and highly reactionary Catholicism versus the

Joven's professed Muslim faith (165), in which it is unclear whether the Joven is serious or being facetious, and then regarding the Espectador's expert marksmanship (165–66).

These sequences are interwoven among the sound effects just mentioned and various bulletins that are delivered about events unfolding outside the theater, a modern adaptation of the *récit* technique used by Jean Racine. According to Espectador 2.°, "Las calles deben estar tomadas militarmente" (The streets must be occupied by the military); the Traspunte reports: "Parece que se acercan más. Todo el vestíbulo está lleno de gente" (It seems as if they are getting closer. The whole foyer is full of people) (155); the Leñador brings the news that "parece que los revoltosos se baten en retirada" (it seems that the troublemakers are beating a hasty retreat) (158); while the Traspunte provides the next update: "La fuerza está ahora cargando en la gran plaza" (The forces of law and order are now charging in the big square) (159); and the Tramoyista the last one: "¡El pueblo ha roto las puertas!" (The people have broken the doors!) (168).

From the Semana Trágica of summer 1909 and the General Strike of August 1917 on into the 1930s, there was a great deal of worker unrest in Spain met by the successive governments with varying degrees of forceful or violent repression. Especially in the wake of the Russian Revolution of 1917, strikes were considered to be revolutionary actions, along with the large-scale street protests, demonstrations, rallies, and marches that usually accompanied them. As a result, over the first three decades of the twentieth century, martial law was declared on many dozens of occasions,[9] and some combination of the police, the mounted police, the Guardia Civil, or the army was almost always sent in to disperse, arrest, and suppress, resulting in a great many casualties. The use of artillery against the civilian population was far from uncommon.[10] This is exactly the situation that is being evoked here: the military taking control of the streets, the withdrawal and flight of the protesters in disarray, who might well seek shelter or refuge in nearby buildings, mounted charges to break up the crowds, and then the use of firearms against them.

Of course, much closer to the date of composition of *El sueño de la vida* is the Asturias uprising of the fall of 1934. In the face of the insurrection launched by the trade unionists, and with the local army detachments and the Civil Guard unable to cope, the government called in Moroccan regulars from its Africa army as well as troops from the Foreign Legion. There were pitched battles involving small arms and cannon, while warships provided an onshore bombardment. Over one thousand workers died. These are doubtless the unspoken points of reference when Espectador 2.° recalls that "tuve de maestro a un teniente alemán que había hecho todas las guerras africanas" (my teacher was a German lieutenant who had fought in all the African wars) (166), when the Hombre (the theater's owner) exclaims: "¡Mano dura!, ¡mano dura! ¡Hagamos una gran rosa de cabezas rebeldes! Adornemos las fachadas, las farolas, los pórticos de la arquitectura milenaria con guirnaldas de las lenguas que quieren destruir lo instituido" (Iron fist! Crack down! Let's make a great rose out of rebel heads! Let's decorate the facades, the streetlamps, the porticoes of the age-old architecture with garlands made out of the tongues that want to destroy the establishment) (157), or when Espectadora 2.ª gives voice to an abiding fear and cries out in panic: "Es la revolución, Enrique. ¡La revolución!" (It's the revolution, Enrique. The revolution!) (159).

Had the play been completed and performed before the outbreak of the Civil War, these events would have been fresh in the memories of the audience. They certainly were in the mind of Margarita Xirgu when Lorca read the first draft of the play to her in the summer of 1935:

> —En aquel primer acto—dice Margarita—se reflejaba el ambiente de los días que se estaban viviendo cuando me lo leyó, y había en él como un presentimiento de lo que ocurriría después . . .
>
> De lo que ocurriría después y de lo que entonces nadie podía sospechar—pensamos nosotros—. Eran los días en que, fracasado el movimiento revolucionario iniciado en Asturias, la República española estaba gobernada por las derechas.[11]

> When he read it to me—says Margarita—the atmosphere of the days that we were living through was reflected in that first act, and in it there was a kind of premonition of what would later happen . . .
>
> Of what would later happen and of what nobody at that time could have suspected—is our additional thought. Those were the days when, after the revolutionary movement that started in Asturias had failed, the Spanish Republic was governed by the forces of the right.

As clear as these contemporary allusions may be, from the metatheatrical perspective, several questions linger. How would the Autor's "prologue" have continued if he had not been interrupted (assuming that the Autor had mapped out a continuation)? Was the original intention that it should lead into some kind of unspecified "main action" had it not been derailed before it reached its conclusion, or was the plan always that it should merge into what actually follows? Could the plants in the audience have been put there in advance by the Autor and form part of his complicated scheme, or—as one might otherwise suppose—are they just part of the work that Lorca has conceived, to draw the Autor into debate with the spectators and thereby insert the audience into the action of the play? Thus, the unresolved ambiguity of the overall situation is a good deal more complicated than has been recognized by other critics.[12] Likewise, over the second half of the act, and within the different levels of reality/fiction on which it operates, is the violence outside the theater something unplanned and unforeseen, or is it prearranged? That is to say, is this event something scripted by the external author—that is, Lorca—an event that he interjects into the action midway through, thereby providing a new development and situation in the face of which his range of characters needs to react? Or alternatively, could this actually be an integral part of the plot that has been mapped out in advance by the Autor for this one-off performance? After all, we never actually see the violence outside the theater: it is evoked by sound effects and later lighting effects and by the aforementioned verbal reports, so could this be seen as literally "staged" and the ultimate curveball that the Autor has carefully prepared for his unsuspecting audience? Mutatis mutandis, might this anticipate what Orson Welles would do in his 1938 broadcast of *The War of the Worlds?* On a given night, a number of audience members might take it for granted that the plants were actually "real" spectators outraged by what was occurring, and however they construed the sum of the events, the denouement of the act would surely have been alarming for someone attending a performance of *El sueño de la vida.* Audience members did indeed respond in a number of different ways when the act was premiered in 1989.[13]

Thematically, the principal focus is on a cluster of related notions that can be organized into a number of binary oppositions: truth-falsehood, the real-the fake, sincerity-pretense, cognizance-avoidance, concern-indifference, kindness-cruelty, and so on. These pairs are manifested in several different spheres of human activity, and Lorca implicitly suggests that there are strong analogies if not direct parallels between them. Where in *El público* he focused on the issues of theatrical performance, individual identity, and interpersonal relations (see chapter 5), in *El sueño de la vida* he ambitiously seeks to revisit all of those topics while also adding another one to the mix—the sociopolitical dimension.

The exploration of the nature of theater, as presented here, revolves around the basic binary of *mentira* versus *verdad* and is exemplified in both plot and in props/pieces of scenery. The topics covered by the Autor in his prologue spill over, in a seamless segue, into the argument with Espectador 1.º, and here the Autor states the dichotomy clearly: "Ahí dentro hay un terrible aire de mentira y los personajes de las comedias no dicen más que lo que pueden decir en alta voz delante de señoritas débiles, pero se callan su verdadera angustia" (Back there inside, there is a terrible atmosphere of falsehood, and the characters in the plays do not say anything other than what they can say out loud in front of frail young ladies, but they silence their true anguish). Although the Espectador 1.º becomes increasingly outraged, his wife has understood all that has happened up to this point to be part of a plotted, if unconventional, action and professes herself intrigued by its novelty or unusualness and so is reluctant to leave: "No me quisiera ir. Me interesa el argumento" (I don't want to go. The plot interests me) (142). In the face of the Espectador 1.º's complaints: "¡Qué exagerado!" (How exaggerated!), the Autor counters that "Dios sabe que digo exactamente la verdad" (God knows that I am telling precisely the truth). Although the Espectador really wants to leave, his wife sees no need as it is all made up and therefore somehow harmless: "En el teatro todo es mentira" (In the theater, everything is made up). When the Autor bluntly contradicts her, "¡No es mentira! ¡Es verdad!" (It's not made up! It's true!), she finally realizes her mistake and is now utterly scandalized by what she has just heard (143).

This episode demonstrates the point that exactly the same stimulus (in this case, what the Autor talks about over these opening pages) can elicit very different reactions depending on the status—invented or factual—that is attributed to it or the context that frames it. Furthermore, what is more than acceptable, if considered to be make-believe, instantly becomes utterly unacceptable if it is found actually to be true. Something quite similar occurs in the scene involving the Criado and various props and pieces of the set. He is afraid of the gauzy material that emulates clouds (145) and hesitant to leave without full illumination because he will again have to pass by this obstacle (149). The Autor is surprised by this "miedo de las cosas pintadas" (fear of painted things) (145), and he reassures the Criado that "no es nada, ya lo verá, unas gasas y unos telones pintados" (it's nothing, you'll see, some pieces of chiffon and painted curtains) (149). In the intervening dialogue between the two, a strong contrast is drawn between this reaction and the Criado's attitude in regard to various events that took place in the café where he works: the brutal, sadistic torture of a child, a turkey, and a cat (145–46), which leave him unmoved or even enthusiastic. The crux of the matter is that even though the stage effects are fake, they *appear* real: "Sí, sí, pero parecen de verdad" (Yes, yes, but they seem real), and it is in some way this very artificiality that is more effective in prompting an emotional response than something genuine or authentic. However, if they were real, the Criado would have no qualms and would deal with them promptly—and violently: "¡Ah!, si lo fueran, con dispararles un tiro." (Oh! if they were, it would be just a question of firing a shot at them) (149). The disjunction that emerges here, as well as the Criado's naïveté, are underlined by the ironic comments offered by the cynical Joven, who first remarks that "este muchacho lloraría con una historia de amor bien narrada" (that lad would weep at a well-told love story) (146) and later, "¡Cántele usted una canción cursi y ya verá qué lágrimas!" (Sing him a schmaltzy song, and then you'll see a flood of tears) (147).

The divide between sincerity and pretense in the sphere of the individual and the interpersonal is exemplified, more or less exclusively, in the relationship between the Autor and the Actriz. In addition, the Actriz's profession, the fact that she is cast in different roles and wears stage costume, and the Autor's accusations of constant pretense all connect this issue of human relationships closely to the theatrical paradigm just analyzed. Evidently, the two of them have been involved in some kind of love affair, which the Autor has recently sought to end, against the Actriz's wishes. We hear her imploring voice crying out for Lorenzo twice (144), and when she is first about to come onstage, he forestalls this action while at the same time establishing the fundamental source of disagreement between them:

"¡No! Te he dicho que no entres. No te quiero ver, ¡estoy cansado de mentiras!" (No! I've told you not to come onstage. I don't want to see you; I'm tired of lies!) (148). When she does finally appear, she is dressed as Titania, from the production that is supposedly going to be rehearsed elsewhere in the building. Again, ignoring the fact that the Autor is onstage and in front of an audience, she wonders why he has not yet come to direct the rehearsal and claims—exaggeratedly—first that "no puedo trabajar sin ti" (I can't work without you) and then that she is only there because of him: "Si no veo la salida del sol que tanto me gusta y no corro por la hierba con los pies descalzos, es sólo por seguirte y estar contigo en estos sótanos" (If I don't see the sunrise that I like so much and I don't run through the grass with bare feet, it's only because I'm following you to be with you here in these cellars). The Autor rejects this and all of her subsequent entreaties as insincere posturing, role-playing, and falsehoods, accusing her of using borrowed words and phrases that she has learned elsewhere. He also rebuffs her protestations of innocence, and of genuine passion for him, with a curt "¡Mentira!" (That's a lie!) (151, 152). Through the course of the scene, she adopts different personas in her attempts to win him over, first a passive and almost masochistic one (152), and then, when that does not work, a much more assertive and indeed a bloodthirsty one, indicated by her shedding of the Titania costume to reveal Lady Macbeth beneath. Their problematic relationship is summed up, in a sense, in this brief exchange: "AUTOR: Tú no me dirás nunca la verdad. | ACTRIZ: "Ni nadie. Pero te cantaría la mentira más hermosa" (AUTOR: You'll never tell me the truth. | ACTRIZ: No one will. But I would sing you the most beautiful of lies) (153).

The episode is brought to an abrupt end by the first gunshots that ring out, and in the latter half of the act, the Actriz shows herself to be cowardly and self-absorbed, hiding her costume under a raincoat and hat, calling for the theater's doors to be barred (155), and pleading with Lorenzo to take cover (157), though still with the same hollow rhetoric: "Aleja el peligro de tu maravilloso talento" (Keep danger away from your marvelous talent) (162). She remains firmly committed to the conventional theater, with all its fake props and stage machinery (156), and in a heavily ironic final appearance, she becomes irritated with Espectadora 2.ª, finding her no doubt sincere cries of anguish for the safety of her children utterly unconvincing:

Estoy harta de oírla gritar mal. No lo puedo sufrir. Su voz tiene un aire falso que no logrará conmocionar nunca. No, así, es así: ¡Mis hijos, mis hijos, mis niños pequeños! ¿Lo ha oído? ¡Mis niños pequeños! Y las manos hacia adelante, imprimiéndoles un temblor como si fueran dos hojas en una fiebre de viento. (168)

I'm fed up with hearing her cry out badly. I can't bear it. Her voice has a false ring to it that will never touch anyone. No, like this, it's like this: My children, my children, my little children! Did you hear that? My children! With your hands out in front of you, making them tremble as if they were two leaves in a feverish wind.

This briefly recapitulates one of the points made by the Criado and the Joven and illustrates that the Actriz, like the Joven, continues to believe in the power of simulation to elicit genuine emotion. Indeed, earlier on, the Joven had commented positively on her imploring cries: "Esa voz que ha sonado dos veces me conmueve a mí mucho más que una verdadera voz de agonía" (That voice that we've heard twice moves me much more than a true voice of agony) (144).

The new, additional element in *El sueño de la vida*—compared to *El público*—is the important sociopolitical dimension. This brings up the question of Lorca's own political stance as of 1935–36, though in general I believe that the text of the play should be allowed to speak for itself. Working with essentially the same corpus of biographical source materials, different critics have arrived at different conclusions. For instance, Andrés Pérez-Simón finds an unequivocal embrace of socialist politics, whereas Emilio Peral Vega traces a considerably more inflected response over the same years.[14] In regard to the play, Lorca stressed both its radical themes and the theatrical experimentation: "Un tema social, mezclado de religioso" (A social theme, mixed in with a religious one); "un acto completamente subversivo que supone una verdadera revolución de la técnica" (a completely subversive act that presupposes a true revolution in technique); "una obra ultramoderna en la que maneja los más audaces procedimientos y sistemas teatrales" (an ultra-modern work in which he deploys the most audacious theatrical procedures and systems); "la obra trata de un problema social agudo y latente" (the work treats an acute and latent social problem).[15]

The Autor's starting point here is the reality of widespread poverty and suffering and, in the face of this, an equally pervasive indifference, denial, or just sheer inhumanity. Thus, his rhetorical question: "¿por qué esa crueldad, ese despego al terrible dolor de vuestros semejantes?" (what is the reason for that cruelty, that detachment from the terrible sorrow of your fellow men?) (138) or the scene depicted on the first painted backdrop: "(Cae un telón pintado con casas y basura.)" (A curtain falls painted with houses and garbage) (139). On the other side of this binary, the Autor points to different tactics adopted principally by city dwellers:

> gentes de la ciudad, que vivís en la más pobre y triste de las fantasías. Todo lo que hacéis es buscar caminos para no enterarse de nada. [. . .] para no ver el inmenso torrente de lágrimas que nos rodea cubrís de encajes las ventanas; para poder dormir tranquilos y callar el perenne grillo de la conciencia inventáis las casas de caridad. (138)

> city dwellers, you live in the most impoverished and sad of fantasies. All that you do is to look for ways in which to not notice anything. [. . .] in order to not see the immense torrent of tears that surrounds us, you cover your windows with lacy drapes; in order to sleep peacefully and silence the constant chirping of your conscience, you invent poorhouses.

Furthermore, the make-believe of the theater—the vacuous, commercial variety—has enabled the theatergoing public to ignore, forget, or deliberately blot out the harsh realities of the world. Thus, the Autor now rejects all the fatuous subject matter of popular drama "adonde dirige el teatro sus luces para [. . .] haceros creer que la vida es eso" (on which the theater trains its lights in order to [. . .] make you believe that that's what life is) and opts instead to "enseñaros esta noche un pequeño rincón de realidad" (show you tonight this small corner of reality) (137).

A few moments later, the Author again disavows the illusionistic theater and makes an even more radical, apparently paradoxical claim: "¿El teatro? Aquí no estamos en el teatro" (The theater? We're not in the theater here) (141; and cf. 142). Taken literally, this is clearly untrue; rather, it conveys in compressed form what the Autor is now aiming to achieve. This he describes to Espectador 1.° before returning to the topic of self-deception and strategies of forgetfulness:

> yo quiero echar abajo las paredes para que sintamos llorar o asesinar o roncar con los vientres podridos a los que están fuera, a los que no saben siquiera que el teatro existe, y usted se espanta por eso. Pero váyase. En su casa tiene la mentira esperándolo, tiene el té, la radio y una mujer que cuando lo ama piensa en el joven jugador de fútbol que vive en el hotelito de enfrente. (141)

> I want to tear down the walls so that we can hear the people who are outside weeping or killing or snoring with their bloated bellies, the people who don't even know that theater exists, and you are terrified by that. But go, leave. In your house, you've got falsehood waiting for you, you have your tea, the radio and a wife who, when she makes love to you, thinks about the young football player who lives in the townhouse opposite.

Against this complacent attitude, the Autor sets the initial inquisitiveness of Espectadora 1.ª and evokes another scene of human misery that apparently he—experimentally?—arranged to have played out in this selfsame theater:

> Quiere decir que [a ella] le interesa la vida. La vida increíble que no está en el teatro precisamente. Hace unos días pude presentar en este mismo sitio a unos cuantos amigos como prueba de lágrimas una escena viva que no creería su marido de usted. En una pequeña habitación una mujer murió de hambre. Sus dos niños, hambrientos también, jugaban con las manos de la muerta, tiernamente, como si fueran dos panes amarillos. (142–43)

> What she means is that she is interested in life. That incredible life which isn't precisely in the theater. A few days ago, I was able to present to several friends in this same place, as a test for tears, a vivid scene that your husband would not believe. In a small room, a woman died of hunger. Her

two children, who were also hungry, were playing with the hands of the dead woman, tenderly, as if they were two yellow bread rolls.

Other obvious examples of cruelty and inhumanity are to be found in the dialogue with the Criado: getting the child and the turkey drunk, the beheading of the turkey, and the torture of the cat (145–46). As before, the points being made here are underscored by the Joven's sardonic commentary. Referring to the acts just listed, he remarks: "Los que se las echan de listos llaman a esto barbarie, otros aberraciones, y dan media vuelta para dormirse mejor" (People who fancy themselves as clever call that barbarity, others call it aberrations, and they turn half over to sleep better), and then continues: "Y esté seguro que recién salidos del sueño, con las cuerdas de una conciencia convencional todavía flojas, la mitad de ellos pediría el manojo de zarzas para restregarlas con fruición sobre el animal crucificado" (And have no doubt that just as they're waking up, with the strings of a conventional conscience still slack, half of them would ask for the bunch of brambles so they could rub them, with delight, on the crucified animal) (147). At best, people will put a convenient label on this kind of behavior that permits them to forget about it; at worst, they will join in.

From all this there emerges another basic opposition: the haves and the have-nots, the haves who are patrons of the commercial theater, and the have-nots who are denied access to any form of theater. Socioeconomic divisions are also depicted as a function of theater tickets, starting with the bourgeois Espectador 1.° and Espectadora 2.ª seated in the expensive stalls, "En butacas" (139); the upper-class Joven, dressed in tails, occupying the even more expensive stage-level box, "En una platea" (144); and the Obrero in the front row of the highest balcony, the gallery or "gods"—"Delantera de paraíso" (160). Notice that the text says "una platea"; as the stage directions establish a distinction with *butacas,* I take this to be a shortened form of *un palco de platea.* In regard to the "Delantera de paraíso," Lorca stated in 1933: "Yo arrancaría de los teatros las plateas y los palcos y traería abajo el gallinero" (I would rip out the stalls and the boxes from the theaters and bring the gallery down), and in 1934: "Yo espero para el teatro la llegada de la luz de arriba siempre: del paraíso. En cuanto los de arriba bajen al patio de butacas, todo estará resuelto" (For the theater I am waiting/hoping for the arrival, always, of the light from above: from the "gods." As soon as the people from up above come down to the stalls, everything will be resolved).[16] Furthermore, at least two of the theater employees—the Traspunte and the actor in the role of Leñador—are passively conformist and conservative and advocate for the status quo, even though the Traspunte has no idea of what "la economía" is, why it should matter to him, or why politicians might invoke it so much (156),[17] and the actor scrapes by on a wage of "unas cuantas monedas" (a few coins) (158) and is content if only he be allowed to play his role.

Stark political sides are drawn after the performance is disrupted by the military violence in the streets outside. A Voz (later identified with the Obrero) shouts "¡Viva la revolución!" (Long live the revolution!) (155), and later the Obrero, "Vestido de mono, levantando los brazos" (Dressed in overalls, raising his arms), calls out: "¡Camaradas!" (Comrades!) (164). The Hombre—the rich owner of the theater (158)—advocates for severe repression (157) and spouts extreme right-wing rhetoric: "¡Mano dura! El bien, la verdad y la belleza han de tener en esta época un fusil entre las manos" (Iron fist! At this time, good, truth, and beauty need to have a gun in their hands) (158). In response to Espectadora 2.ª's cries of worry about her children—left "alone" at home with the governess and the servants (160)— one of the stagehands, the Tramoyista, generously offers to go and check: "No tenga miedo, señora. Yo mismo iré. Yo sortearé las balas y les diré que ustedes están seguros" (Don't be afraid, lady. I'll go myself. I'll dodge the bullets, and I'll tell them that you are safe) (162). This individual, it turns out, is nicknamed "Bakunin el loco" (Bakunin the mad) (163), after the famous Russian anarchist who sponsored Giuseppe Fanelli's important trip to Spain (1868–69). Espectador 2.° jots down his name, telling his wife that it is so he can be rewarded, but in fact it is "Para denunciarlo después" (To report him to the authorities afterward) (163). Somehow overheard by the Obrero, they exchange insults, which rapidly devolve into violence. Espectador 2.° pulls out a flashlight, which illuminates the balcony area, and shouts to the Obrero:

Estás en la sombra, pero yo iluminaré la sombra para cargarte de cadenas. Soy del ejército de Dios y cuento con su ayuda. Cuando muera le veré en su Gloria y me amará. Mi Dios no perdona. Es el Dios de los ejércitos al que hay que rendir pleitesía por fuerza, porque no hay otra verdad. (163)

You're there in the shadow, but I will light up the shadow to weigh you down with chains. I belong to the army of God and I count on His help. When I die, I shall see Him in His Glory, and He will love me. My God does not forgive. It is to the God of the armies that one is necessarily obliged to render homage, because there is no other truth.

Although the extremity of this attitude might seem parodic, consider Raymond Carr's comment on Spanish prime minister Antonio Cánovas del Castillo (who held the office six times between 1875 and 1897): "Cánovas regarded property rights as sacred and the army as the ultimate bulwark against the 'barbarian invasion of the proletariat.' Most conservatives clung to the view that the 'social problem' derived from the increasing secularization of society which had produced a godless working class."[18] Seconds later, Espectador 2.° produces a pistol and shoots and kills the Obrero. Positions are now completely polarized: two women call him "¡Asesino!" (Killer!), while he remains smugly satisfied: "¡pero la mala hierba se arranca así!" (but that's how weeds are uprooted!) (164); "¡Buena caza! Dios me lo pagará. Bendito sea en su sacratísima venganza" (Good hunting! God will reward me for it. Blessed be his most sacred vengeance) (165).

In the simplest of terms, the Autor's goal is to revolutionize the theater by changing radically both the mode of theatrical presentation and the themes treated. His repeated calls to open doors or break down walls can be understood not literally but, rather, as pointing the way to the elimination of the gulf and the barriers between theater and "real life" as well as to greatly expanding the audience demographic: "el autor no quiere que os sintáis en el teatro sino en mitad de la calle" (the author doesn't want you to feel as if you are in a theater but, rather, in the middle of the street) (138); "¡Ésta es la escuela del pueblo!" (This is the school of the people!) (156). This must be done, he believes, to undermine the theater's current complicity and enable it to have an impact on the prevailing sociopolitical situation. The wholesale subversion of conventional theatrical norms that we witness in the course of *El sueño de la vida* is intended to break down the expectations of the audience and hence to prepare it to accept more readily the new and strikingly different presentation that the Autor has in mind and which may arguably take concrete form in the second half of the act.

Various things need to happen to bring this revolution about. The theater must put an end to the stranglehold of the box office that dictates the narrow range of popular plays that can be performed, as exemplified in the statements made by Espectador 1.º: "La única ley del teatro es el juicio del espectador" (The only law of the theater is the opinion of the spectator); "Yo he pagado por ver el teatro" (I paid to see theater) (140). The illusionistic naturalism as well as the fantastic make-believe of commercial theater need to be shown up for what they are; hence those references, on the one hand to "un panorama donde se vea una casa en la que nada ocurre" (a panorama where a house can be seen in which nothing happens) (137) and on the other to a "telón en el que hay pintado un palacio inverosímil" (curtain on which a wildly unrealistic palace is painted) (149) as well as to unspecified plays written by "algún poeta embustero" (some deceitful poet) (151). The scope of theater must be opened both to the genuinely marvelous and the grittily realistic: "debo advertir que nada es inventado. Ángeles, sombras, voces, liras de nieve y sueños existen y vuelan entre vosotros, tan reales como la lujuria, las monedas que lleváis en el bolsillo" (I ought to inform you that nothing is invented. Angels, shadows, voices, snowy lyres, and dreams exist and fly among you, just as real as lust, as the coins that you carry in your pockets) (137); "En una pequeña habitación una mujer murió de hambre. [. . .] los niños descubrieron los senos de la muerta y se durmieron sobre ellos" (In a small room, a woman died of hunger. [. . .] the children found the breasts of the dead woman and fell asleep upon them) (143). In addition, that paradoxical and alluring power of the artificial to move people more than the real thing (mentioned earlier) needs to be combated, presumably by daring to tell the truth—the whole truth: "Por eso yo no quiero actores sino hombres de carne y mujeres de carne" (Because of this I don't want actors but, rather, men and women of flesh and blood) (142); "sólo quiero que la gente diga la verdad" (I only want people to tell the truth) (147)—and also by creating entirely new types of challenging theatrical performance such as the one that the audience is currently experiencing.

Of course, there will be resistance to this kind of profound change, and some of the characters predict failure for the Autor. While the intellectually detached Joven professes that "me interesa mucho su experiencia" (a statement in which the "experiencia" that so greatly interests him might almost be read as *experiment* as much as *experience*), he nevertheless warns the Autor that "como siga así lo dejarán solo" (if you go on like this you'll be left alone) (144), that "creo que esa gente no lo van a dejar. ¡Es tan hermoso el teatro! ¿Qué va usted a hacer de las copas de plata, de los trajes de armiño?" (I believe that those people will not allow it. Theater is so lovely! What are you going to do with the silver goblets, the ermine jackets?) (144), and finally, that "¡Hace falta la escena! ¡Va usted a fracasar!" (The stage is necessary! You are going to fail!) (146). The Actriz states the dilemma more starkly: "La verdad es fea, pero si la digo, me arrojan del teatro. Me dan ganas de dirigirme al público y en la escena más lírica gritarles de pronto una palabrota, la más soez, ja, ja, ja. Pero yo quiero mis esmeraldas y me la quitarían" (Truth is ugly, but if I were to tell it, they'd throw me out of the theater. I have an urge to turn to the audience and in the most lyrical scene suddenly shout at them a swear word, the rudest one, ha, ha, ha. But I want my emeralds, and they would take them away from me) (153).

Undaunted, the Autor pursues his objective from the very opening of the act to its close. Confronted by the Joven's attachment to conventional props and simulated emotion, he boldly claims that "todo eso ha desaparecido ya del teatro" (all that has already disappeared from the theater) (144). He refuses to go to the rehearsal of *A Midsummer Night's Dream* (150) and announces his complete break, at least with this kind of theater: "Es el último día que piso el teatro" (This is the last day that I'll set foot in the theater) (151). As mentioned earlier, this notion of radical rupture is expressed primarily through the figurative (and then possibly literal) idea of the elimination of physical boundaries, a desire to which the Autor gives voice on a number of occasions: "yo quiero echar abajo las paredes" (I want to tear down the walls) (141); "vendrán a echar las puertas abajo. Y nos salvaremos todos" (they'll come to break the doors down. And we will all be saved) (142); "¡Que las abran [las puertas]! ¡El teatro es de todos!" (Have them open [the doors]! The theater belongs to everyone!); "He dicho que abran las puertas. No quiero que se derrame sangre verdadera junto a los muros de la mentira" (I've said to open the doors. I don't want real

blood spilled beside the walls of make-believe) (156). The theater cannot
stand idly by and can at the very least serve to protect the protesters who
are being pursued. Toward the end, the Autor even seems to envisage the
possibility of a violent solution: "AUTOR: ¡Que lo rompan todo!" (AUTOR:
Let them break everything!) (156); "HOMBRE: La pólvora mata a la poesía.
| AUTOR: ¡O la salva!" (HOMBRE: Gunpowder kills poetry. | AUTOR: Or saves
it!) (157); "TRAMOYISTA: ¡El pueblo ha roto las puertas!" (TRAMOYISTA: The
people have broken down the doors!) (168); "AUTOR: Decid la verdad sobre
los viejos escenarios. Clavad puñales sobre los viejos ladrones del aceite y
el pan. Que la lluvia moje los telares y despinte las bambalinas" (AUTOR:
Tell the truth on the old stages. Plunge daggers into the old thieves of oil
and bread. Let the rain soak the fly lofts and strip the paint from the drop
scenes) (169).

In *El público* we witness the near-impossibility of achieving an authentic
and enduring loving relationship and also the attestation that when all the
layers of pretense are stripped away, the ultimate reality left is death (see
chapter 5). The same is true here. The interaction between the Autor and
the Actriz exemplifies the former idea, and while the latter notion receives
considerably more emphasis in the other, earlier work, it is still in evidence
here. In the prologue and referring to the sea, the Autor asserts that "él
sigue llamando a las costas en espera de nuevos ahogados, esto es lo que le
importa al hombre" (it continues calling on the coasts in the anticipation
of more drownings, that is what matters to man) (139). When the Espectador 1.° summarily rejects the truths that the Autor is trying to convey
to him: "Estoy demasiado cerca de la realidad para hacerle caso" (I'm too
close to reality to pay attention to you) (141), the Autor retorts:

La realidad. ¿Usted sabe cuál es la realidad? Óigala. La madera de los ataúdes de todos los que estamos en la sala está ya cortada. Hay cuatro ataúdes
que esperan dentro de los vidrios a cuatro criaturas que ahora me oyen, y
hay quizá uno, ¡quizá!, uno que se puede llenar esta madrugada misma a
poco de salir de este vivísimo lugar. (141–42)

Reality. Do you know what reality is? Listen to it. The wood for the coffins
for everybody in this auditorium is already cut. There are four coffins that
are waiting inside the shop windows for four beings who are listening to

me right now, and there's perhaps one, perhaps!, one that might be filled this very night shortly after people have left this place that is so alive.

Furthermore, the Autor alludes to "las dulces voces desaparecidas" (the sweet vanished voices) (138) of parents of audience members, describes himself as "un agonizante de Dios" (a dying person sent by God) (161), and the Espectador 2.º shoots and kills the Obrero in front of their eyes. But unlike *El público,* this line of thinking does not stop at this point.

Referring to what he sees as the grim message of *A Midsummer Night's Dream* concerning the entirely capricious nature of love, the Autor comments: "Es una verdad terrible, pero una verdad destructora puede llevar al suicidio y el mundo necesita ahora más que nunca verdades consoladoras, verdades que construyan. Se necesita no pensar en uno sino pensar en los demás" (It's a terrible truth, but a destructive truth can lead to suicide and what the world needs now more than ever are consoling truths, constructive truths. People need not to think about themselves but rather about others) (150).[19] The Autor's concern for others and his deep distress in the face of poverty, deprivation, hunger, suffering, and persecution are manifested throughout this first act. In a modern and decidedly secular take on Calderón's message, other people need to "wake up" from their conscious or unconscious self-delusion (*sueño*) and see what is really happening all around them (*vida*). Though *El sueño de la vida,* as it stands, admittedly is short on those "verdades consoladoras, verdades que construyan," the first steps toward them have been taken, and it is more than conceivable that these truths might have found further expression in the remaining two acts of the play, had Lorca been able to complete them before he himself was killed.[20]

Epilogue

For many years, Lorca's experimental theater did not receive the exposure, enjoy the reputation, or exert the influence that, all other things
being equal, might well have been expected. Obviously, his death just a
few weeks after the outbreak of the Spanish Civil War had a tremendous
impact in a considerable number of different ways. His literary production
and associated work were suddenly cut short, which meant that plays were
left unperformed (*Así que pasen cinco años*), unrevised and/or lost (*El público*), and uncompleted (*El sueño de la vida*), as has been detailed in chapter 1. Furthermore, Lorca rapidly became a symbolic martyr figure for the
Republican side in the Civil War, whose ideology was closely linked with a
strong identification with the *pueblo*—the [common] people. For Republi-
cans, Lorca was the poet of the extraordinarily popular *Romancero gitano*
and not of the as yet unpublished and much less tractable *Poeta en Nueva
York*.[1] As a dramatist, Lorca's greatest critical and box office successes had
been with *Bodas de sangre* and *Yerma* (and to a lesser extent *Doña Rosita la
soltera*), the first two normally categorized as rural tragedies and peopled
by characters who lived in villages and were smallhold farmers of one sort
or another. Little wonder, then, that it was the third part of this "trilogy,"
La casa de Bernarda Alba, that was most eagerly and widely anticipated
and that went on to achieve enormous popularity, despite its dark themes.
Or perhaps precisely because of them, for some people saw in Bernarda's
"dictatorship" within the confines of her house a foreshadowing of the
situation in Spain after the Civil War.

After the war ended, the implantation of the Franco regime meant that Lorca, as was the case with numerous other writers, was essentially eliminated from the cultural landscape in Spain. Decades later, his work—or rather, select parts of his work—were gradually and tentatively reintroduced, starting in the 1960s, with productions of *La zapatera prodigiosa, Yerma, Bodas de sangre, La casa de Bernarda Alba,* and *Mariana Pineda.* Abroad, the same works were regularly performed in Spanish in the countries of Latin America, by Margarita Xirgu and many other theatrical companies, and elsewhere, in translations, more sporadically. Given that the text (albeit with some minor flaws) of *Así que pasen cinco años* was available in a printed edition from 1938 onward, it is hard to account for the neglect that it suffered for many years, especially at a time when other forms of avant-garde drama—for instance, the Theater of the Absurd in the 1950s—were rapidly coming into prominence. The situation seems to bear witness to the enduring power of that popular "Andalusian" image of Lorca, whose influence was reinforced by stereotypes about southern Spain lingering on from the Romantic period.

The other factor to be considered here, also treated in chapter 1, is the publication history of the manuscripts and early copies that did survive. As just noted, *Así que pasen* (alongside *Amor de don Perlimplín*) were brought out by Losada in 1938, but *El público* and *El sueño de la vida* were not widely accessible until 1978. *El público* immediately caught the public's imagination, certainly for its remarkable experimentalism, but one suspects primarily for the overtness of its themes concerned with sexuality and identity. In more recent decades, the impact of this play on the perception of Lorca's complete oeuvre has been decidedly mixed, drawing attention to its stablemates—*Así que pasen* and *El sueño*—at the same time as it cast a shadow on them, the one less technically extreme and the other incomplete. It is my hope that the studies offered in this book will demonstrate that each, along with *Amor de don Perlimplín,* stands firmly on its own considerable merits, while at the same time benefiting from being viewed as part of a coherent bloc within Lorca's overall output.

A further, unanswerable question concerns where Lorca would have gone from here, had he not been killed. It is of course unwise even to attempt to speculate on how he might have reacted to the very different circumstances—the war and, subsequently, exile, though we can say with some degree of certainty what his immediate plans were, and there are also a number of traces of other works that he had in mind as possible projects. In the early spring of 1936, Margarita Xirgu had undertaken a tour of Cuba and then moved on to Mexico in mid-April. In late spring or summer Lorca was supposed to join up with her there, but after successive postponements, it is not clear that he would eventually have gone. Thereafter, once Xirgu had returned to Spain and was reinstalled in the Teatro Español, in the fall of 1936, the plan would surely have been to rehearse and premiere *La casa de Bernarda Alba* (whose composition Lorca finished in June); restage *Doña Rosita la soltera* for Madrid audiences, who had not had the opportunity to see it;[2] while he simultaneously worked with Anfistora on the final preparations for the performance of *Así que pasen* and wrote acts 2 and 3 of *El sueño de la vida*.[3]

Over the 1930s, we also find a large number of tantalizing mentions of plays that Lorca had conceived of, most often little more than a title and sometimes a line or two of plot summary, and extraordinarily diverse in nature.[4] These appear on a list of ten titles likely from early 1936,[5] in various interviews, and in the memoirs of several people who knew him. Old Testament plots clearly appealed to him (Samson; Sodom, Lot and his daughters; King David, Tamar, and Amnon; Judith; Cain and Abel), as did provocative and controversial topics (bestiality, patricide, incest, homosexuality, illegitimacy and orphanhood, anti-war protest) but also plays centered on his hometown ("crónicas granadinas" [chronicles of Granada]—he had written one act of *Los sueños de mi prima Aurelia*)[6] and lighter fare based on flamenco with elements of music and dance.[7] Evidently, then, in 1936, Lorca's imagination was at the height of its powers, he envisaged developing his dramatic production simultaneously along many different lines, and as Mario Hernández has succinctly summed it up, "veía ante sí un camino teatral de renovación incesante" (he saw ahead of him a theatrical path of constant renewal).[8]

NOTES

Introduction

1. For a survey and analysis of the types of standard theatrical offerings that were current during this period, see Dougherty and Anderson, "Continuity and Innovation." See also Fernández-Cifuentes, *García Lorca en el teatro*, 12–23.

2. *Comedieta ideal* (1917); *Teatro de almas. Paisajes de una vida espiritual* (1917); *Dios, el Mal y el Hombre* (1917); *El primitivo auto sentimental* (1918); *Del amor. Teatro de animales* (1919); *La viudita que se quería casar* (two versions: pre-1919, 1919–20); *Cristo. Poema dramático* (1919–20); *Cristo. Tragedia religiosa* (1919–20); *Sombras* (1920); *Jehová* (1920); *Señora M[uerte]* (1920); *Comedia de la carbonerita* (1921); *Elenita* (1921); *Ilusión* (1921–22[?]). See García Lorca, *Teatro inédito de juventud* and *4 piezas breves*.

3. Cuesta Guadaño, *El teatro de los poetas*.

4. See García Lorca, *Teatro inconcluso;* and Laffranque's introduction to that volume.

5. Fernández-Cifuentes, *García Lorca en el teatro*, 23.

6. A. Anderson, "The Strategy."

7. Felipe Morales, "Conversaciones literarias. Al habla con Federico García Lorca," *La Voz* (Madrid), April 7, 1936, 2.

8. Martínez Nadal, *"El público": Amor y muerte*, 18.

9. García Lorca, *Amor de don Perlimplín*, 265, 269, 274.

1. Staging the Unstageable

1. Ucelay, "Introducción," 1990, 33–50, 51–73.

2. Ibid., 75–134.

3. García Lorca, *Epistolario completo*, 242, 267, 300. On the subject of what exactly *aleluyas* are, see Ucelay, "Introduction," 1990, 18–26.

4. García Lorca, *Epistolario completo*, 320–22.

5. Ibid., 331.

6. Ibid., 332.

7. Buñuel, *Mi último suspiro*, 100–101.

8. "Sección de rumores. Se dice," *Heraldo de Madrid* (Madrid), October 20, 1927, 5.

9. Letter from Jorge Guillén to Juan Guerrero Ruiz, July 4, 1928: García Lorca, *Epistolario completo,* 568 n. 461.

10. An extensive article detailed their ambitious plans: "Cómicos y autores. La Sala Rex," *La Libertad* (Madrid), November 23, 1928, 3. Here, among a long list of plays they were interested in staging, Lorca's *Amor de don Perlimplín* was already mentioned.

11. Aznar Soler, "El Caracol."

12. García Lorca, *Epistolario completo,* 599, 602.

13. Further details are given in my article "Hiato vital."

14. Ucelay, "Introducción," 1990, 145–53.

15. Antonio de Obregón, "Teatro. Noticias varias," *La Gaceta Literaria* 3, no. 54, March 15, 1929, 2.

16. "Noticiario. Ha embarcado para Buenos Aires la compañía de Irene López Heredia," *Heraldo de Madrid,* May 9, 1929, 5.

17. Ucelay, "Introducción," 1990, 227.

18. Del Río, "Introduction," xv–xvi.

19. Adams, *García Lorca,* 93.

20. García Lorca, *Epistolario completo,* 653, 658, 658.

21. See Walsh, "The Women."

22. Rivas Mercado, *Correspondencia,* 274.

23. Adams, *García Lorca,* 124.

24. Ibid.

25. Excellent photographs of scenes from both plays with their respective stage sets can be seen in "Semana teatral. Espectáculos en el Español," *La Esfera* 18, no. 888, January 10, 1931, n.p.

26. César González-Ruano, "Bajo la sonrisa de la zapatera prodigiosa. Margarita, Federico y Cipriano," *Crónica* 3, January 11, 1931, n.p.

27. In articles published in the *New York Times* on October 25 and December 6, her byline locates her in Act Le Haut, Aisne, France and then in Geneva, Switzerland. There would have been several days' delay between submitting the piece and its appearance in print. Her last byline ascribed to Madrid was printed on January 24, 1932.

28. "En el Círculo de Bellas Artes. Homenaje a la 'Argentina,'" *La Nación* (Madrid), December 3, 1931, 13; "Información y noticias teatrales. En Madrid. Homenaje a Antonia Mercé, 'La Argentina,'" *ABC* (Madrid), December 3, 1931, 46. Adams had met Mercé when the latter was on tour in the United States.

29. Adams, *García Lorca,* 146.

30. Ucelay, "Introducción," 1990, 156. Given certain features of one version of the surviving Adams translation of *Perlimplín* (see n. 34), Ucelay surmises that she and Lorca did indeed collaborate on at least one occasion, an event that led to clarifications of difficult passages as well as new additions (228).

31. Letter of January 26, 1932: Maurer and Currie, "From Stage to Page," 131. Adams published her article on Lorca and La Barraca in the same journal: "The Theatre in the Spanish Republic," *Theatre Arts Monthly* 16, no. 3 (March 1932): 237–39.

32. Adams, *García Lorca,* 146–47.

33. Papers of Mildred Adams, Schlesinger Library, Harvard Radcliffe Institute. Her translation of *Los títeres*, which she did complete, is deposited in the archive of the Hispanic Society of America.

34. The materials related to Adams's efforts to produce a translation of *Perlimplín* are all deposited in the Hispanic Society of America. They consist of a thirty-page handwritten manuscript and the top copy and carbon copy of a typescript of twenty-nine pages (though each copy has different manuscript annotations on it).

35. Ucelay, "Introducción," 1990, 158.

36. Ibid., 159.

37. After completing her edition for Cátedra, Ucelay deposited this typed copy in the Hispanic Society of America.

38. Ucelay, "Introducción," 1990, 161, 216–18, 228.

39. "Sección de rumores," *Heraldo de Madrid*, March 10, 1933, 4; J.G.O., "Anoche, en el Español. Gran función de gala del Club Teatral de Cultura, en honor del poeta García Lorca," *Heraldo de Madrid*, April 6, 1933, 5.

40. "Una interesante iniciativa. El poeta Federico García Lorca habla de los Clubs teatrales," *El Sol* (Madrid), April 5, 1933, 10.

41. A program from this second performance is preserved in the Archivo Federico García Lorca in Granada.

42. José S. Serna, "Charla amable con Federico García Lorca," *Heraldo de Madrid*, July 11, 1933, 5. Indeed, of this list only *Bodas* was published, but not in October 1933 but in 1936, by Cruz y Raya / Ediciones del Árbol.

43. "El poeta español García Lorca, en el Avenida," *El Diario Español* (Buenos Aires), October 25, 1933, 3.

44. García Lorca, *Epistolario completo*, 782.

45. "F. García Lorca habla de *La zapatera prodigiosa*," *La Razón* (Buenos Aires), November 28, 1933, 8. Indeed, *Yerma* was not finished until the summer of 1934.

46. García Lorca, *Epistolario completo*, 799–800.

47. Ucelay, "Introducción," 1990, 177–78.

48. Manuel López-Marín, "Apéndice: Una entrevista. García Lorca ante el teatro. Sus recuerdos de Buenos Aires," Radio Prieto, Transradio Española, March 16, 1935; in García Lorca, *Alocuciones argentinas*, 31–33.

49. Del Río, "Introduction," xv–xvi.

50. García Lorca, *Epistolario completo*, 657.

51. García Lorca, *Autógrafos*, 2:4–41. The Biblioteca Nacional subsequently acquired the manuscript from Martínez Nadal, and today it forms part of their collection.

52. Pérez Coterillo, "La Habana," 41.

53. Loynaz, "Yo no destruí" and "El manuscrito."

54. Cardoza y Aragón, *El río*, 351, 352.

55. García Lorca, *Epistolario completo*, 690. This is not the only occasion on which Lorca described a play of his as a poem.

56. Miguel Pérez Ferrero, "Voces de desembarque. Veinte minutos de paseo con Federico García Lorca," *Heraldo de Madrid*, October 9, 1930, 8.

57. J.L., "La vida escénica. Antes del estreno. Hablando con Federico García Lorca," *La Libertad*, December 24, 1930, 9.

58. Auclair, *Enfances et mort*, 229.

59. Martínez Nadal, "Introducción," 23, 29.

60. César González-Ruano, "Bajo la sonrisa de *La zapatera prodigiosa*. Margarita, Federico y Cipriano," *Crónica* 3, January 11, 1931, n.p.

61. García Lorca, *Epistolario completo*, 706.

62. A. Anderson, "Coincidencias y paralelismos."

63. "Micrófono. *El público*, para unos pocos," *Heraldo de Madrid*, July 2, 1931, 9.

64. Alfaro, "Hombres."

65. "Sección de rumores," *Heraldo de Madrid*, May 4, 1932, 6; "Noticias teatrales. Temporada de verano en el Español," *Luz* (Madrid), May 6, 1932, 4.

66. *La Nación* (Madrid), May 13, 1932, 1 and 11.

67. Martínez Nadal, "Introducción," 23.

68. Correspondence between Guillén and Dámaso Alonso, two of the editors: Monegal, "Una revolución teatral," 13–14.

69. José S. Serna, "Charla amable con Federico García Lorca," *Heraldo de Madrid*, July 11, 1933, 5.

70. Juan G. Olmedilla, "Al margen de la escena consuetudinaria. Se va a crear un Teatro-Escuela de Arte Experimental," *Heraldo de Madrid*, November 21, 1933, 13.

71. "Teatros. Llegó anoche Federico García Lorca," *La Nación* (Buenos Aires), October 14, 1933, 9.

72. García Lorca, *Teatro inconcluso*, 208–13.

73. Suero, "Crónica de un día."

74. Ernesto Pinto, "Federico García Lorca: gitano auténtico y poeta de verdad," *La Mañana* (Montevideo), February 6, 1934, 1 (I have maintained the punctuation of the quotation as printed).

75. "Enviarán a Gustavino 'Un poema para ser silbado,'" *Crítica* (Buenos Aires), March 15, 1934, 16. Enrique Gustavino was head of the Compañía de Teatro Moderno and in 1933 had offered a varied repertoire of classics and moderns at the Teatro Smart in Buenos Aires.

76. Felipe Morales, "Conversaciones literarias: al habla con Federico García Lorca," *La Voz*, April 2, 1936, 2.

77. Gibson, *Vida, pasión y muerte*, 664.

78. Martínez Nadal, "Introducción," 23.

79. Martínez Nadal, *"El público": Amor, teatro y caballos*; García Lorca, *Autógrafos*, vol. 2.

80. García Lorca, *El público y Comedia sin título*.

81. Monegal, "Una revolución teatral," 15.

82. Del Río, "Introduction," xv–xvi.

83. Auclair, *Enfances et mort*, 232.

84. Salazar is speculating and does not know that Martínez Nadal has both of them.

85. Salazar, *"La casa de Bernarda Alba,"* 30.

86. García Lorca, *Autógrafos*, vol. 3.

87. García Lorca, *Epistolario completo*, 711, 712, 716.

88. Morla Lynch, *En España*, 128–33.

89. Pedro, "El destino mágico," May 19, 1949, 20.

90. Ucelay, "Textos," 147–49. Today the typescript is deposited in the archives of the Hispanic Society of America.

91. Ucelay, "Apéndice," 355.

92. José S. Serna, "Charla amable con Federico García Lorca," *Heraldo de Madrid*, July 11, 1933, 5; "founded" is a considerable exaggeration.

93. Ucelay, "Apéndice," 359.

94. Ucelay, "El club teatral Anfistora," 464.

95. Ucelay, "Apéndice," 355.

96. "Teatros. Llegó anoche Federico García Lorca," *La Nación* (Buenos Aires), October 14, 1933, 9.

97. Suero, "Crónica de un día."

98. Suero, *Figuras contemporáneas*, 300–302.

99. "El Club Teatral 'Anfistora,'" *Ahora* (Madrid), December 29, 1934, 17.

100. "Chiquillos actores," *Estampa* 7, no. 363, December 29, 1934, n.p.

101. Ricardo G. Luengo, "Conversación de Federico García Lorca," *El Mercantil Valenciano* (Valencia), November 15, 1935, 5.

102. "El teatro. Eso del Español," *La Libertad*, March 25, 1936, 4.

103. On the hypothetical possibility of Lorca reassigning the play, see Maórtua's comments in Osorio, *Miedo, olvido y fantasía*, 639.

104. "El teatro. Más sobre eso del Español," *La Voz*, March 25, 1936, 3.

105. "El teatro Español, para Ana Adamuz y Benito Cibrián," *La Voz*, March 26, 1936, 4.

106. "Lo del Español. Tres eran, tres, las proposiciones . . . ," *Heraldo de Madrid*, March 25, 1936, 9.

107. "Teatro. Conversaciones. El Español, los autores nuevos, Tirso, Lola Montes y los muñidores ilustres. Eso del Español," *La Voz*, March 27, 1936, 3; "Un banquete a Benito Cibrián," *Ahora*, April 15, 1936, 31.

108. Ucelay, "El club teatral Anfistora," 464; Ucelay, "Apéndice," 355–56; A. Anderson, "La carrera temprana," 196. See also "La actualidad teatral," *Ahora*, May 24, 1936, 29.

109. Felipe Morales, "Conversaciones literarias. Al habla con Federico García Lorca," *Heraldo de Madrid*, April 8, 1936, 2.

110. "*El trovador* de García Gutiérrez, a través del club Anfistora," *Mundial*, no. 2 (May 1936): n.p.

111. Her full name was Ana María Rodríguez-Arroyo Mariscal, and she was the younger sister of Luis Arroyo, who was performing as the protagonist of *El trovador* and had been approved by Lorca for the role of the Joven. See Mariscal, *Cincuenta años*, 33–34.

112. "Obra inédita de García Lorca. Polémico coloquio en la presentación de *El público*," June 24, 1978, unattributed newspaper cutting in the Archivo Federico García Lorca.

113. Ucelay, "Ediciones," 161–62.

114. Suero, *España levanta el puño*, 182.

115. Ucelay, "Ediciones," 159–64.

116. Suero, *Figuras contemporáneas,* 301.

117. Ucelay, "Apéndice," 356; A. Anderson, "La carrera temprana," 200–203.

118. Ucelay, "Textos," 154.

119. Ucelay, "Apéndice," 360; Ucelay, "El club teatral Anfistora," 466.

120. Ucelay, "Apéndice," 361.

121. Osorio, *Miedo, olvido y fantasía,* 630–31; see also Auclair, *Enfances et mort,* 366.

122. This may possibly be an echo of the brief flirtation with Cibrián's company.

123. "Sección de rumores. Se dice," *Heraldo de Madrid,* May 29, 1936, 9.

124. Martínez Nadal, "Nota preliminar," 9; Ucelay, "Textos," 148.

125. González Carbalho, *Vida, obra y muerte,* 69.

126. This is the term in Spanish for the uppermost seats in a theater, the upper balcony or gallery.

127. Alardo Prats, "Los artistas en el ambiente de nuestro tiempo," *El Sol,* December 15, 1934, 8.

128. García Lorca, "Texto íntegro."

129. Proel [Ángel Lázaro], "Galería. Federico García Lorca, el poeta que no se quiere encadenar," *La Voz,* February 18, 1935, 3.

130. Nicolás González-Deleito, "Federico García Lorca y el teatro de hoy," *Escena,* no. 1 (May 1935): 3, 17.

131. Ortega, *Álbum. Una historia,* 66; "Eduardo Blanco-Amor," *El Defensor de Granada* (Granada), July 20, 1935, 1.

132. "Cuentan . . . Verdades y mentiras. Noticias sueltas," *La Nación* (Madrid), July 3, 1935, 9.

133. "Teatro. Conversaciones. Margarita Xirgu hace las maletas y Diéguez rechaza un contrato," *La Voz,* July 3, 1935, 4.

134. "Teatros y cines. Tópicos. La señorita," *Heraldo de Madrid,* July 16, 1935, 8.

135. "Teatro. Conversaciones. Tertulia," *La Voz,* July 25, 1935, 4; "Margarita Xirgu en Madrid," *Ahora,* August 10, 1935, 29. The latter report mentions a period of a month.

136. Pedro, "El destino mágico," May 26, 1949, 12–14.

137. Rodrigo, *García Lorca en Cataluña,* 353.

138. Eduardo Blanco-Amor, "Nueva obra teatral de García Lorca," *La Nación* (Buenos Aires), November 24, 1935, 3; Blanco-Amor claims that he was the first person to receive a reading of the complete play, but it is likely that one was given prior to this in Madrid.

139. El Caramelero, "García Lorca en la Plaza de Cataluña," *El Día Gráfico* (Barcelona), September 17, 1935, 18.

140. García Lorca, *Alocuciones argentinas,* 33, 32.

141. Ricardo G. Luengo, "Conversación de Federico García Lorca," *El Mercantil Valenciano,* November 15, 1935, 5.

142. Rivas Cherif, "Poesía y drama."

143. Suero, *España levanta el puño,* 180.

144. Ibid., 181.

145. Suero, *Figuras contemporáneas,* 55.

146. A.O.S. [Antonio Otero Seco], "Una conversación inédita con Federico García Lorca," *Mundo Gráfico* 27, no. 1321 (February 24, 1937): n.p. The interview was published posthumously, but internal references in it lead most critics to date it to the early months of 1936.

147. "Sección de rumores. Se dice," *Heraldo de Madrid,* February 12, 1936, 9.

148. "Tópicos. Apartado de las peñas literarias," *Heraldo de Madrid,* February 29, 1936, 13. The idea of a lawsuit is of course a joke.

149. Salinas and Guillén, *Correspondencia (1923–1951),* 171.

150. Felipe Morales, "Conversaciones literarias. Al habla con Federico García Lorca," *La Voz,* April 7, 1936, 2.

151. "El teatro. Algo de García Lorca," *La Libertad,* April 24, 1936, 6.

152. "Sección de rumores. Se dice," *Heraldo de Madrid,* May 29, 1936, 9.

153. Cano, "[Desde Madrid]."

154. Laffranque, "Introducción," 275–77.

155. Pedro, "El destino mágico," May 26, 1949, 13–14.

156. It seems that the freezing night referred to here did not occur on Christmas Eve of 1934 but, rather, on the New Year of 1935; Lorca would have made the minor change to enhance the symbolic effect of the event. A long article illustrated with several photographs appeared in the *Heraldo de Madrid* on January 2 and occupied the entire page: Criado y Romero, "Carne lacerada por el frío y por las vicisitudes. Una noche helada de enero por las calles de Madrid. De paseo a cuatro grados bajo cero.—Montones humanos sin comida y sin hogar.—El millonario de ayer y mendigo de hoy.—¡Niños, niños, niños explotados! . . .—De las escaleras de Cuchilleros a los colectores del Manzanares" (10). One photograph shows several people sleeping under the arches of the Plaza Mayor; another depicts a woman with a child who "imploran la caridad pública en la fachada misma del ministerio de Hacienda" (are begging for public charity right outside the Ministry of Finance).

157. León, "Federico y Margarita."

158. Suero, *España levanta el puño,* 181–82.

2. Undecidability in *Amor de don Perlimplín con Belisa en su jardín*

1. Ucelay's introduction and edition (from 1990) are fundamental, and all references will be to this text. For performances see Aguilera Sastre and Lizarraga Vizcarra, "Los tres primeros montajes," and for reception see Fernández-Cifuentes, *García Lorca en el teatro.*

2. See Grant, "Una *aleluya erótica*"; Ucelay, "Introducción," 1990, 12–26; García Castañeda, "Don Perlimplín"; and Pedrosa, "De *Perlinpinpin*."

3. Fernández-Cifuentes, "El viejo y la niña."

4. González Guzmán, "Los dos mundos," 52; Jiménez-Vera, "Don Perlimplín's," 113.

5. Lyon, "Love, Imagination," 238, 239.

6. Borel, *Théâtre de l'impossible,* 34.

7. Lyon, "Love, Imagination," 239.

8. Ibid., 238.

9. Ibid.

10. Ibid., 241; see also Bacarisse, "Perlimplín's Tragedy," 74–75.

11. O., "Guía de espectadores. Un estreno de García Lorca en el Español, en gran función de gala." *Heraldo de Madrid,* April 4, 1933, 5; "Una interesante iniciativa. El poeta Federico García Lorca habla de los Clubs teatrales." *El Sol,* April 5, 1933, 1.

12. Borel, *Théâtre de l'impossible,* 38; González Guzmán, "Los dos mundos," 53, 56; Jiménez-Vera, "Don Perlimplín's," 109–10.

13. Bacarisse, "Perlimplín's Tragedy," 74, 77, 87.

14. Ibid., 74–75, 79; Ucelay, "Introducción," 1990, 184.

15. O., "Guía de espectadores," 5; "Una interesante iniciativa. El poeta Federico García Lorca habla de los Clubs teatrales." *El Sol,* April 5, 1933, 1.

16. Hershberger, "Building and Breaking."

17. Feldman, *"Perlimplín:* Lorca's Drama"; Fernández-Cifuentes, *García Lorca en el teatro,* 122–24.

18. Lyon, "Love, Imagination," 239–40.

19. Bennett and Royle, *An Introduction to Literature,* 276.

20. Wright, *The Trickster-Function,* 40.

3. García Lorca and the New York Theater, 1929–1930

1. Crow, *Federico García Lorca,* 13.

2. Maurer, "El teatro," 134, 139.

3. Gibson, "El insatisfactorio estado," 14.

4. Ibid., 13.

5. Maurer and Anderson, *Federico García Lorca,* 39 (August 8, 1929); 60 (ca. September 21, 1929); 61 (September 23, 1929); 74 (October 21, 1929).

6. Ibid., 39 (August 8, 1929); 60 (ca. September 21, 1929); 74 (October 21, 1929); 75 (October 22–23, 1929); 86 (early December 1929).

7. Maurer, "El teatro," 134.

8. See, for example, Adams, *García Lorca,* chaps. 6–8; and Brickell, "A Spanish Poet."

9. Maurer, "El teatro"; Gibson, "El insatisfactorio estado"; and the section "Cine y teatro," 70–78, in Gibson, *Federico García Lorca,* vol. 2.

10. Eisenberg, "A Chronology"; Gibson, *Federico García Lorca,* 2:9–82; Maurer and Anderson, *Federico García Lorca,* 6, 150–58. The RMS *Olympic* arrived in New York on June 25, but passengers were not able to disembark until the next day.

11. Leiter offers a mine of information, on which I have relied heavily. These figures have been compiled using his "Appendix 1: Calendar of Productions" (*The Encyclopedia of the New York Stage, 1920–1930,* 2:1037–1101), looking at opening dates, length of runs, and consulting the appropriate individual play entries in the body of the encyclopedia. Wherever possible, *Billboard* was also consulted to provide the exact closing date.

12. *Billboard,* in its July 6, 1929, number, noted that "Musicals Outnumbering Dramatic Shows on B'Way" (4). As of June 29–July 2, there would be eleven straight plays running, as against twelve musicals and reviews.

13. Leiter, "Appendix 9, Seasonal Statistics" (*The Encyclopedia of the New York Stage, 1920–1930,* 2:1183–85). Among the 233, there are obviously a number of revivals as well as productions that had run on (continuously) from previous seasons.

14. "B'way Losing Legit. Houses," *Billboard,* February 15, 1930, 5.

15. Leiter, *The Encyclopedia of the New York Stage, 1920–1930,* 1:xiii.

16. Leiter, "Appendix 10: Theatres" (*The Encyclopedia of the New York Stage, 1920–1930,* 2:1187–90); Laufe, *Anatomy of a Hit,* 17.

17. "37 Legit. Shows Promised, Tho' Trade Hit by Market," *Billboard,* November 9, 1929: 6; "Legit. Appeal Remains Bad. Business Still Affected by Stock Market, with Few Shows Doing Sellout," *Billboard,* November 16, 1929, 6; "Legit. Trade Still Down. Three Hits Go Cut-Rate; Stock Crash Is Trade Alibi," *Billboard,* November 23, 1929, 6; "Legit. Trade Hits New Low. Cut-Rates Get Most of Hits—Specs Selling at Half Price," *Billboard,* November 30, 1929, 6; "Pre-Holiday Business Slump Sets New Low Legit. Mark," *Billboard,* December 21, 1929, 4; "Managers Plan 70 More Shows with 101 Now Gone," *Billboard,* December 28, 1929, 5.

18. "Percentage of Flops High as Halfway Mark Nears," *Billboard,* December 7, 1929, 4; "Middle Ground Gone, Plays Are Either Hits or Busts," *Billboard,* December 14, 1929, 5.

19. Cf. Mary Brewster, "Why Our Playwrights Are Trivial," *Billboard,* September 7, 1929, 61.

20. Mantle, *The Best Plays,* 390–91.

21. Leiter, *The Encyclopedia of the New York Stage, 1920–1930,* 1:xxvii.

22. Maurer, "El teatro," 137; Maurer, "Introduction," xii; also Dougherty "Lorca y las multitudes," 78–79.

23. Details of titles and performing companies are generally taken from Leiter, *The Encyclopedia of the New York Stage, 1920–1930,* 2 vols., in which individual entries can be found concerning each of these and all subsequently cited productions; lists of titles in this essay are normally given chronologically by the date of their opening night.

24. Maurer and Anderson, *Federico García Lorca,* 79.

25. See Laufe, *Anatomy of a Hit,* 172–76, 62–63, 105–7, 176–80, respectively; also Leiter, "Appendix 3: Awards" (*The Encyclopedia of the New York Stage, 1920–1930,* 2:1159–62).

26. Leiter has a lengthy entry on it (*The Encyclopedia of the New York Stage, 1920–1930,* 2:871–72); and see also Downer, *Fifty Years,* 63–64.

27. Gibson, *Federico García Lorca,* 2:128.

28. Leiter, *The Encyclopedia of the New York Stage, 1920–1930,* 2:678, 1:567.

29. Ibid., 1:xiii, xvii; Price, *The Off-Broadway Theater,* 1–11.

30. Price, *The Off-Broadway Theater;* see also Leiter, *The Encyclopedia of the New York Stage, 1920–1930,* 1:xvii–xx.

31. Cf. also Leiter's comments on advances in stage direction and stage design during the decade of the 1920s (*The Encyclopedia of the New York Stage, 1920–1930,* 1:xxx–xxxi).

32. For excellent profiles of all the principal groups, see Durham, *American Theatre Companies;* for this group, 311–17.

33. Ibid., 311–12.

34. Leiter, *The Encyclopedia of the New York Stage, 1930–1940,* 77–78; Durham, *American Theatre Companies,* 314.

35. Maurer, "El teatro," 136; Durham, *American Theatre Companies,* 312; "Neighborhood Players Give Indifferent 'Arty' Program," *Billboard,* March 1, 1930, 5.

36. Maurer, "El teatro," 134.

37. Suero, "'La Barraca,'" reproduced in García Lorca, *Palabra de Lorca*, 182. *The Dybbuk* (to which Lorca alludes) had been performed in December 1925 and December 1926.

38. Durham, *American Theatre Companies*, 81–86.

39. Ibid., 433–42, 460–63.

40. The Theatre Guild also survived into the 1930s, but in doing so gradually evolved into a more commercial enterprise: see Durham, *American Theatre Companies*, 440.

41. Mantle, *The Best Plays*, 3.

42. See Leiter, "Appendix 5: Institutional Theatres" (*The Encyclopedia of the New York Stage, 1920–1930*, 2:1167–72).

43. Durham, *American Theatre Companies*, 205–8.

44. Ibid., 489–92.

45. Ibid., 377–89.

46. Ibid., 14–22.

47. Maurer, "El teatro," 137; see also Michel Kraike, "All God's Chillun Got Drama," *Billboard*, September 7, 1929, 65, for a detailed analysis of the function and offerings of the Alhambra.

48. Cf. Leiter on the effects of the Harlem Renaissance (*The Encyclopedia of the New York Stage, 1920–1930*, 1:xxvii–xxviii). These Black, non-Harlem productions are the main focus of Dougherty's article ("Lorca y las multitudes," 79).

49. Maurer and Anderson, *Federico García Lorca*, 77.

50. A. Anderson, "Una amistad inglesa," 3.

51. Loney, *20th Century Theatre*, 163.

52. For more details of these plays, see Dougherty, "Lorca y las multitudes," 79–80 nn. 15–17.

53. Maurer, "El teatro," 139.

54. Maurer and Anderson, *Federico García Lorca*, 37.

55. Leiter, *The Encyclopedia of the New York Stage, 1920–1930*, 2:584.

56. "Charlando con García Lorca." *Crítica*, October 15, 1933, 11; reproduced in García Lorca, *Palabra de Lorca*, 175–77.

57. Leiter, *The Encyclopedia of the New York Stage, 1920–1930*, 1:534; 1:120–21; 1:395–96; 2:715–16; 1:513.

58. Leiter, *The Encyclopedia of the New York Stage, 1920–1930*, 2:1006; Price, *The Off-Broadway Theater*, 6; reviewed quite unfavorably in *Billboard*, November 23, 1929, 7.

59. For the text of this play, see Aguilera Sastre, Soler, and Rivas, *Cipriano de Rivas Cherif*. Curiously enough, Gibson mentions a staging of Bourdet's *La Prisonnière* in Vigo that took place at around the same time (*Federico García Lorca*, 2:108).

60. Maurer and Anderson, *Federico García Lorca*, 21–23 (July 14, 1929); 27–28 (ca. July 24, 1929); and 33–37 (August 8, 1929), among others.

61. Maurer, "El teatro," 136–37; Maurer, "Introduction," xi; see also "Una interesante iniciativa. El poeta Federico García Lorca habla de los Clubs Teatrales," *El Sol*, April 5, 1933, 10.

62. Francisco García Lorca, *Federico y su mundo*, 335–36.

63. Gibson, "El insatisfactorio estado"; for a discrepant view, see Dougherty, "Lorca y las multitudes," 78–79.

64. Rodolfo Gil Benumeya, "Estampa de García Lorca," *La Gaceta Literaria* 5, no. 98, January 15, 1931, 7.

65. Dougherty, "Lorca y las multitudes."

4. Three Expressionist Dramas

1. Suero, *Figuras contemporáneas,* 303–4.

2. Suero, *España levanta el puño,* 181.

3. Gibson, *Federico García Lorca,* 2:418–20, 435; "Sección de rumores. Se dice," *Heraldo de Madrid,* February 12, 1936, 9; "Sección de rumores. Se dice," *Heraldo de Madrid,* May 29, 1936, 9.

4. Among them, Honig, *García Lorca,* 136; Guerrero Zamora, *"Así que pasen,"* 86; Morris, *Surrealism and Spain,* 48 and n. 193; and Cao, *"Así que pasen,"* 186, 192.

5. De la Guardia, *García Lorca.*

6. Kovacci and Salvador, "García Lorca."

7. Jerez-Farrán, "La estética expresionista."

8. On the impact of Expressionism on another dramatist who was a direct contemporary of Lorca, see the book by Ríos Torres on Claudio de la Torre, *El teatro de vanguardia.*

9. A. Anderson, "Bewitched, Bothered, and Bewildered."

10. Benson, *German Expressionist Drama,* 7; Sokel, *The Writer,* 34, 97; Sprinchorn, "Introduction," 385; Styan, *Modern Drama,* 16–38.

11. Benson, *German Expressionist Drama,* 7, 23; Kenworthy, *Georg Kaiser,* 24; and Samuel and Thomas, *Expressionism in German Life,* 26. For the filmmakers, see Barlow, *German Expressionist Film;* and Eisner, *The Haunted Screen.*

12. Styan, *Modern Drama,* 42–46, 97–114.

13. There was at least one Italian translation of *The Road to Damascus* (*Verso Damasco*) that Lorca could conceivably have seen.

14. Dougherty and Vilches de Frutos, *La escena madrileña,* 243, 251, 381; McGaha, *The Theatre in Madrid,* does not list any production for 1931–36.

15. These five one-act plays, *La más fuerte; Debe y haber; Amor maternal; Ante la muerte; El primer aviso,* were translated by the young Alejandro Casona who published them under his real name of Alejandro Rodríguez Álvarez.

16. García Lorca, "Texto íntegro."

17. Gibson, *Federico García Lorca,* 2:449.

18. Videla, *El ultraísmo,* 101–3; C. García, *El joven Borges.*

19. Borges, "Lírica expresionista"; "Antología expresionista"; "Lírica expresionista"; "La antología expresionista"; Colin, "Letras alemanas"; "El teatro alemán contemporáneo"; "El teatro alemán contemporáneo"; as well as the pieces by A. de G., "El teatro alemán," and Panxsaers, "La pintura expresionista." To these we should add mention of Torre's book, *Literaturas europeas,* of 1925, which devotes some pages to Iwan Goll and to the German movement; and the essay by Lafora, "Estudio psicológico."

20. "Información teatral," *El Sol,* December 29, 1928, 3.

21. Kaiser, *De la mañana a medianoche;* Kaiser, *Gas [I];* Kaiser, *Un día de octubre;* Díez-Canedo, "Georg Kaiser."

22. Benson, *German Expressionist Drama*, 114; and Kenworthy, *Georg Kaiser*, 24, 114–15.

23. "Margarita Xirgu estrena hoy *Un día de octubre*, primera obra de Georg Kaiser en España," *Heraldo de Madrid*, May 6, 1931, 5.

24. All data from multiple reports in the contemporaneous Madrid press.

25. Ricardo G. Luengo, "Conversación de Federico García Lorca," *El Mercantil Valenciano*, November 15, 1935, 5, in García Lorca, *Palabra de Lorca*, 436.

26. See Julio Álvarez del Vayo, "Cómo se hace y deshace una república de soviets," *España* 6, no. 280, September 11, 1920, 8–9; A. de Tormes, "Teatros de vanguardia. Alemania: el teatro de Ernesto Toller," *La Esfera* 12, no. 576, January 17, 1925, n.p.; *La Gaceta Literaria* 2, no. 33, May 1, 1928.

27. Ernst Toller, "De nuestra colaboración extranjera. La literatura dramática alemana de la postguerra. El expresionismo y sus hombres," *La Voz*, April 1, 1929, 4.

28. "Ernst Toller, German Playwright, Held on Ship; His Red Activities in 1919 May Bar Him Here," *New York Times*, September 27, 1929, 21.

29. "[Classified ad]," *New York Times*, October 8, 1929, 40.

30. Toller, *Hinkemann*. Carlos Fernández Cuenca published a long review of the translation: "Teatro nuevo. Los dramas de Ernst Toller," *La Época* (Madrid), October 10, 1931, 3.

31. Multiple reports in the contemporary Madrid press.

32. O'Neill, *"El emperador Jones"*; Baeza, "Nota" and "El teatro."

33. J.G.O. [Juan González Olmedilla], "Guía de espectadores. *Anna Christie*, la heroína universal del dramaturgo norteamericano O'Neill, lucha por ser buena y purificarse del fango de su juventud," *Heraldo de Madrid*, January 20, 1931, 5.

34. "Recitales de arte. Elvira Morla en la Sala Pleyel y González Marín en el Calderón," *Heraldo de Madrid*, February 26, 1934, 6.

35. "Gaceta teatral madrileña," *Heraldo de Madrid*, March 3, 1934, 6. Of course, at this time Lorca was in Argentina.

36. "Noticiario. Inauguración en el Lyceum Club del curso literario 1934–1935," *Heraldo de Madrid*, December 10, 1934, 6.

37. J.G.O. [Juan González Olmedilla], "Guía de espectadores. Los tres estrenos de esta noche: *La calle*, en el Español; [. . .]," *Heraldo de Madrid*, November 14, 1930, 7.

38. On the impact of cinema on Spanish literature from between the world wars, see Morris, *This Loving Darkness;* Gubern, *Proyector de luna;* and Puyal Sanz, *Cinema y arte nuevo* and *Cine y renovación estética.*

39. Eisner, *The Haunted Screen*, 269–74.

40. First session of December 1928 and seventh of May 1929; Gubern, *Proyector de luna,* 279, 317.

41. Multiple reports in the contemporary Madrid press; Gubern, *Proyector de luna,* 361.

42. Benson, *German Expressionist Drama*, 113–14.

43. Luis Buñuel, *"Metrópolis,"* *La Gaceta Literaria* 1, no. 9, May 1, 1927, 6. See also Barlow, *German Expressionist Film,* 112–13, 133. *Der müde Tod* was called in French *Les trois lumières.*

44. In order not to overburden the endnotes excessively, in what follows I have incorporated into my analysis several points made by Novacci and Salvador, Jerez-Farrán ("La

estética expresionista"), and others without citing each individual occasion on which we agree in our findings.

45. Benson, *German Expressionist Drama*, 23; Samuel and Thomas, *Expressionism in German Life*, 41; Styan, *Modern Drama*, 5, 53.

46. Kenworthy, *Georg Kaiser*, 54.

47. Eisner, *The Haunted Screen*, 111–12.

48. All page references are to the translation of Kaiser's *De la mañana a medianoche*, in *Revista de Occidente*, 187, 198, 211, 184, 207.

49. All page references are to the translation of Kaiser's *Gas [I]*, in *Revista de Occidente*, 37, 39, 209, 342.

50. All page references are to Monegal's edition of *El público. El sueño de la vida.*

51. All page references are to Ucelay's edition of *Así que pasen cinco años.*

52. All page references are to Monegal's edition of *El público. El sueño de la vida.*

53. Benson, *German Expressionist Drama*, 8; Styan, *Modern Drama*, 5.

54. Sokel, "Introduction," xxv; Baeza, "El teatro," 224.

55. Styan, *Modern Drama*, 22.

56. See chapter 5.

57. Benson, *German Expressionist Drama*, 7; Kenworthy, *Georg Kaiser*, 24; Samuel and Thomas, *Expressionism in German Life*, 40; Styan, *Modern Drama*, 13–14.

58. Benson, *German Expressionist Drama*, 23, 39, 107; Styan, *Modern Drama*, 4, 49, 53.

59. Strindberg, *Selected Plays*, 473.

60. Sokel, *The Writer*, 38–45; Sokel, "Introduction," xiii–xviii.

61. Sokel, *The Writer*, 44; Styan, *Modern Drama*, 4.

62. Benson, *German Expressionist Drama*, 23–24; Samuel and Thomas, *Expressionism in German Life*, 45–46; Sokel, "Introduction," xv. Samuel and Thomas give examples of other playwrights who also used this approach: Boetticher and Johst (*Expressionism in German Life*, 40–41).

63. Barlow, *German Expressionist Film*, 24; Styan, *Modern Drama*, 4, 53.

64. Sprinchorn, "Introduction," 383; Styan, *Modern Drama*, 27.

65. Strindberg, *Selected Plays*, 460.

66. Barlow, *German Expressionist Film*, 111. Sokel in *The Writer*, 39, has also commented on the acceleration of time; evidently, Claudio de la Torre makes use of the same notion in his play *Tic-Tac*.

67. See chapter 7; Huélamo Kosma, "Algunas claves"; Huélamo Kosma, "La influencia de Freud," 63–65; Martínez Nadal, *"El público": Amor y muerte*, 70–110.

68. García Lorca, *Teatro inédito de juventud*, 95.

69. Barlow, *German Expressionist Film*, 24; Benson, *German Expressionist Drama*, 24; Eisner, *The Haunted Screen*, 209; Sokel, *The Writer*, 35–36, 40; Sprinchorn, "Introduction," 383–84; Styan, *Modern Drama*, 25, 27.

70. Baeza, "El teatro," 205.

71. Samuel and Thomas, *Expressionism in German Life*, 129; Sokel, "Introduction," xx.

72. Strindberg, *Selected Plays*, 462, 469–70.

73. Benson, *German Expressionist Drama,* 24–30; Styan, *Modern Drama,* 45; Barlow, *German Expressionist Film,* 130.

74. See Menarini, "L'uomo dei dolori," for a detailed commentary on this Cuadro.

75. Barlow, *German Expressionist Film,* 35–37; Sokel, *The Writer,* 38–39, 49; Styan, *Modern Drama,* 4, 27, 53.

76. Benson, *German Expressionist Drama,* 35–36; Sokel, *The Writer,* 41.

77. Morris, *This Loving Darkness,* 123–24.

78. Sokel, "Introduction," xvi; Styan, *Modern Drama,* 32–33.

79. Sokel, "Introduction," xvi–xvii.

80. Ibid., xviii; Jerez-Farrán, *El expresionismo,* 35; Barlow, *German Expressionist Film,* 42.

81. Sokel, *The Writer,* 206–7.

82. Sokel, "Introduction," ix–x; Styan, *Modern Drama,* 3.

83. Styan, *Modern Drama,* 53.

84. See chapter 9.

85. Styan, *Modern Drama,* 40.

86. Just two disparate examples from among many: Oliver, "The Trouble," 12; and Fernández-Cifuentes, *García Lorca en el teatro,* 260.

87. "El misterio evidente," 221, as Sánchez-Biosca also does ("El expresionismo," 201–3).

88. García-Posada, "Lorca y el surrealismo," 8; Lázaro Carreter, *"El público"*; Jerez-Farrán, "La estética expresionista," 113–14; Martínez Nadal, *"El público": Amor y muerte,* 78–80.

5. Theme and Symbol in *El público*

1. All page references to *El público* are drawn from the edition by Antonio Monegal (*El público. El sueño de la vida*). The manuscript of *El público* is reproduced in facsimile in García Lorca, *Autógrafos,* vol. 2, which I used extensively in preparing my own edition of the play (1996). There is also an earlier edition edited by María Clementa Millán (1987), which I reviewed in 1989.

2. Edwards, *Lorca: the Theatre,* 86; Martínez Nadal refers to "el carácter poemático de la obra" (*"El público": Amor y muerte,* 71).

3. Cf. Edwards, *Lorca: The Theatre,* 68–69.

4. Brotherton, *The "Pastor Bobo."* Rubia Barcia was one of the first to propose this rearrangement ("Ropaje y desnudez," 390, 393), and he was seconded by Menarini ("L'uomo dei dolori," 66). For a fuller treatment, see Vitale, *El metateatro,* 65–73.

5. In Spanish, *careta* and *máscara* are near synonyms, and the *DRAE* makes no functional distinction between them. *Antifaz* is often used for the partial mask that only covers the area around the eyes, while *mascarilla*—not mentioned here—is used for masks that cover the nose and mouth.

6. Monegal incorrectly gives *cabellera* instead of *manzana,* which appears in the manuscript.

7. Cf. Martínez Nadal, *"El público": Amor y muerte,* 102.

8. See Curtius, "Theatrical Metaphors," 138–44. Cf. the remarks of Huélamo Kosma, "Algunas claves"; Jerez-Farrán, "La estética expresionista," 111–13; Lázaro Carreter, *"El público"*; and Millán, "Introducción," 29–30, 50.

9. Other possible though more tenuous equations, such as the "focos de gas" (gas spotlights) with "lumini dei mort" (lights of the dead) and "anuncios" (advertisements) with "epigrafi mortuarie" (mortuary inscriptions), are established by Melis, "*El público:* metamorfosi," 164.

10. Feal, "El Lorca póstumo," 47.

11. Gide, *L'Immoraliste*, 60, 61, 65, 68.

12. García Lorca, *Autógrafos*, 2:48–49.

13. Cf. Daverdin-Liaroutzos, "*Le Public* à Paris"; Mazzotti Pabello, "Una lectura," 161, 164, 166.

14. Mazzotti Pabello, "Una lectura."

15. Feal, "El Lorca póstumo," 49.

16. Belamich, "*El público*," 81–82. Aspects of Mazzotti Pabello's viewpoint are echoed by Smith in his chapter on "Lorca and Foucault" in *The Body Hispanic*.

17. See also Lacomba, "*El público*," 80.

18. For the "view from the grave," see R. Anderson, *Federico García Lorca*, 147; Edwards, *Lorca: The Theatre*, 69; Feal, "El Lorca póstumo," 47; and Martínez Nadal, "*El público*": *Amor y muerte*, 45.

19. Brenan, *South from Granada*, 135.

20. Smith, *The Body Hispanic*, 127; Fernández-Cifuentes, *García Lorca en el teatro*, 275–93.

21. Cf. Belamich: "Si, vista desde las sepulturas, la persona no existe, ¿qué será del amor?" (If, seen from the graves, the person does not exist, what happens to love?) ("*El público*," 82).

22. See Balboa Echevarría, *Lorca: El espacio*, 113.

23. Menarini, "L'uomo dei dolori," 104; Londré, *Federico García Lorca*, 45; Martínez Nadal, "*El público*": *Amor y muerte*, 68.

24. DeLong-Tonelli, "The Trials," 159–60.

25. "Aesthetic Distance."

26. Ucelay, "Introducción," 1990, 39 41.

27. Cf. R. Anderson, *Federico García Lorca*, 152–53.

28. See the section on *El público* in chapter 1.

29. E.g., Figure, "The Mystification"; García Pintado, "19 motivos"; Ladra, "El teatro bajo el agua"; or Marco, "Sobre una obra inédita."

30. See Edwards, *Lorca: The Theatre*, 60–92; Millán, "Introducción"; Vitale, *El metateatro;* and even, to an extent, Martínez Nadal (*"El público": Amor y muerte*).

31. "La estética expresionista."

32. "*El público*," 12.

33. Cf. "Imaginación, inspiración, evasión," in García Lorca, *Conferencias*, esp. 2:13–31. See Edwards, *Lorca: The Theatre*, 77, 86; Huélamo Kosma, "Algunas claves," ix; Millán, "Introducción," 81.

34. Monegal, "Entre el papel"; Menarini, "L'uomo dei dolori."

6. Juliet and the Shifting Sands of *El público*

1. Martínez Nadal, "*El público*": *Amor, teatro y caballos*; García Lorca, *Autógrafos*, vol.

2. The work finally became widely available with the publication in 1978 of the Seix Barral

edition, *El público y Comedia sin título.* Cf. Fernández-Cifuentes, *García Lorca en el teatro,* 277–78.

2. Fernández-Cifuentes, *García Lorca en el teatro,* 275–93. For more on "these strange mechanics of textual transmission," see the section on *El público* in chapter 1.

3. Fernández-Cifuentes, *García Lorca en el teatro,* 282–87. See chapter 5 for a treatment of the essentialist versus existentialist debate in connection with concepts of self.

4. All quotations are drawn from Monegal's edition: García Lorca, *El público. El sueño de la vida.* Where necessary, I have compared this text with the facsimile manuscript and Martínez Nadal's transcription (in García Lorca, *Autógrafos,* vol. 2) and with the version offered by Millán in her edition of 1987, along the lines suggested in my review of 1989.

5. A. Anderson, "Some Shakespearian," 202.

6. David and Tapp, *Evidence Embalmed,* 40–41.

7. Cf. Martínez Nadal's remarks on Elena, 69, 88; all references and quotations come from the third and most recent edition of his study (*"El público": Amor y muerte*).

8. Ibid., 48, 65, 73.

9. Gómez Torres, *"El público,"* 902–3.

10. In the section of his "Introduction" devoted to sources, Brian Gibbons points out that the story originated in folklore, developed in European (principally Italian) *novelle,* and first gained currency in Britain via Arthur Brooke's poem *The Tragicall Historye of Romeus and Iuliet* (1562) (Shakespeare, *Romeo and Juliet,* 32–42).

11. This is a slightly different formulation from the one that I advanced a number of years ago: A. Anderson, "Some Shakespearian," 201.

12. Shakespeare, *Romeo and Juliet,* act 5, scene 3, 215–17.

13. Martínez Nadal, *"El público": Amor y muerte,* 84.

14. "Juliet's Tomb," *The Literary Tourist* (blog), January 17, 2014, https://www.open.ac .uk/blogs/literarytourist/?p=49.

15. Martínez Nadal offers a more univocally figurative view, writing of "el bisturí del análisis" (the scalpel of analysis) (*"El público": Amor y muerte,* 49).

16. Rennert, *The Spanish Stage,* 169–70.

17. Martínez Nadal, *"El público": Amor y muerte,* 54–55.

18. This would be an example of the kind of apparent arbitrariness or lack of signifi-cation that Fernández-Cifuentes believes creates indeterminacy and undermines readings of the play that seek thematic or imagistic logic and cohesion. In spite of local instances such as these, Gómez Torres nevertheless reaffirms the existence of considerable symbolic coherence on both linguistic and visual levels (*"El público,"* 741).

19. García Lorca, *Autógrafos,* 2:26.

20. Monegal alerts us to the fact that "the association between desire and knowledge can be traced back to Plato's *Symposium.* The object is at once object of desire and object of knowledge" ("Un-Masking the Maskuline," 210).

21. Hughes, *The Shock,* 66.

22. García Lorca, *Autógrafos,* 2:8; 2:24–26.

23. Gómez Torres, *"El público,"* 801, 817.

24. García Lorca, *Autógrafos,* 2:64.

25. Ibid., 2:130.
26. Ibid., 2:112; *para enterarse* was presumably discarded because of the previous nearby usage of the same verb.
27. Ibid., 2:114, 2:136.
28. Russell, *The Problems of Philosophy*, 23.
29. Fernández-Cifuentes, *García Lorca en el teatro*, 86.
30. For a discussion of this particular "mistake," see the previous chapter.
31. García Lorca, *Autógrafos*, 2:68.
32. Gómez Torres, *"El público,"* 321, 322.
33. Monegal, "Un-Masking the Maskuline," 205, 213.
34. Harris, "Introducción," 33.
35. Monegal, "Un-Masking the Maskuline," 214, 215.

7. Destiny and Denial in *Así que pasen cinco años*

1. I have compiled a listing of over 150 articles and book chapters/sections concerned wholly or primarily with *Así que pasen cinco años* and have consulted them all. The addition of the play to the reading list for the CAPES and Agrégation exams led to a noticeable boom in the publication of French articles and collections of essays in the late 1990s.
2. Honig, *García Lorca*, 135.
3. Sánchez, *García Lorca*, 47.
4. Nourissier, F. *García Lorca*, 66.
5. De la Guardia, *García Lorca*, 306, 318. Ironically, this first list is one of the most complete among those offered by a variety of critics. Only in 1992 did I publish an essay that provided greater coverage: see chapter 4.
6. De la Guardia, *García Lorca*, 306, 309.
7. Machado Bonet, *Federico García Lorca*, 67.
8. Ibid., 67, 71, 69.
9. Ibid., 71, 78.
10. Xirau, *"Así que pasen,"* 97, 97, 99.
11. Arce, "Palabras de introducción," 176.
12. Granell, "Esquema interpretativo," 180, 180, 186.
13. Kovacci and Salvador, "García Lorca," 90, 97.
14. Lima, *The Theatre*, 158.
15. Knight, "Federico García Lorca's *Así que pasen cinco años*," 33, 32.
16. Pedro, "El destino mágico," May 16, 1949, 14.
17. Sapojnikoff, "La estructura temática."
18. Allen, *The Symbolic World*, 64, 150.
19. F. Anderson, "The Theatrical Design."
20. Martín, "Una leyenda."
21. Fernández-Cifuentes, *García Lorca en el teatro*, 250–54.
22. Soufas, *Audience and Authority*, 69.
23. Huélamo Kosma, *"Así que pasen,"* 29; Oxman, "As Time Stands," 60.
24. Oxman, "As Time Stands," 60; Ucelay, "Introducción," 1995, 97–98.

25. All references are to Ucelay's 1995 edition of the play.

26. Lavergne, "Les voix de l'homme," 174; Valente, "Pez luna," 195.

27. Lavergne, "Les voix de l'homme," 170; Valente, "Pez luna," 194.

28. Unfortunately, this utterance, combined with the date of completion of the manuscript of the play, have given rise to a range of wild and unwarranted speculations of a quasi-biographical nature.

29. Granell, "Esquema interpretativo," 181; Ucelay, "Introducción," 1995, 80–81; Ly, "Grammaire et dramaturgie," 129; Doménech, "Doble lectura," 252; Harretche, *Federico García Lorca,* 138–39.

30. The *Légende du beau Pécopin et de la belle Bauldour* is story no. 21 in Victor Hugo's *Le Rhin* (Brussels: Société des Bibliophiles Belges, 1842).

31. "Teatros. Llegó anoche Federico García Lorca," *La Nación* (Buenos Aires), October 14, 1933, 9.

32. Saillard, "F. García Lorca."

33. Ucelay, "Introducción," 1995, 79; Ly, "Analyse d'un fragment," 25; Lavergne, "Les voix de l'homme," 168.

34. García Lorca, *Teatro inédito de juventud,* 95, 92.

35. Afata, "Candor y tragedia."

36. Ricardo G. Luengo, "Conversación con Federico García Lorca," *El Mercantil Valenciano,* November 15, 1935, 5.

37. González Ramírez, "La escenificación," 318–19.

38. García Lorca, "Presentación del auto sacramental," 219, 220.

39. "Sección de rumores. Se dice," *Heraldo de Madrid,* February 12, 1936, 9.

40. Ibid., May 29, 1936, 9.

41. In the Ptolemaic system, there were eleven crystalline spheres.

42. Calderón, *Autos sacramentales;* all quotations are drawn from the edition by Valbuena Prat.

43. Cf. Xirau, *"Así que pasen,"* 99; Lima, *The Theatre,* 159; Ucelay, "Introducción," 1995, 69; and Martínez Nadal, "Estudio," 248.

44. All references to Calderón's *La vida es sueño (comedia)* are to the edition by Ruano de la Haza.

45. All quotations are drawn from Ruano de la Haza's edition.

46. See, however, Granell, "Esquema interpretativo," 181; Ly, "Grammaire et dramaturgie," 133–35; Ramond, "Figuras del eclipse," 94–98; Doménech, "Doble lectura," 246–47.

47. Ucelay, "Introducción," 1995, 123–27.

48. Ly, "Grammaire et dramaturgie," 135.

49. Marful Amor, *Lorca y sus dobles,* 172.

50. Doménech, "Doble lectura," 246–47; Ramond, "Figuras del eclipse," 94–95.

51. Marful Amor, *Lorca y sus dobles,* 172.

52. Ly, "Analyse d'un fragment," 27. More generally, see as a representative example Álvarez Miranda, *La metáfora y el mito.*

53. Harretche, *Federico García Lorca,* 140; Lavergne, "Les voix de l'homme," 176–77.

54. Huélamo Kosma, *"Así que pasen,"* 23.

55. Ibid., 29.

56. Afata, "Candor y tragedia," 255.

57. See, for comparison, Shaw's conclusions with respect to Lorca's "rural trilogy" in his essay "Lorca's Late Plays."

8. *Así que pasen cinco años,* Act 3, Scene 1

1. All page references are to Ucelay's 1995 edition.

2. Martín, "Una leyenda."

3. Martínez Nadal, "Estudio," 248; Thiollière, "Du chant de l'Arlequin," 515.

4. Rodríguez, "L'Arlequin," 169.

5. Huélamo Kosma, "Pastor y Arlequín," 64–65, 73–74, 80.

6. Ibid., 74, 77.

7. Ucelay, "Introducción," 1995, 88.

8. Huélamo Kosma, "Pastor y Arlequín," 75, 77.

9. Ibid., 75.

10. Martínez Nadal, "Estudio," 247.

11. Huélamo Kosma, "Pastor y Arlequín," 76–77.

12. Ibid., 82–83; Oxman, "As Time Stands," 62.

13. Ly, "Grammaire et dramaturgie," 138.

14. Ucelay, "Apéndice," 357.

15. Francisco García Lorca, *Federico y su mundo,* 331, only mentions two.

16. Rodríguez Marín, *Cantos populares españoles,* 87. Another lullaby reads: "A la nana, nanita, / perdí mi caudal; / a la nana, nanita, / lo volví a ganar" (6).

17. Álamo Hernández, *Mi barrio y yo,* 60. There are many slight variants of the text.

18. Santiago y Gadea, *Lolita,* 51–52.

19. *PajaraPinta 2° (juntadeandalucia.es),* consulted April 5, 2023.

20. Orringer, "Lorca's *Así que pasen,*" 109.

21. Knight, "Federico García Lorca's *Así que pasen cinco años,*" 40.

22. Samper, "Espacios y decorados," 59.

23. Francisco García Lorca, *Federico y su mundo,* 330.

24. Courgey, "Le réseau," 47.

25. Roux, *"Así que pasen,"* 61, 66.

26. Samper, "Espacios y decorados," 51–52; Lavergne, "Les voix de l'homme," 176.

27. Allen, *The Symbolic World,* 73, 109.

28. Ucelay, "Introducción," 1995, 71; Lavergne, "Les voix de l'homme," 175.

29. Lázaro Carreter, "Final de *Así que pasen.*"

30. Ucelay, "Introducción," 1995, 72; Orringer, "Lorca's *Así que pasen,*" 109.

31. Knight, "Federico García Lorca's *Así que pasen cinco años,*" 42.

32. Lázaro Carreter, "Final de *Así que pasen*"; Ucelay, "Introducción," 1995, 73.

33. Fernández-Cifuentes, *García Lorca en el teatro,* 271.

34. Francisco García Lorca, *Federico y su mundo,* 325.

35. Ucelay, "Introducción," 1995, 73.

36. Knight, "Federico García Lorca's *Así que pasen cinco años,*" 33.

37. Here I would disagree with the reading put forward by Wright in *The Trickster-Function,* 70–73.

38. Martínez Nadal, "Nota preliminar," 231; Lázaro Carreter, "Final de *Así que pasen.*"

39. Evidently, there are quite close connections with the forest in Victor Hugo's *Légende du beau Pécopin et de la belle Bauldour* but not to the exclusion of many other examples.

40. Lázaro Carreter, "Fracaso de amor." Huélamo Kosma calls the pair "aurigas de la muerte" (charioteers of death): "Pastor y Arlequín," 84; cf. Rodríguez, "L'Arlequin," 171. Certainly they are nothing like the Virgil who accompanies Dante in his "selva oscura."

41. R. Anderson, *Federico García Lorca,* 139.

42. Knight, "Federico García Lorca's *Así que pasen cinco años,*" 40.

9. Social Concern, Metatheater, and the Audience's Experience in *El sueño de la vida*

1. See Laffranque, "Introducción"; R. Anderson, "*Comedia sin título*"; Edwards, "'Comedia corriente'"; Giménez Micó, "Lorca: Teatro posible"; Menarini, "Federico García Lorca"; Soufas, *Audience and Authority;* Allinson, "'Una comedia sin público'"; and Harretche, *Federico García Lorca.*

2. See, for example, Peral Vega, "Introducción," 50. All page references are to Monegal's 2000 edition of Lorca's play: *El público. El sueño de la vida.*

3. Allinson, "'Una comedia sin público,'" 1028.

4. On the complex relationships that can exist between the prologue, the person delivering it, the play, and the audience, see Colecchia ("The 'prólogo'") and R. Anderson ("*Prólogos* and *advertencias*").

5. From the 1933 interview "Charlando con García Lorca," in García Lorca, *Palabra,* 176.

6. See García Lorca, *Palabra,* 335–471.

7. Peral Vega, "Introducción," 48–50.

8. See Gutiérrez Cuadrado, "Crónica de una recepción"; Allinson, "Lorca and Pirandello"; Chirico, "Lettura pirandelliana"; and Pérez-Simón, *Baroque Lorca,* 89.

9. Carr, *Modern Spain,* 53–61, 75–93, 130–31; González Calleja, *La razón de la fuerza,* 65–73.

10. Romero Salvado, *Spain, 1914–1918,* 122, 130.

11. Pedro, "El destino mágico," May 26, 1949, 14. Xirgu and Pedro both refer, of course, to the military uprising that led to the Spanish Civil War.

12. Menarini, "Federico García Lorca," 152, 155; Peral Vega, "Introducción," 47.

13. Edwards, "'Comedia corriente,'" 349; Allinson, "'Una comedia sin público,'" 1028; Delgado, "*Other*" *Spanish Theatres,* 214.

14. Pérez-Simón, *Baroque Lorca,* 89, 94–95, 99, 101; Peral Vega, "Introducción," 19–33.

15. Ricardo G. Luengo, "Conversación de Federico García Lorca," *El Mercantil Valenciano,* November 15, 1935, 5; "Sección de rumores. Se dice," *Heraldo de Madrid,* February 12, 1936, 9. See also García Lorca, *Palabra,* 391, 459, 489; and "Sección de rumores. Se dice," *Heraldo de Madrid,* May 29, 1936, 9.

16. García Lorca, *Palabra,* 176, 340.

17. Allinson, "'Una comedia sin público,'" 1034.

18. Carr, *Modern Spain,* 37.

19. Menarini traces this idea back to an early poem by Lorca, "[Yo estaba triste frente a los sembrados]," and thence to *El maleficio de la mariposa* and later *El público* ("Introducción," 55–60, 67–68).

20. Elsewhere I considered Lorca's attempts over 1935–36 to reconcile his existential pessimism with his social conscience and humanitarian preoccupations ("El último Lorca," 142–45); cf. also Monegal, "Una revolución teatral," 34–35. According to Valentín de Pedro ("El destino mágico," May 26, 1949) and León ("Federico y Margarita"), act 3 was to take place in heaven "con ángeles andaluces."

Epilogue

1. For the notion of Lorca as "poeta del pueblo," see Barea's early book *Lorca, the Poet and His People*.

2. "Lo del Español. Tres eran, tres, las proposiciones . . . ," *Heraldo de Madrid*, March 25, 1936, 9; "La Xirgu serà de retorn a la peninsula a primers d'octubre," *L'Instant* (Barcelona), June 24, 1936, 4; "La Xirgu, al Español," *Ahora*, July 1, 1936, 30.

3. In this regard, see the gossip column "Tópicos. Apartado de las peñas literarias," *Heraldo de Madrid*, February 29, 1936, 13, and the editorial "La barbarie. Se ha confirmado la ejecución del gran poeta García Lorca," *La Voz*, September 8, 1936, 1, both of which contain information from Lorca about his plans for the coming fall theatrical season.

4. García Lorca, *Teatro inconcluso*, 216–31.

5. Ibid., 344–45.

6. Ibid., 286–341. *Los sueños de mi prima Aurelia* is identified as a "crónica granadina" on the first page of the manuscript, while on the list of titles *Las monjas de Granada* is given an identical subtitle. According to a newspaper article, Lorca was also planning to premiere *Los sueños* that fall and had already promised it to the actress María Fernanda Ladrón de Guevara ("Sección de rumores. Se dice," *Heraldo de Madrid*, May 29, 1936, 9).

7. Hernández, "Introducción," 8–30; A. Anderson, "The Strategy," 219; Laffranque, "Estudio y notas," 48–97.

8. "Introducción," 23.

BIBLIOGRAPHY

A. de G. "El teatro alemán." *Cosmópolis* 3, no. 32 (August 1921): 669–75.

Adams, Mildred. *García Lorca: Playwright and Poet.* New York: George Braziller, 1977.

Afata, Stefano. "Candor y tragedia: Federico García Lorca y la poética de La Barraca." In *Textos, géneros, temas. Investigaciones sobre el teatro del Siglo de Oro y su pervivencia,* edited by Fausta Antonucci, Laura Arata, and María del Valle Ojeda, 245–63. Pisa: Edizioni ETS, 2002.

Aguilera Sastre, Juan, and Isabel Lizarraga Vizcarra. "Los tres primeros montajes de *Amor de don Perlimplín con Belisa en su jardín,* de Lorca: Breve historia de tres experimentos teatrales." *Boletín de la Fundación Federico García Lorca* 6, no. 12 (1992): 111–26.

Aguilera Sastre, Juan, Manuel Aznar Soler, and Enrique de Rivas, eds. *Cipriano de Rivas Cherif: retrato de una utopía. Cuadernos El Público* 42 (booklet insert in *El Público* 75) (December 1989).

Álamo Hernández, Juan Antonio. *Mi barrio y yo.* Seville: Punto Rojo Libros, 2015.

Alfaro, José María. "Hombres, aconteceres y nostalgias. Federico y *El público.*" *ABC,* June 18, 1978, 28.

Allen, Rupert. *The Symbolic World of Federico García Lorca.* Albuquerque: University of New Mexico Press, 1972.

Allinson, Mark. "Lorca and Pirandello (and Not Unamuno): Modernism, Metatheatre." *Journal of Iberian and Latin American Studies* 3, no. 1 (1997): 5–14.

———. "'Una comedia sin público': Metatheatre, Action, and Reaction in Lorca's *Comedia sin título.*" *Modern Language Review* 95, no. 4 (2000): 1027–37.

Álvarez de Miranda, Ángel. *La metáfora y el mito.* Madrid: Taurus, 1963.

Anderson, Andrew A. "Bewitched, Bothered, and Bewildered: Spanish Dramatists and Surrealism, 1924–1936." In *The Surrealist Adventure in Spain,* edited by C. Brian Morris, 240–81. Ottawa: Dovehouse Editions, 1991.

———. "Coincidencias y paralelismos: las carreras teatrales de Ricardo Baeza y Cipriano Rivas Cherif." In *Actas del XII Congreso Internacional de Hispanistas. Birmingham 1995*, vol. 4: *Del Romanticismo a la Guerra Civil*, edited by Derek W. Flitter, 41–49. Birmingham: Department of Hispanic Studies, University of Birmingham, 1998.

———. "El último Lorca: unas aclaraciones a *La casa de Bernarda Alba, Sonetos y Drama sin título*." In *Lecciones sobre Federico García Lorca*, edited by Andrés Soria Olmedo, 131–45. Granada: Comisión Nacional del Cincuentenario, 1986.

———. "Federico García Lorca, *El público*, edited by María Clementa Millán." *Bulletin of Hispanic Studies* 66, no. 3 (1989): 296–97.

———. "Hiato vital: La actividad de Federico García Lorca durante la primera mitad de 1929." *Nueva Revista de Filología Hispánica* 72, no. 2 (2024): 741–69.

———. "La carrera temprana de Germaine Montero como actriz (1933–1938): García Lorca y el Club Anfistora, Max Aub y Francia." *Anales de la Literatura Española Contemporánea* 47, no. 2 (2022): 193–215.

———. "Some Shakespearian Reminiscences in García Lorca's Drama." *Comparative Literature Studies* 22, no. 2 (1985): 187–210.

———. "The Strategy of García Lorca's Dramatic Composition 1930–1936." *Romance Quarterly* 33, no. 2 (1986): 211–29.

———. "Una amistad inglesa de García Lorca." *Ínsula* 40, no. 462 (May 1985): 3–4.

Anderson, Farris. "The Theatrical Design of Lorca's *Así que pasen cinco años*." *Journal of Spanish Studies: Twentieth Century* 7 (1979): 249–78.

Anderson, Reed. "*Comedia sin título*: Some Observations on the New García Lorca Manuscript." *Pacific Coast Philology* 14 (1979): 5–12.

———. *Federico García Lorca*. London: Macmillan, 1984.

———. "*Prólogos* and *advertencias*: Lorca's Beginnings." *Confluencia* 2, no. 1 (1986): 10–20.

Arce, Margot. "Palabras de introducción." *La Torre. Revista General de la Universidad de Puerto Rico* 3, no. 9 (1955): 175–78.

Auclair, Marcelle. *Enfances et mort de García Lorca*. Paris: Seuil, 1968.

Aznar Soler, Manuel. "El Caracol y la Sala Rex (1928–1929)." *(Pausa.) Quadern de Teatre Contemporani* 4 (1990): n.p.

Bacarisse, Pamela. "Perlimplín's Tragedy." In *Lorca: Poet and Playwright. Essays in Honour of J. M. Aguirre*, edited by Robert Havard, 71–92. Cardiff: University of Wales Press, 1992.

Baeza, Ricardo. "El teatro de Eugenio O'Neill." *Revista de Occidente* 7, no. 71 (May 1929): 189–234.

———. "Nota sobre *El emperador Jones*, Eugene O'Neill." *Revista de Occidente* 7, no. 70 (April 1929): 74–75.

Balboa Echevarría, Miriam. *Lorca: El espacio de la representación*. Barcelona: Edicions del Mall, 1986.

Barea, Arturo. *Lorca: The Poet and His People*. Translated from the Spanish by Ilsa Barea. London: Faber and Faber, [1945].

Barlow, John D. *German Expressionist Film*. Boston: Twayne, 1982.

Belamich, André. "*El público* y *La casa de Bernarda Alba*, polos opuestos en la dramaturgia de García Lorca." In *"La casa de Bernarda Alba" y el teatro de García Lorca*, edited by Ricardo Doménech, 79–92. Madrid: Cátedra / Teatro Español, 1985.

Bennett, Andrew, and Nicholas Royle. *An Introduction to Literature, Criticism and Theory*. 5th ed. Abingdon, Oxon, UK: Routledge, 2016.

Benson, Renate. *German Expressionist Drama: Ernst Toller and Georg Kaiser*. New York: Grove Press, 1984.

Billboard 41 (July–December 1929); 42 (January–March 1930).

Borel, J.-P. *Théâtre de l'impossible*. Neuchâtel, Switzerland: La Baconnière, 1963.

Borges, Jorge Luis. "Antología expresionista." *Cervantes* (October 1920): 100–112.

———. "La antología expresionista. Die Aktions-Lyrik, 1914–16." *Ultra*, no. 16 (October 1921): n.p.

———. "Lírica expresionista." *Grecia* 3, no. 47 (August 1920): 10–11.

———. "Lírica expresionista." *Grecia* 3, no. 50 (November 1920): 10–11.

Brenan, Gerald. *South from Granada*. Harmondsworth: Penguin, 1963.

Brickell, Herschel. "A Spanish Poet in New York." *Virginia Quarterly Review* 21, no. 3 (1945): 386–98.

Brotherton, John. *The "Pastor Bobo" in Spanish Theatre before the Time of Lope de Vega*. London: Tamesis, 1975.

Buñuel, Luis. *Mi último suspiro*. Barcelona: Plaza & Janés, 1982.

Calderón de la Barca, Pedro. *Autos sacramentales*, vol. 1: *La cena del rey Baltasar. El gran teatro del mundo. La vida es sueño*. Edited by Ángel Valbuena Prat. Madrid: Espasa-Calpe, 1972.

———. *La vida es sueño*. Edited by José M. Ruano de la Haza. Madrid: Castalia, 1994.

Cano, José Luis. "[Desde Madrid, José Luis Cano nos envía este artículo . . .]." *La Gaceta del Fondo de Cultura Económica* 8, no. 84 (August 1961): n.p.

Cao, Antonio F. "*Así que pasen cinco años* de Federico García Lorca: teatro y antiteatro." In *Actas del IX Congreso de la Asociación Internacional de Hispanistas*, edited by Sebastián Neumeister, 2:185–94. Frankfurt: Vervuert, 1989.

Cardoza y Aragón, Luis. *El río. Novelas de caballería*. Mexico City: Fondo de Cultura Económica, 1986.

Carr, Raymond. *Modern Spain, 1875–1980*. Oxford: Oxford University Press, 1980.

Chirico, Domenico Pio. "Lettura pirandelliana di una trilogia lorchiana." *Status Quaestionis: Language, Text, Culture* 18 (2020): 256–62.

Colecchia, Francesca. "The 'prólogo' in the Theater of Federico García Lorca: Towards the Articulation of a Philosophy of Theater." *Hispania* 69, no. 4 (1986): 791–96.

Colin, Paul. "El teatro alemán contemporáneo." *Cosmópolis* 11, no. 42 (June 1922): 154–60.

———. "El teatro alemán contemporáneo." *Cosmópolis* 11, no. 43 (July 1922): 242–50.

———. "Letras alemanas. Introducción." *La Pluma* 2, no. 12 (May 1921): 299–303.

Courgey, Paulette. "Le réseau des allusions et des signes dans *Así que pasen cinco años* de Federico García Lorca." In *Hommage à Amédée Mas,* edited by Aaron August Lawton, 29–56. Paris: Presses Universitaires de France, 1972.

Crow, John A. *Federico García Lorca.* Los Angeles: by the author, 1945.

Cuesta Guadaño, Javier. *El teatro de los poetas: formas del drama simbolista en España (1890–1920).* Madrid: Consejo Superior de Investigaciones Científicas, 2017.

Curtius, Ernst Robert. "Theatrical Metaphors." *European Literature and the Latin Middle Ages,* 138–44. Princeton: Princeton University Press, 1967.

Daverdin-Liaroutzos, Chantal. "*Le Public* à Paris." *Magazine Littéraire,* no. 249 (January 1988): 48–50.

David, A. Rosalie, and Eddie Tapp, eds. *Evidence Embalmed: Modern Medicine and the Mummies of Ancient Egypt.* Manchester: Manchester University Press, 1985.

Delgado, Maria M. *"Other" Spanish Theatres: Erasure and Inscription on the Twentieth-Century Spanish Stage.* Manchester: Manchester University Press, 2003.

DeLong-Tonelli, Beverly J. "The Trials and Tribulations of Lorca's *El público.*" *García Lorca Review* 9 (1981): 153–68.

Díez-Canedo, Enrique. "Georg Kaiser." *Revista de Occidente* 13, no. 37 (July 1926): 121–24.

Doménech, Ricardo. "Doble lectura de *Así que pasen cinco años.*" *Boletín de la Fundación Federico García Lorca* 4, nos. 7–8 (1990): 233–54.

Dougherty, Dru. "Lorca y las multitudes: Nueva York y la vocación teatral." *Boletín de la Fundación Federico García Lorca* 6, nos. 10–11 (February 1992): 75–84.

Dougherty, Dru, and Andrew A. Anderson. "Continuity and Innovation in Spanish Theatre, 1900–1936." In *The Cambridge History of the Theatre in Spain,* edited by David T. Gies and María Delgado, 282–309. Cambridge: Cambridge University Press, 2012.

Dougherty, Dru, and María Francisco Vilches de Frutos. *La escena madrileña entre 1918 y 1926. Análisis y documentación.* Madrid: Fundamentos, 1990.

Downer, Alan S. *Fifty Years of American Drama, 1900–1950.* Chicago: Henry Regnery, 1951.

Durham, Weldon B., ed. *American Theatre Companies, 1888–1930*. Westport, CT: Greenwood Press, 1987.

Edwards, Gwynne. "'Comedia corriente de los tiempos actuales': Lorca's *Comedia sin título*." *Journal of the Institute of Romance Studies* 2 (1993): 337–50.

———. *Lorca: The Theatre beneath the Sand*. London: Marion Boyars, 1980.

Eisenberg, Daniel. "A Chronology of Lorca's Visit to New York and Cuba." *Kentucky Romance Quarterly* 24 (1977): 233–50.

Eisner, Lotte H. *The Haunted Screen: Expressionism in the German Cinema and the Influence of Max Reinhardt*. Berkeley: University of California Press, 1969.

Feal, Carlos. "El Lorca póstumo: *El público* y *Comedia sin título*." *Anales de la Literatura Española Contemporánea* 6 (1981): 43–62.

Feldman, Sharon G. "*Perlimplín:* Lorca's Drama about Theatre." *Estreno. Cuadernos del Teatro Español Contemporáneo* 17, no. 2 (1991): 34–38.

Fernández-Cifuentes, Luis. "El viejo y la niña: tradición y modernidad en el teatro de García Lorca." In *El teatro en España, entre la tradición y la vanguardia. 1918–1939*, edited by Dru Dougherty and María Francisca Vilches de Frutos, 89–102. Madrid: CSIC / Fundación Federico García Lorca / Tabacalera, 1992.

———. *García Lorca en el teatro: la norma y la diferencia*. Zaragoza: Universidad de Zaragoza, 1986.

Figure, Paul. "The Mystification of Love and Lorca's Female Image in *El público*." *Cincinnati Romance Review* 2 (1983): 26–32.

Freud, Sigmund. *The Interpretation of Dreams*. Translated by A. A. Brill. 3rd ed. New York: Macmillan, 1913.

García, Carlos. *El joven Borges y el expresionismo literario alemán*. Córdoba, Argentina: Universidad Nacional de Córdoba, 2015.

García Castañeda, Salvador. "Don Perlimplín, Don Crispín y otras vidas de aleluya." *Salina: Revista de Lletres* 17 (2003): 103–9.

García Lorca, Federico. *Alocuciones argentinas*. Madrid: Fundación Federico García Lorca, 1985.

———. *Amor de don Perlimplín con Belisa en su jardín*. Edited by Margarita Ucelay. Madrid: Cátedra, 1990.

———. *Así que pasen cinco años*. Edited by Margarita Ucelay. Madrid: Cátedra, 1995.

———. *Autógrafos*, vol. 2: *El público*. Edited by Rafael Martínez Nadal. Oxford: Dolphin, 1976.

———. *Autógrafos*, vol. 3: *Así que pasen cinco años*. Edited by Rafael Martínez Nadal. Oxford: Dolphin, 1979.

———. *Conferencias*. Edited by Christopher Maurer. 2 vols. Madrid: Alianza, 1984.

———. *4 piezas breves*. Edited by Andrés Soria Olmedo. Granada: Comares / Fundación Federico García Lorca, 1996.

———. *El público.* Edited by Andrew A. Anderson. Granada: Comares / Fundación Federico García Lorca, 1996.

———. *El público.* Edited by María Clementa Millán. Madrid: Cátedra, 1987.

———. "*El público.*" *Los Cuatro Vientos* no. 3 (1933): 61–78.

———. *El público. El sueño de la vida.* Edited by Antonio Monegal. Madrid: Alianza, 2000.

———. *El público y Comedia sin título. Dos obras teatrales póstumas.* Edited by Rafael Martínez Nadal and Marie Laffranque. Barcelona: Seix Barral, 1978.

———. *Epistolario completo.* Edited by Andrew A. Anderson and Christopher Maurer. Madrid: Cátedra, 1997.

———. *La zapatera prodigiosa.* Edited by Mario Hernández. Madrid: Alianza, 1982.

———. *Palabra de Lorca. Declaraciones y entrevistas completas.* Edited by Rafael Inglada and Víctor Fernández. Barcelona: Malpaso, 2017.

———. "Presentación del auto sacramental *La vida es sueño,* de Calderón de la Barca, representado por La Barraca." In *Obras completas,* vol. 3: *Prosa,* edited by Miguel García-Posada, 218–21. Barcelona: Galaxia Gutenberg / Círculo de Lectores, 1997.

———. *Teatro inconcluso.* Edited by Marie Laffranque. Granada: Universidad de Granada, 1987.

———. *Teatro inédito de juventud.* Edited by Andrés Soria Olmedo. Madrid: Cátedra, 1994.

———. "Texto íntegro de la formidable proclama del joven e ilustre autor dramático." *Heraldo de Madrid,* February 2, 1935, 6.

García Lorca, Francisco. *Federico y su mundo.* Edited by Mario Hernández. Madrid: Alianza, 1980.

García Pintado, Ángel. "19 motivos para amar lo imposible." *Cuadernos El Público,* no. 20 (January 1987): 7–11. (Insert in *El Público,* no. 40.)

García-Posada, Miguel. "Lorca y el surrealismo: una relación conflictiva." *Ínsula* 44, no. 515 (November 1989): 7–9.

Gibson, Ian. "El insatisfactorio estado de la cuestión." *Cuadernos El Público,* no. 20 (January 1987): 13–17. (Booklet insert in *El Público,* no. 40.)

———. *Federico García Lorca,* vol. 2: *De Nueva York a Fuente Grande (1929–1936).* Barcelona: Grijalbo, 1987.

———. *Vida, pasión y muerte de Federico García Lorca, 1898–1936.* Barcelona: Debolsillo, 2016.

Gide, André. *L'Immoraliste.* Paris: Mercure de France, 1973.

Giménez Micó, José Antonio. "Lorca: Teatro posible e imposible." *Anales de la Literatura Española Contemporánea* 20, no. 3 (1995): 351–64.

Gómez Torres, Ana. "'El público' de Federico García Lorca y su teoría teatral." PhD diss., University of Málaga, 1991. Málaga: Universidad de Málaga, 1992. 11 microfiches.

González Calleja, Eduardo. *La razón de la fuerza: orden público, subversión y violencia política en la España de la Restauración (1875–1917)*. Madrid: Consejo Superior de Investigaciones Científicas, 1998.

González Carballho, J. *Vida, obra y muerte de Federico García Lorca*. Santiago de Chile: Ercilla, 1938.

González Guzmán, Pascual. "Los dos mundos de don Perlimplín." *Revista do Livro* 4, no. 16 (1959): 39–59.

González Ramírez, David. "La escenificación de *El gran teatro del mundo* (Granada, 1927). Consideraciones sobre la 'vuelta a Calderón.'" *Boletín Millares Carlo* 28 (2009): 305–24.

Granell, Eugene F. "Esquema interpretativo." *La Torre* 3, no. 9 (1955): 178–88.

Grant, Helen. "Una *aleluya erótica* de Federico García Lorca y las aleluyas populares del siglo XIX." In *Actas del primer congreso internacional de hispanistas*, edited by F. Pierce and C. A. Jones, 307–14. Oxford: Dolphin, 1964.

Guardia, Alfredo de la. *García Lorca: persona y creación*. Buenos Aires: Sur, 1941. (Quotations drawn from 4th ed. [Buenos Aires: Schapire, 1961].)

Gubern, Román. *Proyector de luna. La generación del 27 y el cine*. Barcelona: Anagrama, 1999.

Guerrero Zamora, Juan. "*Así que pasen cinco años*." *Historia del teatro contemporáneo*, 85–87. Barcelona: Juan Flors, 1961.

Guillén, Claudio. "El misterio evidente: en torno a *Así que pasen cinco años*." *Boletín de la Fundación Federico García Lorca* 4, nos. 7–8 (December 1990): 215–32.

Gutiérrez Cuadrado, Juan. "Crónica de una recepción: Pirandello en Madrid." *Cuadernos Hispanoamericanos*, no. 333 (1978): 347–86.

Harretche, María Estela. *Federico García Lorca. Análisis de una revolución teatral*. Madrid: Gredos, 2000.

Harris, Derek. "Introducción." In *Romancero gitano. Poeta en Nueva York. El público*, by Federico García Lorca, 9–46. Madrid: Taurus, 1993.

Hernández, Mario. "Introducción." In *La casa de Bernarda Alba*, by Federico García Lorca, 7–42. Madrid: Alianza, 1998.

Hershberger, Robert P. "Building and Breaking the Metadramatic Frame in *La zapatera prodigiosa* and *Amor de Don Perlimplín*: The Dilemma of Social Convention." *Estreno. Cuadernos del Teatro Español Contemporáneo* 23, no. 1 (1997): 23–28.

Honig, Edwin. *García Lorca*. Norfolk, CT: New Directions, 1944.

Huélamo Kosma, Julio. "Algunas claves sobre un drama profundo." *ABC Literario,* January 10, 1987, ix–x.

———. *"Así que pasen cinco años:* La memoria recuperada." In *La mirada joven. (Estudios sobre la literatura juvenil de Federico García Lorca),* edited by Andrés Soria Olmedo, 13–41. Granada: Universidad de Granada, 1997.

———. "La influencia de Freud en el teatro de García Lorca." *Boletín de la Fundación Federico García Lorca* 3, no. 6 (December 1989): 59–83.

———. "Pastor y Arlequín: dos personajes paralelos en el teatro imposible de García Lorca." *Hispanística XX* (1999), special issue "Voir et lire Federico García Lorca: le théâtre de l'impossible," edited by Jean-Marie Lavaud, 63–85.

Hughes, Robert. *The Shock of the New.* Rev. ed. New York: Knopf, 1991.

Jerez-Farrán, Carlos. *El expresionismo de Valle-Inclán.* La Coruña: Ediciós do Castro, 1989.

———. "La estética expresionista en *El público* de García Lorca." *Anales de la Literatura Española Contemporánea* 11 (1986): 111–27.

Jiménez-Vera, Arturo. "Don Perlimplín's Poetic Inspiration." *García Lorca Review* 5, no. 2 (1977): 104–13.

Kaiser, Georg. *De la mañana a medianoche. Revista de Occidente* 13, nos. 37–38 (July–August 1926): 77–109, 174–224.

———. *Gas [I]. Revista de Occidente* 21, nos. 61–63 (July–September 1928): 33–60, 204–33, 322–50.

———. *Un día de octubre. Revista de Occidente* 25, nos. 73–75 (July–September 1929): 40–62, 201–23, 329–51.

Kenworthy, B. J. *Georg Kaiser.* Oxford: Basil Blackwell, 1957.

Knight, R. G. "Federico García Lorca's *Así que pasen cinco años.*" *Bulletin of Hispanic Studies* 43, no. 1 (1966): 32–46.

Kovacci, Ofelia, and Nélida Salvador. "García Lorca y su *leyenda del tiempo.*" *Filología* 8 (1961): 77–105.

Lacomba, José M. "*El público* de García Lorca." *Sin Nombre* 9 (1978): 77–84.

Ladra, David. "El teatro bajo el agua." *Primer Acto,* no. 182 (December 1979): 31–35.

Laffranque, Marie. "Estudio y notas." In *Teatro inconcluso,* by Federico García Lorca, 5–99. Granada: Universidad de Granada, 1987.

———. "Introducción." In *"El público" y "Comedia sin título." Dos obras teatrales póstumas,* by Federico García Lorca, 273–316. Barcelona: Seix Barral, 1978.

Lafora, Gonzalo R. "Estudio psicológico del cubismo y expresionismo." *Archivos de Neurobiología* 3, no. 2 (June 1922). (Collected in *Don Juan, los milagros y otros ensayos.* Madrid: Biblioteca Nueva, 1927, 187–259.)

Laufe, Abe. *Anatomy of a Hit: Long-Run Plays on Broadway from 1900 to the Present Day.* Introduction by Jack Gaver. New York: Hawthorn Books, 1966.

Lavergne, Gérard. "Les voix de l'homme et de l'ombre dans *Quand cinq ans seront passés* de Federico García Lorca." *Cahiers de Narratologie. Analyse et Théorie Narratives* 10, no. 2 (2001): 155–84.

Lázaro Carreter, Fernando. "*El público*, de García Lorca." *Blanco y Negro* 97, no. 3604, July 24, 1988, 12.

———. "Final de *Así que pasen cinco años*." *Blanco y Negro* 97, no. 3660, August 20, 1989, 12.

———. "Fracaso de amor." *Blanco y Negro* 97, no. 3659, August 13, 1989, 12.

Leiter, Samuel L. *The Encyclopedia of the New York Stage, 1920–1930*. 2 vols: *A–M, N–Z*. Westport, CT: Greenwood Press, 1985.

———. *The Encyclopedia of the New York Stage, 1930–1940*. Westport, CT: Greenwood Press, 1989.

León, María Teresa. "Federico y Margarita." *El Nacional* (Caracas), October 11, 1956.

Lima, Robert. *The Theatre of García Lorca*. New York: Las Américas, 1963.

Londré, Felicia Hardison. *Federico García Lorca*. New York: Frederick Ungar, 1984.

Loney, Glenn. *20th Century Theatre*, vol. 1. New York: Facts on File Publications, 1983.

Loynaz, Dulce María. "El manuscrito." *ABC*, October 8, 1989, 24.

———. "Yo no destruí el manuscrito de *El público*." *ABC*, May 30, 1987, 42.

Ly, Nadine. "Analyse d'un fragment de *Así que pasen cinco años* (Duo 'Le Jeune Homme et le Mannequin')." In *Le Théâtre impossible de Lorca. "El público." "Así que pasen cinco años*," edited by Michèle Ramond, 19–40. Paris: Éditions du Temps, 1998.

———. "Grammaire et dramaturgie du temps dans *Así que pasen cinco años*." *Les Langues Néo-Latines* 92, no. 307 (1998): 129–64.

Lyon, John. "Love, Imagination and Society in *Amor de don Perlimplín* and *La zapatera prodigiosa*." *Bulletin of Hispanic Studies* 63, no. 3 (1986): 235–45.

Machado Bonet, Ofelia. *Federico García Lorca. Su producción dramática*. Montevideo: Imprenta Rosgal, 1951.

Mantle, Burns, ed. *The Best Plays of 1929–30 and the Year Book of the Drama in America*. New York: Dodd, Mead, 1930.

Marco, Joaquín. "Sobre una obra inédita de Federico García Lorca." *La nueva literatura en España y América*, 163–67. Barcelona: Lumen, 1972.

Marful Amor, Inés. *Lorca y sus dobles. Interpretación psicoanalítica de la obra dramática y dibujística*. Kassel, Germany: Reichenberger, 1991.

Mariscal, Ana. *Cincuenta años de teatro en Madrid*. Madrid: El Avapies, 1984.

Martín, Eutimio. "Una leyenda de Víctor Hugo en la obra de García Lorca." *Ínsula* 37, no. 427 (June 1982): 1, 10.

Martínez Nadal, Rafael. *"El público": Amor, teatro y caballos en la obra de Federico García Lorca*. 1st ed. Oxford: Dolphin, 1970.

———. *"El público": Amor y muerte en la obra de Federico García Lorca.* 3rd ed. Madrid: Hiperión, 1988.

———. "Estudio." In *Autógrafos,* vol. 3: *Así que pasen cinco años,* by Federico García Lorca, 229–48. Oxford: Dolphin, 1979.

———. "Introducción." In *"El público" y "Comedia sin título." Dos obras póstumas,* by Federico García Lorca, 13–29. Barcelona: Seix Barral, 1978.

———. "Nota preliminar." In *Autógrafos,* vol. 3: *Así que pasen cinco años,* by Federico García Lorca, 9–12. Oxford: Dolphin, 1979.

Maurer, Christopher. "El teatro." In *Federico García Lorca escribe a su familia desde Nueva York y La Habana (1929–1930),* by Federico García Lorca, edited by Christopher Maurer, 133–41. Special double number of *Poesía* 23–24 (1985).

———. "Introduction." In *Poet in New York: A Bilingual Edition,* by Federico García Lorca, xi–xxx. Translated by Greg Simon and Steven F. White, edited by Christopher Maurer. New York: Farrar, Straus and Giroux, 1988.

Maurer, Christopher, and Andrew A. Anderson. *Federico García Lorca en Nueva York y La Habana. Cartas y recuerdos.* Barcelona: Galaxia Gutenberg / Círculo de Lectores, 2013.

Maurer, Christopher, and Lincoln Son Currie. "From Stage to Page: A *Perlimplín* Chronology." In *Zóbel Reads Lorca. Poetry, Painting, and "Perlimplín in Love." Federico García Lorca,* by Fernando Zóbel, 127–38. Chicago: Swan Isle Press, 2022.

Mazzotti Pabello, Honorata. "Una lectura de *El público* de Federico García Lorca." In *Tres ensayos sobre Federico García Lorca,* by Honorata Mazzotti Pabello, Gabriel Rojo Leyva, and Jesús Villegas Guzmán, prologue by James Valender, 153–78. Mexico City: Universidad Autónoma Metropolitana, 1990.

McGaha, Michael D. *The Theatre in Madrid during the Second Republic.* London: Grant & Cutler, 1979.

Melis, Antonio. "*El público*: metamorfosi e travestimento." In *L'"imposible/posible" di Federico García Lorca,* edited by Laura Dolfi, 155–75. Naples: Edizioni Scientifiche Italiane, 1989.

Menarini, Piero. "Federico García Lorca y el teatro de su época. En torno a *El sueño de la vida." Boletín de la Fundación Federico García Lorca* 10, nos. 19–20 (1996): 145–55.

———. "Introducción." In *El maleficio de la mariposa,* by Federico García Lorca, 9–73. Madrid: Cátedra, 1999.

———. "L'uomo dei dolori (Struttura ed esegesi del Quadro V de *El público*)." In *Lorca, 1986,* edited by Piero Menarini, 65–106. Bologna: Atesa, 1987.

Millán, María Clementa. "Introducción." In *El público,* by Federico García Lorca, 13–112. Madrid: Cátedra, 1987.

Monegal, Antonio. "Entre el papel y la pantalla: *Viaje a la luna* de Federico García Lorca." *Litoral,* special issue "Surrealismo. El ojo soluble," edited by Jesús García Gallego, nos. 174–76 (1987): 242–58.

——. "Una revolución teatral inacabada." In *El público. El sueño de la vida,* by Federico García Lorca, 7–42. Madrid: Alianza, 2000.

——. "Un-Masking the Maskuline: Transvestism and Tragedy in García Lorca's *El público.*" *Modern Language Notes* 109 (1994): 204–16.

Morla Lynch, Carlos. *En España con Federico García Lorca.* Edited by Sergio Macías Brevis. Seville: Renacimiento, 2008.

Morris, C. B. *Surrealism and Spain, 1920–1936.* Cambridge: Cambridge University Press, 1972.

——. *This Loving Darkness: The Cinema and Spanish Writers, 1920–1936.* Oxford: Oxford University Press, 1980.

Newberry, Wilma. "Aesthetic Distance in García Lorca's *El público:* Pirandello and Ortega." *Hispanic Review* 37 (1969): 276–96.

Nourissier, François. *F. García Lorca, dramaturge.* Paris: L'Arche, 1955.

Oliver, William I. "The Trouble with Lorca." *Modern Drama* 7 (May 1964): 2–15.

O'Neill, Eugene. "*El emperador Jones.*" *Revista de Occidente* 7, nos. 70–71 (April–May 1929): 76–101, 235–62.

Orringer, Nelson R. "Lorca's *Así que pasen cinco años:* A Symbolist Vision of Crisis." In *Studies in Honor of Donald W. Bleznick,* edited by Delia V. Galván, Anita K. Stoll, and Philippa Brown Yin, 101–15. Newark, DE: Juan de la Cuesta, 1995.

Ortega, Jesús, ed. *Album. Una historia visual de la Huerta de San Vicente.* Granada: Delegación de Cultura del Ayuntamiento de Granada, 2015.

Osorio, Marta, ed. *Miedo, olvido y fantasía. Crónica de la investigación de Agustín Penón sobre Federico García Lorca, Granada-Madrid (1955–1956).* 2nd ed. Granada: Comares, 2009.

Oxman, Steven. "As Time Stands Still: Federico García Lorca's *Once Five Years Pass.*" *Theater* 22, no. 3 (Summer–Fall 1991): 58–62.

Panxsaers, Clément. "La pintura expresionista alemana." *Cosmópolis* 11, no. 42 (June 1922): 161–63.

Pedro, Valentín de. "El destino mágico de Margarita Xirgu. Conoce a García Lorca." *¡Aquí Está!* (Buenos Aires), May 16, 1949, 12–14.

——. "El destino mágico de Margarita Xirgu. Una obra de don Manuel Azaña." *¡Aquí está!* (Buenos Aires), May 19, 1949, 20–22.

——. "El destino mágico de Margarita Xirgu. Una obra de García Lorca, desaparecida." *¡Aquí Está!* (Buenos Aires), May 26, 1949, 12–15. (Partially reproduced in Rodrigo, *García Lorca en Cataluña,* 358–61.)

Pedrosa, José Manuel. "De *Perlinpinpin* a *Perlimplín: féerie* francesa, *Cyrano*, ale-luyas, cuentos de Calleja . . . y Lorca." *Liburna* 8 (2015): 117–63.

Peral Vega, Emilio. "Introducción." In *Comedia sin título (seguida de "El sueño de la vida" de Alberto Conejero)*, by Federico García Lorca, 9–62. Madrid: Cátedra, 2018.

Pérez Coterillo, Moisés. "La Habana: donde Lorca escribió *El público*." *El Público*, nos. 10–11 (Summer 1984): 39–43.

Pérez-Simón, Andrés. *Baroque Lorca: An Archaist Playwright for the New Stage.* New York: Routledge, 2020.

Piscator, Erwin. *El teatro político.* Madrid: Cenit, 1930.

Price, Julia S. *The Off-Broadway Theater.* New York: Scarecrow Press, 1962.

Puyal Sanz, Alfonso. *Cinema y arte nuevo: la recepción fílmica en la vanguardia española (1917–1937).* Madrid: Biblioteca Nueva, 2003.

———. *Cine y renovación estética en la vanguardia española.* Seville: Renacimiento, 2018.

Ramond, Michèle. "Figuras del eclipse en *El público y Así que pasen cinco años*." *Hispanística* 20 (1999), special issue on "Voir et lire Federico García Lorca: Le théâtre de l'impossible," edited by Jean-Marie Lavaud, 87–101.

Rennert, Hugo Albert. *The Spanish Stage in the Time of Lope de Vega.* New York: Dover, 1963.

Río, Ángel del. "Introduction." In *Poet en New York*, by Federico García Lorca, ix–xxxix. Translated by Ben Belitt. New York: Grove Press, 1955.

Ríos Torres, Félix. *El teatro de vanguardia: Claudio de la Torre.* N.p.: Gobierno de Canarias, 1985.

Rivas Cherif, Cipriano. "Poesía y drama del gran Federico. La muerte y la pasión de García Lorca." *Excelsior. Diorama de la Cultura. Suplemento dominical*, January 27, 1957, 3.

Rivas Mercado, Antonieta. *Correspondencia.* Edited by Fabienne Bradu. Xalapa, Veracruz, Mexico: Universidad Veracruzana, 2005.

Rodrigo, Antonina. *García Lorca en Cataluña.* Barcelona: Planeta, 1975.

Rodríguez, Marie-Soledad. "L'Arlequin de *Así que pasen cinco años:* un retour au mythe?" In *Lorca: L'Écriture sous le sable*, edited by Pascale Thibaudeau, 169–76. Poitiers: La Licorne–UFR de Langues et Littératures, 1999.

Rodríguez Marín, Francisco, ed. *Cantos populares españoles*, vol. 1. Seville: Francisco Álvarez, 1882.

Romero Salvado, Francisco J. *Spain, 1914–1918: Between War and Revolution.* New York: Routledge, 1999.

Roux, Lucette-Élyane. *"Así que pasen cinco años" de F. G. Lorca ou Le désir d'éternité.* Perpignan, France: Imprimerie Catalane, 1966.

Rubia Barcia, José. "Ropaje y desnudez de *El público.*" *Cuadernos Hispanoamericanos,* nos. 433–34 (1986): 385–97.

Russell, Bertrand. *The Problems of Philosophy.* Oxford: Oxford University Press, 1959.

Saillard, Simone. "F. García Lorca. *Así que pasen cinco años.*" *Introduction à l'étude critique. Textes espagnols,* 47–74. Paris: Armand Colin, 1972.

Salazar, Adolfo. "*La casa de Bernarda Alba.*" *Carteles,* April 10, 1938, 30.

Salinas, Pedro, and Jorge Guillén. *Correspondencia (1923–1951).* Edited by Andrés Soria Olmedo. Barcelona: Tusquets, 1992.

Samper, Edgard. "Espacios y decorados en el acto tercero (cuadro primero) de *Así que pasen cinco años:* variaciones sobre el teatro en el teatro." *Hispanística 20* (1999), special issue "Voir et lire Federico García Lorca: le théâtre de l'impossible," edited by Jean-Marie Lavaud, 47–61.

Samuel, Richard, and R. Hinton Thomas. *Expressionism in German Life, Literature, and the Theatre, 1910–1924.* Philadelphia: Albert Saifer, 1971.

Sánchez-Biosca, Vicente. "El expresionismo: hacia una relectura de las vanguardias." *Ideologies and Literature* 2, no. 2 (Fall 1987): 201–9.

Sánchez, Roberto G. *García Lorca. Estudio sobre su teatro.* Madrid: Jura, 1950.

Santiago y Gadea, Augusto C. de, ed. *Lolita. Cantares y juegos de las niñas.* 2nd ed. Madrid: Est. Tip. de los Hijos de Tello, 1910.

Sapojnikoff, Victor. "La estructura temática de *Así que pasen cinco años.*" *Romance Notes* 12, no. 1 (1970): 11–20.

Sartre, Jean-Paul. *L'Être et le néant.* Paris: Gallimard, 1943.

Shakespeare, William. *Romeo and Juliet.* Edited by Brian Gibbons. London: Methuen, 1980.

Shaw, Donald L. "Lorca's Late Plays and the Idea of Tragedy." In *Essays on Hispanic Themes in Honour of Edward C. Riley,* edited by Jennifer Lowe and Philip Swanson, 200–208. Edinburgh: Department of Hispanic Studies, 1989.

Smith, Paul Julian. *The Body Hispanic: Gender and Sexuality in Spanish and Spanish American Literature.* Oxford: Clarendon Press, 1989.

Sokel, Walter H. "Introduction." In *Anthology of German Expressionist Drama: A Prelude to the Absurd,* edited by Walter H. Sokel, ix–xxx. New York: Anchor Books, 1963.

———. *The Writer in Extremis: Expressionism in Twentieth-Century German Literature.* Stanford: Stanford University Press, 1968.

Soufas, C. Christopher. *Audience and Authority in the Modernist Theater of Federico García Lorca.* Tuscaloosa: University of Alabama Press, 1996.

Sprinchorn, Evert. "Introduction to *To Damascus.*" In *Selected Plays,* vol. 2: *The Post-Inferno Period,* by August Strindberg, 381–86. Translated by Evert Sprinchorn. Minneapolis: University of Minnesota Press, 1986.

Strindberg, August. *Cinco dramas en un acto.* Translated by Alejandro Rodríguez Álvarez. Madrid: Mundo Latino, 1929.

———. *Selected Plays,* vol. 2: *The Post-Inferno Period.* Translated by Evert Sprinchorn. Minneapolis: University of Minnesota Press, 1986.

———. *Verso Damasco.* Translated by Nino Frank. Milan: Alpes, 1927.

Styan, J. L. *Modern Drama in Theory and Practice,* vol. 3: *Expressionism and Epic Theatre.* Cambridge: Cambridge University Press, 1983.

Suero, Pablo. "Crónica de un día de barco con el autor de *Bodas de sangre.*" *Noticias Gráficas* (Buenos Aires), October 14, 1933, 10. (Reproduced in García Lorca, *Palabra de Lorca,* 161–69.)

———. *España levanta el puño.* [Buenos Aires]: [Noticias Gráficas], [1937].

———. *Figuras contemporáneas.* Buenos Aires: Ediciones Argentinas / Sociedad Impresora Americana, 1943.

———. "'La Barraca' del poeta García Lorca." *Noticias Gráficas* (Buenos Aires). October 15, 1933, 12. (Reproduced in García Lorca. *Palabra de Lorca,* 178–85.)

Tamayo y Baus, Manuel. *Un drama nuevo.* Madrid: Imprenta de José Rodríguez, 1867.

Thiollière, Pierre. "Du chant de l'Arlequin au serviteur porteur de lumière. Chronique d'une mort annoncée. (À propos de l'acte III de *Así que pasen cinco años*)." In *Mélanges en hommage à Jacques Soubeyroux,* edited by Philippe Meunier and Edgard Samper, 513–28. Saint-Étienne, France: Éditions du CELEC, 2008.

Toller, Ernst. *Hinkemann. Los destructores de máquinas.* Translated by Rodolfo Halffer. Madrid: Cenit, 1931.

Torre, Guillermo de. *Literaturas europeas de vanguardia.* Madrid: Caro Raggio, 1925.

Ucelay, Margarita. "El club teatral Anfistora." In *El teatro en España: entre la tradición y la vanguardia 1918–1939,* edited by Dru Dougherty and María Francisca Vilches de Frutos, 453–70. Madrid: CSIC / Fundación Federico García Lorca / Tabacalera, 1992.

———. "Introducción." In *Amor de don Perlimplín con Belisa en su jardín,* by Federico García Lorca, 11–231. Madrid: Cátedra, 1990.

———. "Introducción"; "Textos"; "Ediciones"; "Apéndice." In *Así que pasen cinco años,* by Federico García Lorca, 9–145, 146–58, 159–71, 355–61. Madrid: Cátedra, 1995.

Valente, José Ángel. "Pez luna." *Trece de Nieve,* 2nd epoch, nos. 1–2 (December 1976): 191–201.

Videla, Gloria. *El ultraísmo. Estudios sobre movimientos poéticos de vanguardia en España.* 2nd ed. Madrid: Gredos, 1971.

Vitale, Rosanna. *El metateatro en la obra de Federico García Lorca.* Madrid: Pliegos, 1951.

Walsh, John K. "The Women in Lorca's Theater." *Gestos* 2, no. 3 (1987): 53–65.

Wedekind, Frank. *Despertar de primavera.* Translated by Manuel Pedroso. Madrid: Biblioteca Nueva, 1910.

Wright, Sarah. *The Trickster-Function in the Theatre of García Lorca.* London: Tamesis, 2000.

Xirau, Ramón. *"Así que pasen cinco años." Prometeus. Revista Mexicana de Literatura,* 2nd epoch, no. 2 (March 1952): 96–111.

INDEX